THE DRUM SET
Finding Love and Happiness

The Drum Set. Printed in the United States of America. No part of this book may be used or reproduced in any manner whatsoever without written permission, except in the case of brief quotations embodied in critical articles and reviews.

ISBN 9781080352616

Cover photo by Matthijs Smit from Unsplash; drum set icon by Mohamed Assan from Pixabay; drum quotes from WiseOldSayings.com

As long as the ideas keep coming...

The Drum Set: Finding Love and Happiness
Life Reimagined: A What-If Kind of Love Story
Pre-Bound Girl: Learning Life's Lessons

Reunion Trilogy
The Amulets of Power
The Cabal
The Prophecy Fulfilled
Finding Magic: The Legend of Sorcha and Aidan+
+Prequel

CHAPTERS

INTRODUCTION (2019)

My mother was right.

I hate to admit it, but she was.

Buying a house, selling two houses, and getting married in the same month was a terrible idea. A really terrible idea. A ridiculously awful, terrible idea.

But we had survived a lot already.

I wanted to celebrate that.

I could do it.

I knew I could.

Or rather, I knew we could. The Drum Set could do anything.

CR ℰℂR ℰℂR ℰ

BEGINNINGS (2014)

I actually asked Tom McDonnell to marry me. I knew if I waited for him to ask, it would never happen. He wasn't sure he ever wanted to get married. Live together – sure. But marriage? He didn't see the point.

I thought just living together would work for me, too. I really just wanted Tom in my life. All the time. However I could get that to happen.

But then things happened, and things changed, and I needed the security of being married. And fortunately, he saw the wisdom of being married, too. We'd come a long way together, and we looked forward to our "ever after".

℃ ℅℃ ℅℃ ℅

Tom McDonnell and I met on a blind date. Sort of. Like so many things in life, it was sort of this and sort of that.

We had met before, but only briefly and had not really talked that much to each other. In 2012, our mutual friends, Jane and Peter Greene, had had a party. There were forty or so people there. Jane, who I worked with, had introduced me to Peter's friend, Tom. I was smitten with another man at the moment, and I'm afraid I paid absolutely no attention to poor Tom. The other man was having nothing to do with me, and that, of course, only made me more obsessed with him. Jane and Peter, knowing that I was obsessed and knowing that it was a mistake of gigantic proportions to be obsessed, had tried to steer me toward Tom. Nice, lovable, sensible Tom. Instead of crazy, erratic, and going-to-break-my-heart Richard.

I'll admit when Jane then suggested a date with Tom a few months after Richard had in fact broken my heart by going on exactly two dates with me before sleeping with another woman, I didn't remember our previous meeting. The more fool I. I could have met the love of my life years earlier and saved myself from a great deal of stupid and foolish behavior.

But no.

So, to Tom. We met, as I said, for a sort of blind date, sort of fix-up, sort of getting to know you again.

Through Jane, Tom had suggested drinks after work Monday. An innocuous way to meet after work and decide whether there's anything more to say and decide whether dinner is something you want. Or not.

I'm afraid I was tired from having been out the night before and taking things very literally. So, when I met Tom for drinks, that's what I thought it was going to be. Drinks. Or perhaps only one drink as I'm not much of a drinker.

It turned out Tom doesn't drink at all. Ever. So I had my one glass of wine, while he ordered a glass of water. And I thought, 'This doesn't seem like an auspicious beginning.'

And yet somehow, I managed to babble my way through the next three hours. As I nursed my one glass of wine, and he drank his frequently replenished water. I finally asked our poor server for a glass of water too. And the guy looked at me like he was ready to kill. We'd already taken the table for longer than a typical after-work dinner would have been. The server was looking to turn over the table to someone who might actually get more than one glass of wine. But no, here we were, talking and laughing, and not eating or having any more wine. Finally, I said, "I have to go home. My poor cats must be starving."

"They must be," Tom responded. "Are they used to being fed when you get home?"

Tom, I knew from our conversation, had never had a pet. "Yes, I usually am greeted at the door by meows begging for food."

He smiled and laughed. He really had a wonderful smile and a ready sense of humor.

If you ask 100 women what they look for in a man, a good sense of humor will be at the top of most women's lists. Certainly top ten. I appreciated that Tom found me funny, and I had to admit I laughed at his witticisms quite a lot. It reminded me of a time when I realized two of my friends were perfect for each other because one laughed at the other's jokes, which I didn't find all that funny. Sense of humor, I tell you. It means a lot.

So, he paid the check. I noticed, because I tried to, that he left a very generous tip. The kind of tip one would have left if one had eaten dinner – and then some. The restaurant may not have made much from our meal, but I really appreciated that Tom made it up to the server.

Another thing women care about. Being generous and treating people kindly. I remember the story of a famous person – I don't remember who – who would meet prospective business partners for a meal. He or she took note of how they treated the servers and the other people around them. If they were not kind or generous, this person wouldn't take a second meeting.

I felt much the same way, but my reasons were personal. As well as looking for kindness, I had many friends in the restaurant business.

Servers live off their tips, as most restaurants don't pay them a salary to speak of. I've been a server. I know how one bad tip can hurt your whole night. So, Tom's generosity was definitely not lost on me. In fact, it made him more attractive.

Not that he wasn't aesthetically pleasing already. Medium height and build, dark brown hair – what was left of it at 35 – starting to go gray at the edges. I didn't mind that he was going bald, and I appreciated that he didn't try to cover it up, as some men do. He had a neatly trimmed beard, though he told me he went back and forth on having one. He was slim, bordering on skinny, despite his telling me he didn't workout at all. He was average height for a man at 5'8". Thomas Edward McDonnell, Jr., wasn't stunning, but then again, neither was I.

My name is Tiffany Catherine Johnson. Quite a mouthful. My parents gave all of us "fancy" first and middle names to make up for our rather pedestrian last name. And I suppose Tiffany was better than something plainer like Ann, though it did inspire more than one reference to the classic movie, *Breakfast at Tiffany's*. I'm average height for a woman at 5'4". Also medium build. I had always wanted to be one of those model-thin women so I could wear the clothes, though I did like having curves. It was a quandary. My hair was blond, though dyed that color. It was really gray, driven by genetics – my mother, who never colored her hair, had been mostly gray by the time she was 30. On the other hand, I had started coloring my hair in my 20s. So, I honestly didn't know how gray I was at 36, but probably mostly. As far as Tom knew, however, I was a blond.

After he paid the check, leaving a generous tip, Tom walked me to my car. Now, this was hardly the first time I'd been walked to my car by a guy I'd met on a sort of blind date. I had done the internet dating thing a few times. And inevitably, though I often tried hard not to let him, the guy would want to walk me to my car. For my safety ostensibly. Even though I am a black belt in tae kwon do. And even though most of the time, the person I most wanted to get away from in that moment was the guy. Even in the 21st century, guys feel the need or right to protect women. And of course, try to get a goodnight kiss. Even the guys who never wanted to see me again wanted a goodnight kiss.

Anyway, Tom walked me to my car. And I realized as we were walking that I didn't mind. In addition to the realizations about his sense of humor and his tipping. That meant I liked this guy. Perhaps a lot.

He didn't try to kiss me good night. I wasn't sure if I was happy or sad about that. I wondered immediately if that meant I was more attracted than he was. But I'd also gotten the distinct impression, both from Tom and from Jane, that Tom was a slow mover.

Jane had said, "He's one of the best guys I know. I wouldn't set you up with anyone not worthy of you. But he's also very shy. And hasn't dated much. So, cut him some slack at first, okay?"

I had said I would. And I was.

But then he said, "Jane gave me your number, so I could text if I was running behind tonight. Would it be okay if I called you? I enjoyed our date."

And my heart sang. I said, "Yes," quite calmly, I thought considering I was bouncing around inside.

Of course, that also might have been the hunger pangs. It was, after all, past 8 pm, and I hadn't had anything to eat or drink since noon except a glass of wine. Which meant the wine had also gone to my head. I tampered my enthusiasm and drove home. And fed the cats. And then myself. Cats first, always. There was no point in eating before them. They would just curl and meow around me until they were fed.

A word about my cats. I had two. Still do. Growing up, we'd always had pets; sometimes dogs, sometimes cats, occasionally both. I loved pets of all kinds. But I had a very demanding, time-consuming job. Some days, I'd get to the office with the plan to leave on time at 4. And by 3 pm, the day was blown, and I still had several hours of work to do. I say this not to complain, but rather to explain why I had cats. Cats, you can leave until 8 pm to get fed. Dogs, you just can't. Cat also didn't need to be let out a couple of times a day. Cats, you could not worry too much about when you suddenly had to work later than planned. Hence, I had cats.

And I had two because the rescue people convinced me kittens would be less destructive in pairs. The theory is two means they have someone to play with and chase around, and they are therefore happier. And less destructive. In reality, two kittens can be amazingly destructive. One had only to look at my sofa to see that. But I loved them anyway. They were litter mates, my two girls. When I had that first date with Tom, they were three years old and still very energetic. We still have them. They were part of all the logistics around houses and weddings, though of course they had no idea about any of it till they were packed up one day and moved to a new house. Our new house. Tom's and mine. And theirs too.

CR SOCR SOCR SO

Tom did, in fact, call me, but not for another two days. I was almost panicked by then, convinced that I had had a great time, but he had not. Then he called and explained that he'd wanted to call the next day, to find out how the cats had fared, he said. But that Peter had told him he must wait three days. So, he'd waited two, and he hoped I didn't mind that he didn't wait the one more day. I carefully said I didn't mind, while I was smiling ear to ear and shaking my hand by my face and mouthing to my co-worker, Jane, 'He finally called!'

Jane smiled knowingly. She was, after all, married to Peter.

"Did the cats survive?" Tom asked.

"They are used to it, I'm afraid. I just don't always know when I'm going to get home," I said.

"You mentioned that your job can change quickly."

"Yeah. I arrive in the morning with a plan for the day. And then things happen. Sometimes, it's the big boss needing something rewritten. Sometimes, it's a new project that just landed earlier than expected."

"I don't think I'd like that chaos," Tom admitted.

And my heart sank. If a man was going to share my life, he had to be able to adjust to this crazy schedule. Because it came with the job, which I loved. Most of the time. "It's not that bad," I backpedaled. I didn't want to scare Tom off before a second date.

"No, I mean, for me. I like things a little more ordered. But I could tell from the way you talked about it, that your job is very important to you."

Or dear. Did I sound like a woman with no time for love? All about my career? Was that my problem with men? I was suddenly second-guessing everything I'd said the other night. "It is. Though I try not to let it run my life."

Tom laughed. "That's the cats' job."

I smiled and laughed. I liked that he teased me, which was fascinating because I usually hated being teased. My brothers could attest to that. "Most definitely," I replied.

"Well, would you like to go out again?"

"I'd love to," I replied.

"Dinner? Since apparently I didn't feed you the other night."

I wasn't sure what that meant. It sounded like he was teasing me, but I didn't get it. "Dinner sounds good."

"What's your favorite kind of food?"

One of the things Tom and I had in common was a limited palate. Some might call us picky eaters, but that just wouldn't be nice.

"Italian is usually good. Burgers. I like PF Chang's."

"How about Italian? Macaroni Grill?"

"Sounds great. There's one in Fairfax. How about there?"

"Great! Saturday?"

It was Thursday. "Great! About 5:30? I usually like to eat on the early side."

"Except when you're meeting for drinks."

And I finally got it. He was teasing each about the fact that we hadn't had dinner on our first date. "Yes, except then."

"5:30 at Macaroni Grill in Fairfax on Saturday."

"It's a date."

"Yes, it is." Tom's tone was teasing, but there was a serious undertone. I sensed he was as pleased at the idea of a second date as I was. Good.

We met on Saturday night. I'm usually early to things. It's a joke in my family. If you invite the Johnsons somewhere, you can count on two things. One, we will be early. And two, we will all arrive at about the same time. It had happened more than once. So, I was expecting to be the first one at the restaurant.

But Tom was already there. He was standing outside, waiting for me. I appreciated that I didn't have to go in and find him.

"I put our names in the list, though they don't really have one because it's early," he teased.

I laughed. "Saturday night can get crazy! I like things calmer than they will be later tonight."

"I do too. I'm not a big fan of crowds."

I would learn later that this was a tremendous understatement.

"Shall we?"

"Let's!"

The hostess asked if we wanted to sit inside or outside. It was a lovely evening in July, cool relatively. But I'm not a fan of eating outdoors. I looked at Tom, and he looked at me.

"Your choice," I said, trying not to be any pickier than I already was about food.

"Outside," Tom told the hostess.

She led us outside, and it was a nice evening. There were only a few tables outside, and it was quieter there. I think that might have been Tom's motivation for choosing outdoors. I would cope.

He ordered salmon, which I don't like at all. I had fettuccine Alfredo with chicken, one of my favorites. I noticed, as we started to eat, that he was very polite in his eating. He flaked the salmon and delicately ate each piece. I tend to eat quickly. Not sure whether that's from years of eating too much on the go or something else. But I took note of his deliberate eating and slowed down. I didn't want to finish before him.

I ordered a glass of wine with my dinner. Since this was our second date, I felt like I could ask some more personal questions.

"Have you never drunk alcohol for personal reasons? Or is it something else?" I wanted to ask if he was a recovering alcoholic but had no idea how to do that. I knew more than one, and it wouldn't bother me. But he didn't know that.

"I just don't like it."

"So, you've had a drink and didn't like the feeling?"

He laughed. "Actually, I've never tried anything alcoholic."

"So, you don't know if you'd like it," I teased.

"I guess not," he said, with a laugh. "I just never wanted to try it."

"I feel that way about drugs. No interest."

"Me too."

I generally didn't drink much or often, so Tom's abstention was not an issue. Certainly preferable to a guy who drank and then got stupid. I knew a few of those too, including my ex Richard.

I mustered up my courage for another question to confirm my thoughts. "What did you mean when you said something about not feeding me?"

"Well, I offered to buy you dinner the other night, but you said you didn't want any." He smiled to let me know he was teasing me.

"But we were meeting for drinks."

"I would have bought you dinner."

"But when I asked if you wanted dinner too, you said no. I wasn't going to eat alone."

"Did I say that?"

"You did. So, I thought I'd just eat when I got home. I didn't expect it to be so late." I smiled to let him know I was happy about it having been late.

"Me either. And you had been up late the night before."

I had been to a concert the previous evening. It was, in fact, two late nights in a row. It was a testament to how much fun I'd been having with Tom that I didn't mind two late nights. I'm not usually that social.

"Sarah McLachlan. I enjoyed her show."

"I know the name, but I'm not sure I know her music."

"Oh? She's had quite a bit on the radio." Music was one of my things. I needed to be with someone who enjoyed music. It's part of the reason I'd dated quite a few musicians over the years. Including Patrick, who had been a summer fling.

"I think I have one of her CDs. Ecstasy or something."

"*Fumbling towards Ecstasy.* It's her most famous."

"That's the one. I liked it, though I don't think I've listened to it in a while."

"She's touring for a new CD of course. It's pretty good too. In general, I like singer-songwriters."

"I'm stuck in the 80s."

"Really? You're too young to be a fan of that decade."

"Yeah. Not sure where it came from. College, I think? My roommate loved Depeche Mode. The one before Peter. He converted me."

"I know the name, but I'm not sure I know the music."

"You probably know *Personal Jesus.*"

"Oh yeah. I remember that song."

"I like 80s alternative music."

"Interesting." I thought that was an okay genre, though it depended on how alternative. I wasn't a big fan of the more extremes of the style. In general, though, I liked to think I was open to lots of options. As long as he liked music, that was the important part. And being open to going to concerts. I generally went to several a year, and I would want my partner to go with me. In fact, it was one of the things I was looking forward to if I finally got a boyfriend. Going to a concert with friends was nice and all – I had done it for Sarah McLachlan – but it wasn't the same as sharing music with someone I loved.

We ate a while longer and chatted more. I debated about another glass of wine, but opted not to. Generally, one glass is my norm. Two occasionally. As Tom wasn't drinking at all, I stuck with one.

Tom paid the check, leaving another generous tip. So, that meant the first night was not just because we had taken up a table for most of the night. Good.

Tom again walked me to my car.

"You know I can take care of myself," I said boldly.

"I'm sure you can," Tom said, a little taken aback.

"I did tell you I'm a black belt, didn't I?

Most guys, when I say this, say something to the effect of "ooh, should I be worried?" Which is annoying, because I don't tell people about my black belt to scare them, but rather because it's one of the major accomplishments of my life.

Tom said, "That's cool. Hard work."

I appreciated his reaction. And it had been.

"I haven't practiced in a while though." I didn't want to sound too fierce. "I stopped after getting my first degree black belt, just after grad school."

"I remember Jane saying you had a master's degree. I stopped at bachelors."

I could tell Tom was smart, so I wondered about that a little. But I would ask more another time. For now, we had been standing at my car for a while. And this time, I wanted a goodnight kiss.

"I have an MBA to supplement with my BA in English."

"Useful for your job," he said.

I was in marketing, so his observation was true. "Yeah, though I originally had intended to get my PhD." Oh dear. I was talking too much again.

"What stopped you?"

"I decided I didn't want to be a professor after all. That had been the plan. But it just wasn't my thing. Academia."

"I get that." Tom was a programmer, he told me.

"Well, I should head out. It's not far to home, but I didn't feed the cats yet."

"They are going to hate me," Tom teased.

I laughed. "More likely me. But yes, they need to be fed again."

"I promise not to make them starve any longer."

"It's a short drive. They'll be fine." I didn't want my cats to be a thing either, though I thought Tom was mostly giving me a hard time.

"You live near here?"

"A couple of miles."

"Me too."

"Which way?" I asked.

"That way," Tom said, pointing south.

It was the same direction in which I lived. "Me too."

"I live in Ridge Drive," Tom explained.

"How funny! I'm in the next development over – Stone River."

"So, we're neighbors!"

"It would appear so."

"Wonderful!"

I stood there quietly for a second.

"Well, you should go. Feed the cats."

"I should."

And he kissed me. Gently. On the lips. No tongue. No hug. Just a peck goodnight. I thought it was very respectful. But I also wanted more. Oh well. I thought there would be more opportunities to come.

I got in my car. Tom got in his. He followed me out of the parking lot. We turned the same way. It was a little weird, I'll admit. Then, he turned, which made sense as his development was closer to the restaurant, but also made me stop feeling like I was being followed. I turned at the next intersection.

As I opened my garage, I got a text.

"Had fun again. Enjoy the rest of your evening."

It was from Tom. Nice move. I saved his phone number to my contacts, so I'd know it was him in the future.

I opened my door, walked upstairs, being followed by my felines howling for dinner as usual. I put down my purse and started toward the cabinet where I kept the food. I still had my phone in my hand. I was smiling at Tom's text and trying to figure out some witty thing to say in response. In the meantime, Sabrina and Cassandra were talking up a storm, waiting for me to open their can of food and put it down. As soon as I did, they shut up as their mouths were full.

"The girls have been fed," I texted. "They thank you."

I waited for his response.

It seemed like it was taking a long time.

I grabbed some water and headed upstairs to get ready for bed. I took my phone, not because I was waiting for a text. Though I was. But because I kept my phone beside me in the night. Mostly in case my family needed me. But also for work. Or sometimes other inspiration struck.

I brushed my teeth. Still no text. Wasn't my text funny? I thought it was.

I went to sleep disappointed not to hear back.

ભ ૭૦ભ ૭૦ભ ૭૦

I awoke to a series of texts.

"Sorry I missed your text last night."

"I crashed as soon as I got home."

"Sorry again."

These started at 5:30 am. I vaguely remembered Tom saying something about being a morning person. I, most definitely, was not.

Which is not to say I didn't get up early in the morning. I did. Most weekday mornings, I left the house around 7 or 7:30. But I don't like it. And I always tell people I'm not really awake until about 10.

In college, I was a serious night owl. Often, I wouldn't go to sleep until after midnight. I spent many late nights talking with my then-boyfriend, Ian, until the wee hours of the morning. Or reading a good book just for fun. I would even read my literature textbooks late into the night, though sometimes that wasn't productive as I wouldn't always remember the details. So late-night reading was usually for romance novels or pulp fiction that didn't require a lot of brain power.

These days, I usually crashed around 10. I slept on my side, usually facing the empty side of my queen-sized bed. Sabrina, also known as Brie, would lie across my arm, while Cassandra or Cass curled into her sister. It was adorable.

They knew my routine and usually woke up around 5:30, sometimes after my alarm, sometimes before. It being Sunday, the alarm wasn't set. But that didn't stop the cats from wanting to be fed early in the morning. On the weekends, I got up to feed them around 5:30 or 6, and then I would go back to bed for a few more hours. I had to close the door when I got back in bed because otherwise the cats, who would now be awake, would try to get me up to play. Or they would just come and go all morning, which would keep me from a restful sleep. They didn't like the closed door – no cat would – but they understood. Most mornings.

One thing that's still true about me, which has been true all my life, is that I don't just bounce up out of bed in the morning. I like to set my alarm for about an hour before I really have to get up. And I laze in bed during that time, convincing myself to get up. I wake up to music, and the alarm clock radio default is to play for an hour. So at the very longest, I will laze for the full hour. Most workday mornings, though, I get up 30-40 minutes after my alarm goes off.

Anyway, apparently, Tom had been up early this morning. Even on a non-work morning. Yawn!

"Ah. I didn't realize that." I texted back after I'd fed the cats again.

"Figured," he responded quickly. "Glad the cats were happy to have been fed."

I appreciated his good grammar. Even in text, I still use all my words. Too many years of training. "They were. They ate heartily. I just fed them again, in fact."

A little witty?

"Names?"

I hadn't told Tom their names yet? That was strange. I guess I just called them "the cats" or "my girls".

"Sabrina and Cassandra. Brie and Cass if I'm in a hurry."

"Great names! They are black cats, right? I love Salem."

I knew he was referencing the cat from the show *Sabrina the Teenage Witch*. I had thought about that name. But they were girl cats, and somehow the show had made Salem a male name. "Thanks. Yes, they are black." I was ready to go back to sleep now, but wasn't sure how to tell Tom that. Him being a morning person.

"Your familiars?"

I laughed. That was sort of where the inspiration for their names had come from. I had been interested in witches and witchcraft as a teenager, and I read most of the books published about the Salem Witch Trials. I loved fantasy novels and all things magic. Plus, black cats were beautiful, but often among the last of the cats or kittens to be adopted because of silly superstitions. I was proud to have given two of them a forever home.

"Of course!" I wrote, wondering if he'd appreciate my response. Some people were freaked out by references to witchcraft.

"Cool!"

Okay, he got it. Whew.

"Are they sassy like Salem?"

I laughed. "Sometimes!" I was missing out on my weekend sleep. How to explain that to a new beau? "Is it okay that I'm not really awake right now?"

"Not a morning person?" Tom asked.

"Not at all."

"Only got up to feed the cats?"

"Pretty much."

"Later then."

"Later." My sleeping-in was another thing Tom apparently got. Cool.

CR ℰꙄCR ℰꙄCR ℰꙄ

Tom and I had our third date the following weekend. I was determined this time to find out more about him. On our previous dates, it seemed as though we ended up talking about me most of the time. Now, I love me, but even I get bored talking about myself. Ha!

"How was your day?" I asked. It seemed like an innocuous place to start.

"Fine. Uneventful."

We were having dinner again, pizza this time at a local place adjacent to our respective neighborhoods. We'd both been before though not together, of course. We might even have been there at the same time. Who knew? It was a little weird that we had lived less than a mile from each other for the past six years and not known it. When Jane had tried to fix us up the first time, she must not have realized that we lived so close to each other. The irony wasn't lost on me that I drove past Tom's house every day on my way to work. Literally every day.

"Uneventful is good. I know you do computer programming. But what kind?"

"You mean what language?"

I knew there were different computer languages, but he could have said 'pink', and it wouldn't mean anything to me. "No, for what purpose?"

"Whatever my client wants," he replied with a grin.

"Who's your client?" I asked. I knew Tom was a government contractor. We'd talked about that on our first date. I knew a bunch of people who were.

"I can't say."

"One of those kinds of clients?" I replied, my tone mysterious, though I wasn't 100% sure I even knew what that meant. My brother, Xan, and sister-in-law, Jennifer, had top secret clearances, and most of the time, they couldn't talk about what they did. I inferred Tom had a similar situation.

"Yes. One of those clients." He smiled.

"You can't tell me even the acronym?"

"I'm afraid not. Is that okay? Some people are really bothered by not being able to know more."

"If I'm not allowed to know more, then that's the way it is. I sometimes work on projects that I can't talk about, too."

"Good. I wouldn't want it to be an issue between us."

There was more there, I knew. I could sense Tom was holding something back. But it was too early in our relationship for him to tell me his deep-seated secrets. Still, I did want to find out more about him.

"You work at home, though? You don't need to be in a clandestine location?"

Tom chuckled. "I work about half the week at home. The other half, when I need to apply the programs to real data, I have to go to the SCIF."

"Skiff?" I asked. As far as I knew the word 'skiff' was a kind of boat. I didn't think that's what Tom meant.

"Sensitive Compartmented Information Facility. S-C-I-F. SCIF."

"Oh."

"I do have a special safe for my laptop. I put it away every night. But that's more for my feeling of security than a requirement of my job."

"I remember reading about laptops with sensitive information getting stolen."

"Right. Some people aren't diligent about keeping the class and unclass separated. It can get you in real trouble. I do have another laptop, for company stuff, too."

"So you have two laptops, and you use one for the stuff that you can't talk about. And the other for stuff you can?"

"Yeah."

"So, are you like Captain Nemo and rolling from laptop to laptop? I had a job once where I had three computers, and I used to roll my office chair around all day. I felt like Captain Nemo on his keyboards."

"Well, I never thought about it that way. But yes!"

"Do you ever get confused and do the wrong thing on the wrong laptop?"

Tom shrugged. "Not really. I don't really think about it much anymore. I've been doing it for a long time."

"How long?"

"Since I finished college."

"You've never worked anywhere else?"

"I've worked for different companies. But always the same end client."

I looked at him confused; my head cocked to the side like a dog. I had no idea what that meant.

"I've been working for the same agency of the government for many years. But the contract I work on has had different companies leading it."

"How does that work? Can you talk about this?" I didn't want to cause any problems.

"Sure. This stuff isn't classified. It's pretty common. It's called badge swapping."

"Okay. I have no idea what that means."

Tom laughed. "The government contracts out a fair amount of work."

"Right. I know there are a lot of companies that are government contractors in this area. My brother and his wife work for State."

"Directly?"

"Yeah. They are feds. But they've talked a little bit about having contractors they work with. And I have other friends who are government contractors. So, I know a little bit about it."

"All right." Tom took a breath. "A fair amount of government contracts change hands over time."

"Meaning?"

"Say Northrop Grumman wins the work to start with."

"I've heard of them. I've seen their name on lots of buildings around town."

"They are one of our biggest competitors."

"Okay. So Northrop wins a contract. What's next?"

"So, a few years down the road, usually five, the government will recompete the contract."

"Recompete?"

"Meaning they want the work to continue."

"Why don't they just continue with Northrop then? Or are they unhappy with Northrop's work?"

Tom smiled. "Sometimes the government is unhappy with the prime contractor. That's what Northrop Grumman would have been in this case. The prime."

"This is a whole new world," I said, fascinated. But at least I got Tom to talk about himself, sort of.

"It really is its own world. Anyway, it might be that the government doesn't like the prime. But sometimes, they just want another company to try, to see whether they would do something differently. And sometimes, if a prime has had the contract for a long time, the government just feels obligated to change primes."

"Weird. Okay. I get it, I think."

"Yeah. It's a little weird. The other thing to know is that, depending on how big the contract is, how much it's worth, the government can't do a sole-source contract. They can't give the work to one contractor directly. They have to compete the work."

"To be fair to everyone," I inferred.

"Something like that. There are very convoluted rules about government contracting."

"I can tell!"

"Anyway, when I first started on the contract where I work, the prime was SAIC."

"I've heard of them. They are as big as Northrop Grumman."

"Not quite, but close. Similar. I worked for them. SAIC. I got a job there right out of college. Working for this contract."

"Got it."

"SAIC had the contract for two cycles already. So we knew when it came up for renewal, for recompete, another contractor was likely to get the award."

"Because the government doesn't like to keep the same prime for too long."

"You're quick! Yes, that's right."

I smiled, but didn't say anything about being quick. I was. But so was Tom from what I could tell. It's one of the things I looked for in a guy. I inherited my intelligence from my two overachieving parents. And I was a lifelong learner. But I didn't flaunt my brain. It just wasn't done in my family.

"So, if I wanted to continue doing the work I was doing – and I did – then I was going to have to switch companies when the work was recompeted. To whoever won the new contract."

"That makes sense."

"So, I would keep doing the same work – the work I'm still doing now – but someone else would sign my check."

"Where does the badge thing come in?"

"We all have badges to show we don't work for the feds. I mean, they have badges too. But theirs say they are feds. Mine says I work for General Dynamics. The feds like to know who is a fed and who is not."

"So General Dynamics won the recompete."

Tom nodded. "Three years ago. So, now I work for them. The benefits are pretty much the same. I like my new boss. So that's good."

"So, you do the same work, but you have a different company name on your badge. Badge-swapping."

"Yup! You got it."

"Doesn't seem very efficient."

"It can be good to change primes. GD – that's my company's nickname – has different priorities than SAIC did. At SAIC, my contract wasn't very important. It wasn't part of their larger strategy, so it didn't get much care and feeding. At GD, it's part of their focus area. So, that's better for me."

"More attention?"

"Well, I don't really like attention."

One place where we differed, Tom and me. Maybe it was because my name was Tiffany – which had always gotten a fair amount of attention – but I didn't mind being the center of attention. I even sometimes made a point of becoming the focus in the room. In my current job, I was often presenting important information to important people. That necessitated being comfortable being the center of attention.

But Tom hated being the center of attention. He had told me that on our first date, and everything he'd done since then had convinced me that he wasn't being coy. Including his asking me a lot of questions, but not offering much about himself. Now that I knew he worked on a classified project, I understood his reticence even more.

But it did make me wonder how I was going to create intimacy with someone who didn't share? Or perhaps the better way of thinking about it was someone who *couldn't* share a lot of his life.

CR ЄꙀCR ЄꙀCR ЄꙀ

Our first date had been in July. Tom's birthday was in April, so we hadn't been together to celebrate it. But my birthday was at the end of September, and so it was fast approaching. And I didn't want Tom to feel a lot of pressure to get me a great present. We barely knew each other!

For me, birthdays also are a time for reflection. This year, I was happy to be dating Tom. And I felt as though there was potential for our relationship. But we still hadn't said "I love you."

I was a little frustrated with Tom, to be honest. I knew he couldn't talk about work. I got that restriction. But I was having trouble getting him to talk about his family, too. And that shouldn't have been off limits.

"We just don't talk about things like that," he said, when I asked him what his sisters thought about our relationship.

"Your sisters haven't asked you about me?"

"Well, sure. But it's more like 'what does she do?' or 'what are you doing this weekend?' than the state of our relationship."

"They know we're dating, right?"

He looked at me, insulted. "Of course they do."

I just looked back at him, nonplussed. "Well, you say you don't talk about these things."

"Tiffany, why are you pushing on this?"

I could tell he was annoyed, but so was I. "I'm trying to get you to talk about yourself. About your feelings."

That was the rub. Feelings. The last guy I'd dated had told me he didn't love me. Just flat out said it. I had been heartbroken, even though I wasn't yet sure I loved him. I mean, it had been early in our relationship. But no one likes to hear those words.

"What about my feelings?"

"Do you have them?"

"About you?"

"No, about Sabrina." My sarcasm was a defensive mechanism.

"Tiffany…" Tom's tone was not happy.

I wasn't happy either.

We were sitting on my couch in my living room. I almost never used this room. It was a true living room, off the dining room, with a couch and two comfy chairs, a china cabinet that had been custom-made for the room, and a glass coffee table.

Most evenings, Tom and I sat downstairs in the family room. That's where the TV was, and when we hung out at my house, that's where we were. Watching TV. And talking. And laughing.

Tom usually walked over from his house. It was summer, and the weather was conducive to being outside, if hot during the day. Tom came over most evenings. When he worked from home, he started early, so he was usually done working before I got home. Even on days he went to the office, he would get there as soon as the offices opened and would end his day about an hour or two before I did. I would come home, feed the cats, have a bite to eat, and then Tom would come over to spend the evening with me. About 8, he would leave, so he could go to sleep early. I would stay up another hour or two. He texted me when he got home to say good night. And I woke up to a text from him wishing me a good morning. As August turned to September, that had become our routine. It was very nice and comfortable. And his evening and morning texts were things I looked forward to.

Today was Saturday. So he'd stayed a little later than normal, even though he got up early even on the weekends. He'd been on his way out when I'd confronted him about his family and how much they knew about us. And then about his feelings. When the conversation started being longer than a minute or two at the door, I started to sit on the stairs that led down to the front door. Tom didn't like that, so he decided to go sit on the couch. So that's where we were having this conversation. This very uncomfortable, but necessary conversation.

"I'm sorry, Tom, but I'm confused."

"What are you confused about?"

"How you feel about me?" I was on the verge of tears. I had decided to talk to Tom about this topic today. But I had chickened out all evening.

We had been having a nice time, as we usually did. We had similar tastes in most things, including TV. One of the things we'd found we both enjoyed were documentaries and science-based shows. He didn't like my family and medical dramas, so I watched those after he left. I didn't like his zombie shows, so he watched those at home. All in all, I could see us living together pretty comfortably.

The cats had even adjusted to having him around regularly. My cats were not fond of other people. When I had guests over, they usually hid. Tom had been around enough that they had gotten used to his presence. Cass had even taken to Tom so much that she sometimes sat on his lap when we were watching TV. At first, Tom hadn't understood how to pet a cat. But between Cass and me, we'd trained him. Brie wasn't nearly as friendly. She still hissed at him from time to time. But she did come into the room when we were watching TV. She just usually skirted around Tom to get to me.

With tears on the edges of my lashes, I looked at Tom. He was staring at me, and he still wasn't happy.

"Why are you so upset?" Tom asked.

"Because I don't know how you feel about me!" I wailed. A tear escaped.

"Don't do that," he said angrily.

"What?" I was taken aback at his tone. I genuinely didn't know what Tom was angry about.

"Don't cry."

"Don't cry? Why?" My tears were drying up as I got mad instead.

"It's not nice."

"How is it not nice?" I was furious now.

"It's manipulative."

"You're saying I'm crying to manipulate you?"

"Aren't you?"

I got up off the couch. I couldn't sit there any longer, as angry as I was.

I walked into the dining room. And around the table. And then into the kitchen. Tom didn't say a word.

That was one thing I'd learned about Tom. When he was uncomfortable, he just shut up. Me, I'd get angry and yell. I wasn't sure which method was more effective. Or more manipulative.

I was in the kitchen debating with myself about what I was going to do. Was I going to break up with Tom? I was sad and infuriated. I didn't really want to break up with him. But I didn't know how to go on from here.

And I *was* manipulating Tom right now. I was well aware that's what I was doing. I hadn't been before when I was crying. But now I was. I wanted to see whether he would fight for me. For us. Or at least be willing to make himself uncomfortable by coming to me, instead of my having to come back to him.

And then I heard the front door shut. Tom had just left.

THE NEXT LEVEL (2018)

Tom and I had been dating for more than three years when 2018 started. At three years, it was the longest relationship I'd ever had and, for Tom, second in length only to the relationship he'd had with Priya.

I started in 2018 taking steps to take our relationship to the next level, whatever that meant. Tom, I knew, would be fine if everything just stayed the same. Tom wasn't good with change. He was like a cat that way. I had had cats in my life for a long time, so I thought I knew how to handle Tom's fear of change. The same way I did with my cats. Either very incrementally or very abruptly.

I had a plan to change our relationship incrementally.

Then things happened. And change became abrupt.

CR EOCR EOCR EO

Early on in our relationship, I had talked to Tom about marriage in a general way. This was in our get-to-know-you phase, as we shared things we had learned from past relationships, about ourselves and about what we wanted.

Tom told me about Beth and Priya, the substantive two relationships in his life. Beth had been a college girlfriend, Tom's first real girlfriend, as high school had been largely consumed by his mother's illness and taking care of Meghan. They'd dated all through Tom's junior year, when his mother was seemingly in remission. Tom said it was a "typical" college relationship in that it lasted as long as they were away at college in Chicago. But as soon as they went home for the summer – Tom to Virginia and Beth to Florida – it wasn't sustainable. Still, Beth had been important to Tom because she helped him realize he was appealing to the opposite sex, and that dating could be fun.

He didn't like to talk about his relationship with Priya, other than to say it had ended badly. I knew they had dated for several years, and that she had been important to Tom mostly because he learned how to say no from being with her and was better about standing up for himself as a result. I was sure I would find out more about that situation as time went on, but at this point in our relationship, I wasn't going to push.

Tom had dated others off and on between Beth and Priya, but no one he considered a significant relationship.

For myself, I had had a few "great loves". Like Tom, I had had a significant college relationship with Ian. We were both night owls and enjoyed many of the same books, music, and television. We'd talk for hours and never run out of things to say. Our main source of friction was religion. Ian went to church on Sundays, and he went to a men's Bible study during the week. For my part, I didn't care much about this. As long as he didn't try to convince me to join him, it didn't bother me that he went to church. My family had been very involved in the Lutheran church in previous generations, including a grandfather and uncle who were ministers. Once things started to get serious, though, Ian insisted that he needed a partner in life who would share his faith. He tried to talk me into being that person, into embracing his religion. I loved him deeply, so I tried. I went to church with him a handful of times. I enjoyed the music, but I couldn't believe as he did. We broke up for a while, and then got back together. And broke up, and got back together. We just couldn't seem to let go of each other because the only thing keeping us apart was this one thing. Every other aspect of our relationship was perfect. But despite how much we loved each other, I just wasn't able to be the partner he needed. It had been heart-wrenching, but we had parted as friends and had actually kept in touch for the remainder of our college years.

Vic was another college relationship, perhaps a bit more like Tom and Priya than I would like to admit. Vic played in the college orchestra, and I sang in the college choir. The two organizations played concerts together several times a year, and it was during the rehearsals for one of these that I had first met Vic. He was a brilliant man with a beautiful voice who also played several instruments. I love music, and I think our mutual love of music was a big part of why we fell in love in the first place. But Vic was a snob about music. He believed that only classical music was worthy of his attention. He belittled my interest in rock and pop music, dismissing those genres as trivial and pedestrian. I tried, for many months, to convince Vic of the quality of the singer-songwriters I loved. The talent they possessed. The complexity of the music. The beauty of the lyrics. He didn't listen. For a while, I wondered if I was wrong. Was Vic right to argue that modern music had no value? He twisted my arguments and made me doubt them.

After years of just dating here and there, with no real success in love, I finally met Chris through an online dating service. He was the first man in a very long time who made me feel like I was worthy of male attention. He laughed and loved with me. We explored the countryside and even took a vacation together, something I hadn't done with a boyfriend before. Our connection felt strong and secure. Unfortunately, he was also going through a tough emotional time as his father was dying. He spent a lot of time going back and forth between his home in Virginia and his childhood home in New Jersey, trying to support his mother and father through this difficult situation. It ultimately became too much for him to try to develop a relationship with me and be there for his family. When the time came to choose, I knew what his choice would be, should be. I was sorry to lose him, but I understood his decision. Had the situation been reversed, I would have made the same choice.

Telling Tom about these three seminal loves in my life made me recognize even more the value of my relationship with Tom. Which had brought me to the realization that I wanted Tom in my life as more than just a boyfriend.

○ ○○ ○○ ○○ ○

One weekend, Tom and I were lying in bed, getting ready to go to sleep. Brie was curled up next to me, on the opposite side from Tom. In typical Tom fashion of giving everything a nickname, he had started called her "Cheese Omelet" though it didn't seem to make much difference in her level of affection. As the vet told me, Sabrina was my cat. I was her person. She didn't like sharing me.

Cassandra, on the other hand, had almost become more Tom's cat than mine. Tom's nickname for her was "Little Mama" after Cass Elliot from The Mamas and the Papas. She sat on his lap almost every evening as we watched TV. And she slept on his side of the bed. She'd start off next to him. Then gradually she'd lump. That was what Tom called it – another nickname – after we'd discovered her a few times, particularly on a colder day, sleeping between the top sheet and the blankets, making a lump. I'm not sure how she breathed, and I don't remember her doing it before Tom came into our lives. But she loved to lump now. Particularly next to Tom as he slept.

In other words, at night, Tom and I were sandwiched between the cats. It was a good thing we liked each other!

Anyway, we were lying there talking, as we did most every weekend night. It was one of the best parts of the day. Not that we hadn't spent most of the day together already. No, we had. But somehow in the evening, settling down to sleep, we still had things to say. Quiet things. Intimate things. Personal things.

This particular night, however, I was nervous. I had had an idea, one that I wasn't sure Tom was going to like. But once it had taken hold, I really wanted to make it happen.

"Tom," I said, as we nestled in, cats surrounding us. Cass hadn't yet gone into lump mode. "I was wondering if, maybe, we should move in together?"

Tom looked at me, not quite surprised, but his eyes said he was tentative. I knew, because I knew him pretty well by now, he was carefully weighing what to say. He knew this would be a big deal to me. And it was. I hadn't ever lived with a man, not even the couple I'd come close to marrying. Neither had Tom, with a woman that is. "Where do you think you would want to move?"

That wasn't the question I was expecting. But then again, sometimes Tom surprised me with how he thought things through. "I don't know. I was thinking maybe Reston?"

"Why Reston?"

"Or maybe somewhere around there. I like being near shopping and restaurants and stuff like that." I was fumbling in my nervousness.

"We have that here."

"True. But," confession time, "I've been looking around a bit. I think I can afford a single-family house in Reston."

"Single-family vs. townhouse?"

We both lived in townhouses now. I never, ever thought I'd be able to afford a single-family house. But I could now. And once I'd figured that out, I really wanted to do it. It felt so, well, grown up. Before the divorce, my parents had had single-family homes, but they had had two incomes. I, who had originally planned to be a college professor, never thought I'd make enough money to live in anything bigger than a townhouse. Especially not in the DC metro area.

The reality was, going a little farther west and north, I could buy a house. A real house. Like I'd lived in growing up. I didn't need Tom's income to afford it. But, if I was going to move, I wanted him to live with me. It was a big step, but I thought we were ready for it.

"Yeah, single-family. I can afford it in Reston. Or Herndon. Maybe even Sterling, though that might be too far."

"You want all that responsibility?"

"You mean a yard and all that?"

"Yeah."

"I mean, I had more of a yard in my last townhouse, because it was an end unit." An end unit was a possible alternative to my dream of a single-family house because it had the benefit of extra space and only one connecting wall with a neighbor. Single-family was still my ideal, mostly because it meant I had achieved more than I thought possible. But an end unit, particularly a three-bedroom one, would be almost like a single-family house. Almost.

Tom knew I had just missed out on an end unit when I bought my current house. In the same row of townhouses, the one with the enclosed brick staircase to the front door had gone on the market the week after I'd put in the offer on the townhouse I owned now. It had made me sad, though I did like my current home quite a lot.

"I have terrible credit. I would be a detriment to your buying."

"If I put you on the loan?"

"Yeah. Your rates would go way up."

I wasn't sure that was true, since I had pristine credit. But then again, I didn't need Tom's assistance to finance the house. But having him pay for half the mortgage after the fact, and help with the utilities, would definitely make the house much more affordable. "If you say so."

"I do. At least, I assume so."

"Well, we can talk about that another time. I can do it on my own if I have to. But the more important part is do you want to live together? You can sleep on it and tell me in the morning."

"Do I have to?" He looked at me with a playful, scared look on his face.

I laughed. "Not if you want to tell me what you think now?"

His face got serious again. "I think I love you. And living together in Reston or Herndon or some such would be nice."

'Nice? I was looking for a little more than that. But then again, I had thought he might say no altogether. I guessed I should count my blessings and be quiet.' To Tom, I said, "Great!" And we kissed to seal the deal.

We turned out the lights and settled in to sleep. As usual, Tom started gently snoring long before my mind and body had settled down enough to let me sleep. So, I lay there wondering if he was really okay with the idea of living together. Or just mollifying me in the moment, since it was late, this was a big deal, and I was invested in his answer. I decided I would find out tomorrow. Or the next day. For now, I would trust that what he said was what he meant. It usually was. And believing that, really believing it, let me sleep.

With Tom and Cass snoring on one side, Brie snoring on the other, and me sandwiched in between.

As usual, Tom was up and out of the house before I got up. All these years into our relationship, it had become routine for him to feed the cats before he left to do whatever it was he did before I woke up. He would kiss me goodbye, shut the door behind him – the cats having preceded him down the stairs – feed the cats, and walk or drive home. I would wake up a couple of hours later, usually to a text or two from Tom.

"There are some cool houses in Reston," was this morning's text.

I smiled as I replied, "Yeah. I like the modern look."

"Me too!"

I honestly had had no idea what Tom's taste in houses and furnishings might be, but I assumed he didn't care all that much. He'd never paid much attention to the way my house was decorated. And his house was decorated the same as when he moved in 10 years earlier. It had been the model townhouse for the development, and it still had the same wallpaper and fussy curtains that decorators loved and I hated. Tom, when I asked, had said he didn't much care, as long as the house was functional. He paid attention to the appliances and utilities. He didn't seem to care much about anything else.

Given that, I was both surprised and pleased that he'd expressed a preference for a modern style house. And even more excited that he'd been enthusiastic enough about the idea of living together to do a little research himself on houses.

"I can afford a 3bd, 3ba, I think," I wrote back.

"Great! Cheese Omelet and Little Mama need their space."

"Hahaha"

The texts went quiet, which usually meant Tom was back to work.

They say we are often attracted to people who resemble our parents, either physically or otherwise. In this case, Tom was much like my father, as both almost always worked on the weekends. In my father's case, I think working evenings and weekends was part of his driving ambition, though they made being a divorced father even more of a challenge. In Tom's case, I had learned that working at his own pace on the weekend made him less stressed about the amount of work he had to do during regular working hours.

And that thought, in that moment, made me realize that Tom's weekend working was something I was going to have to adjust to if we were going to live together. Currently, with our respective townhouses, his leaving in the morning and going home to work or do errands or whatever he wanted to do didn't really affect me. In fact, I enjoyed it because it gave me the chance to do my errands or whatever I wanted to do without worrying about Tom or Tom's schedule. Most weekends, we had one day where we did this – spent much of the day apart and doing whatever we needed to do to keep life organized and relatively under control. The other day of the weekend, we would spend together, doing some kind of activity or just hanging out together. We were both homebodies, so we didn't always like to go out and do things. But there were also some things that I had been wanting to do with a partner, like going to the zoo in the spring or summer and driving down Skyline Drive in the fall. Now that I had one, I'd asked Tom to join me. And most of the time, he was happy to come along.

But if we were going to live together, that day apart was going to go away. That made me realize that, as both of us were introverts, one of the things were would need in our house was space for each of us to be by ourselves; an office or some other space – where we could go if we needed time to recharge.

Not only that, as I thought more about it, we had some different tastes in television. We did like a lot of the same kind of TV, though; television was actually a source of compatibility. For example, in addition to documentaries – shows that taught us about new things and shows about animals – we enjoyed a lot of the same competition or game shows. There were only a few dramas Tom liked, a couple he had introduced me to in the past few years, which I had come to like as well. There were some comedies, too.

On the other hand, I liked a bunch of procedural and medical dramatic shows, which Tom found tiresome or overly dramatic. Tom liked several shows I found borderline offensive, too silly or making fun at others' expense.

But with those differences, in order for us not to have evenings when only one of us got to watch what he or she wanted, we needed a house with more than one TV room. Especially as neither of us liked having a television in the bedroom.

So, as I started to really think about the characteristics of "our" house, I recognized there was going to be more to it than just neighborhood and price.

⚬ ℘⟩⚬ ℘⟩⚬ ℘⟩

I contacted my realtor, a woman I had worked with to buy my last two homes. I told her the news about moving in with Tom and the general parameters of our plans to buy. Sarah asked some more questions, as good agents do.

"Are you selling both houses to be able to afford the new one?"

"No," I replied. "Just mine. The new house will, initially, be only in my name."

"Okay. Will you be selling his house, though?"

I wasn't sure. We'd talked about maybe keeping it and renting it out. It was in sad shape, though. "We're not sure, yet."

"What's your timeline?"

I knew spring was the best time to sell. And I knew I needed to do some fixing up of my place before it would be sellable. I figured I'd need at least a month for that. If we decided to add Tom's house to the mix, it would be at least a couple of months before we would be able to get it ready for sale. So, the timing might be perfect. To Sarah, I said, "I think we're pretty flexible. Next couple of months?"

"You know spring is the best time of year to sell," Sarah reminded me.

"Yes, I know. But we just made this decision, and we have some work to do on our houses first."

"Okay. I'll come by in the next week to get the paperwork started. I know your house, obviously."

Since she'd helped me buy it, that was a given. "Yeah."

"Where's Tom's house?"

"Just up the road, actually. In the Ridge Drive neighborhood."

"Funny. Did you meet him there?"

"Not at all. We met through friends. It just turns out we live really close to each other."

"Interesting coincidence."

"Yup. I literally have driven by Tom's house on my way to work every day since I moved into this neighborhood."

"That's funny!"

"I know!"

"Where are you thinking about buying?"

"Reston, Herndon, Sterling."

"That's a lot of territory."

"I know. But we are flexible with that too."

"Flexible is good, but it would be more effective to narrow down the search."

"Let's start with Reston, and we can expand from there."

"Good."

So, I made a list of the things that I thought I needed to do to ready my townhouse for sale. Sarah reviewed it and added a few things. I started lining up contractors. But it was looking like the list was going to take more than a month. Spring was looking likely but not definite.

Tom, in the meantime, decided he was going to keep his place as a rental. I was okay with that, but I told him it was his project. If he wanted to rent the house out, he was going to need to do the repairs to get it ready and figure out how to get it rented.

"There are companies that do that, you know," he argued.

"I know. I used one when I couldn't sell my first condo. But they take a cut of the rent. Can you get enough to pay for the mortgage and the fees?"

"Maybe. Maybe not. Good question. I'll look into it."

So, we both had our to-do lists for our current homes. But more importantly, we were starting to build a life – together.

"Music is like a conversation. One person says one thing that speaks with a harmonica, with a bass, with a drum. They're all conversating, and we're just trying to find a way to make conversation, rather than blah, blah, blah. But it's not really so hard a thing to do if you know the way to approach it." --
Stephen Marley

THE BIG FIGHT (2014)

I stood in my kitchen for a minute after the front door shut behind Tom, wondering what in the world just happened and what I should do next.

CR EOCR EOCR EO

In my younger years, I would have just let Tom go and then had a good cry and assumed the relationship was over. In my younger years, it probably would have been.

But we were not teenagers or even in our 20s. We were grownups, theoretically mature individuals. So, I decided in that moment that, if I wanted to know what had just happened, rather than assume, I should ask.

I ran to the door and down my front steps. Tom was about a block away at this point. But since he was walking, I had a decent chance to catch up to him. I ran after him, yelling his name.

"Tom!"

He stopped and turned to see me running down the street. The look on his face was pure confusion.

I caught up to him a minute later, out of breath. He hadn't moved since I yelled his name.

I tried to remain calm. I was still furious and scared and sad and a whole bunch of other emotions. But I knew if I flung my emotions at Tom, he would just stare at me and then, probably, start walking away again.

I took a deep breath, both to catch it and to try not to cry or scream. "Why did you leave?" I asked, as calmly as I could under the circumstances. It wasn't all that calm, but it was the best I could do.

Tom looked at me, still confused. "You left first," he replied.

"I just went to the kitchen."

"Was I supposed to go after you?"

I thought about that comment. Of course he was supposed to come after me. Wasn't that the right response to my dramatic exit? But, I reminded myself, we weren't teenagers any longer. Drama shouldn't be part of our relationship. We should be able to talk about things. I should be able to talk about things. And he should be able to talk about things.

I laughed, which only confused Tom more.

"I'm not sure what's so funny," he said, partially confused and partially annoyed.

I stopped laughing. "I'm sorry. I was having an internal discussion with myself about being a fool."

"What?"

"Will you come back to the house?" I asked, changing topics for a second, sort of. "I'd like to talk this through, but I'm not sure the street is the right location for it. I know it's late."

"Is it important?"

"I think this might be the most important conversation of my life."

Tom was still very confused, but he replied, "Okay."

We walked back to my townhouse in silence. I took his hand, though. I needed the reminder of how much I was starting to love this man.

I'd left the front door unlocked, of course. I didn't even have my keys with me. I had just run out the door after Tom before he got too far away.

I went to sit down on the foyer stairs again, but Tom again walked past me to sit on the couch.

Chuckling under my breath, I joined him.

"I don't like sitting on stairs," he explained, very seriously.

"Okay. I didn't know that." I got serious too.

Tom just sat there, waiting for me to say whatever it was I had to say.

I took deep breath. "Do you like me?" I started. It was an awkward start.

"Tiffany…"

"I know it's a weird question, but bear with me. I need to understand."

He sighed. "Yes, I like you."

"We've been dating for six weeks now."

Tom looked at the ceiling for a second. I assumed he was doing the math in his head. "Right."

"You like me, you just admitted. I like you."

"Okay…"

"My birthday is coming up."

"Right. End of the month."

"Correct."

"It's late, Tiffany. I'm tired. What does all this have to do with anything?"

"Birthdays make me retrospective. Do they do that for you?"

"To be honest, I don't care much about my birthday."

"Really?" This was news.

"Really. My family doesn't do much about birthdays. Except for Meghan. She's into birthdays."

"Well, I have traditionally had issues with my birthday, usually because I have expectations related to it. My family is very into birthdays. We always had parties. Since my birthday is close to the new school year, though, my birthday almost never worked out the way I wanted it too. I'd invited new friends, and it would be awkward. I usually ended up crying."

"That's awful."

I shrugged. "I explain this mostly to tell you where my head is right now."

"Got it. I think."

"As I said, birthdays make me retrospective. They make me think about the past year and what's happened. Where I've come from. And where I want to go."

"Okay."

"First, I don't want you to get me a big birthday present this year. Maybe next year, if there is a next year. But this year, it's too much expectation."

"And you don't do those well."

"Right. I don't. I will try to assign meaning to whatever you give me."

"Wouldn't it be easier to just take whatever I give you at face value?"

"That's what I'm trying to do. Reduce my expectations. So, just get me something small. Or silly. Or just take me to dinner. Okay?"

I could see the wheels in Tom's brain spinning. He was still confused. "Okay."

"But I do want to also talk about feelings."

"What about them?"

"I know you haven't had very many relationships."

"Two. I've had two relationships," Tom replied. I already knew this about him.

I smiled. "I've had a few more…"

"A lot more."

"A lot more than you, but not that many really."

"Compared to who?"

It was a valid question. Tom's older sister, Lauren, had married her college sweetheart, a guy named Charlie. That had been 15 years ago. Though she'd dated a bit in high school, she'd basically married her first serious love.

His younger sister, Meghan, had recently gotten engaged to a guy she met at work, George. She hadn't dated much before then.

The McDonnells, as a family, didn't do relationships well.

"Compared to most people."

"How many serious relationships have you had?" Tom asked, already knowing the answer as well.

"Four," I replied sheepishly. "Ian in college, and a few after college – Chris most recently. Others have not been so serious." I was thinking of Patrick, significant, but not serious.

"I rest my point."

"Okay. So, I've dated more than you have and more than your sisters."

"Right."

"Have you ever been in love?"

Tom looked at me. He held my gaze for a second. "I'm not sure I know what love would feel like."

Oh boy. The wind went right out of my proverbial sails. I had thought that might be his answer. But to hear it so boldly took my breath away.

I had to think about how to approach this logically. Tom was nothing if not logical. Programmer and full-blown nerd. I wasn't sure whether his pure logic led to the programming, or vice versa. Either way, they fed each other. He thought things through. Carefully. Fully.

I got that. I was highly logical too, even if I was also emotional and artistic in my way. I wasn't really a believer in astrology, but my sign was Libra, the scales. I liked to think I could see both sides of most issues. Or that I weighed out the pros and cons before deciding. And so I was logical in that way.

"Do you love your dad?"

"Of course," Tom said, reflexively.

"And your sisters?"

"Most of the time." He smiled.

I got it. I felt the same way about my brothers.

"But that different, isn't it?" he said. "Family love is different."

"Yes, it is. But I just wondered how deeply you felt things."

"Not very deeply, I don't think."

"I think you feel more than you let on," I argued.

Tom looked at me, confused again.

"You enjoy my company." It wasn't a question.

"Yes."

"You like me."

"Tiffany…"

"I have a point, I promise."

Tom was silent.

"Do you want to sleep with me?"

Tom and I had had some serious make-out sessions, but no sex yet.

"Am I a boy?"

"Is that all it is? Boy and girl? Because I don't think you'd just sleep with anyone."

Tom thought for a second. "Well, I haven't had that many opportunities."

I'll admit I didn't really understand that. Tom was a good-looking guy. He was shy or introverted. But I liked that in a guy. And I surely wasn't the only one.

"Granted," I said, only because it was easier than arguing about opportunities at this point. "So, you like me, and you'd like to have sex. With me."

Tom pretended to leer. "Are you asking?" he said, raising his eyebrows up and down like they do in B-movies.

I laughed. Tom's silliness was one of his most endearing qualities. "Maybe later."

"Promise?"

I smiled. "Maybe."

Tom grinned.

"Anyway, getting back to feelings..."

Tom stopped grinning.

"You've really never been in love?"

"I really don't know what that means."

"Have you ever wanted to be with someone all the time?"

"Not really."

"Have you ever cared more about someone else's feelings than your own?"

"Sure. My family. My friends. Priya, though you know how that went."

That wasn't helping. "Have you ever wanted to take care of someone? Be there for them? Someone not your family."

"Not really. Not like you mean."

Oh dear. "Were you sad when you broke up with Priya?" Priya was Tom's last serious relationship. It hadn't ended well.

"No, I was relieved."

"Why?"

"Because she wasn't good for me."

"Why do you say that?"

"She wouldn't let me be myself. She was always trying to change me."

I knew what he meant. I had finally come to realization with my last boyfriend, Chris, that part of what I really needed from him was to feel completely comfortable. To not feel like I had to be something I wasn't for him. A lot of the time, I felt that way with him, that I could just be myself. But not always. Not enough of the time. I don't think he felt that way either. I think he felt like he had to be on guard with me. Once I realized it was true that both of us had to pretend to be something we weren't, I realized we were not going to make it in the long haul. Which was sad, to me, because I did love Chris.

Tom was different. With Tom, I really felt as if I had nothing to prove, nothing to explain, nothing to justify. I was who I was with Tom. And he still liked me. I thought he felt the same way about me, but I wasn't sure.

"Do I let you be yourself?" I asked.

"You do."

"I feel like that too. I feel like you let me be my authentic self, as cliché as that sounds."

"It's pretty cliché."

"Yes, but I've never felt that way before," I admitted.

"Not even with Ian?"

Ian was one of the guys I'd almost married. "No. He wanted a religious wife, remember?"

"I remember. Then he married a woman who didn't believe in God."

"Yeah. After he'd become a minister. Not sure what he was thinking there," I said, shaking my head in memory.

Tom nodded.

"But I'm not here to talk about Ian. Or Richard. Or Chris. They all helped me realize, though, how different you are. To me. For me."

"Because I let you be you?"

"Because I don't feel like you want me to be anyone other than who I am. Maybe it's because I finally grew up. But I say what I mean with you."

"Which I appreciate."

"And you don't let me get all dramatic."

Tom smiled.

"Or rather, you let me, but it doesn't do any good with you."

"I don't like drama." He smiled, to let me know he didn't just mean my dramatic behavior, but was teasing me about my love of drama television and his not liking it.

"Haha."

He smiled a little more.

"But I do need something from you, Tom."

"Uh-oh."

"I need you to not walk away when things get uncomfortable."

"I can try. But I don't know if I can."

"Fair enough. Trying is all I can ask for. Because sometimes I'm going to cry. And it's not to manipulate you."

He looked at me skeptically.

"Really. Tonight, I wasn't trying to manipulate you. I was trying to figure out what I meant to you. And it was making me sad to think I might not mean as much you to you as you're coming to mean to me."

"Okay."

"Do you get it?"

"I guess. I don't think I've ever felt that way, though."

"Like you wanted to cry?"

"Yeah."

"Not even when your mom died?"

"I was sad, of course. And mad. And I missed her. Still do. But I didn't cry."

"Never?"

"No."

"Wow."

Tom shrugged.

I wasn't sure what to do with tonight's conversation. But it had helped me understand Tom better. And I thought he knew how to love. I thought he just didn't know that's what the feeling was when he felt it.

"Do you want to just crash here?" I asked, changing the subject.

"It's not very far to home."

"I know. But I'm feeling very close to you right now, and I don't want you to go."

"Okay."

"Really?"

"I'm a boy. I'm not going to turn down a girl asking me to spend the night."

"I don't know about sex, though."

"That's okay. That part of girls I have a lot of experience with." He smiled to let me know he was teasing. But I also knew he was serious. His relationship with Priya had had a very long spell of no sex, I knew. She had been manipulating him that way. I promised myself I would never do that to Tom.

CR ᏚᎧCR ᏚᎧCR ᏚᎧ

We went to bed. The cats came in to join me and were super confused to find their side of the bed already occupied.

"They usually sleep there," I explained to Tom as Cass and Brie jumped on and then off the bed.

"Of course."

"They may come back."

"Okay."

"Are you comfortable?" I asked, wanting to be sure he was before I tried to go to sleep.

But Tom was already asleep. I watched him for a minute in shock. Not only had we just been talking, but the light was still on. But he was well and truly asleep. I heard a soft snore. It made me chuckle. This would be interesting. I was a light sleeper. I hoped Tom's snoring didn't keep me awake.

As usual, it took me a good 20 minutes to fall asleep. I thought about our conversation tonight, Tom and I. I thought more about how to describe the feeling of both being in love and loving. Because they were different, or rather, two sides of the same coin.

This evening, I felt the pangs of being in love start to stir in me for Tom.

CR EOCR EOCR EO

Morning came, and I woke up around 6 am to feed the cats. Tom was awake, very awake, and looking at me.

"What's going on?" I asked, completely forgetting that he was an early riser.

"I'm awake. But I didn't want to wake you."

"So, you're just lying there?"

"Yeah."

"For how long?"

"About an hour, I think."

"Oh, my goodness! You could have woken me."

"You don't sleep well."

Too true. I nodded.

"I was waiting for you to wake up to feed the cats."

He remembered that I got up to feed the cats early in the morning? "Right." I wasn't really awake.

"Are you going to feed the cats, or would you like me to?"

'What?' I thought. 'That's nice of him, but they are my cats.' To Tom, I said, "Thanks, but I'll get up."

"Okay."

I got up. He got up.

"Would it be okay if I went home now?"

"You're awake, right?"

"Yeah. And I don't want to keep you from sleeping more."

He was right. I wouldn't have been able to sleep knowing he was awake. Even if he went downstairs or something. He really was one of the kindest people I knew. "Nice of you. Yes, it's okay if you go home. Text me when you get there, though. Okay?"

"I don't want to keep you from sleeping."

"I won't be able to sleep until I know you're home and safe."

Tom smiled. "Okay."

So, we headed downstairs. I kissed Tom goodbye at the front door. "Thanks for last night," he said.

"Really? But you didn't get any." I was teasing him.

He smiled. "That's okay. There will be another time."

I smiled too. Yes, there would be.

I locked the door behind Tom, fed the girls, went back upstairs, and closed the door behind me. About 15 minutes later, I heard my phone ping.

"Home!"

"Good."

"Sleep tight."

"Thanks!"

CR ᏕᎧCR ᏕᎧCR ᏕᎧ

It took Tom a long while to get comfortable with the words, "I love you".

After that first night, he started spending the night more frequently. Mostly on the weekends, but a few times during the week. We spent most evenings together, usually at my place, but sometimes at his to be equitable. We hung out with his sister Meghan and her husband George.

In fact, I was Tom's date to their recent anniversary party, where I met his extended family of uncles, aunts, and cousins on his mother's side of the family, the Youngs. The McDonnells stopped with Tom's dad, as the elder Tom had no siblings or cousins with whom that he was in contact. But Tom's mother, Mary, had been part of a large, very interconnected family. In addition to his sisters, these people were Tom's family. I had been somewhat nervous about meeting them.

"Hello, Tom-Tom!" yelled a middle-aged woman from across the reception hall. She ran over and gave Tom a huge hug, which he looked marginally uncomfortable returning. He glanced at me with something of an apology in his eyes.

'Tom-Tom?' I thought. As Tom was a junior, I guess that nickname made some sense. But yuck. My own childhood nickname was Tiff, which I now hated. Only my mother could get away with using it, and then only sparingly.

When she let him go, Tom turned to introduce me. "Tiffany, this is my cousin, Cathy. Cathy, this is my girlfriend, Tiffany."

I startled a bit internally at that title. It was the first time Tom had said those words out loud. We'd been dating for about six months now, and I'd introduced him to my family as my boyfriend a few times. But with Tom's family, his father and his sisters, I'd always been introduced with just my name. So I was surprised that Tom used the term "girlfriend" now.

In fact, we'd explicitly avoided some of the traditional boyfriend / girlfriend stuff during the recent holidays. As with my birthday, the holidays often loomed large with expectations. Therefore, I'd had much the same conversation with Tom about Christmas and New Years that we had had about my birthday. Low-key presents. Low-key celebrations. He would spend Christmas with his family celebrating as they usually did, while I would spend Christmas with mine.

The Johnsons had a fairly elaborate set of Christmas rituals that I had told Tom about, but didn't think he needed to participate in just yet. I celebrated Christmas twice: once on Christmas Eve with my father, my brothers, and their families; and then again on Christmas Day with my mother, stepfather, my mother's children, occasionally my stepfather's children, and their significant others. I didn't have one of those yet, though Tom was getting close to that designation. But my brothers did. Alexander Christopher Johnson had married Jennifer Murphy, and they had two children, Peyton and Samantha. Phineas Harrison Johnson, my younger brother, was partnered with Joseph Rodriguez, with whom he'd adopted an orphan in the aftermath of Hurricane Sandy they had named Eliza Harrison-Rodriguez.

The McDonnells were much more low key about the holidays, apparently even more so since their mom had died nearly a decade ago. Now, the holidays were much like their birthdays; only Meghan made a big deal of them. Their father, Tom, probably would have preferred to just stay home by himself. But Meghan put on a feast and expected her father and Tom to show up for at least that meal. Their other sister, Lauren, lived in Colorado. She and her family, from what Tom had told me, came to Virginia for the holidays every other year, alternating between the McDonnell side of the family and her husband Charlie's family. This year was a year without the Davises from Colorado, which made it easier for me not to participate in their plans.

Cousin Cathy. As soon as I'd connected with Tom, Meghan, and Lauren on social media, Cathy had sent me a request to become friends. I looked her up and knew she was connected to Tom somehow. I recognized her maiden name, Young, as the same maiden name as Tom's mother. So I figured she was a cousin. It was the first time we'd talked about that side of the family.

"She's one of my Young cousins," Tom had explained, when I asked who Cathy was. "She likes to know what's going on with everyone."

"She's a busybody?"

"The McDonnells, as you've learned, aren't very demonstrative. It drives the Young side a little crazy, because they are strong proponents of family ties. Since Mom died, they've been really trying to hold onto our bond. My sisters and I go visit once a year, usually. We like our cousins, even if they do get to be a little much sometimes."

I laughed at Tom's characterization of the McDonnells as not "very demonstrative". That was putting it mildly. I'd met the elder Tom a few times now. The first time, he didn't even shake my hand, just nodded his head when I was introduced. The second time I met him, I'd hugged him goodbye, and I'd startled everyone by doing so. That was the Johnson way, at least my branch of it. The first time my Tom met my mother, she'd pulled him in for a big hug. I had a feeling the Youngs and the Johnsons had more in common than the Youngs and McDonnells did.

"Ah," I said in response to Tom's description of Cathy. "I don't accept friend requests from people I don't know."

"I'll tell Cathy. You'll meet her soon, I'm sure."

And now I had. Which meant I was going to have to accept that friend request. Oh well. Time would tell if that would be a problem or not.

Cathy grabbed my hand and pulled me away from Tom. "We'll be back," she said over her shoulder as she took me across the room.

Tom followed in our wake, for which I was grateful, even though Cathy clearly had not expected him to do so. She presented me to more of the Youngs.

"Everyone, this is the infamous Tiffany," she announced dramatically to a table with a half dozen other middle-aged cousins at it.

'Infamous?' I wondered.

Tom whispered in my ear, "Sorry about this."

I smiled at him. I'd suspected what I was getting myself into by coming to Meghan and George's anniversary as Tom's date. I knew his family, like mine, would be excited to see him paired off finally. It didn't help that his last relationship with Priya had been a toxic one. I think they wanted to be sure they approved of me.

"I like being infamous. What am I infamous for?" I said, teasing Cathy and immediately winning her over to my side, as I knew I would. Cathy reminded me of my friend Jane, in fact. Heart of gold, but not much of a filter.

"For snagging Tom-Tom, of course!" Cathy replied, with a laugh.

'Snagging?' Was I destined to question every comment out of Cathy's mouth? I thought I might.

"Well, I'd like to think we snagged each other. It's nice to meet you collectively, but who's who?" I asked, to steer the conversation. So, I met the other cousins, but I'm not sure I retained anyone's names then. I've met them all several times now, and now I know their names. And yes, I was correct. The Youngs have much more in common with the Johnsons than with the McDonnells.

After the party, Tom and I drove back to my townhouse. We settled in, after feeding the cats, exhausted not only by the long day of family, but by being 'on' all day. The introverts in us needed time to recharge.

"I had a good time today," I said as I turned out the light.

Cass was already lumped next to Tom. It was January, and she loved to lump in the colder months. Brie was sitting next to me, not having settled down yet as she waited for me to adjust the blankets to be just so.

"You did? Cathy wasn't too much, was she?"

"A little. But in a good way. She's already re-sent a friend request, you know?"

"Has she? Did you accept this time?"

"I did. She's already liked my post about the joy of being home after a long day."

"The other cousins are all on social media too. I'm sure you'll get friend requests from them, too."

"Okay. Do you mind their connecting to me?"

"Not at all. It's what they do."

"And I'm your girlfriend," I teased.

Tom looked at me and laughed. "Caught that, did you?"

"Yes. I was happy to hear the designation."

"I figured you would be."

"You're my boyfriend, too, you know."

"I know. You already called me that a few times."

"I did? Oh, yeah, with my family, huh?"

Tom nodded. "And with your office friends. I don't think you even realized you'd done it. But when we went to that office party, you introduced me a few times as 'your boyfriend Tom'."

"I really don't remember that."

"I figured."

"It didn't bother you?"

"No. I'm comfortable with that – what did you call it – designation?"

I laughed. "Yes, that's what I called it."

"Oh, and something else."

"What's that?"

"I love you."

Both cats got displaced as I kissed and hugged Tom. "I love you, too."

"I know. You've said that too."

"What?!" Now, *that* I was sure I hadn't said. I had promised myself I wasn't going to make Tom uncomfortable with telling him I loved him – though I had grown to – until he said it first. "No, I haven't!"

"You have. Again, I don't think you realized it."

"When?" I really didn't think I had.

"In the mornings. When I leave. You're half asleep, still in bed."

I thought about it. And I realized I'd said "See you later. Love you." I blushed, though Tom couldn't see it. "Sorry. I really was trying not to say it first."

"Why?"

"Because I didn't want you to be uncomfortable or feel obligated to say it back."

"But I wasn't, and I didn't."

I loved that Tom was honest about things like that. He didn't say things he didn't mean. "True."

"But it was nice to know how you felt."

"Really?"

"Really. And it made me realize that I loved you too."

"I thought you didn't know what love was?"

"I didn't."

"But now you do?"

"Now, I do."

For that, Tom got more than just a kiss. The cats got banished from the room for a while.

RENTING OUT HIS HOUSE (2018)

Now that the most important decision had been made – and we were going to live together! – it was time to get our houses ready for sale and rent, respectively, and look for a new one.

Tom's house definitely needed more work than mine did. He had lived there for years, and other than keeping the major systems running, had done nothing to the house. One of the first times I was there in 2014, in fact, I had noticed there was a hole in the cooktop of the stove.

‿ ‿‿ ‿‿ ‿

"Tom, there's a hole in your stove!" I had said, in alarm.

"Oh that. It's been there for a while. It's not hurting anything," he had replied cavalierly as he was making omelets for us. Cheese omelets were his specialty, hence Sabrina's nickname.

I freaked out. It was a gas stove. A hole seemed like a bad idea. "I think you should get a new one," I had said, trying to remain calm and also not be seen as a nag. It wasn't my house, after all. I really had no say.

"The oven doesn't work either. I don't need it, as I never bake or anything."

"Well, I suppose that's okay. But a hole in the top seems like you're asking for trouble. It is a gas stove."

"I could use a new microwave too. That I do use, and this one isn't very reliable anymore."

I had kept my mouth shut. I could tell Tom was not a guy who cared a lot about his surroundings. His computers, definitely. And he did like the house to be comfortable. But up to date or stylish? He couldn't have cared less.

"If it bothers you, I can get a new one," he had said, sheepishly, though I hadn't said anything more.

"It should be a good time of the year to buy." It was right around Thanksgiving, a good time to buy big ticket items.

"Okay!" Tom was a guy who agreed in exclamation marks. He texted them too. It was adorable.

"We can look this weekend."

"I will check for sales. There's bound to be a few." He had smiled.

"Yup!" I could exclaim too.

So, on Saturday, we went to a local big box store. I had assumed we would go to a couple of stores and check out the competition. But that wasn't Tom's way.

"I think this will work, don't you?" he had asked me, after we'd been in the store for maybe five minutes.

"Suuure," I had replied hesitantly. I had thought we would go to more than one store. I had thought we'd look at multiple options, including more high-end options. But no. Tom had found basically what he already had. It had worked before. It would work again.

"What?" he had asked me. I have a terrible poker face.

"I guess I thought this was only the first stop."

"Why?"

"Big purchase. Don't you do comparison shopping?"

"I did. Online. Before we came. This is the best deal for the money. It has all the major functionality. The microwave is rated highly. The oven/stove too. I don't need much."

"What about resale?"

"Tiffany, you've seen my house. And my neighborhood. These are not homes the rich buy."

He had a point. There was no reason to get a six-burner Wolf or something like that. "You have a point," I had responded. "Basic and functional it is."

"Just like me!"

"Well, I don't think you are basic or just functional."

"All my parts work!" Tom had kidded.

"That they do," I had laughed. "That they do."

"We aren't fancy, the McDonnells. But we get the job done."

"If you say so!"

He had looked at me, pretending to be aghast. "Are you saying I haven't been getting the job done?"

"Oh dear."

He waggled his eyebrows at me. "You just say the word, and I will endeavor to get it done right."

I giggled. Tom did make me laugh. A lot. "Later."

"Promise?"

"Yes, you. Now, buy the appliances already!"

"Yes, ma'am!"

I had laughed again. I left Tom to finish his purchases. I wandered into another part of the store, where I was immediately greeted by a "friendly" salesperson.

"May I help you?" he said.

"No, thank you. I'm just wandering."

"We have a big sale going on."

"Yes, my husband is buying some appliances over there. See?"

He looked across the showroom floor and saw Tom. "Ah. I see." And he left.

I don't know why I said "husband" instead of "boyfriend". I think I was trying to get the salesperson to leave me alone, and I thought making our relationship more significant would help. But it did make me think. We'd only been dating for a few months, but I could see myself with Tom. Of course, I hadn't even broached the idea of being in love yet.

CR ᏕᎦCR ᏕᎦCR ᏕᎦ

Other than the stove, microwave, and an updated furnace, Tom hadn't done anything else with the house in the four years I'd known him. Not only were the living room curtains hideously ugly – they had large red roses on them – they also were filthy. Tom admitted they were original to the house, as he'd bought the model unit. He'd never replaced them, had never taken them down to wash them, and so I was correct in guessing that after 10 years, they were dusty beyond belief. With my fear of spiders and other things that nest in dirt, I had a hard time sitting in his living room without squirming.

Not that I was great about cleaning curtains. I wasn't sure the last time I'd washed mine. I did buy new ones when I'd moved in, but I made a mental note to get mine cleaned as well. My house also would show better with freshly ironed curtains.

In addition to the dirty, ugly curtains, one wall of the dining rooms was completely mirrored. I'm sure the designer thought it made the space appear larger. But it also made it so you saw every movement on that floor, from kitchen to dining room to living room. I'm sure Tom didn't even notice it any longer, as it had just always been him in the house. But I found it more than a little creepy. Not only that, but mirrored walls were very '70s, I thought. Like the red rose curtains, they were décor that hadn't aged well.

Tom slept in the downstairs bedroom, which had a bathroom across the hall. That meant it wasn't an "en suite", but it was close. And as that was the only bedroom in that floor, he essentially had the floor to himself. I was thinking about how we would use this to market the home for rental as a mother-in-law suite or more likely a teenager wanting privacy. The other rooms on that floor were the laundry/utility room and the family room, complete with fireplace and walk out to a nice patio.

The bedroom itself was decent size – Tom had a queen-sized bed in the room, along with a couple of dressers. So, I didn't mind sleeping over sometimes. The furnace was a little noisy at night, but not horrible. It was, again, one of those things you wouldn't notice after a little while of living in the house.

But the bathroom was hideous. The size of the large standing shower was the only plus. The shower floor was stained yellow from the hard water we have in Virginia – not a good look in a shower. And the bathroom was wallpapered, and the wallpaper was quite literally peeling off the walls from years of steamy showers. It didn't bother Tom in the slightest. But it wasn't going to be possible to rent the house out with that bathroom like that. If the dirty shower stall didn't discourage renters, the falling wallpaper would! Tom was aware of this once we decided to move. But in the month since our decision, I had gotten several of my to-do items done. Tom hadn't even started on his.

"It's been cold, and work has been busy," he explained.

Again, I didn't want to nag. It was his house after all. But my plan had been for Tom and me to share the mortgage on the new house. If he couldn't rent this one – or even sell it – then I would have to pay the mortgage myself. I could; I just had a bunch of other ideas of what I could do with the extra money if I had it. So, I tried to let Tom move at Tom's pace. But it wasn't easy.

The top floor was also problematic, too, though not as bad for the most part. The main challenges were the carpet on the stairs, stained from many spills of coffee and years of use, and the relentless use of wallpaper. Here, the wallpaper wasn't peeling, as it was in the downstairs bathroom, but it was still ugly. 'Wallpaper does not age well,' I thought. Another reason to never use it. The master bedroom upstairs did, indeed, have an en suite bathroom, easily large enough for two adults to move around each other in the mornings. The bathtub had leaked, however. Evidence of that was seen on the ceiling of the dining room below. Tom had had the leak fixed, or so he thought.

"I just turned off the water to the tub. That way, I didn't have to worry about it any longer," he explained.

"So, you don't know if the tub is really fixed?"

"Well, the plumber said the whole thing needed to be recaulked. It was expensive, and no one was using the bathroom. So, I put it off."

"Okay," I replied evenly. The list of to-dos at Tom's house was very long, even if all we wanted to do was get it rented. Needless to say, being able to use the whirlpool bathtub in the master suite was going to be a selling point. But only if it worked!

Aesthetically, the house had good 'bones'. It was four bedrooms, and three and half baths, so it was a good size too. It didn't have a garage, which I was spoiled by having, or so Tom teased, but it did have an assigned parking space. But, boy, did it need a lot of work!

It was also going to need to be staged or redecorated internally for rental. Tom's four computers occupied the dining room, across three desks. Two of the laptops were for work, but he also had an old desktop he'd restored years earlier, and a personal laptop. There was a large box in one corner, which I assumed was the security safe for his classified laptop. There was no dining room table and chairs. Just wires everywhere.

That made sense since Tom worked half the week at home, and using the dining room for his office was more comfortable than one of the guest rooms upstairs. But the current situation wouldn't be good for showing other people.

"I know I'll have to rearrange things upstairs," Tom admitted, "once I get the upstairs ready. No point in moving the computers upstairs until the rooms have been refurbished."

"True," I agreed, though I also thought it was a convenient excuse. Still, we weren't in a terrible rush to get Tom's place ready. Not like my place.

"I guess I need to find someone to strip and redo the walls first. Then paint, of course. After that, deal with the carpeting."

"And the plumbing. You might need to do the plumbing first, in case it involves holes in the walls."

"Good point!" he agreed.

We were sitting in his living room after our tour to make the list of what needed to be done. It was amazing how exhausting that had been. And how long the list was. I felt badly that I was making Tom spend all this time and money on his house, just so we could live together, when he was perfectly content with the way it was already. But then again, I thought, if he'd only maintained it along the way…

Finally, I felt as though I had to do something. Anything.

I stood up and crossed to where the incredibly ugly curtains, with their years of dust, were hanging. I turned and said to Tom, "Can I?"

He knew without my saying it what I was asking. I wanted to tear those curtains. Now!

He laughed. "Sure! But it's going to be messy."

"I know. But I'm already dirty and sweaty from walking around the house. And I can't stand these another minute!"

He laughed louder. "I'll help."

There were actually two sets of curtains, one over the window by the television and the other over the door to the deck. So, Tom could take down one set while I did the other. I was going to enjoy this!

But it was harder than it looked. Each window had a set of curtains and a valance, in the matching fabric. But neither was on a rod. I had assumed that there were two rods, one for the valance and one for the curtains. That's how it was in my house.

But not so in Tom's.

The valance was nailed to a 2x2" that had been nailed to the ledge that ran the length of the living room. Removing it meant making holes in the ledge. Ugh.

"This is the strangest décor I've ever seen," I complained.

Tom just shrugged. "Model house." It was his answer for every house-related challenge.

"You okay with another project?" I asked, knowing the ledge would have to be repaired and new curtain rods installed.

"Sure! We'll just add it to the list."

"Oh dear."

But we were committed now. So we pulled at the valance. Tom had to help me; I couldn't remove the valance by myself. We did my window first and then did his. Without the valances, the windows let in so much more light. I loved that. I was a big fan of light. Tom was a bit of a vampire. He didn't really like sunlight, and his fair skin made him like it even less.

"Well, that will make you happy, huh?" Tom said, anticipating my response to more natural light.

Natural light was another reason a single-family house had appeal. With an interior townhouse, I only got light on two sides. Same for Tom's townhouse. My townhouse faced east-west, so it got a lot of light and pretty sunrises and sunsets. Tom's house was more north-south, so it rarely got direct light. With the valances removed, however, it would be better. And again would show better.

Next, we tackled the curtains. Again, there was no rod. The curtains had been tacked to the underside of the ledge. That explained why they hung in perfect drapes for all these years. They literally could not move. They couldn't even be drawn. Oh, what was the designer thinking!?

As we took the curtains down, dust flew everywhere even as we were trying to be careful about moving the fabric much. It was just impossible after 10 years of buildup.

"Achoo!" I let out. I'm very allergic to dust, mold, and mildew. I'm sure all three were in those curtains.

Tom chuckled a bit, then let out an "Achoo!" of his own.

Luckily, Tom had the foresight to get some garbage bags for the now-discarded curtains while I worked on getting them into a semblance of order. It took one bag per curtain, but we felt better when the dust was contained. The valance-wrapped pieces of wood were another story. There wasn't much we could do about putting them in anything. We put them on the deck instead, so at least the dust and whatever else was on them would be outside. With the curtains in the garbage can and the valances out back, the house already felt cleaner and airier.

What I hadn't known either, because I'd never really looked behind the curtains, was there were blinds too. So that meant Tom wouldn't be exposed to light sitting in his living and dining rooms if he didn't want to. I felt better about taking down the curtains knowing that Tom wouldn't have to see the sun if he didn't want to.

And then I realized that, if the curtains hadn't been cleaned in 10 years, then neither had the blinds. Oh dear.

I got up again, got a sponge and some paper towels from the kitchen and set to work on cleaning the blinds. Tom helped, of course. By the end of the evening, the blinds were clean, and the house looked infinitely better without the hideous curtains. Now if only taking down the mirrors could be that easy…

CR ℰℭ ℰℭ ℰℭ ℰℭ

Another month passed, and Tom still hadn't even lined up contractors to give him estimates.

"Work is really busy right now," he explained.

"Your house. Your call," I insisted. Though it bothered me that Tom was such a procrastinator. Was I going to have to do all the organizing if we needed repairs done on the new house? I resigned myself to the idea. After all, I'd been doing these tasks myself for as long as I'd owned homes. Just because I was moving in with a man didn't mean I wasn't capable. Or responsible. And as Tom still planned to work from home, just our new home, we had the advantage of being able to have flexibility in setting appointment times. That almost made up for my having to be the one to do the planning. Almost.

CR ℰℭ ℰℭ ℰℭ ℰℭ

Another month passed. Tom said he'd called a few people, but they hadn't had time to come yet to give him estimates. The one who said he would come had never showed, which ticked Tom off. I got it.

CR ᔓᗤCR ᔓᗤCR ᔓᗤ

Finally, three months after we made the list of what needed to be done, Tom finally arranged for the wallpaper to be taken down in a few of the rooms, and the walls reskimmed for painting later.

"I knew it wasn't going to be cheap," he said as we were having dinner, "but, boy, it's really expensive."

"Hard work," I countered.

"Yeah. I know. I tried to do some of it myself. Even in the bathroom where the wallpaper was falling down, it was almost impossible to get that stuff off."

"I guess that's the idea, right, that you don't want the wallpaper to come off the walls. But yeah, it's a pain."

"So, we won't be wallpapering our new place?" Tom teased.

I looked at him in mock horror. "No, we will not!" I mock-yelled.

And we cracked up at ourselves.

"It's going to take a week, too. So, I warned my co-workers."

"Warned them why?"

"Because I'm going to be crabby."

I chuckled. "I know. Having strangers in the house for a week. That will be awful."

"You laugh. But it will be."

"I know. And you don't even have cats who will take out on you their annoyance in the changes in their environment."

"Cass would never. She loves me. Cheese Omelet, on the other hand…"

"Just you wait. You'll see. You've only seen the nice side of the cats so far."

"Oh really? You mean when Little Mama puts her paws in my face at 3 am, that's being nice?"

I laughed. "Well, she's hungry, and she wants to make sure you know it."

"I'm sure."

"At least I don't make you clean their litter boxes."

"True. I would, if you wanted me to."

"No, that's my job. I appreciate that you feed them a couple of times a week, though. Saves me from getting up early."

"Well, sort of. I mean, you still wake up when I leave."

"True. But I get back to sleep that much faster!"

Tom laughed. "You and George do love your sleep." Tom's brother-in-law, George, was a late sleeper like me. It explained why Tom was so understanding of my habits.

"And you and Meghan both snore!" I quipped.

"Can't deny it. You have proof!"

I had recorded Tom one night when he was being particularly loud. He and Cass were also snoring in unison. It had been too funny not to memorialize. "That I do!"

CR ꇄꁍCR ꇄꁍCR ꇄꁍ

The walls were finished. Ready for paint.
But the additional chores went undone.
No painting.
No new carpet for the stairs.
No new curtain rods, much less curtains.

I loved Tom deeply, but I also knew he had his flaws. We both tended to procrastinate, but Tom was taking it to new levels. Or rather, I should say he was bipolar about getting things done. He either did something immediately, as with the appliances, or it took him forever to get it done. Very rarely anything in between. And so the question of whether Tom's house would be ready to rent in time for the purchase of our new home was hardly answerable.

"My version of a stress dream is, really, showing up on a concert stage with a drum set and not knowing the chart." -- Damien Chazelle

Memories (2011-2013)

"Tom," I asked carefully, "do you need help from me to get your house done? I could call people. Let me know."

I sent this text and waited. I was being a chicken by texting this offer instead of waiting until I saw Tom later that night and making the suggestion in person. But I was also trying to keep my nagging low key. So, after thinking about how to handle the situation, I decided on this course of action. I still wasn't sure it was the best one.

No immediate reply.

So, now I started to rethink my strategy. Had I just pissed Tom off so much he wasn't even willing to write me back?

I didn't think he'd break up with me over this. We were pretty solid. And when we did have problems, we usually were able to talk them through. I didn't think he'd be willing to throw away our relationship over this. Certainly not without talking to me first. We'd gotten that far in our relationship. Hadn't we?

An hour went by, and still no response.

I'm starting to panic. I really didn't want to lose Tom over his procrastination over his house. It wasn't that important. 'Oh, Tiffany, what did you do!?' I cried to myself.

Two hours later, I was inconsolable. I had started a million other texts, apologizing for overstepping. Begging Tom not to leave me. Telling him I would never ask about the contractors again.

I hadn't sent any of them.

I was trying to wait, to see what he really would say.

Because I did have a tendency to be dramatic. To assume the worst. To make more of things than they were.

I spent another hour convincing myself that's what was going on here. I tried to distract myself with house-hunting. And I redid my finances again to make sure I really could buy a house without Tom if I had to. Though without Tom, I wasn't sure I wanted to buy a single-family house.

After all, the dream of a single-family house also included someone to share it with. Just me and the cats wouldn't be enough. Wouldn't complete the ideal.

I also had another long conversation with myself, about the value of listening over pushing. Of letting others do things in their own time. That Tom's house was Tom's house – not my circus, not my monkeys.

Finally, four hours after I'd sent the text, I got a reply.

"We'll talk tonight."

'Well,' I thought, 'at least I'm going to get to see Tom one more time.'

CR ՋՈՇ ՋՈՇ ՋՈ

Tom usually came to my house in the evenings. He knew I didn't like his house very much, especially after the situation with the curtains. It wasn't just that the townhouse needing fixing up; it was also that it seemed musty to me. I didn't have an allergic reaction as with mold or mildew. I couldn't really justify my feelings. I felt badly for how I felt, and because Tom knew.

In typical Tom fashion, however, he had always accepted my antipathy and not taken it as an affront against him. After all, even his sister Meghan had to wonder, "She saw your house, and she still wants to go out with you?" He knew the house wasn't his selling point.

I should also mention that Tom drove a 25-year-old car. With a bumper that had been reattached with duct tape and windows that didn't go up and down any longer. When I'd first seen his car, after our second date, I had had my doubts. I'm not a 'keeping up with the joneses' kind of person. I didn't care that he wasn't driving the latest sports car. I wasn't either. But I think it was weird that Tom didn't drive a nicer car. He could certainly afford it.

And that was really the crux of it for me. I wasn't extravagant in my purchases. But I liked to live comfortably. And, as was obvious from my interest in buying a new house, I had certain ideas about what I should have achieved in my life.

Tom didn't have these ambitions. He'd essentially been in the same job for his whole career, without any increase in responsibility or managerial role, and that was just fine with him. He did good work, was compensated appropriately, and in his case, the work he did was also important for the nation's security. I knew that much, even if I still didn't know which agency he worked for – CIA, DIA, NSA – I was sure it was one of them.

No, Tom didn't have ambition in the way I thought of it, and he would be the first to tell you that. His ambition was to do his job well, to live his life the way he wanted, and to enjoy the company of others around him. Beyond that, what kind of car he drove or whether his house was perfectly maintained, just wasn't important.

I knew this. I accepted this. I even thought this was admirable in a lot of ways. My brother Alexander had some of the same qualities. He'd had the same government job for more than two decades, and he was perfectly fine with that. He had made a point to his bosses that he had no interest in managing other people. Projects, sure. But not people. He didn't want the headache. Xan – Alexander's nickname –

had always been like that, and I certainly didn't think any less of him for his lack of ambition in the traditional sense of the word. So, when I had met Tom, I had seen the similarities and thought about all the good qualities both men shared. A strong commitment to family. Good ethics. Caring about those less fortunate than themselves. Not being a Type A was fine. There were too many of us out there in the world anyway. And I did wonder if two Type As would work as a couple. Certainly Xan's wife, Jenn, had more in common with me than with Xan. She wasn't quite a Type A the way I was. But she was close. Certainly closer than Xan. And Tom.

Anyway, I was waiting for Tom to arrive, nervously pacing in my living room and looking out the window for his car to pull onto my street. Terrified of what this evening would bring.

CR ЄⁿCR ЄⁿCR Єⁿ

"Hey Tiffany!" Tom greeted me, as he got out of his car.

I had come down the stairs to see him. I didn't usually do this. I usually waited for him to ring the bell, even though most of the time when I knew he was coming over.

But today I couldn't wait. My nerves were shot. Like taking off a band-aid, I wanted to get through the pain and to the other side.

So, imagine my surprise at Tom's cheerful tone. I had tears on the brims of my eyes, tears I was trying hard not to shed because Tom didn't like tears, even real ones.

I ran across the driveway and into his arms. Tears were flowing now, though some of them were hopeful.

"What's going on, babe?" he asked. Tom rarely used terms of endearment. It wasn't his style.

So, I pulled back from having my face buried in his shoulder at the word 'babe'. "Babe?"

"Sorry," he said, running his hand through what was left of his hair, "It's been a day. I'm sorry it took me so long to return your text this morning," he explained, as he reached for my hand and started walking toward the door. Everything seemed completely normal.

I wiped away the tears and took his hand. He squeezed mine in response. Maybe all was well?

We started up the narrow stairs, forcing us to go single file. Tom pushed me in front of him, as he always did. He was my backup in this as in all things.

"Lauren called this morning. Charlie fell. He's okay, but he's in the hospital. So, then I had to call Meghan. And Dad. And we needed to figure out whether one of us needed to go help Lauren with the kids. She said she's good, she doesn't need help. After all, Tom's parents live nearby. But we spent a good portion of the morning trying to figure out if she was just being Lauren or whether she really did need help."

"Is Charlie going to be okay?"

"Yeah. That's why we ultimately decided we didn't need to go. He's going to need ACL surgery. He'll be in the hospital for a while and then recovering at home. But he'll be fine."

"Thank goodness," I thought. And then I realized I'd let my overdramatic self run rampant all day for no good reason. Tom wasn't mad at me. He just had had other things to do.

"What's up with you? Why the tears?"

So, he had noticed them. I'd wondered. "I'll tell you later. Tell me more about your day. How are Meghan and your dad?"

"The same. You know Dad. He's never one to complain. Or tell me much of anything."

Like father, like son, I thought.

"Dad's been having some heart issues, apparently. Meghan knew – she's the one who took him to the doctors when he wasn't allowed to drive himself. He had a pacemaker put in. I didn't even know!"

"Oh dear. You have had a day!"

"Yeah. It's been all family, all day. I'm beat."

"I can imagine."

We went inside. I led Tom to the living room instead of downstairs.

"Not downstairs?"

"Let's finish this conversation first."

"Okay. As long as we don't sit on the steps."

"Yes, dear."

Tom smiled at my words. I was hardly the 'yes, dear' type.

"You've been crying a lot. Your eyes are all puffy. What's going on, Tiffany?"

I started to cry again. How much should I confess, I wondered?

But this was Tom. He was the one person I could always be myself with, right? He would get it.

"You remember the text I sent this morning?"

"The one about helping with contractors. I probably should let you help with that. I'm terrible with those kinds of things. You're much more organized."

I laughed inside. What a ridiculous ninny I was.

Then I laughed out loud. "I spent the day thinking I'd pushed you away."

"What? What are you talking about?" Tom sounded genuinely confused.

Which made me realize how utterly absurd I had been all day. Thinking that he had been ignoring me on purpose. Or to hurt me. I knew Tom better than that!

"Well, I've been trying not to bug you about the house."

"You have?"

"I have."

"Why?"

"Because it's your house."

"Yeah. So?"

"So, it should be yours to fix up."

"It is. I'll pay for it."

"That's not what I meant."

"Well, what did you mean?"

"I meant that I shouldn't be bugging you about getting it done. It's not my circus, not my monkeys."

"You do love that expression."

"Well, it seems appropriate in this case," I said, smiling, teasing Tom.

"Oh, so now I'm a monkey?"

"Absolutely!" I said, kissing him. "Oh Tom!" Tears were surfacing again, but this time because I was happy. I wasn't going to be alone.

"What?"

"I love you!"

"Love you too. What's really going on?"

"I told you. I was worried that I had ticked you off by interfering with your house plans. And that you were so mad at me that you were never going to talk to me again."

"Tiffany..." Tom warned.

"Yes, I know. You don't work that way. That's what I have to remember when I get like that, all worried about you and what you're thinking."

"You know you can always just ask me. I'll tell you."

"I know. Same here. It's why we're good for each other. Because we can talk about the hard things."

"So, why didn't you just text me again?"

"Because I was afraid. When I didn't hear back. Because, well, I was being stupid."

"And..."

"And dramatic. It's a bad habit."

"I understand. I still have a few of those myself."

"Yeah, like not telling me you're talking to your family and busy."

Tom grinned. "Point taken. Yes, I'm not good about telling you what's going on."

"Is Charlie really going to be okay?"

"Yeah. He was playing soccer. He tore his ACL. It happens to a lot of people."

"And Lauren is okay. Should I call her?"

"Maybe later."

"Okay.

Tom got serious. He took my hand again. There was something he was going to tell me. And I wasn't going to like it. I could just tell. Maybe I did have something to worry about?

CR EDCR EDCR ED

"I should tell you about the house."

"What about it?" Now, it was my turn to be terribly confused.

"I know I've been delaying getting the work done. I realized that today. When I was talking to Meghan about Dad, and she was asking about the house."

"Okay…"

"I don't mind that you asked about my getting the contractors lined up. Really, I don't. But…"

"But what?" I was afraid again.

"But…there's a reason I haven't done anything with the house in years."

'What was going on? Did he lose all his money somehow?' I thought I knew Tom really well.

"Priya."

"What does she have to do with it?"

"She pushed me on the house. A lot."

"She pushed you on everything." I didn't know all the details of their relationship. I just knew she was a manipulator of the first order. Meghan had told me that much. And I knew that some of Tom's touchiness about tears came because of her.

Tom laughed, but it was a bitter laugh. "Yes, she did."

"Like I do?" It was one of my fears when I tried to encourage Tom to do things. I really tried not to manipulate him.

"No, you don't manipulate me."

"I just tell you what to do."

Tom laughed, this time more genuinely. "Sometimes. When I need it. Like with the house. I know it's been bugging you that I've been dragging my heels. And I have been. I just didn't realize it, didn't confront it until I was talking to Meghan."

"Because of Priya?"

"Yes. She was very Type A."

"So, am I." I owned my Type A.

"Yes you are, but you aren't afraid to admit it. Priya was. She liked to pretend she was vulnerable."

"The two aren't opposites, you know. You can be vulnerable and Type A."

"True. But she pretended to be vulnerable to manipulate. Not just me, but everyone."

"She doesn't sound like a nice person."

"Oh, she's a sweetheart. Really. If you met her, you would love her. You wouldn't realize what a snake she is for a while. She's very good."

"And she pushed you about your house?"

"And my car."

I stayed quiet.

"And my job. And my eating habits. And my taste in clothes. And, well, just about everything."

"If she wanted to change everything about you, then why was she with you?"

"Very good question. One that I finally asked myself. And her. And her answer was that I was fixable."

"Fixable!?"

"Fixable. She thought she could make me the perfect man."

"Oh dear."

"Yeah."

"She didn't accept you for who you are."

"She liked some of the things about me. She said I smart."

"You are."

"Not like her. Or you."

"You don't give yourself enough credit." We'd had this conversation before. I had a lot of formal education, and Tom seemed to equate this to being super smart. I was smart. But just because I had more degrees than he did didn't make me smarter than him.

Tom smiled. He knew I was very serious about this. I wouldn't, couldn't be with a guy who didn't match my intelligence. I had tried it in the past. And it was not good. I might be more word smart, with a bigger vocabulary. But I couldn't begin to program the way Tom could. I didn't even understand most of what he did try to tell me about what he did with his day. Algorithms and the like. I got the concept. But that was it.

"Okay, I'll admit I have a brain or two."

"Good, because you do." I was very serious.

"Anyway, she did admit that my smarts attracted her. And she actually liked that I can't talk about my job. She found the mystery enticing."

"I could see that. James Bond-ish."

"Not hardly."

"Well, you know what I mean."

"I do. And yes, the mystery was intriguing to her, apparently. But everything else about me she didn't like. But thought she could change."

"How exactly?"

"Tears. And sex. Lots of sex." Tom smiled.

"Well, you are a boy." It was one of our running jokes. It stemmed from that first night when I'd invited him to stay.

"Never denied it," Tom said, with a fake leer.

I laughed, well and truly laughed. It felt good. And it reminded me of Tom's best quality. He made me laugh. Every time we were together. Usually over something silly. Often a play on words that was groan-worthy.

But it was more than that. It wasn't just that Tom could be and was silly with me; it was that his being silly let me be silly. I had spent a lot of my life being a serious person. But the kid in me still liked to laugh and be silly, and not be judged for it.

"But seriously, let me tell you what I finally realized today," Tom said.

CR ED CR ED CR ED

"Priya ruled my life. For almost three years, every thought I had was what could I do to make her happy, to make her love me, to keep her with me."

"Those aren't bad goals. But I know it wasn't a good thing."

"No, it wasn't.

"When I met Priya, I thought she was the most beautiful thing I'd ever seen. And I couldn't imagine why she would want to be with a guy like me."

"Again, you don't give yourself enough credit," I interjected.

Tom smiled, but didn't respond. He was good for my ego, and I liked to think I was good for his. Our mutual admiration was healthy for both of us, because we'd both struggled with self-love for a long time.

"Anyway, she was gorgeous. Her skin was lustrous, her hair silky, her body, well, let's just say she knew how to use her assets very well. And she's very smart.

"We met at a party. Through Peter. Sound familiar?"

I startled. I had no idea that's where they had met.

"Peter knew Priya through work. As you know, he and I went to University of Chicago at the same time. We were roommates who developed a genuine friendship in time."

"He's good people."

"He is. He didn't see through Priya either. Not until we started dating. When he saw how she treated me, he tried to tell me. But I didn't listen. I didn't listen to anyone. Peter, Meghan, even my dad. They all saw through Priya before I did."

"It's hard to see what's right in front of you, sometimes."

"Some of what Priya wanted to change about me, I wanted to change too. I wanted to be more hip, more of the kind of guy that other people like."

I didn't say anything, but Tom looked at me. He knew what I was thinking.

"When she suggested shopping for new clothes, I was all for it. I had, have no idea about fashion. I wear what's comfortable."

"Nothing wrong with that."

"True. But I wanted to fit in more. Priya has ambition. She got herself invited to lots of parties with important people. Lots of them were work-related, but she also donated to charities, enough to be invited to galas and the like. She needed a date. She wanted me to go with her. But I needed better clothes, more fashionable clothes."

"But you hate parties."

"I tried to like them, or at least tolerate them."

I looked skeptical.

"Really, I did. For Priya. Because they meant so much to her. And I thought it was admirable that she gave money to these causes. They were causes I supported as well. Environmental causes. Pro-choice. The arts. So, we went shopping. We bought me a tux. A couple of other suits. I spent a small fortune on new clothes.

"We went to party after party. Every weekend it seemed like there was another one. I tried to make small talk, but I'm no good at it. Priya would tell me afterward that someone said something about my awkwardness."

"Did they really?"

"I have no idea. But I tried to be more social. I thought there was something wrong with me that I couldn't make small talk, could never think of something witty to say. I really wanted to be better at that. I read the newspaper for topics to discuss. But I still didn't know the right things. The things these important people cared about, well, I just didn't. So, I suffered through party after party. Priya tried to help me, tried to suggest things for me to study. She always knew just what to say. She was in her element, charming and gracious. She laughed at the jokes. And of course, she looked fabulous. I was grateful for her help. I was flattered to be seen with her, that she was with me. But somehow, I always fell just a little bit short. I was good, but not great.

"The parties were exhausting. I came to hate them. I would try to suggest we not go. Just one weekend. It wasn't going to hurt, right? And Priya would either tell me someone was going to be there that she just had to meet, for her job or some such. Or she would promise she'd make it up to me if I would just muddle through. Just one more time. And she did!"

"Sex."

"Sex. I was enthralled with her. And as I said, some of the things she wanted to 'fix' about me, I also wanted to fix. Or at least agreed were things that were wrong with me. You know how I never eat at parties?"

"Yeah. Usually because there's no food there you like. I have the same problem."

"Right. Priya insisted I was being rude by not eating. She would bring me a plate of food when she brought her own. Everyone around us would think 'Isn't she nice? Bringing a plate for her guy.' But she wasn't being nice. I see that now. She was forcing me to do something I didn't want to do. I would try to eat a little from the plate, to be polite. And then try to discretely dump the food at a later point. I'd excuse myself to go to the restroom and put the plate down where I knew the caterers would take it. I had a lot of tricks to avoid eating. But Priya wasn't fooled. She told me I needed to learn to just eat what was put in front of me. And for a while I thought she was right. I hated that I was a picky eater. I knew it was a social failing."

"How old were you at this point? 34?"

"32 or 33. But close enough. I know. You understand the pain, the feeling of being ostracized for not enjoying the same foods that everyone else seems to be able to eat."

"I do. I still feel that way sometimes. It's hard."

"Yes, it is."

"So you went to parties you hate to eat food you didn't like. Sounds as though you were having a ball." Sarcasm was dripping from my every word.

Tom smiled a rueful smile. "I didn't see it. I thought I was being a supportive boyfriend. I started to lose weight though, because of the stress."

"And being forced to try to eat food you didn't want to."

"That too. Meghan noticed. She asked me what was going on. She told me to tell Priya I just wouldn't go. To let her go alone, if she wanted. But I was afraid if Priya went by herself, she would meet some cooler, hipper guy. That I would lose her. She was always telling me about other guys who hit on her. And how she turned them down for me."

"Oh goodness!"

"It was also interesting how often her parties conflicted with things I really did want to do. Peter and Jane's parties, for example. Or family functions. That's when my dad called me on the carpet about Priya. When I stopped going to spend time with him and Meghan."

"You didn't see them as much?"

"You know how we often have breakfast, just the three of us?"

"Right."

It was a McDonnell thing. George and I didn't go. It was a chance for the three of them to share their stories without the in-laws. They would talk about the trips they took as kids. They would talk about their mom. I wasn't sure these breakfasts were good for Tom Senior, as they kept him rooted in the past. But at the same time, I knew it was important for the local McDonnells to bond. I sometimes wondered if Lauren felt excluded. She knew about the breakfasts, from what Meghan had told me. But Lauren had made her life away for most of her life now. I supposed she was okay with her choices.

"It was interesting how often we, Priya and I, would have to go to a party the night before and be out until late."

"Late is not your thing."

"No. Again, I'm the anomaly. I tried to be more like I thought the rest of the world was. I would stay at parties until well after midnight."

"I can't even imagine you doing that."

Most of the time, Tom was asleep before 9 pm. Because he was up at 5 am. That was just Tom. I understood that.

"Well, I did. And that meant I either missed breakfast altogether. Or I was barely awake. Or grumpy. I was grumpy a lot."

"Unhappy but not quite aware of it," I asserted. I knew that feeling.

"Exactly. Trying to fit into Priya's world, and failing miserably at it. Not able to be myself. Because myself wasn't good enough for Priya, and I really wanted to be good enough for her. I wanted to be the man she thought I could be."

"Oh dear."

"Then she started wanting to throw parties of her own. She said her apartment was too small. But my house would be perfect for an intimate gathering or two. But only if I redecorated. She even hired a decorator."

"She didn't!"

"Well, she set me up with one. He came to the house one day when I was working from home. I didn't even know he was coming, and that created a problem."

"Because your work is top secret."

"Well, not when I'm not in the SCIF." Tom was serious about this, where I had been teasing.

"I was just kidding."

"I know. But it was really uncool of Priya to put me in that position. I told her that, and she cried that I didn't love her anymore."

I grimaced.

"She did that a lot. If I wouldn't go to a party with her, she'd cry and accuse me of not loving her enough."

"Manipulative tears. I get it."

Tom nodded. He'd learned to cope with my tears, trusting that I wasn't crying to try to get him to change. But it had taken years to get to that point.

"What did Priya think about your beard?"

Tom often grew a beard in the winter. And then shaved it off in the spring. I thought it was sexy. But I could see where Priya might not have thought beards were fashionable.

"She told me it prickled her."

"It does. But in a good way." I leered playfully at Tom.

He laughed. "Be careful what you tease." He currently sported a beard since it was March. I knew he'd shave it off soon.

"Later." Another of our running jokes.

"If I must wait," Tom teased. He gave me a quick peck.

"What finally made you see what Priya was doing as bad?"

Tom smiled. "Dad told me that no amount of sex was worth giving up my sense of self."

"He said that?!"

"He did. I blushed to the roots of what little hair I have. My dad and I haven't talked about sex since I was ten and he told me about the birds and the bees."

I laughed.

"He told me that the beauty of his love for my mom was that she loved him no matter what, for who he really was. Not for who he might be or become."

"And that opened your eyes?"

"Not for a while. Eventually, though, I just couldn't do it anymore. I couldn't be the person Priya wanted me to be.

"She threatened to leave me. She said there were men waiting in the wings, others who would be happy to be her plus-one. To meet these important people. Didn't I realize how much they could help me in my job?"

"But you love your job!"

Tom nodded. He'd been in the same job for most of his adult life, and he was just fine with that. "And I didn't need any of these people for my job. Most of them didn't have the first clue what I do. Just like Priya. She had only vague ideas."

"Well, we all do."

Tom laughed. "True. But it doesn't seem to bother you."

"I do wonder sometimes. And it did bug me at first. Not to know what you do for a living. It's a big part of who we are. And also part of how we relate to other people. So, when you couldn't talk about what you do, I wondered how we would really get to know each other."

"You did?"

"Yeah. But then I realized that your job is only a small part of Tom. An important part. I get that. But still a small part of the larger person. My job is a much bigger part of me. It's part of how I define myself. You don't seem to have that."

"I do. I mean, what I do is really important to me."

"I know. I'm not explaining this well."

"I know what you mean, though. I've never been able to talk about my job outside of work. Since I started working in Intel after undergrad. So, I'm used to it."

"And we have a million other things to talk about. And you love your job. To me, that's the important part. If you hated your job and couldn't talk about it, that would be awful."

"I don't know that I love my job. Well, I guess I do." He smiled remembering that he'd said he did just a minute ago. "There's a challenge to it. And the challenge has changed over time."

"Oh?"

"New technology. New complications."

"Got it."

"So, I'm always having to learn new things. And I love that."

"Me too. I can't imagine a job where I didn't have new challenges."

"You get it."

"I do, even if I don't know what you do beyond coding or who you work for!"

Tom smiled. "I work for a government contractor."

"Which one is it now?" I teased. His contract had been recompeted recently, but I knew the same company had won. He hadn't had to 'badge-flip'.

He laughed. "You know!"

"I do," I laughed. "So, I do know who you work for. Just not which part of the government you support."

"Yeah. Well, if it helps, neither does anyone else in my life."

"I know. That's why I'm okay with it. I know it's not me. It's you!" I said, as I pointed my finger at Tom.

Tom got serious again. "So, do you understand a little better what makes me resistant to change?"

"I do."

"Good. Then remembering was worth it."

I smiled.

"And, yes, it's okay for you to call contractors on my behalf."

"As long as I'm sure to tell you before they show up at your house!"

Tom laughed. "Yes, dear."

SELLING HER HOUSE (2018)

As I had fewer items on my to-do list, I thought getting my townhouse ready for sale would go quicker than for Tom and his townhouse.

My list included new carpeting for the stairs, new carpeting for the downstairs family room – which was honestly the room that got the most use – and some thinning of the number of clothes and shoes in the master closet so it would show better.

Unlike Tom, I had done some renovations over the years I had lived in my townhouse. The previous owners had two small boys. What were now my guest rooms had been the boys' rooms. One was painted bright green, and the other was bright blue. Lovely colors for small boys, but not so much for a 40-year-old woman. Fortunately, I quite enjoy painting.

I had carefully taped off the doorway, windows, and baseboard. This was a several-day process. It's tedious, but it's really important, especially if you don't want to have to paint the ceiling, baseboards, or trim. I did buy a can of white paint, just in case. But I was also pretty diligent in my painting. Fortunately, one of the skills I had inherited from my artistic father was a pretty good sense of a drawing a line and edging with paint. My father could quite literally draw a straight line across a page. Between years of drawing and architecture school, he had had a lot of practice. I, on the other hand, had a keen eye for art – which had played a role in my choice of work – but not much artistic ability. That's what I had Jane for. Well, her and her team, though originally it had just been Jane. But I was pretty good at free-handing edges of paint. The tape just made it that much more likely that I wouldn't bleed over.

I painted the green room all in one weekend. It would have been one day, but it had taken three layers of light brown to cover the bright green, even with a layer of primer. The green was that bright; it saturated through the primer! Finally, the bright green room was a more moderate brown, a more neutral color for when I decided to sell.

The bright blue had been easier because I just painted that room a lighter version of blue. Having learned my lesson from the green paint, I used a layer of primer to mute the color, but then chose a slightly lighter shade of blue than I had intended the room to be. Sure enough, even with the primer, the original blue bled through. The end result was a light blue.

The final room that had been the boys' domain was the hallway bathroom. It was an aqua that was sort of a blend of the blue and green that the bedrooms had been. The color wasn't quite as bright, however, so I didn't think it would be that hard to repaint. I chose a cream –

again, using a neutral to make the house marketable. By the time I was finished, I realized the original aqua was, in fact, coming through the cream, making it a very, very light green. I decided that was okay. It just looked as though the cream had a touch of green in it. I used Sarah as my gauge, and she agreed.

The one paint choice I had made that was a bit controversial was painting the foyer powder room deep red. When the door to the half bath was open, it was the first thing you saw when you opened the front door. So, red?

But I love a strong red wall. And somehow it works well as either an accent wall in a living room or in a small bathroom. So, I chose to paint that bathroom a deep red hue. Sarah wasn't sure about the color, but said she'd keep track if prospective buyers seemed to have a problem. I was willing to repaint the bathroom for a sale, if needed.

As I said, I enjoy painting, and all this painting had been done over the course of several years. There are those who would argue that, to sell a house, you should make it all neutral, if not all the same color, as houses are when they are first built. But I didn't like buying houses that were so uniform in color. And honestly, the colors of the townhouse were part of what had attracted me to the home in the first place. I knew my kind of buyer would feel the same way. Fortunately, when Sarah came by to review my checklist, she agreed that painting was off the list of things that needed to be done. I privately wondered if Liz, her partner in real estate, would have felt the same way.

However, the carpeting on the stairs between the main floor and the downstairs was worn from years of use. I hadn't had it replaced when I moved in, and we – Sarah and I – were pretty sure the previous owners hadn't replaced it before they put the house on the market. That meant it had at least a few years of two little boys running up and down the stairs, plus six years of me and the cats. I agreed it needed to be redone before the house would show well.

The stairs going upstairs to the bedrooms were the same carpet, though not as worn. Clearly, the previous family had used the downstairs as much as I did. The floor in between the two sets of carpets was hardwoods. So, the carpet on the stairs did not touch. The question had been whether to replace the carpet on both sets of stairs or just the one that was faded from use. In the end, because I appreciate symmetry, I decided both carpets should be the same.

I could have gone to a big box store and gotten the carpet and installation services. But I was trying to 'buy local', so I wanted to hire a small company contractor. I used the internet to find a couple of suggestions for contractors who could do a good job. Unfortunately, I had two agree to appointments and then stand me up. An unfortunate consequence of not using a big box store, I was discovering. I remembered that Xan had had some of the same challenges. He and Jenn had redone a lot of their house, and they had found some contractors were reliable and others were not. There was no way to know. They had even had one guy draw up and get plans approved by the county for work they wanted to do. The plans had been approved, Xan knew because he was on the application. But the contractor disappeared. Alexander and Jennifer had tried email, phone, and text, to no avail. So, I wasn't pleased the first two guys bailed, but I also wasn't entirely surprised.

A third contractor came, we agreed on a particular Berber carpet, and then he disappeared, refusing to return my calls. I was amazed. Like Xan, I struggled to understand how contractors who exhibited such behavior made a living. But I supposed it was possible his contractor had overextended himself and just hadn't wanted to 'fess up. So strange.

Finally, the fourth contractor gave me an estimate, helped me pick out another Berber carpet – very similar to the one that was already there – and showed up for the installation. I was thrilled. Finally, progress!

However, he installed the carpeting on the last three stairs sideways. Now, you may wonder how I could tell. Did I mention I'm in marketing? I look at designs and patterns a lot. The pattern, while it was just a multicolor blend, was meant to be 90 degrees from how he'd done the installation. I was honestly surprised, in fact, that the carpet hadn't already been trimmed to lay down in the correct direction. But apparently it hadn't been, because the contractor had had to take an extra day to finish while he got the last piece of carpet edged. That was the piece that was installed in the wrong direction. As what was supposed to be a one-day job was already on day three, I had agreed to just let him in before I went to work, and he would let himself out after he was done, locking my front door behind him. He expected to only be another couple of hours for that last piece of carpet.

All this to say, I wasn't home when the last piece of carpet went in. And I had already paid for his services, had had to pay before he would buy the carpet, in fact.

When I noticed the carpet was installed incorrectly, I immediately called the contractor. He was incredulous. I was obviously mistaken. He'd been doing house maintenance and construction for 30 years. What did I know! I tried to maintain my composure as I explained that it was quite clear the pattern between the last three steps and the four steps above it on that run of stairs were not the same. I sent him a picture. He maintained he was correct. He patently refused to even consider that I was correct. And he refused to fix the problem.

This, I have found, is one of the problems with dealing with a one- or two-person organization. There's no higher-up to complain to.

I was stuck.

Just to be certain I wasn't going crazy, I asked Sarah for her opinion when she came by a couple of days later. She saw the problem immediately.

Tom didn't. I loved Tom dearly, but he had little sense of style.

I scoured what little paperwork I had from the contractor, but nothing listed the type of carpet or the color. I had no way of getting another set for just those few stairs and ensuring it would match.

So, I had two choices: 1) redo all the stairs again, which meant paying for another installation and staying home to watch the work being done, or 2) hope that the prospective buyers of my townhouse weren't as observant as I was.

I opted for Door #2.

CR SOCR SOCR SO

After the debacle with the stairway carpet, you can bet I went to the big box stores for the other work that needed to be done.

For the family room, I went a little off the beaten path. Sarah was none too certain about my choice, but Tom loved it. I wasn't sure if that was a good thing.

I decided to install carpet squares rather than wall-to-wall carpeting. The advantage of carpet squares is that they are easier to replace. In fact, when you buy carpet squares, I discovered, you have to buy quite a bit more than you need for the edges and such. And because the carpet squares come a certain number to a box, you end up with quite a few extra. Perfect, I thought, for the next owner.

I picked a square that was a pattern in black, white, and gray, and then black and gray squares. The man at the shop showed me the pattern on the computer, what it would look like on my 15x12' room, and I was sold. It was elegant and interesting, a complex checkerboard. If the next owner didn't like the pattern, there were enough leftover black and gray squares that he or she would be able to make a simpler checkerboard pattern. The carpet squares also were a name brand, and the colors would – in theory – be available for some time into the future.

All good.

The installation went fine, which I was thankful for. Except it turned out there was a hole in the concrete edge of the floor. The installer told me this was on purpose – that was where some of the pipes were – but it made putting a relatively small piece of carpet over the top challenging. Because, since we didn't know that hole was there, he had started on the other wall!

In the end, the installer was able to make it work. And the beauty of the carpet squares was, when I noticed one of the gray tiles was facing in a different direction than all the others, I just picked it up, rotated it 90 degrees, and stuck it back down. I was very pleased.

CR EOCR EOCR EO

I found out how really useful carpet squares could be a few weeks later. I had decided to change out the kitchen faucet.

The one I had was quite serviceable. But it was a boring chrome. I liked the look of a dark metal one instead. So, I bought one. I talked to Xan about installing it, as he'd done one in his home just a few weeks earlier. He was encouraging that I could do the change myself. I read through the instructions, and it seemed pretty straightforward. I had all the right tools already. I turned off the water to the sink. I removed the old faucet. I put the new faucet in place. It worked. I was so proud of myself!

Until I went downstairs the next morning. There was a bubble in the ceiling of water being held from splashing onto the floor by paint. A very large bubble of water.

I immediately called a plumber, who came within hours and fixed the hose connections I had broken without knowing. Many dollars later, the sink was no longer leaking.

However, the family room ceiling had to be taken apart, as well as part of the wall, to dry everything out so there would be no mold issue. The restoration company had fans going for a couple of days to make sure.

Then I had to pay for someone to rebuild the wall and ceiling, and repaint them to match the existing colors.

But...I did not have to replace the carpet. I just took up the sodden carpet squares and replaced them with some of the spares I had in my storage room. It helped that the subfloor of the family room was only cement. If there had been wood or another layer, then I might have had to do more. But in this case, a few spare carpet squares, and that part of the repair was completed.

CR ED CR ED CR ED

The final requirement from Sarah was to make the master walk-in closet look bigger by removing about half of the clothing and shoes in it. The closets had been "designed" at some point. The back wall was all hanging closets, but the center third had two rods across it – presumably one for pants and one for shirts for the man of the house. The right wall of the closet had a shoe rack built-in. This was nice, but it meant that there was less hanging space in the closet than one might assume for a walk-in closet. Further restricting the amount of hanging space was a dresser and shelving that took up the entire left side of the closet. I used the dresser for my winter sweaters and all my workout clothes. That worked well. But the dresser was not butted to the door of the closet, but centered on the left wall. Which meant that about a third of the left part of the back wall's hanging space was behind the dresser. It wasn't that you couldn't hang clothes in that part of the closet. You could. But it did mean that you did not *see* those clothes. As I was thinning the clothes, I found dresses back there I had forgotten I owned.

You also have to understand, I already had clothes in all the other closets in the house, so I wasn't going to be able to just move the clothes from one closet to another.

It was late spring, so my summer clothes were in the master closet. My winter clothes were in the blue bedroom's closet. The brown bedroom had built-ins in the closet, which reduced the amount of hanging space – there was a built-in dresser taking up the center third of the closet. The two guest rooms were meant to be children's room or only guest rooms, so they had smaller closets than the master, of course. That meant that my winter clothes took up the entire blue bedroom closet and spilled over a bit in the brown room. There was not going to be room for my "extra" clothes in either of those closets.

The one thing I didn't like about this townhouse was a dearth of storage. The kitchen had a plethora of cabinets, which I had found out was important when my previous home did not. But I hadn't really noticed the lack of other storage when I bought this place. It wasn't until I was unpacking my belongings that I realized there was no storage in the bottom part of the house. There was a big room off the garage for storing things. But it was not enclosed – it was just part of the garage that had been partially walled off. Which meant you wouldn't want to store anything in that space that couldn't stand up to being exposed to weather. If only from the garage door opening and closing. And the occasional spider or other critter that made its way into the garage.

So, clothes were a problem. That's when Tom and I agreed to rent a storage unit. We would put my extra clothes in there, as well as whatever else needed to be stored to make my house show. For example, Sarah also wanted me to thin out the number of books I had. You might imagine I have a few books. I had six bookcases full of books downstairs, two rows deep on most shelves, plus three two-shelf bookcases in other parts of the house, like the entrance way. Sarah said I needed to reduce the number by half, so the bookcases didn't look so stuffed. I carefully culled through my books, packed up six boxes of books for storage, and packed up another four boxes for donation to the local library.

Sarah approved of the reduction. We agreed we would live with the wonky stair carpeting. We were ready to show!

CR ℰⓇCR ℰⓇCR ℰⓇ

The agency's photographer took what seemed like a million pictures of my townhouse in the "perfect" light for the real estate listing. Sarah put together the description, which I only changed a little. I couldn't help myself.

I thought we were ready to go.

"The insistent drums were an unwelcome reminder of the existence of another world, wholly autonomous, with its own necessities and patterns. The message they were beating out, over and over, was for her; it was saying, not precisely that she did not exist but rather that it did not matter whether she existed or not, that her presence was of no consequence to the rest of the cosmos. It was a sensation that suddenly paralyzed her with dread. There had never been any question of her "mattering"; it went without saying that she mattered, because she was important to herself. But what was the part of her to which she mattered?" -- Paul Bowles, The Spider's House

TIFFANY'S BAD LUCK WITH HOUSES (2005-2009)

I had met Sarah, and her real estate partner Liz, in 2005. I was a year out of graduate school, and I had finally found a job that paid me enough money to be able to move into a bigger place.

I lived in a one-bedroom condo then, which I rented. Now, I had had gotten my first real job in management, working for a small polling firm that did both political and market research polling. It was perfect for me; a way to use my English undergraduate degree and my MBA to pursue my interest in marketing.

I notified my landlord of my desire to move. He was fine with my decision and planned to take the opportunity to get rid of the rental he no longer wanted.

Unfortunately, I learned one-bedroom condos are notoriously hard to sell, regardless of the economy. And this one was particularly tricky as the neighborhood was going through a rough patch – there had been some incidents of vandalism and an apparent drug connection. These facts were not going to help me with getting a decent price for my home.

The condominium association, recognizing the challenge this combination had wrought, had hired a real estate firm to work with owners on selling. Sarah and Liz specialized in that part of the area and in selling difficult properties. They brought the condo association some new ideas for marketing the property, and they encouraged the association to build a fence between the condos and the neighborhood behind our development, where the troubles had happened. The separation really helped with making it feel as though whatever happened over there wasn't relevant to the condos. At least a little bit.

"We have a campaign going in the local papers," Liz explained, "to show the crime statistics and resale statistics."

"To show that these condos are a good investment," Sarah finished.

The three of us were at the condo, as they were explaining to me the role I'd have to play in getting the condo sold.

"As you know, this is a good location," Liz added.

I nodded. It never occurred to me that as a renter I would have to be involved in this process. I was feeling very overwhelmed. "Do you think it's possible to sell? And get a decent price?" I didn't want to leave my landlord in a bad situation, but I honestly felt as though it was really his problem, not mine.

"We have been having some good luck," Sarah said. "The marketing seems to be working."

"We think he can get a good price. Especially if he's to put in some money upfront."

I didn't know what that meant. My expression must have shown that.

"If he does some small upgrades, it will help sell the condo better. New carpet, things like that. We will come by in the next couple of days and let you know what he's decided to do," Sarah clarified.

The two of them again visited the condo the following Saturday. I had cleaned, of course, but I wasn't sure what else to do to make a good impression on prospective buyers.

"You should cull your bookcases," Sarah said. "Houses show better when the bookcases aren't stuffed."

"Get rid of my books?" I was horrified at the idea. I loved books.

"Store them somewhere else. You can rent a storage locker for not much," Liz offered.

I thought I'd see about putting some boxes at my mom's home, which was not too far away. I didn't want to get rid of any of my books.

"Same with the closets. You have two?" Sarah mentioned.

"Yes, side by side in the bedroom," I responded.

"You know how they show clothes in magazines, with lots of space in between? Do that. It makes the closets seem bigger," Liz suggested.

"Okay. I can take my winter clothes to my mom's."

"Perfect!"

"The kitchen looks good," Sarah said. "I think the carpet is okay. People generally want to put in their own anyway."

"Okay. Your décor is fine, fits the space well, not too much," Liz declared.

'Thanks. I think,' I thought. Aloud, I said, "This is a lot."

"We know. We do this every day. Sometimes we forget," Sarah added, with a laugh. "You'll be fine. We should be able to sell without too many issues. It could take a while, though."

"Well, I'm not required to stay, am I?"

"No, of course not!" Sarah said. "But the place will show better if it's occupied. People are weird about empty spaces. Some can see the potential; others have a hard time."

"Though the same can be sad for decorating," Liz added. "Some people can't see past what's been done to what can be done. Not so much of an issue in a one-bedroom place like this, though."

I nodded.

"What are your house plans?" Sarah asked. "Have you found a new place?"

"Actually, I'd like to buy a place. A two-bedroom, so I have a little more room," I explained. "Condo or townhouse."

"You have money for a down payment?" Liz asked.

I thought that was kind of a personal question, but I supposed they were used to asking it in their business as realtors. "I'll be borrowing the money from my family."

"Be sure to research the laws," Sarah said. "You can only get so much from each family member."

"And they have to sign a letter to say what the money is for, for their taxes," Liz amended.

I nodded again. I had no idea about any of this.

And then I realized I needed a realtor to buy a new place, and here were two realtors right in front of me. "Would you be interested in helping me?" I asked.

Sarah and Liz laughed. "Of course, we would!" Sarah said.

"Great! I've never owned before, so I'm very new, as you can tell."

"We'll lead you through everything," Liz explained. "It's not that complicated."

"Sounds good. We will be in touch," Sarah said. "We have another unit on the market now, and an open house for it tomorrow. Okay if we show your place then too, if someone is interested?"

Thinking it would be great to sell so quickly, I said, "Sure."

"It may not happen. We are obligated to sell the condo we are showing tomorrow," Liz explained.

"But yours in bigger and on the top floor. Some people will like that."

That was one of the reasons I had rented it. No upstairs neighbors to be noisy. "Yes, I had the same idea," I agreed.

"Terrific. We will try to give you some warning if we are coming down. Will you be here?"

"I'm guessing the answer should be no."

"Ideally," Sarah confirmed.

"I can go to my mom's. Take my clothes and books."

"Do you have boxes?" Liz asked.

"Enough to thin things a little."

"Great!" they said in unison.

And so, I packed up my car with my belongings and spent some time at my mother's. It's always a mixed bag to visit with her.

"So, you're moving? Are you sure that's a good idea with the job market right now?" Mom asked.

"I think I will be okay."

"Well, it seems like a bad time to me. Why now?"

"I just got that promotion. I'm making enough money to be able to afford a bigger place. You know I've been wanting one."

"Yes, Tiffany. I know. But you just got the new job. What happens if it goes badly?"

My mother liked to play what-if with everyone's life but her own. And even though I was in my late-20s, she sometimes forgot and talked to me as though I was 10.

"I think I'll be okay," I said firmly, trying to shut down the topic. "Have you talked to Phin?" I asked, changing the subject. Phineas was Mom's favorite.

And that launched her into a discussion about my brother and his life choices. Phin had just told the family he and Joseph were trying to have a baby, though I don't think any of us was really surprised. Still since they were gay, that wasn't going to be easy, even in the 21st century. Fortunately, Phin had Joseph. And we all loved Joseph. And their relationship was so, well, normal. Just like Xan and Jenn. Mom was adjusting the idea of her son being in love with another man, but she had to tell me all about how Phin's decision was affecting her life. I shouldn't have used Phineas like that, I knew. But I just needed her to stop focusing on me. It backfired.

"Tiff?" Mom asked, using the nickname only she could get away with.

"What, Mom?"

"Do you think you'll ever get married?"

I knew she meant well, but I had enough stress with my new position at work and trying to sell a difficult-to-sell condo. I didn't want to get into my love life.

"I don't know, Mom. I never meet any nice men."

"Well, if Phineas can find someone, surely you can. I mean, how hard can it be?"

"Mom, please."

"All right. I know you don't like talking about this."

"No, I don't. It's not like I can wave a magic wand and find the perfect guy."

"I think you could look harder."

"Mom..."

"Fine. Subject closed."

"Thank you. Besides, Sarah and Liz should be done by now. So, I need to go home and get ready for tomorrow's workday."

"Hope they have good news."

"We will see. Don't get your hopes up."

"I have faith."

'Oh, dear,' I thought. And yet I had hopes too.

❧ ❧❧❧ ❧❧❧ ❧

I went looking at two-bedroom condos and townhouses with both agents. Liz was perfectly nice, and she and I had a good time looking at a bunch of listings at least two weekends during my search. But I preferred Sarah's demeanor because I felt Liz was a little obsequious. I'm sure it was a good quality to have in sales. And most people would probably see the fact that she rarely contradicted their opinion as a plus. Whether I found a townhouse to be acceptable or whether I thought it was too small, too dirty, weirdly laid out, whatever – Liz agreed with all of it. Sarah, on the other hand, had her own opinions and wasn't afraid to express them. Given my own personality, I needed someone to give me a different point of view, not just agree with me. I was also still pretty new to this homeowner thing, and Sarah pointed out flaws in townhouses that I hadn't considered.

Between the three of us, we found a nice two-bedroom end-unit townhouse, with a decent size kitchen and a large yard for a townhouse. The master en suite bathroom had a second door to the hall, which meant it was really a shared bathroom. But it could be called a classic en suite, which I thought would be good for resale. There was another bathroom, too, though it was on the bottom floor with the family room. The second bedroom was small, only wide enough for a single bed. Clearly, the townhouse was intended for a small family of three – parents and a child. But it worked for my purposes, too. I wanted that second bedroom for the rare times when I had guests, but also because of my experience with the one-bedroom condo. Sarah had advised that two-bedroom homes were easier to sell. I figured it couldn't be much worse than my only previous experience.

I really enjoyed that townhouse. When I moved in, a very nice couple lived next door. They were older than I was, but not by much. He was a cop, and she was a schoolteacher, which explained why they, combined, were only making about what I was making as a middle manager in a marketing firm. They were friendly, saying hello and goodbye whenever we saw each other. While there were no garages for the townhouses, we each had an assigned space. I always let Marvin and Milly know if I wasn't going to be around overnight, so they could use my space if they wanted. One night, when I got home particularly late from work, I noticed Marvin's face at their window, and I realized he was watching to make sure I made it home all right. It gave me some comfort to know that help was living right next door if I needed it.

Three years after I moved in, Marvin and Milly moved out. A young man moved in. He was a decade younger than I was, and I was surprised he could afford the townhouse. But, being an affable guy, he explained to me immediately that his parents had bought the unit as an investment, and given him the townhouse as a residence while he was in graduate school for computer programming, so he could save on rent. I thought that was darn nice of them! Michael was a nice young man, and not very noisy at all. I lucked out.

ᏒᏕᏕᏒᏕᏒᏕ

But then, my luck ran out when it came to selling and buying.

The Great Recession collapsed the worldwide economy in 2008. A large part of the economic challenges in the United States was the collapse of the real estate market.

But I didn't know all that when I decided to move in early 2008.

I called Sarah, my favorite of the two real estate agents. She and Liz were still working in tandem, which I took in stride. Although I would have preferred to work only with Sarah, I could deal with Liz as needed.

Sarah assured me that selling my two-bedroom townhouse wouldn't be too hard, even as the economy was having some challenges. The harbingers of things to come weren't showing yet.

She and I walked through to see what needed upgrading before I listed. I had already put in hardwood floors on the main level, including the kitchen. Sarah wasn't wild about the mahogany hue of the floors, as she thought the choice would be difficult for some people. The upstairs bedrooms were painted a generic white, which I hadn't changed. Sarah agreed that was a good idea. The bathtub in the en suite was one of those all-in-one piece things that seemed like they were made of plastic, but probably weren't.

"I was thinking about changing this out," I said, pointing to the bathtub/shower combination, "with a more conventional bathtub and shower."

"I think that would help with your resale. You also might think about changing out the doors up here."

"Really? Why?"

"These are all builder grade. They aren't real wood, and they aren't very soundproof," Sarah explained.

"Oh? I had no idea."

"You wouldn't, but it's my job to tell you these things. A family would appreciate having some more solid doors to help with keeping down the noise of the kid in the second bedroom."

"I get that. It's three doors. I can probably swing that."

"Nice one," Sarah said, laughing.

I hadn't even realized I had made the pun, but laughed along.

We visited downstairs to see if there was any work needed down there.

"How old are the washer and dryer?" Sarah asked.

"They predate me," I replied.

We checked the dates on the inside of the lids. Both had been bought in 2001.

"You might think about switching those out for newer ones," Sarah suggested.

"They work," I said with a shrug.

"Again, a family will have more laundry than you do. Particularly if the child is young, a good washer and dryer is important."

"I'll think about it."

Sarah nodded. It was her job to advise, but ultimately my decision. I thought the bathtub and doors made sense. But I didn't see the point of replacing a working set of appliances, just to be fancier.

I thought I better hire a professional to take out the shower/tub combo and to replace it with a tub and tile the walls. Fortunately, I had had one recommended by someone at work. Steve was a very tall, very thin black man about the same age as I was. "Well, ma'am," he said, when I asked about the tile, "yes, I can do that."

"Please call me Tiffany." Ma'am was not a term I was comfortable with.

"Yes, Miss Tiffany."

"Tiffany."

"Yes, Miss Tiffany."

I gave up. I knew some people just grew up with those terms. Steve seemed to be one of them.

"How long do you think the project will take?"

"Two days, Miss Tiffany. My guys and I will have to take out the toilet to get the shower out. That's gonna add to the time."

"Take the toilet out?"

"Yes, Miss Tiffany. And to put the new tub in. There's not much space in this room, though it do help that there are two doors."

I was thinking it was a good thing there was a second full bath downstairs, since apparently this one was going to be out of use for a couple of days.

"Did you pick out a new tub?"

"I just want a basic tub, Steve. Nothing fancy."

"Did you buy one?"

I had not. "Please include that in your estimate."

He nodded. "How about the tile? What color you want?"

"Just white, please."

"Subway tile or those little tiles or octagons?"

"Subway, please. Simple is good in this case."

"Yes, ma'am. White grout, I imagine."

I hadn't thought about all these choices. "Yes, otherwise, I think it will look funny."

"I agree, Miss Tiffany. Most definitely. White tub, white tile, and white grout. We fix you up real nice."

"Thank you, Steve. How much do you think it will be?"

"I reckon about $1,500. Including the tub and tile."

I was a little shocked, but I did some quick math in my head. I thought a tub alone was about $500. A couple of guys for a couple of days. Some tile. Grout. Taking out the toilet. Okay, I could see that. It was just more than I had hoped for. "Okay, Steve. I agree."

"Let me give you a more formal estimate. I got the forms in my truck. And we can start work in about a week?"

"Not this weekend?"

"No, Miss Tiffany. We got another project this weekend. Next weekend, okay?"

"Okay. Guess it has to be," I said, smiling to let him know I was really okay, though inside I was disappointed.

"We will be here next Saturday. We will be done by Sunday. We got you." Steve smiled. He really was a very nice man, and if he did good work, I would be happy with a little delay.

"See you then!"

8 am the next Saturday morning, there was a knock on the door. I'll be honest, I was still in bed. I had forgotten Steve and his "guys" were coming first thing this morning. I scrambled to get dressed. I grabbed my shampoo and conditioner, and a towel. Later, perhaps, I would take a shower in the downstairs full bath. I thought in some ways this was a good opportunity, as I had never used that shower. Maybe it needed a little something too.

I opened the door. Steve was there, wearing a very beat-up sweatshirt and a pair of blue jeans that looked like they had been through a war. The other guys weren't dressed any better. It was a little jarring, as they looked like hoodlums with their pants barely on their hips. But the work was going to be messy, so it ultimately made sense. Steve was also a freelancer. He'd given me a "formal" estimate, but it was just a handwritten list of the work with a total cost of $1,500 at the bottom. It wasn't like it said labor would be this much vs. the cost of the tub vs. all the other costs. Steve was just winging how much things were going to cost. I just hoped he knew what he was doing. I reminded myself that he'd come recommended, as the crew piled into my house and upstairs to start work. They put a plastic runner on the stairs as they climbed. That made me feel good about their professionalism. I didn't have the budget for new carpeting.

"Steve, how late do you plan to work today? You'll stop sometime in the afternoon?" I asked. I was now thinking that I wasn't entirely comfortable taking a shower with a bunch of strange men in my townhouse. I also didn't know if they planned to turn off the water at some point. Probably. Oh dear.

"You tell me, Miss Tiffany. You have somewhere to be today? I can vouch for my guys. You can leave, and I promise we won't hurt anything."

That wasn't really the issue, though I appreciated the show of support for his crew. "I will probably run some errands today, so I'll be in and out. I was just wondering how long you thought it would take."

"We'll be here most of today, Miss Tiffany. I told the guys to plan to work till 5 pm if that's okay. Then come back tomorrow to finish up the cleanup after the grout has dried, 'round this same time tomorrow. Wanna see your new bathtub?"

I nodded, and he led me out to the truck, which had a perfectly normal bathtub in the back, along with a bunch of white subway tile and a few bags of grout.

A few minutes later, I saw the toilet come down the stairs and out to the truck. It was wrapped in heavy plastic against leaks, I supposed. "We'll store the toilet here, Miss Tiffany."

I hadn't thought about where they would put the toilet.

"It won't hurt nothing if it leaks a little back here," Steve added, because apparently I looked confused.

I nodded. "Makes sense. Thank you."

"No problem. It's what we generally do. Works well."

We headed back in.

"I'm going to go help, Miss Tiffany, unless you have any other questions?"

"No, Steve. I'm good. I'll be downstairs in the family room if you need me."

"Yes, ma'am."

Chuckling internally at Steve's inability to just use my name, I went downstairs. The first bang made me cringe and realize I'd reached the point of no return. Steve had explained, when he'd brought me the estimate, that they'd be breaking apart the all-in-one tub/shower to get it out.

"It won't fit past the doorway any other way," he'd explained.

I nodded. Made sense to me, and I didn't need it anyway.

Remembering that, I knew the noise meant they had started taking out the tub/shower combo.

I opened up my laptop, prepared to work a little this morning. I planned to work a little and read a little, and perhaps find a movie to watch, to occupy myself. I did have those errands to run, as I told Steve. But they wouldn't take very long. I had to figure out how to fill the rest of the day, stuck in the downstairs, as far away from the chaos and noise as I could.

Another loud bang. Then I heard someone shout, "SHIT!"

I resisted the urge to run upstairs, though I did get off the couch and move to the bottom of the stairs so I could listen better.

"DAMNIT!"

I didn't mind the language, but I was surprised by it. What was going on?

A few minutes later, Steve appeared at the top of the stairs to the bottom level.

"Miss Tiffany. Ma'am. We got a problem."

"I wondered," I admitted. "What's going on?" I asked, as I started up the stairs.

"Better you see for yourself, Miss Tiffany."

That did not sound good. I followed Steve upstairs, scenarios running through my mind and wondering what I was going to do about them.

"There's no wall," Steve explained as we entered the bathroom.

I looked, and sure enough, where the shower wall had been, there was a hole, and I could see the studs of the wall behind it.

"I'm not sure I understand what happened."

"When they put in the tub combo, they apparently didn't put in a wall behind it," Steve offered. "So, to put up the tile, we're going to have to put in a wall."

My mind exploded. Put in a wall? How long would that take and how much was it going to cost? My heart sank in my chest. I didn't have that much more money. "That does not sound good. You didn't know that beforehand, I guess."

"I should have thought about it, ma'am, but I just assumed they had put in a wall."

"I guess they saved a little money not putting in one."

"Yes, ma'am."

I noted that the "ma'am" was back. I guessed it was his bad news habit.

"How much?" I asked, trying not to panic.

"We have to buy drywall, put in the wall, and then skim it before we can put the tile up. You're going to need to paint what isn't covered by the tile, with waterproof paint."

"How much?" I asked again, nodding at his list.

"Another $500." He looked apologetic, but resolute.

I knew it wasn't his fault. But I was very glad I hadn't yet ordered the new doors. Or decided to buy the washer and dryer. I nodded. "It is what it is. We can't go backward. Another day or two to do the work?"

"I'm going to send Billy to buy the materials while we finish taking out the tub. Should be done by the time he gets back. This means another full day tomorrow, but we should be able to finish tomorrow."

"What about the cleanup day?" I asked.

"I think we can do it tomorrow. But I'll let you know at the end of today, depending on our progress. Okay?"

"It is what it is," I said, shaking my head at the situation. "Good thing there are two bathrooms in this house."

"Yes, ma'am," Steve agreed, with a slight smile.

"Keep me posted, okay. And let me know if there are any other problems. Okay?"

"Of course, ma'am."

I headed back downstairs, calculating as I went whether I could find the money to still get the doors. I called my brother. I explained the situation to him, including my need to cut costs down any way I could. "Xan? Can you help me put up the new doors?"

"Sure, Tiffany. It's not that hard. We can do it together, I'm sure. Have you ordered them?"

"Not yet."

"You might want to do that. It can take a while to get them in. What size doors do you need?"

"What size?" I thought doors were pretty standard in size.

"Measure the ones you have. Are you planning to replace the door frames, too?"

"Door frames?"

"The doorways. You can buy just the door, and take down the ones you have and hang new ones. Or you can replace the entire frame with the door already attached."

"That sounds more expensive."

"It is. But that way you know the doors will hang right."

"Xan, I have no idea what you're talking about." I knew my tone was exasperated.

He took a deep breath. "Tiffany, no doorway is truly square, just like no wall is truly square."

I looked around the room. "They look square to me."

"They are close. But they aren't exact. I learned all this when I redid our master bathroom."

Xan and Jenn had pretty much redone their house in the 10 years they'd lived in it. Alexander had done a lot of the work himself, which is why I knew I could ask him all these questions. And why I knew he could help with my doors. "Which is why I'm asking you!" I said, making my voice brighter than I felt. It wasn't Xan's fault or Steve's fault what was going on. No need to take my frustration out of them.

"I know. Tiffany, really, in the long run, it's better to get the doors with their door frames. It takes more effort to take the old ones out and put the new ones in. But you can jimmy the doorway more easily to fit the new doorway – carve down some of the drywall if needed – than trying to shave a door to fit a slightly off doorway. Trust me."

"I do. Thanks, Xan. I'll check on the costs and let you know."

"Sorry about the wall, Sis."

"Thanks. It sucks."

"Believe me, I know. Good luck!"

"Thanks!"

True to his word, Steve and his crew were able to get the new wall installed on Saturday. I checked on them a few times, but they clearly knew what they were doing.

About 6:30, Steve shouted down the stairs, "We're done for today, Miss Tiffany."

I was glad to be back to that name vs. "ma'am". I figured it meant things were relatively under control. I got off the couch and walked up the stairs. "Thanks, Steve," I said as I walked into the living room to meet him. "Tomorrow around 8?"

"Yes, Miss Tiffany. We've got your toilet on the truck, too, as well as your new tub. We'll give the wall the night to settle. Then we'll put in the tub and tile tomorrow."

"Thanks. Sorry about the extra work."

"These things happen, Miss Tiffany."

"I guess they do," I said, ruefully.

He chuckled. "Be back in the morning. Have a good evening."

"You too."

I was ready for the guys in the morning this time, having taken a shower downstairs before they arrived. I even had made coffee, which I didn't drink, for them.

"Thank you, ma'am," they all repeated as they took their cups upstairs to work.

"The wall looks good," I told Steve.

"Thank you, Miss Tiffany. One more day, I hope."

"Me too," I said, with a chuckle before I headed downstairs. "Feel free to drink the rest of the coffee. I don't drink the stuff. There's more grounds in the freezer, too, if you want."

"Awfully nice of you. Thanks."

I just smiled as I headed downstairs.

I heard lots of banging and a few curses as the day wore on. But there was no sign of Steve, which made me believe that things were progressing as best they could.

When I came up at lunchtime to make a sandwich, Steve told me the tub was in. "Toilet next."

I nodded, grateful for small favors.

Smack, scrape was the sound I heard as the tiles were going on. They put in spacers, I saw when I peeked, to make the tiles even. I had wondered how that worked! The rows looked straight, which was important for my sense of aesthetic. As Xan indicated, most people might not notice a slight tilt. But I was sure I would.

In the afternoon, I went to the store to check out doors. Xan wasn't kidding when he said the full doorways were more expensive. But the salesman agreed with Xan that it would be better to replace the entire system. And the research I had done on the Internet agreed. I bit the bullet to buy door frames and doors together. It would take three weeks for them to get in. Another delay. But that would make it easier to schedule the install with Xan.

Around 4 pm, Steve shouted down the stairs, "We done, Miss Tiffany."

"Really? That's great," I said, as I got off the couch to come up the stairs.

I followed Steve up the two flights of stairs, with a little fear in my heart that the bathroom wasn't going to look as nice as I hoped. I was mentally preparing myself. After all, Steve and his crew weren't professionals. You get what you pay for, right?

I walked into the bathroom, and was astonished. It looked perfect! The white walls, tile, and tub made the room look so much bigger. The tub looked good. The whole room looked professionally done, but also refreshed. I was beyond happy.

I looked at Steve with a big smile on my face. "Thank you!" I said, shaking his hand.

"Glad you're happy, Miss Tiffany. I'll let the guys know."

I realized I had never even learned the other guys' names. I should have, I supposed. "Please do. This is perfect."

Steve smiled, his white teeth showing brightly against his brown skin. I realized I hadn't seen him smile before. That, too, was a shame.

"Here's the check." I had written it out before. I made it out to Steve, as he'd asked, and he said he would take of the rest of it. "I added a little extra." It wasn't much, I knew, but I had made the total $2,200 as a little tip. As long as I was going underwater for these repairs, I figured a little more wouldn't hurt.

"Thank you very much, Miss Tiffany. You got any other jobs, you let me know."

I felt badly that Xan and I would do the doors without any contractors, but I had to. I couldn't afford it. "I have your card. I'll keep you in mind for any future projects." I wasn't lying. I would for anything beyond the doors. Especially now that I trusted he would do a good job.

Once they had left, I went back and looked at the room in more detail. It really was well done. Steve had told me not to use the shower for another day, but on the scale of things, I could live with that.

A month later, Xan came over to help me install the new doors. He brought his truck, which had some scars from his own home improvements. He also brought one of his friends, Bill.

"The doors are going to be heavy, Tiffany," he explained. "I know you're strong, but Bill is stronger."

"But…" I started.

Xan cut me off. "Buy us some beer and pizza."

I nodded. Least I could do.

So, I helped where I could without trying to get in the way. Bill and Xan knew what they were doing, and I did not. That was really what Xan was trying to tell me by bringing Bill.

"What are you going to do with the old doors? I asked, as Xan and I were carrying one of the old ones to his truck.

"I'll take them to the dump," Xan explained. "They know me there." He chuckled.

"I can imagine. Thanks again, Brother. I owe you more than beer and pizza."

"Comes with the territory," Xan replied.

It was handy to have a handy brother. I knew Phin could do some of these kinds of things, too, though Joseph was the handier of the two of them. But it was comforting to have Xan take the lead. He and Bill worked well together. I mostly helped by getting tools and making coffee. I felt like a 50s housewife, but I wasn't going to say a thing. I knew I was getting the better part of the deal.

"Tiffany, want to see what I meant by the doorways being off?" Xan asked.

"Sure." I was a little nervous given my experience with the shower. All I needed was another disaster.

"It's not bad. Just a little off," Xan explained when he saw my face. He put the level against the drywall from where the door threshold had been. The bubble was not in the middle, where it should have been, but distinctly to the left.

"Oh dear," I said.

Bill chuckled.

Xan smiled. "No biggie. Really."

"If you say so," I said, with trepidation.

Bill nodded. "Most of them are off."

"The other one was off too. I just forgot to show you," Xan explained.

I looked across the hall at the door they had already finished. It was the door to the master bedroom. It looked just fine, straight, to my eye.

"We cut a little of the drywall for the new doorway. We leveled it. And put in the new doorway," Bill told me.

"Thanks!" I meant it. I saw what Xan meant now. And if the end result was indistinguishable from perfectly straight, what did I care?

"We're almost done with this door. One more after that, right?" Xan asked.

"Right."

"Got beer?" Xan wondered.

I laughed. "Amstel's and meat lovers pizza,"

"Works for me," Xan echoed.

Bill just smiled.

The new doors really made the place look good. On top of the updated bathroom, I thought I'd make back my investment in the sale.

A couple of hours later, the beer had been drunk, the pizza had been eaten, and I had three beautiful, new doors. Not bad, I thought, grateful against for Xan's help.

"Take care, Tiffany," Bill said, as he climbed into Xan's truck.

"He's a good guy," Xan whispered to me.

I realized Xan had also been trying to fix me up with Bill. I had been so focused on getting the house done, I hadn't noticed. Maybe my mother was right, as much as I hated to admit it. "Seems like it," I replied.

"Okay if I give him your number?"

"Yeah. Thanks for asking. And thanks for today. I would have been lost without you."

"I got brother points?"

"Big time," I said, with a kiss on his cheek. "My love to Jennifer and the kids."

He climbed into the truck. "See you later!"

I went back inside, cleaned up the kitchen, and then went upstairs to admire the work that had been done. I was confident it had been worth it.

Sarah agreed when she came to see the house a few days later. "Nice doors!" she exclaimed. "And I love the white bathroom. So elegant for such as small bathroom."

"Thanks. Best we could do with the space we had." I hadn't told her the sad tale of woe of the missing wall.

"I'll get the photographer out here this week. I've got your spare key. The listing should go up toward the end of the week."

"Great! Thanks!"

While I was working on getting my house ready, I had started house-hunting with Sarah and Liz. We'd gone out several weekends already, but hadn't found THE house yet. Now that my house was ready, I felt more urgency to find my next place.

Sarah was in the midst of a sale with another client, so I ended up going on looking with Liz. She picked me up so we could ride together.

"Ready to go?" she asked

"Yes. I saw the list you sent. I like all the options, I think."

"Great!"

So, we headed out to see what there was to be seen.

The first townhouse was in a neighborhood with almost no parking. Although the townhouse came with a garage - one of my new requirements - I had learned my lesson about not having enough parking from where I lived now. My family liked to gather for occasions, and I ended up not being able to host very often because the plethora of cars couldn't find places to park in my neighborhood. It wasn't the only thing that townhouse had going against it, but it was probably the biggest strike.

The next townhouse was perfect. Big airy kitchen, with skylights. I loved all the light! Great neighborhood within a reasonable drive to work. Two-car garage. Three bedrooms. Three and a half baths. I was excited.

"This is it!" I said to Liz.

"Hmmm…"

"What is it?" Liz had never been negative when I was positive. That didn't bode well.

"Let me talk to the agent."

This was an open house, so of course there was an agent on site. And of course, we weren't the only ones walking through.

Liz came back to the kitchen, where I was standing anxiously. I really thought this house would be wonderful. I was getting excited at the idea. But Liz's expression when she returned wasn't positive.

"It's as I thought," she said quietly. Clearly, she didn't want the agent or the others touring the house to hear.

"What?" I whispered in return. "Should we go out front?"

"Good idea," she replied.

We went out the door and to the sidewalk a few yards from the house.

"This is a very popular neighborhood," Liz started.

"I can see why!"

"And there have been lots of people by today. The agent said she's expecting at least two offers from people who have been to the open house."

"Oh. That doesn't sound promising."

"Not unless you want to get into a bidding war. I know this townhouse is at the top of what you're willing to spend. How much flexibility do you have?"

The truth was I was stretching to get to the price already. "Not much." My heart was breaking. I wasn't going to get this house.

"I was afraid of that. We could try, if you want." Liz's voice was sad. She could tell I really liked the house.

I raised my chin. "No, there are other houses. I'm sure we can find another one I like just as much."

"I'm sure we will. I'll check on the listing tonight. See if those offers really came in. We can always put one in tomorrow."

"That's great. Thank you."

Sad but optimistic, I piled into Liz's car to head to the next listing.

Unfortunately, that house wasn't even supposed to be available for appointments that day.

"Oh dear. I told them I wasn't going to be able to show today. The baby is sick!"

Liz replied quickly, "We understand. We'll just be going."

The relief on the mother's face was palpable. "Thank you for understanding."

We quickly put the key back in the lockbox and got back into Liz's car to head to the next house.

I looked around at the next neighborhood. There was a nice pond next to the main drag. I liked that. One of the things I loved about where I was living now is the pond with a fountain in the middle of the development. There was a long walking/running path around it, which I used on many occasions. So, I liked that this community had a similar pond and path. The pond even had a fountain!

The townhouse was an interior unit, where I had an end unit now. I'd really like another end unit, but I was open to possibilities given my budget. It looked like it was a four-story townhouse! Wow.

Liz got the key from the lockbox, she knocked on the door, and fortunately, this time no one answered.

The townhouse had a small foyer when you first got in the door, with a half bath. There were five steps up to the main floor, which included a dining room, living room, and kitchen. The living room was a step down from the dining room, which I sort of loved.

The kitchen is the width of the house with a little family room off to the side, including a fireplace. There was a nook where you could put a small table for meals for two. I didn't have a "two", but I liked the idea of it. Not that I ate breakfast much and dinner was usually in front of the television in the evening. But it was the idea of the thing I liked. Actually, I realized that nook would be the perfect place for the cats' bowls. Laughing to myself, I followed Liz upstairs.

"There are three bedrooms up here. The master, with an en suite bathroom, and two other bedrooms. You can tell the current owners have two little boys."

"How so?"

"You'll see." Liz liked to be cryptic.

We turned right at the top of the stairs into the master. There was a closet just outside the room, which Liz opened to reveal the washer and dryer.

"That's weird to me. To have the laundry upstairs," I said.

"It's good for families. You don't have to haul the laundry downstairs."

I nodded. I could see that. "Convenient, I suppose."

The master bedroom had two large windows, so there was a lot of light, which I loved. The master closet was technically a walk-in, but it wasn't like the walk-in I had now because someone had "remodeled" the closet with built-ins. The result was you couldn't see all the clothes on the back wall of the closet. 'Weird,' I thought.

"Nice closet," Liz said, contradicting my thoughts.

"I like the built-in shoe cubbies, and it would be nice to have the extra storage for sweaters." I was trying to be positive, but I really didn't like the layout of the closet. One strike against the house.

We wandered into the master bathroom. It was huge! There were two sinks on different sides of the room. I thought that was so smart. If I did have a visitor or maybe someone to share the house with eventually, we wouldn't be bumping elbows getting our teeth brushed and other morning and evening activities. The house just went up in my estimation.

There was a huge jetted tub, plus an oversized shower. I was used to a walk-in shower/tub, which I had just upgraded a bit with the new tile. But this was so much fancier. I was surprised I could afford it. The toilet was in its own little room, which also had a phone jack.

"This cracks me up," I said to Liz. "People put phones in the bathroom?"

"All the time," Liz assured me.

"I can't imagine." I shrugged. I didn't have to put a phone in the jack.

We walked down the hall toward the other bedrooms. There was another bathroom in the hall for the other bedrooms. We ducked our head in there, and I understood what Liz was hinting at about the small boys. The bathroom was covered in sailboats and other water-related things. It was painted a seafoam green, which I actually liked. It looked like the water.

The two bedrooms were bright blue and bright green. 'I can change that,' I thought. I enjoyed painting, so I wasn't put off by the colors.

"Bright, aren't they?" Liz asked.

"Yes, but paint is paint," I replied.

"You don't mind?"

"No. I like to paint actually."

"So many people can't see past the colors to the rooms themselves."

"Really? There are two nice closets in the rooms. They have two windows for lots of light. I love the ceiling fans."

"I noticed there was one of those in the master, too."

"Yes, I noticed that too. I like ceiling fans."

"Great!"

We headed down two flights to the family room, and I realized what I thought was a fourth floor was just an attic with two dormer windows. Bummer.

But the family room was large and very useable. The current owners were using it for a mother-in-law suite, but I could see the possibilities.

"This should be a family room," Liz explained.

I nodded. "I can see that. Creative of them to make it into another bedroom, though."

They had hung a curtain over the entrance from the bottom of the stairs to separate the space.

"There's another full bath here," Liz added, flicking on the light.

The bathroom was nicely appointed, with what was obviously not builder grade tiling. "Very nice."

"And here's the entrance from the garage," Liz said, pulling open the door to our right.

There was a large two-car garage. The idea of having a garage was thrilling. I was used to having assigned parking, so I didn't have to drive around looking for a place to put my car. But being able to have the car inside, so I didn't have to clean off the snow or balance an umbrella in the rain – I was excited to be moving up to such luxury!

"There's two storage rooms off the garage," Liz explained, as we toured it. "One for whatever you want to store, and another that includes the furnace and hot water heater. What do you think?" Liz asked, as we headed up the stairs to the kitchen again.

"I like it. It's got a good layout."

"I agree," Liz agreed. "It's good that you're not put off by the wall colors."

"No, I like having painted walls. I don't like houses that are all white."

"Great. So, do you want to make an offer?"

"Yes, let's put in an offer."

We drove to Liz's office, which was Sarah's office too, of course. Sarah was there, as well, doing paperwork.

"You found a place?" she asked when she saw us walk in together.

"Yes, the Stone River house," Liz replied.

"I really like it," I echoed.

"Great!" Sarah said. "I thought that might be a good fit for you. Good neighborhood. Nice layout for the house. Good sized kitchen."

Liz nodded. "Yes. I know you were hoping for an end unit. Too bad you weren't looking a couple of months ago. We sold one then."

"You did?" I was instantly jealous of that.

"Yes. Nice couple. A few streets from the house we looked at today," Liz offered.

"Well, I probably can't afford an end unit, anyway," I said, trying to console myself.

"They are $10-15k more," Sarah said, with a nod.

I did the calculation in my head. Unfortunately, I could afford an end unit, given the price for the townhouse we looked at today. "Any chance an end unit might come on the market anytime soon?"

"I can look," Sarah said.

"Thanks."

"In the meantime, let's get started on the paperwork," Liz suggested.

"Okay," I replied.

We worked on the offer, while Sarah searched whatever database it is that realtors use.

"I don't see any pre-listings for that development," Sarah explained. "Sorry."

"Oh well. I'm sure the one we saw will be lovely. And I can always move."

Liz looked at me askance. "Are you sure you want to finish this offer?"

I debated for a minute. I didn't really want to wait any longer. "Yes. Let's do it!" I said with enthusiasm. I still had the townhouse with multiple offers in my head. I didn't want to get locked out of another house I wanted. "Did you check on the other house?" I asked Liz, having reminded myself of the first house I thought I might want.

Liz frowned. "I did. There have been four offers today."

Sarah laughed. "It's going to be a blood bath!"

"Four offers?" I said, crestfallen.

"Yes. All above the asking price," Liz clarified. "Sarah is right. This is going to be a bidding war, just as we feared."

I nodded. "Let's just move on with the offer on the last townhouse. I think it's just perfect!" I was trying to convince myself as much as them.

"Okay. Just sign here, and here, and here," Liz pointed to the documents in front of me.

I signed, and they submitted the offer.

The owner and his agent responded a few hours later. They asked for another $10,000.

"Have there been other offers?" I asked Sarah when she called to tell me the news.

"No. They are just negotiating."

"Well, then I say no. I mean, what is the basis of their negotiation?"

"Well, they can refuse your offer and hope for another one."

"I suppose." I was beginning to hate house-hunting.

"How about we split the difference and offer an additional $5,000?"

"Okay," I said. I was reminding myself why I liked the house. And I really did. And we had looked at about a dozen in the past month, most of which I didn't like. Finding a townhouse I did like had proven harder than I thought.

That did the trick. The owners accepted my revised offer. I was thrilled.

Sarah and I went to do the home inspection, and I realized that I really loved the place. It was perfect. Really.

I also realized it was in a development I had admired for years.

"I didn't know," I explained to Sarah, "but when I first started thinking about getting a place, I started looking around when I was driving around. And I saw this set of townhouses off Rt. 50 when I was driving to work. I really liked their look."

"Yeah?"

"I just realized those are the townhouses on the front side of this neighborhood. I didn't make the connection because Liz and I came in from the other direction."

"Really?"

"Really. I've been looking at these townhouses for about six months!"

"Funny!"

While Sarah and I were doing the home inspection, Liz was holding an open house at my current townhouse. In a bit of kismet, one of the people who toured the townhouse said they would be making an offer.

"They might not," Sarah cautioned.

"I hope they do. Then we would be in great shape!" I wasn't sure how I was going to get together a down payment otherwise. I could borrow from Xan, but I didn't want to do that.

"We'll see."

Fortunately, the offer did come in. Unfortunately, it was for less than the list price.

"Can we ask for more?" I suggested. "Like the owners of my new place did?"

Liz nodded. "Sure. It's a risk, but you can try."

"Let's ask for $10,000, and we'll take $5,000."

"Okay."

And just like that, the dominoes fell into place. Now, we just had to work out the timing, so I could use the proceeds from the one sale to purchase the other. Sarah and Liz worked with the other two agents – coming and going – and they were able to make it all work. All seemed in order.

CR ЄОCR ЄОCR ЄО

"I'm sorry, Tiffany," said the HR director. "I really am."

I was trying hard not to cry. I had just been laid off. I knew the company was struggling, but it never occurred to me that I would be let go. "What happens now?" I asked.

"You'll get two weeks' severance. And you have two weeks before you have to leave. We have a program to help with finding your next position. Please make use of it. It's a tough economy right now."

I had just bought my new townhouse. My mortgage was substantially more than it had been, based on my ability to pay based on my current job. Now, I was starting to panic. I couldn't afford to be out of a job. I had JUST bought a house.

I started to get angry. The whole office knew I had just bought a house. And it wasn't like this had to happen right now. The layoffs. I took some consolation that I wasn't the only one being laid off. It wasn't a personal decision or based on my performance. The company just wasn't making as much money as they'd hoped. They needed to cut back. I was a junior marketing manager, one of three. They only needed two, they explained. And I was the last one hired, so I was the first one laid off. Same with a couple of the production folks.

"Who should I talk to about that?" I inquired, trying to keep my voice level. I was seething and crying internally. But I wanted to remain professional. I could tell there were tears at the edges of my lashes, though. I blinked hard to make them go away.

"Marian is handling the replacement process," Gretchen, the HR director, explained.

"Thank you." I calmly stood up. I walked to the door and opened it.

And ran to the bathroom to cry. And panic. What was I going to do?

I talked to Marian. She wasn't very helpful, though.

"The market is glutted, I'm afraid. So many mid-sized firms like ours are having to lay off people."

"So, what do I do?"

"Get your resume together quickly. Post it everywhere you can think of. Share with your friends. You never know."

'Obviously!' I thought, but didn't say. I had thought Marian would have more to suggest. "Are there any company contacts we can use?"

Marian shook her head. "I'm afraid not. None that I'm aware of."

And so I updated my resume and posted it to all the usual job sites. I sent it to all my contacts, including my clients. I knew my company wouldn't be happy with me about that. They didn't want clients to know they were in trouble. I didn't care. This was my life.

In the meantime, I did what I had done when I had been laid off before. I became a temp. I listed myself as an editor and writer, both skills I used extensively in my marketing position. I knew temp marketing wasn't really a thing. But editors and writers were.

"Can you do desktop publishing?" the coordinator asked.

"Sure!" I said. I knew how to layout documents in several different programs, in fact.

"I have a position for that. Doesn't pay as well as editing. But it includes overhead, if you're willing to work extra hours."

"Anything," I agreed.

So, I became a desktop publisher. I worked 50-60 hours a week, and got time and a half for the extra 10-20 hours. It was almost as much as I was making in marketing. Amazingly, I was going to be able to keep my house. I was exhausted, but I could keep my house.

It took me six months to find another marketing job. I applied to every job I could find, reviewing the listings every night when I got home and on the weekends. I had lots of interviews, mostly for positions that would be a step backward.

But the economy wasn't getting any better. As 2008 rolled into 2009, I despaired of ever getting out of desktop publishing.

Then, a longshot position called. They were looking for a marketing manager. Perfect! I interviewed three times, with different groups of people.

Finally, I got the offer.

I breathed a deep sigh of relief.

BUYING THE NEW HOUSE (2018)

Now that my house was ready to be listed, Sarah started taking us out looking at new houses. Or new-to-us houses because Reston's communities had mostly been built in the '60s and '70s.

The timing was going to be challenging. I needed the money from the sale of my house to buy the new house. The plan was to sell my house, move my furniture and most of my belongings into storage until closing, move me and the cats in with Tom for a few weeks, and then close on the new house and move both houses' worth of furniture and boxes to the new house.

That was the plan.

But Sarah was concerned because contingent sales, like the one we would be making to buy the new house, were harder. In her ideal, we would sell my house, move into Tom's house for a little while, and then start house-hunting after closing on my townhouse. That way, we wouldn't have to make the buying of a new house contingent on the sale of my current townhouse.

"Don't most people have to do it that way? I mean, I've never bought a house without needing to sell the previous one," I said to Sarah, as she was driving Tom and I to some possible listings.

"Yes. But your offer will be stronger if you can do it without the contingency. That's all I'm saying."

"Do you think we won't get the house we want if we have a contingent offer?" Tom asked.

"I'm not saying that. But the market is tight. There aren't a lot of houses for sale right now. And scrutiny of offers is harder than it used to be."

"Doesn't that mean the same for whoever is buying my house?" I wondered.

"Yes. And because the market is so tight, and lenders are being pickier about deals, the offer on your house could fall through. Then, because the offer you put in is contingent, you could lose the new house. It's a domino effect."

"Which also means, if the buyer of Tiffany's house is also in need of the funds from the sale of his or her house to buy the townhouse, that domino could fall too," Tom stated.

I gasped. "That's crazy."

"Yes, but Tom's right. It's possible. But your townhouse might be a starter home for someone, Tiffany. We can hope," Sarah said.

My plan was not very good, I thought.

CR EOCR EOCR EO

I could have sold my townhouse and moved the cats and myself into Tom's place for a while, until we closed, before we started looking. We could do it as Sarah wanted.

I didn't want to. For two reasons.

First, that would mean leaving my stuff in storage for that much longer, which was expensive.

Second, I really didn't want to live in Tom's place any longer than I had to. He'd had some work done, but not all of it. The old curtains were down, but the new blinds had never been put up. The upstairs walls had been stripped and rebuilt, but still weren't painted. The downstairs rooms hadn't been touched. I wasn't sure why Tom hadn't had all the wallpaper stripped at the same time, including the bathroom he used, but he had not. The bathroom was usable, even with the paper hanging over the edge of the shower. But it drove me crazy.

And in keeping with my agreement with myself not to bother him too much about his place, I had decided not to ask why. Tom had talked about how expensive it was to get walls stripped and readied for painting. Maybe he could only afford a few rooms at a time. I didn't know much about his finances. We hadn't meshed ours and weren't planning to even after we moved in together.

But, selfishly, I just didn't want to live in that townhouse any longer than I absolutely had to.

If it turned out we couldn't get a new house with a contingent offer, then I would reconsider. Carefully.

CR ಐCR ಐCR ಐ

As we looked, we started coming up with even more parameters for what we wanted in a house. We had already told Sarah we wanted a three-bedroom, three-bath house. Single-family. With a garage.

"Is this cul-de-sac too busy? We don't want to have to stress out every morning getting our cars out of the driveway," Tom mentioned.

I had never considered getting in and out of the driveway as something we needed to worry about. But Tom was right. This particular house was near the entrance to the cul-de-sac. There were a half dozen houses on the cul-de-sac. Just in the few minutes we'd been there, we'd seen a bunch of cars coming and going. On a weekday morning, when everyone was going to work or school at about the same time, getting out of the driveway, backwards of course, might be difficult.

Requirement – easy driveway access.

"There are a lot of trees around this house," I said. "Trees make me think about spiders." I had once rented a house nestled in the trees. It was a lovely place. But there were spiders in the house all the time. I hate spiders.

We didn't see any spiders when we walked around the house. But then again, it had been cleaned for showing, of course.

"You also love the sun," Tom pointed out. "There might not be as much in this house with all those trees."

Another requirement – fewer trees.

"I like this place. There are several ways to get out of the neighborhood." Another Tom requirement or at least preference.

"This house has a good place to put the litterboxes out of the main traffic areas of the house." Another Tiffany suggestion.

"I'd like to be able to walk to the grocery store. In a snowstorm, that can come in handy." Tom's suggestion.

"Ooh, I never knew I liked houses that sit on a corner at an angle. I really like that." Tiffany's idea.

And so, in time, the list grew longer. Lots of houses met most of the requirements. But very few met them all.

CR SOCR SOCR SO

We looked most Saturdays. Sarah would send us a list of houses she thought we might like to see on Thursday. We would reply with yesses and noes, and send her a few others to add to the list.

We could only see about four or five houses on a given Saturday. In part, this was because of the amount of time it took to really look at a house. In part, this was because there was only so much time we could devote to house-hunting.

Saturdays were also for errands and work and other things. While we were prioritizing finding a new house, we couldn't spend our entire Saturday doing it.

Most Sundays, I ended up at Tom's place while Sarah or one of her fellow realtors held an open house at my place. I knew the cats would be okay, because they would just hide while strangers were traipsing through our house. But I had to go somewhere else. That was usually Tom's place.

Every time I spent more than a few hours there, my nose would twitch. There was a mustiness to the house that even getting rid of the old curtains hadn't cured. Also, Tom's couch, which fortunately he didn't mind leaving behind once we moved, was not comfortable. At least not to me. It didn't have enough back support. And the cushions were thinned from age and use. I also wondered if the mustiness was coming from the couch, and once that idea had sprung, I could barely stand to sit on the couch for any amount of time.

Tom would usually work when I was there on Sundays. Or at least he'd be in the dining room on his computers. I never did learn which laptop was which, though I assumed the classified one was stored in the safe when I was there since I didn't have a clearance and Tom was meticulous about security. When I'd ask what he was doing, Tom would say he was working or just browsing. Either way, he spent most of his Sunday afternoons in front of his screens.

I brought over my laptop, too. Sometimes, I would work. Sometimes, I would browse. Sometimes, I would just look at social media or spend money for things I probably didn't really need. I usually also brought a physical book to read.

One of the differences between Tom and me was preferred method of reading. We both were pretty voracious readers; it was one of the things we enjoyed about each other. While we enjoyed many of the same television shows, Tom primarily read short stories or articles about computing or math. I always had at least one novel going, though sometimes I read marketing or business books. He loved his ebooks. I had actually never read a book that way, preferring the physical heft of a book, though most of the time mine were paperback.

"See, if you read ebooks, Tiffany, you wouldn't have to carry so many things," Tom teased. "You could read on your laptop – two for one!"

"I don't mind carrying both," I responded tartly but playfully. "I like my books!" I insisted.

"You do? I had no idea."

"Oh, you."

I was amazed, however, at how slowly a Sunday afternoon could pass when I was trapped outside my house.

CR ଔଔ ଔଔ ଔ

We looked at a lot of houses in Reston. We were taken with the midcentury modern look. A lot of my furniture was also midcentury modern, so the two would work well together.

But we didn't find anything that really worked for us.

"Too small." Even with the requisite 3BR, 3BA, the house was cut in a way that made it seem smaller than the 2,500 square feet.

"Too many trees." We'd thought it would be light enough. But it just wasn't.

"This street is crazy!" We loved the house, but it was on a major road in Reston. That just wasn't going to work for us.

"Who clears the pipe stem when it snows?" It turned out a lot of the houses for sale were on pipe stems, not really a cul-de-sac but a long driveway with two or three houses on it. "What do you do if your neighbor doesn't help with that?" "I think most people pay for a plow to come." "Added expense?" Sarah shrugged. "Next!"

○₹ ℰↄ○₹ ℰↄ○₹ ℰↄ

This was taking a very long time. Weeks were turning to months.

No one had made an offer on my place either. I was surprised. I thought my townhouse was lovely. I was a little insulted, in fact.

"There are a lot of end units for sale, for whatever reason," Sarah explained. "Those go first."

"I can see that. I would have bought one if I could, as you know."

"What will you do if you get an offer before you find a new place?" Tom asked.

"Move in with you?" I teased.

"Isn't that the plan?" Sarah questioned, not used to the teasing between me and Tom.

"Yes, Sarah. He's just being silly," I explained.

Tom laughed.

○₹ ℰↄ○₹ ℰↄ○₹ ℰↄ

We looked and looked, and looked some more. I was beginning to think our house – the house we really loved – was a unicorn. We had looked all over Reston. We had found several houses that we liked, but they all had some kind of flaw. Too many trees. Too chopped up. Down a pipe stem. The only one we saw and fell in love with was almost twice our budget. It was a lovely house. But not for us.

We expanded our search parameters to include Herndon and Fairfax. I thought about adding Sterling, too, but wanted to make that a last resort as it was further north and west than I really wanted to live.

Part of the reason we had looked in Reston to start with was the mid-century modern architecture. There weren't many of those houses in Herndon or Fairfax. We had to let go of that wish. It just wasn't practical.

We were both open to Fairfax, as that's where we currently lived. Part of me thought it would be ironic if we ended up in Fairfax, having lived so close to each other these past few years. But Fairfax is a fairly good-sized town, and we didn't want to get too close to the university on the east side of town. Mostly because of traffic, but also because we were afraid the college-aged folks might be a little too much for us. It was a sad realization that I was now a little more than middle-aged, and I liked my peace and quiet. Our current residences were on the other side of Fairfax, in two quiet townhouse communities, more full of families. We soon found, however, that the single-family inventory in Fairfax was pretty limited. Most of the homes that looked interesting were beyond our ability to buy. Or rather my ability as I was the one doing the financing.

Meghan and George lived in Herndon, so we thought it would be amusing if we ended up there. They had bought their home two years earlier. It was on a dead-end street and off a major roadway. I knew Tom would never want to live in the same neighborhood, which was fine with me. I loved Meghan and George, but I didn't want to live within walking distance.

However, the first house we saw in Herndon with some potential was in the next community over from where they lived. You could walk from one to the other, but it wouldn't be easy. More importantly, the house was on a good-sized cul-de-sac, so we didn't feel like we would have difficulties getting in and out. It had a two-car garage, three bedrooms, and three-and-a-half baths. I liked the front porch, mostly because I liked the idea of a front porch more than any intention of sitting out on it. Phin and Joseph had a large porch, and as a family, we sometimes ate outside in the summer when they had a barbecue for everyone. I would inevitably be bitten by some creature or another at these events. And Tom wasn't a fan of sitting in the sun. So, no, I didn't think the porch would necessarily be used. But it was a cute element to the house.

The kitchen was not very large, but then again, we didn't really cook. There was a decent-sized dining room, which would fit my table that expanded to fit 16 people. I hadn't entertained that many people often, but I didn't want Phin to feel like he was the only one who could fit the family. Xan and Catherine had the space to host everyone, but they never did. They were so busy with their kids, it was a challenge just to get them to find the time to come to a family event. Both children played a variety of sports, as well as participating in plays and such at school. Getting Xan to host would have required more planning than seemed to be possible, given all the other demands on their time. So, I was pleased with the possibility of a dining room where I could not only fit my big table, but also fit the leaves to expand it if needed.

The house had two spaces we could use for televisions, one of our other requirements – a living room upstairs and a family room downstairs. That way, Tom could watch his horror movies and dystopian shows, while I watched my family dramas. The living room would probably end up as our primary television room, which reminded me that I wanted to get a cabinet to house the TV, so it wasn't always out when we were entertaining.

The master bedroom was nice, with the requisite en suite bathroom. It had two sinks, also something that we had decided would be key to compatible living. Although Tom was usually up, dressed, and working before I got up, there would be times – usually bedtime – when we would be sharing the bathroom. Two sinks would make this infinitely easier.

After we finished our tour, we sat on that cute front porch and discussed the house.

"Do you think the road is okay?" Tom asked.

"What is your concern?" I countered, knowing Tom had more driving issues than I did.

"The basketball net."

"I hadn't even noticed."

"If there's a group of kids playing, that will be difficult to navigate."

"Not to mention noisy."

When Tom worked at home, noise in the neighborhood was a bit of a round-the-clock concern.

"Not to mention," Tom replied with a chuckle.

"Well, I did like the house," I said.

"We can think about it," Tom conceded.

Sarah intervened, "There are lots of other houses. Let's find one you just love."

We nodded, though we were not as convinced as Sarah that finding one we loved was possible.

CR ᏯᎧCR ᏯᎧCR ᏭᎧ

"Sarah says she thinks the owners will accept my offer."

Tom was quiet for a minute, though I could hear his breathing so I knew he was still on the phone. "What offer are you talking about?"

"The offer. On the Kings Farm house."

"The one we saw Sunday?" Tom asked, his tone acrid.

"Yeah. That one. I told you I met with Sarah to finalize an offer. We faxed over the paperwork last night." It was Wednesday.

"No, you didn't," Tom said, his voice flat.

"I'm sure I did."

"Tiffany, I would remember if you said you were going to put in an offer. You didn't tell me."

"You liked the house, right? I thought we decided?"

"Sounds like you decided."

"No, we decided," my voice was no longer calm. "You were there. With Sarah and me. We all liked the house."

"Yes, we liked the house. I'll agree to that."

"So, I put in an offer."

"Without talking to me first." It was a statement, not a question.

"Oh, I guess so. I was excited! Aren't you excited? It's a great house!"

"You guess so?"

"I should have told you. I'm sorry."

"Yes, you should have."

"I didn't mean to exclude you from the decision. I really thought we had decided. Together. On Sunday. Sarah and I met on Tuesday to finish the paperwork."

"So, you decided on Monday to buy the house?"

"We decided on Sunday to buy the house."

"No, we decided on Sunday that we both thought the house had all the elements we were looking for. We..." – he emphasized the word – "...did not decide to put in an offer."

"It's my money."

I immediately regretted saying that. I tried to backpedal quickly.

"Tom, I'm sorry. I shouldn't have said that. It's our house. I'm just buying it. Really. I don't think of it as my house."

Tom's breathing was more audible. I could tell he was really angry. But at least he'd stayed on the phone. A year ago, he wouldn't have. He would have hung up.

"Tom? Are you there? I'm so sorry. Really. I'm sorry I said what I just said. And I'm sorry I didn't tell you about the offer. I really, truly thought we had agreed to put in an offer. We had talked about what a good neighborhood the house was in. How you could get into and out of the driveway easily. It's a catty-corner house, which you know I love. It has two rooms we can use for televisions, so you don't have to watch those medical dramas with me. And you can watch all the scary movies with Meghan you want to, while George and I watch, well, I don't know what we'll watch. But something…" I was being silly. I was trying to get Tom to smile. I couldn't see his face. I didn't know if it was working. But I knew I had dug myself a pretty deep hole. I needed to find a way out. And humor often worked.

"Tiffany…" he said warningly.

I could tell he was teasing me now. "Yes, dear?"

He burst out laughing. "I'm still angry."

"I know. I'm sorry. I really did think we'd both decided on the house. But maybe we hadn't finished that discussion. Are you okay? If they accept the offer, should we buy the house?"

"I don't think we can back out now, can we?"

In a small voice, I said, "No, I don't think we can."

Tom took a deep breath. "It is a nice house."

I breathed a sigh of relief. "Yes, it is."

CR ∞CR ∞CR ∞

Tom wasn't going to walk out the door this time. But it was a close thing.

"The most persistent sound which reverberates through man's history is the beating of war drums." -- Arthur Koestler

The Big Fight: Round Two (2017)

Tom and I had almost broken up a couple of years ago. Because I was stupid and selfish.

CR ꙮCR ꙮCR ꙮ

"Cathy said she's fine with Craig sleeping on the floor," I told Tom. We were sitting downstairs, as we did most nights, watching TV and looking at our respective smartphones. I had just gotten an email from Tom's cousin, Cathy, with whom I'd been emailing for the past few days.

"What are you talking about, Tiffany? Cathy, as in my cousin Cathy?"

"Right. Craig and Isabelle have been learning about American history, and Cathy figured it was about time they came to DC to see some of it in person."

"And what does that have to do with Craig sleeping on the floor?" Tom asked, his voice tight.

"Why are you mad at me? She's your cousin."

"Agreed. So why are you talking to her?"

"She emailed me after I posted a picture of our trip to the Smithsonian to social media," I explained.

"Got it. And?" Tom's voice still had an edge.

"She said they wanted to visit."

"Got it. And?"

"Tom, I've told you all this."

"No, you haven't."

I thought about it. In fact, I might not have. Cathy, being Cathy, liked to get things done, and quickly. So did I. It was possible we'd made arrangements, and I hadn't told Tom. "Okay, maybe I didn't remember to tell you before. I'm telling you now."

"And what exactly are you telling me?"

"Cathy, Mitch, Craig, and Isabelle are coming to DC in June. Cathy asked if they could stay with us. You know with two teachers' salaries, they don't have a lot of discretionary income. They will drive down, to save the airfare. And most of the museums are free. So, they just needed a place to stay for it to be a pretty inexpensive trip."

"You volunteered to let them stay with you?"

"Well, the plan is for the kids to stay with me, Isabelle in my spare bedroom and Craig on the floor of my downstairs. Or the futon downstairs. His choice. Cathy thought he might prefer the floor, since he's a big kid at 6'3" and the futon is not that long and pretty narrow."

"And where are Cathy and Mitch staying?"

"Well, I told Cathy they could stay with you."

"You did, did you?" Tom's voice was all sarcasm.

I got sheepish. Looking at the plans from Tom's perspective, I understood why he was angry.

"We were emailing back and forth, and I only have the one room for guests, and she's your cousin, and I guess we just assumed you'd be okay with it."

Tom shook his head. "When in June?"

"The 10th through the 15th."

"Five days!"

"Well, there's a lot to see. They will drive down over the weekend, be here Monday through Friday, and then drive back the following weekend."

"Do you remember my telling you I had to go out of town for work?"

"Vaguely…" I admitted.

"And when am I going?"

"Oh, crap! It's the same week."

"Exactly," Tom said, his voice cold. "You have to stop doing this."

"Doing what? Arranging vacations with your cousin?" I was being defensive, and I knew it. But I couldn't seem to help myself.

"Running our lives without me. Aren't we supposed to be partners?"

"Of course! I didn't mean it that way."

"And yet, that's the end result."

"I should have talked to you. I'm sorry."

"Tiffany, I don't know if I can do this," Tom said sadly.

"Do what?"

"Live life the way you do."

"I'm not sure what that means."

"I'm not sure either. But I can't be this person. I can't be passive in my life."

"I'll talk to Cathy. We can change the week, I'm sure."

"That is so not the point."

"I know. But this time, I will talk to you first. So, I will make sure you're available."

"Again, not the point. Do you really think I want Cathy and Mitch to stay with me?"

"You don't?"

"No, I don't. I'm pretty mad at Cathy too, to be honest. She's tried this before. Through Meghan. Meghan was smart enough to push back and tell Cathy that we would be happy to meet them for dinner while they were here, but not to let them stay with us."

"Smart enough?" I said, with grit in my voice.

"Savvy enough. With emotional intelligence," Tom said with more sarcasm. "You know I barely tolerate my cousins. Sort of like you with your stepsiblings."

"I have good reason to not like them."

"And I have decades of history with Cathy and the rest of the Youngs that you know nothing about," Tom explained.

"But we go visit every year? You've been going since you were a kid."

"For essentially 36 hours."

I thought about it and realized that was true. Even the anniversary party had been a limited timeframe.

"But you're still missing the point," Tom said, his voice now sad.

"I am?" I was genuinely confused.

"If you don't see what you've done, then I don't know if I can do this."

"Do what?"

"Be with you."

CR ƎƆCR ƎƆCR ƎƆ

As Tom and I had discussed several times before, neither of us had dated all that much, and so intertwining our lives with another person was something we just hadn't done much of.

Except with Priya. Tom had let Priya into his life, integrated her into his world, included her in family functions, communications, and made her his partner. That she hadn't done the same was part of what made Tom realize that she was controlling their relationship.

"Be with me, as in date me at all?" I said, tears starting to well up in my eyes. I knew Tom hated tears, but these were genuine tears. He was breaking up with me over vacation plans?

"I think you need to figure out your priorities."

"You're my priority. I've shown that a thousand times in a thousand ways."

"I'm not sure. I'm not trying to be mean or cryptic, Tiffany. But you have this tendency to just run with things. It's part of being a strong woman, and I wouldn't want you not to be that."

"Well, that's good, because I wouldn't know how, nor would I want to be with someone who wants me to be anything other than strong." I had an edge in my voice.

Tom looked at me. "There's strong, and there's controlling. I think you haven't quite learned the difference."

"I do not control you!" I shouted. And I knew as soon as I did, it was a mistake. Tom had learned to deal with my tears. But he was still nonconfrontational. And as soon as my temper flared, he stopped all communication.

So, I wasn't really surprised when he stood up and said, "We'll talk again later. I don't think now is a good time." And he went up the stairs, out the front door, and left. Much as he had all those years before.

Only this time, I didn't go after him. Because this time, I was right, and he was wrong.

∞ ∞ ∞ ∞ ∞ ∞

Okay, so maybe I was a little wrong. I mean, I apparently did invite Cathy and her family to stay with Tom and me without checking with him first. Obviously, I had, otherwise I wouldn't have invited them for a week when Tom was going to be out of town on business travel. Especially since his going out of town was a rarity.

But Tom wasn't entirely right either. He had his issues, too, mostly stemming from his relationship with Priya or his anxiety about crowds. In this case, both were at work, I realized, as I analyzed every word of our fight / discussion. His relationship with Priya had made him distrustful of certain things, like women's tears. Just because she had used hers as a weapon didn't mean I was doing the same. In a similar fashion, he tended to believe my intentions were to control things when I just saw it as planning and organizing – and part of my personality.

And yet, I did try to be mindful of Tom's crowd phobia and avoid circumstances where he would be forced into large groups of people with little chance of an exit. Going downtown to see the DC monuments and museums during the height of tourist season definitely qualified as pushing that boundary. Which also made me realize that Cathy was dismissive of this fear of Tom's, which she also had known about since they were kids together, and that was yet another reason why Tom and the rest of the McDonnells tended to limit their time spent with the Youngs.

The question now was what to do about all this. First and foremost, I needed to tell Cathy to find alternative plans. And to warn Meghan that those plans should not include staying with her and

George. Not that Meghan would give in to Cathy's machinations. But still.

So, I texted Meghan to tell her about the whole situation, including the fact that her brother had apparently broken up with me. She texted me back immediately, as I hoped and feared she would. Meghan was almost always on Tom's side, as well she should be. But she also knew his foibles as well as anyone. I hoped, in this case, she would see my side.

"You shouldn't have done that," she wrote, confirming my fears that she was with Tom on this. "Tom and I barely tolerate the Youngs."

"I didn't think it was THAT bad," I texted back.

"You have no idea."

"Okay. I'll admit I don't."

"I'll be on the lookout for Cathy's self-invitation to stay with George and me. I appreciate their desire to see the sights, and their limited budget. But I couldn't take a week."

"Good."

No response to that was forthcoming. And I hadn't asked the most important question.

"Do you think Tom will forgive me?"

"Have you asked him?"

"Well, no…"

"He's not going to be the first to call, you know."

"He'll just cut me out of his life?"

"He might. I couldn't say for sure. He loves you. I know that."

"If he loves me, why would he leave?"

"You know the answer to that."

It was my turn to be silent. I did know. I just didn't like it.

CR ED CR ED CR ED

When I reached out to Cathy to tell her the plans weren't going to work out, I understood a little better about why the McDonnells had issues with their Young cousins.

I sent her an email explaining that Tom was going to be out of town the week they had planned to come. So, I was sorry, but it wasn't going to work out after all.

Cathy's response was almost instantaneous. "We'll just change weeks! When should we come instead?"

I, of course, had thought about this possibility. But I had hoped that, what with our email exchange being close to their travel dates, changing the week wouldn't be so easy. I assumed Cathy and Mitch would have already taken the days off.

And then I realized my mistake. With Cathy and Mitch being schoolteachers, they had much of the summer off. I knew they both took summer jobs, but apparently it wasn't that hard to change their plans. The kids, of course, were off for the summer from school.

So, chastened, I wrote back. "I don't think this summer will work for us. There's just too much going on."

Again, Cathy's response was quick. "What have you got planned? Anything fun? We can work around whatever. Just let me know!"

Ugh. We didn't really have plans. And Tom wasn't speaking to me at all at the moment.

I had been trying to be nice in my responses to Cathy. But she wasn't getting it. Instead, the responses were quintessential Cathy. So quick you hardly had a chance to think. A bit pushy. Definitely nosy.

The private McDonnells must be horrified by this behavior. If there was one thing Tom was definitely not, it was nosy. He was reticent to the point where I had to ask a lot of questions to get information.

But what to do about Cathy? Should I lie again? Or confess that Tom just didn't want them to stay with him? No, it wasn't fair to open that particularly can of worms, certainly not without Tom's okay.

So, I just let the last email go without a response. As far as I was concerned, my last email to Cathy stood. We were not available this summer. End of story.

ॐ ୫)ॐ ୫)ॐ ୫)

I missed Tom. It had been three days since he'd walked out. Three days since we had broken up. Or maybe had broken up.

I thought of the infamous *Friends* storyline of Ross and Rachel, and whether they were on a break or broken up. And it made me realize that what I should do was actually talk to Tom, rather than making assumptions about what was or was not going on with the two of us.

ॐ ୫)ॐ ୫)ॐ ୫)

I wasn't brave enough to call. I texted.
"I emailed Cathy and told her we weren't available this summer."
No response.
"She asked a million questions. LOL"

No response.

"I understand better what you find challenging about her."

No response.

"I'm sorry. I know I should have talked to you first."

No response.

CR ℰↃCR ℰↃCR ℰↃ

Since Meghan wasn't going to help, I went to Jane. Even though Peter knew Tom better since they had been college roommates, Jane also knew Tom well, as their friendship predated my involvement. And I knew Jane better than Peter since we worked together. She was my work BFF.

"So," I concluded the long, complicated story, "I don't know where things stand.

"Because Tom didn't respond to your texts?" Jane asked.

"Yes."

"Seems to me you know what you should have done," Jane said, pulling no punches. "You should have called, rather than texted. And you shouldn't have made plans without talking to Tom in the first place."

"I'm too chicken," I confessed.

"To call?"

"Yeah. I'm afraid he'll say he's done with me."

"Wouldn't it be better to know?"

"Not really. I guess so. I don't know," I vacillated.

"You do know. Just like you know what you need to do."

"I guess."

"Tiffany, I love you. You know that. But if you're going to make things work with Tom, you're going to have to back off from your Type A personality. Just a little."

"I know. I just don't know how."

"Think of him like a colleague," Jane suggested.

"What do you mean by that?"

"Do you tell me what to do all the time?" She smiled, because sometimes I did. But mostly, no, I trusted her expertise.

"I try not to. You're the visual expert."

"Right. How about Jim?" Jim was one of my direct reports. His job, unlike Jane's, was essentially a more junior version of what I did – managing accounts and helping with their branding and messaging.

"What about him?"

"Do you tell him what to do?"

"Sometimes…" I admitted.

Jane smiled. "Well, sometimes I do, too. But mostly you let him deal with his clients and only come to you when he's stuck. Or he needs another opinion. Or someone is being a jerk. Right?"

Jane had a point. I did try to let my team of marketing managers actually manage their accounts. We had weekly meetings to talk through approaches and strategies. But day to day, I wasn't involved in every decision. I couldn't be. I had my own accounts to manage. And Jim and the others had been hired to lead their own accounts, not just to help me with mine. "Okay. I get your point about Jim. I'm not sure how that applies to Tom."

"When the two of you are planning something, how much does Tom help?"

"Well, usually it's my idea, so I do all the planning," I argued.

"Do you think Tom likes it that way?"

"He's not much of a planner."

"Do you know that for a fact?"

"Well, have you seen his house?"

Jane laughed. "Not in years. But that's not the same thing."

"Isn't it? He hasn't gotten the curtains redone since he moved in."

"Does he want them to be redone?" Jane led me onward.

"Well, I don't actually know. They're hideous!"

"To you. My impression is that they don't bother Tom, though."

"No, I don't think they do. I don't think he cares at all." I sighed.

"So, it's not that he's not organized. He just has other priorities. Right?"

"I guess."

"He's good at his job, right?"

"Definitely. They love him. He may not talk about his job much, but every time the contract changes, the new company hires Tom – usually for more money – because the customer loves him."

"Do you really think they would keep him on and pay him more money if he wasn't organized? And a planner?"

"Sure. But that's work."

"And your life together is different how?"

A lightbulb went off. What Jane was trying to tell me, or get me to see, was that just because Tom did things differently, didn't mean he did them wrong. That was something I learned a long time ago as a manager. Jim did his job differently than I did. But he got to the same endpoint. And his customers thought he did good work. So, the fact that he got there in another way was okay. Jane was arguing I needed to let Tom do things in our lives, even if he did them in a way that I disagreed with, as long as the end product was what we wanted. "You're saying I should treat Tom like Jim, and let him be himself."

Jane nodded. "Hardest thing in the world not to try to change the other person. But don't you love him?"

"I do. I really do."

"As he is?"

"Yes, and more than that, for who he is. He's the only person I've ever dated who made me feel like I was good enough."

Jane laughed sardonically. "Don't you think he wants the same thing?"

I blushed. "But I do think he's good enough!" I argued.

"Not when you don't let him be involved in your decisions, your planning, your organization. If I were him, I would think you didn't think I was good enough to help."

I nodded. "I get it."

"Now, call him!" Jane ordered.

I laughed. "Yes, ma'am."

CR SOCR SOCR SO

I went back to my office and closed the door. I didn't often make personal calls on work time, and this could be a longer call depending on Tom's receptivity. But I didn't want to wait. I wanted to talk to Tom while Jane's arguments were still fresh in my head. And heart.

The phone rang. I waited with my heart in my throat to see if Tom would pick up the line. It was the middle of his working day too. He could be in a meeting and unable to answer for that reason, I told myself, as the phone continued to ring. One more ring and it would go to voicemail. 'Should I leave a message,' I wondered.

"Tom McDonnell," I heard him say.

I started to cry. But I needed to talk. So, I pushed the tears back. "Hi."

"Tiffany? I almost didn't answer. What number is this?"

"My work phone."

"Must not have that programmed."

I guess I didn't call Tom from work often, and if I did, I must have used my cell phone. I had used my work phone because I wanted the connection to be clear. Sometimes my cell cut in and out when I was in my office.

"Funny. I'm glad you answered."

"Me too."

"Are you really?"

"Tiffany…"

"No, I'm serious. I wasn't sure you would want to talk to me."

"I'm mad at you. And I think we need to talk things over. But I'm not going to not talk to you."

"You didn't respond to my texts."

"I didn't think texting was the right way to talk."

"Okay. I get that. That's what Jane said, too."

"Jane is a smart woman."

"She is. She's the one who told me I was bossing you around. Is that what you feel?"

"Sometimes. Listen, I do want to talk, but I'm not sure now is the best time. You're at work; I'm at work. Can we talk tonight? In person?"

The tears were starting again. I wasn't sure if Tom was going to break up with me when he saw me. "Okay."

"Great. Text me when you get home, and I'll come over."

"Okay." I put my big girl shoes on. "Tom, are we broken up?"

"Let's talk tonight, okay?"

That wasn't what I wanted to hear, but I had to let Tom be Tom. "Okay. Have a good rest of your day."

"You, too."

I hung up not sure if I should feel better or not. Tom's vague answer about whether we were broken up only added to my anxiety.

The rest of the day was kind of a blur. Fortunately, I didn't have any critical client meetings; just routine stuff. I hoped I would rally if I needed to – I was confident I would – but I also mostly just stayed in my office.

"Did you call?" Jane IM'd me.

"I did. But he didn't want to talk over the phone."

"Oh no! In person okay?"

"Yes. Tonight."

"Good luck. Peter says good luck, too. We're rooting for you two!"

"Thanks!"

As I was walking to my car, I text Tom, "On my way home." I was cheating a bit, I knew, since he had said to text when I got home. But I had waited as long as I could to make sure I was going to be able to see him, to talk things through. As Jane said, I needed to know one way or another.

"Text me when you get home" came the response.

So much for pushing the boundaries.

I texted again after I had pulled my car into the garage and was going up the stairs to the main floor of my house. Cass and Brie were curling around my legs meowing for their dinner.

"Yes, girls," I said, as I waited for Tom's response. "I'm getting the can out right now."

I put my phone down on the counter, so I could pick up their food bowls. My ear was very attuned to the phone, even as I rinsed out breakfast and opened the can for dinner. The cats meowed and circled me until I put down their bowls, with food in them.

"Here you go, you silly children!"

I heard my phone ping. It was the text ping. I was almost afraid to look at it.

"Be over in about 10?"

"Sounds good," I responded quickly. I would just have enough time to change before Tom got here. Ten minutes meant he was essentially leaving his house now.

I walked up another flight to the floor with the three bedrooms, including the master. I took off the day's work clothes and put on what Tom and I referred to as "indoor" clothes, aka sweatpants and a sweatshirt with a t-shirt underneath. Most of the year, Tom wore shorts instead of sweatpants. But I only wore shorts in the summer. In the fall, I needed more warmth. I put my work clothes in the hamper and headed back downstairs. About five minutes had passed. Five more until Tom arrived.

I stood by the living room windows where I could watch for Tom's car. He only lived a couple of miles away, but he also didn't drive fast. I debated about moving away from the windows and trying to distract myself by doing something else. But I couldn't seem to make myself do it. I just stood there looking for his headlights.

Five minutes seemed like a lifetime. I wasn't crying, but my emotions were very close to the surface. I knew, because Tom struggled with other people's tears, it would be better if I could keep from crying. So, I tried to keep my emotions in check. I tried to focus on the positive. Tom was coming over. After four days, I was finally going to talk to him.

Finally, I saw his car's headlights. He pulled into my driveway and put the car in park. He didn't get out of the car right away. I thought maybe he was trying to get his emotions under control, too. I just didn't know if that was a good or bad thing.

He got out of the car, closed the door and locked the car behind him, and walked over to the stairs to my front door. He didn't look up. He didn't see me waving at him from the window.

The doorbell rang, and I jumped even though I knew it was going to. Nerves!

I walked across the living room, down the foyer stairs, and unlocked the front door. 'Should I kiss him hello?' I thought. 'Let him decide,' I told myself.

I opened the front door, and there was Tom. My heart leapt. I loved him so much. Did he still love me?

He smiled. "Are you going to let me in?" he asked with a laugh.

I stepped back to let him into the house. He walked across the threshold and gave me a quick kiss on the lips. 'A good sign,' I thought.

"Do you want to talk here in the living room or downstairs?" I asked, as we walked up the foyer stairs. I remembered Tom didn't like sitting on those stairs, and I smiled. We knew so many little things about each other after three years together.

"What's the smile for?" Tom asked, as he sat on the living room couch.

"I was just remembering your aversion to the stairs."

Tom smiled, too. "Not conducive to conversation."

"So you've said."

"They aren't comfortable."

I laughed. "I guess not."

We settled in on the living room couch, not quite next to each other, but not at opposite ends either. Normally, when we sat on the couch downstairs, we sat hip to hip. But I wanted to be able to see Tom's face, and I couldn't if we were sitting like that. I missed the intimacy of touching. But I thought the exchange was worth it.

Tom sat quietly. I wasn't sure if that was just Tom being Tom or he was waiting for me to start the conversation. In keeping with letting Tom be Tom, I decided to let him start the conversation.

"Interesting," he said, after a few minutes of silence.

"What is?" I said, wondering what he was talking about.

"I expected you to start talking as soon as I got here."

"Did you want me to? Because I could," I said with a smile, trying to keep the mood from getting too heavy.

"No. But I expected it."

"Well, I'm trying to let Tom be Tom."

"What does that mean?" Tom asked, genuinely curious.

"It was Jane's advice. To let you be you."

"Okay. But what does that mean in actuality?"

"Not to jump to start the conversation in this case. To let you do things in your own time, in your own way."

"You can do that?"

"Probably not all the time. But I can try."

"That's a lot."

"I know. But you're half of this relationship, and I tend to dominate."

"Yes."

"I'll try to be better. Really."

"That would be good," Tom said, with a smile.

I smiled back, though the tears were just at the edge of my heart. "Is it enough?" I asked, fearful of the answer.

"Let's talk this through a little more, okay?"

"Okay," I said in a small voice.

"I don't want you to not be you," Tom said, echoing my words. "And you are a powerful, strong woman. And I love that. I don't mind you're being in charge. Most of the time. But you have to let me participate in our lives."

"I know. I thought I did. I guess I didn't?"

"Not always. Not enough."

"Okay. Can I ask you for something, though?"

"What?"

"Can you let me know when I'm being too much before it gets to the point where you're mad?"

Tom looked at me. "Why is that my job?"

"It's not. Not entirely. I have to pick up my side, too. But I'm not sure I always know when I'm being too much in charge."

"You don't?"

"No. This is new for me. I have been on my own most of my life. I'm used to just doing things. I was the only one in charge on my life. Now, you have to be in charge of my life, too. And I'm not sure how to do that. Not yet anyway."

"I don't want to be in charge of your life, Tiffany," Tom warned. "I just don't want you to be in charge of my life. Or rather, I want our lives to be our lives. Together."

"I know. I get it. I do. I just am not sure where the line is."

"It's wherever your life stops being yours and starts being ours," Tom replied logically.

"I get it when it's things like going out to eat or something like that. It's when it gets to the big things that I get lost."

"Well, those are actually more important to share, don't you think?"

"I guess. But you don't like confrontation."

"What does that have to do with it?"

"Sometimes big things involve confrontation. So, sometimes I make the decisions, so you don't have to. To save you from the confrontation."

"Tiffany…"

"Well, that's how I see it."

Tom sighed. "While it's true I'm not the best at facing difficult things, it doesn't mean I can't. I do all the time. At work. With my family. Just because I don't like it, doesn't mean I shouldn't do it. Or rather that you should do things for me. For us."

I looked at Tom like a dog who is listening really hard, with my head cocked slightly to one side. I was really trying to understand what he was telling me. I just wasn't sure I was. "I understand what I did wrong with Cathy. I should have talked to you before we made plans for her and Mitch to stay with you."

"You should have talked to me before you told them it was okay to come and stay with us, either of us."

I nodded. "Right. I didn't realize, or maybe I did but it just seemed like a quirk, how pushy Cathy is."

"You have no idea," Tom said, repeating what his sister had said.

"Meghan said the same thing. Someday, maybe you'll tell me the stories."

"They don't really make sense, I think, unless you were there. And you've gotten the point now. Give Cathy an inch, and she'll take a mile. So, in general, we don't give her an inch. She's a nice enough person. But she doesn't know when enough is enough." Tom looked at me pointedly.

"I'm not THAT bad," I countered, smiling to hopefully get a positive response.

Tom grinned. "You have your moments."

I grinned back. "Yeah. I guess I do. Jane said I should think of you like a colleague."

"Intriguing. What does that mean?"

"She pointed out that I let Jim – and her, of course, but she's different – I let Jim run his accounts. He doesn't always do things the way I would do them. Or even things I appreciate. But his customers are satisfied with him, and in the end, the results work."

"So that's where the 'let Tom be Tom' comes from?"

"Exactly!"

"Well, it's not a bad plan."

"I need to remember that you have a different way of doing things. Doesn't mean it's wrong. Just different."

"Yup!"

"And I need to make you feel like you're in charge of your own life."

"I am in charge of my own life," Tom said with a bit of heat in his voice.

"That's not what I meant. I meant – oh, I'm not saying this right."

"Just say what you mean, Tiffany."

"I told Jane that one of the things I love about you is that I can be myself with you. You don't want to change me."

"And…"

"And I don't want to change you either!"

"Sometimes I'm not so sure."

"No, really. I don't! I love you just the way you are. That's what I have to remember. That and to not make all the decisions. To let you make the decisions in your own time, in your own way."

"Sounds about right."

"So, do you still love me?" I said it with a half smile, trying to tease, but the answer was too important to me for the smile to be full. And the emotions threatened to break free.

"Tiffany, I never stopped loving you."

"So, are we still a couple? I mean, did you break up with me?"

"Well, I threatened to. I almost did. I can't deal with another controlling person in my life. I have to be able to trust you."

"You can!"

"And you have to trust me."

"I do!"

"I'm not sure you do. Not always."

"It's not a matter of trust. Not really. It's more a matter of not thinking about what's mine is mine and what's ours is ours. I'm so used to it all being mine. I'm still learning the 'ours' part."

"Okay. But you'll try, right?"

"I promise!"

"Really?"

"Yes, dear."

Tom cracked up. And I had intended him to.

CR EOR EOR EO

I can't say I was perfect. I can't say I always remembered where the line of 'ours' was. But I was better. And Tom was Tom.

WHEN THINGS DON'T GO AS PLANNED (2018)

Now that we had found a house to buy, selling mine became even more imperative. Fortunately, Sarah had plans for several open houses, hosted by either her or Liz. While they were conducting the open houses, I would stay at Tom's for the afternoon – and try not to obsess about strangers in my house.

The Saturday before the next open house, Sarah had dropped by one her way to another client's showing to drop off more flyers. She'd redone the layout a bit and swapped out some of the pictures.

"I think these might be more appealing," she explained.

"Whatever you think is best," I said, trusting her opinion.

"Great! We've had a few calls from realtors in the past few days, so I'm expecting a good turnout this Sunday."

"No one who wants to come see the townhouse earlier?" I asked.

"No. Just inquiries to make sure the house is still available. You never know. It only takes one!"

"True!"

We were just wrapping up when my cell phone rang. Caller ID told me it was my doctor's office. I figured they were just calling to tell me the results of the mammogram I'd had earlier in the week. So, I motioned for Sarah to wait a second while I excused myself to take the call; I didn't expect it to take long. I moved into the living room from the kitchen.

"This is Tiffany," I said, answering the phone.

"Tiffany. This is Dr. Kessler."

Hmmm…Normally, one of her assistants or the nurse practitioner would be calling with the results. Often, they just sent me an email. The doctor didn't usually call, especially not on a Saturday. "Hi there," I said with some trepidation.

"We'd like you to come in for another test. There are some shadows on your right breast. We need to examine them further."

My heart dropped. Breast cancer? Tom's mother had died of breast cancer. I wasn't sure how he would take this news. I wasn't sure how I was taking this news. "All right."

"I have an opening on Monday, at 2?"

A Monday appointment? As in the day after tomorrow? She was serious. "Let me look at my calendar. Hold on."

Fortunately, I had my work calendar synced to my phone. I quickly pulled up Monday. I had several meetings, but I could put them off for this. "I can do that," I told Dr. Kessler.

"Great. See you then."

I walked back to the living room, where Sarah was looking at the curtains. "These convey?" she asked without turning, having heard me come into the room.

"What? Oh, yes, the curtains can stay. And the blinds elsewhere."

"Excellent!"

Sarah turned and looked at me. I must have had a weird look on my face. I'm sure I had a weird look on my face. "What just happened?" she asked.

"That was my doctor. My mammogram wasn't clear."

Sarah rushed over to the dining room where I had stopped walking, and she hugged me. And I started to cry. More from the shock of it than anything else, I think. I didn't really believe I had breast cancer. And if I did, I knew the chances were good we'd caught it early – last year's mammogram had been clear – and so my chances were very good. But the word 'cancer' is still a very scary word, even when you're pretty sure you'll be okay.

"Anything I can do?" Sarah asked.

I pulled back, wiping my eyes. "Sorry about that," I said.

"Nothing to be sorry about. It's scary. I've been there."

That was news to me. "You have?"

"Yup. I had a lumpectomy about five years ago."

I had known Sarah then. But she never mentioned it. I guess that's because I was not really her friend, just a return customer. "I'm sorry to hear that."

"It wasn't fun. But I got through it. If you have cancer, you will too." Sarah's voice was very positive. I took comfort in that.

"I'm telling myself that."

"You will. I'm sure of it. Tom will help."

Tom! I needed to tell Tom. "Speaking of whom, I should call him."

"Definitely."

"Thank you."

With a wave, Sarah let herself out the front door as I went into the kitchen to call Tom. The reception on my cell phone was best on that side of the house. I wanted to be sure he could hear me.

His phone rang, but he didn't answer. Tom often didn't answer his phone, though. Especially if he was concentrating on something.

So, I sent him a text. "Need to talk. It's important. Please call ASAP."

I stood in my kitchen for an agonizing 10 minutes, waiting for Tom's call and playing back the doctor's call in my mind again and again. Trying to glean any little bit of good or bad news from her tone. Unfortunately, she had been very doctor-like. And, unlike Sarah, she hadn't offered any positive platitudes.

"What's up?" Tom said, when he called.

"I got some bad news."

"Oh noes!" Tom said. 'noes' was one of Tom's catchphrases. There were many. I had learned to love them all.

Despite what I was feeling, I smiled at his words. "The doctor called."

"What doctor?"

"My PCP. Remember, I had a mammogram this past week?"

"Yeah. But the doctor doesn't usually call with test results. Or is that stuff different for women?"

"No, they don't usually call. But apparently, the mammogram wasn't clear."

"Oh, honey! Are you okay?"

I started to cry.

"I'll be right there," Tom responded.

I still couldn't talk.

"Hold on," he replied. "I'm coming."

I nodded, though he couldn't see me.

Another 10 minutes passed as I waited for Tom's car to appear in my driveway. It always seemed to take much longer to drive the 1-1/2 miles between our houses than it should. This time was no different.

He raced up my front stairs, I saw as I watched from my living room window. I had already unlocked the front door. I met him at the top of the foyer stairs. I was still crying.

He took me in his arms and just held me. There's an old 3 Doors Down song called *Your Arms Feel Like Home*. That's how I felt about Tom's arms. They were my home. Never more so than now.

We just stood there for a while. Tom didn't say anything. He wasn't a platitudes kind of guy, which I appreciated. He wouldn't say everything was going to be okay, just to say it. Because he knew, firsthand, it might not be. I appreciated that too.

Finally, the tears stopped long enough for me to talk. "Sorry about that," I said.

"Sorry for what?" Tom asked, genuinely confused.

I didn't cry nearly as often these days as I had in my 20s and 30s, and after our first big fight, I'd learned not to cry with Tom unless I was genuinely hurt – emotionally or physically. Some of that change was maturity. But a lot of it was Tom. The safety and security I felt with him calmed my emotions in a way no one else ever had.

"Sorry for crying all over you," I said, laughing a little and pointing at Tom's shoulder, which was soaked through.

"Pish posh," he said in reply, another catchphrase. "You cry all you want."

I smiled more easily. Tom was so good for me. "Thanks."

"So, what did the doctor actually say?"

"She said there was a shadow. So, I need more tests."

"Okay. That's good. That's nothing dire."

"She scheduled an appointment for Monday."

"Woah. That's a little more serious."

"Yeah. I thought so too. And she called on Saturday."

"Yeah. Valid point. I hadn't thought about that."

"Yeah."

"You scared?"

"A little. Though breast cancer is usually survivable." I wanted to be respectful of Tom's history. He didn't often talk about his mom, but I knew, mostly from his sister, that she'd been sick for a long time. She'd been through chemo and radiation and the mastectomies. And they had thought she'd beaten the cancer. Until it came back. So, I didn't want to minimize Tom's experience. But I needed the hope of the odds being in my favor.

Tom knew that. He knew what I was thinking. It was one of his best qualities that he often knew what I was thinking. "My mom's experience was 15 years ago," he said, knowing I was holding back because of his history. "Things have changed a lot."

I smiled warily. "I'd like to think so."

"You should. And if you have cancer, it's got to be really early, right? I mean, I remember last year's tests were fine."

Another of Tom's qualities. He remembered things like that. Often better than I did. "Yes, they were."

"So, at most you've had cancer for less than a year. I'm sure you'll be fine. And we don't even know yet."

"Right." I was trying to be brave. But that word was looming.

"Do you want me to go with you on Monday?"

Oh, that was so sweet! "No, I think this appointment is just more tests. If something shows up, then maybe."

"Okay. You can change your mind about that until Monday morning."

I smiled at Tom. He really was my sanctuary.

CR ഉ)CR ഉ)CR ഉ)

Monday came. I had rearranged my schedule so I could go to the appointment. I had only told my boss something personal had come up. I didn't share the details. There would be time to share them if I was going to need surgery, chemo, or radiation. There was no need to create drama now just for the sake of creating drama.

I did tell Jane, though. When the annual employee satisfaction survey asked "do you have a best friend at work?", Jane was who I thought of as I answered yes. She and Peter had become our go-to couple, since they knew us and knew our history. We also enjoyed a lot of the same things, so that helped cement our friendship.

"Are you scared? Nervous?" she asked via IM Monday morning from her desk just down the hall. She was our lead graphic designer. Over the years, she and I had spent many hours reviewing her team's creations for our marketing firm, to ensure they were sending the right messages and fit with our clients' aesthetics. She was very good at her job.

"A little. I vacillate between being confident it's nothing to being terrified it's cancer," I responded. Just typing the words was making me tear up. I didn't want anyone to notice. They would either ask questions I didn't want to answer or just sit and wonder what was going on. Many would assume something had gone wrong with Tom and our move, since my fellow marketeers did know that much about my life.

"I'm sure you'll be fine" was her reply. Unlike Tom, Jane was all about platitudes. She had several motivational posters on her office wall. Though she often said they were just great examples of marketing, I also knew she was inspired by the words and images.

Personally, I fell somewhere between Jane and Tom. I had been known to spout platitudes: "I'm sure it will be fine" "You're better off without him" etc. But I did try to keep them to a minimum and make my advice contextual and meaningful.

"I'll let you know!"

She replied with a happy face emoji.

Tom texted later in the morning. "Good luck!"

"Thanks!"

I left for the appointment about 1:30, assuming I would be back at work by 3 or 3:30. I brought my laptop with me, so I could go home and work from there, though. My doctor was closer to home than to the office so that just made good sense.

The doctor was on time, which was one of the reasons she was my PCP. I really appreciated that her schedule was almost always maintained. My previous PCP had kept me waiting as long as an hour, though that was actually the last time I had gone to her. Not only did they keep me waiting for over an hour, they were completely unapologetic about it. For a busy professional like myself, and most of the DC population, an hour was a long time. The cavalier attitude was unacceptable, which is what I had said in the letter sent to tell her she would no longer be my doctor.

Dr. Kessler's nurse called me back to the exam room. They did the usual height, weight, blood pressure vitals. Not surprisingly, my blood pressure was higher than normal. The nurse didn't say anything about it. It wasn't that high, just higher than my usual, which was pretty low.

"The doctor should be with you shortly," the nurse said as she left me. I knew this wasn't just another platitude. It was, in fact, the case.

Dr. Kessler walked in about five minutes later. I had just checked my work emails on my mobile phone and replied to a few of the more urgent ones. The others could wait until after the appointment.

She was a medium-sized woman with light brown hair and a ready smile. She was probably at least five years younger than me, perhaps more. I liked her immensely for her no-nonsense attitude. She answered my questions, and she never made me feel like she was in a hurry to get to another appointment.

"Hello, Tiffany," Dr. Kessler started. "Thank you for making the time today."

"It seemed pretty urgent when you called," I responded.

"We don't like seeing abnormal mammograms."

"I'm not wild about it either," I joked.

She smiled. "I'm ordering some blood work and a few other tests. We'll have you return to the radiologist for another mammogram and an ultrasound, as well. I've set up a 3:30 appointment for you."

"Oh." It looked like getting back to work today was not going to happen.

"As I mentioned on the phone, the shadow was on the right breast." She put up the film on the screen in the examination room. She pointed to a small dot at the top of my right breast. "It may be nothing. It may just be a shadow on the film itself or a small benign cyst."

"We know I have fibrous breasts."

"Yes, you do. And that makes mammograms that much more challenging. You also had the 360 view done, which was great. I can't share that here, as it requires imaging software. But the shadow did seem to be on those images as well."

"Well, that's concerning."

"Yes. So, we will do the bloodwork, a return mammogram, the ultrasound, and see what, if anything, those show."

"Okay." My heart had sunk in my chest. I needed to text Tom, my rock.

"I'll call you as soon as we know. Probably tomorrow afternoon."

"Okay. Thanks for telling me the timeline."

She smiled. Then she left, and the nurse returned to take my blood for processing.

After that was done, I headed to the imaging center, which was five miles in a different direction than either home or office. I texted Tom as I walked to my car. "Bloodwork done. Off for mammogram and ultrasound."

"Today?"

"Yes, Dr. Kessler set it up."

"I see. Do you need me to come?"

Part of me was screaming 'Yes!' But I said, "No, I'm okay. But thank you for offering!"

"Of course!"

I spent the next week getting tests. The mammogram showed the same spot. The ultrasound as well. That meant I had at least a cyst. I went back to see Dr. Kessler again, and she withdrew some of the tissue for a biopsy. Tom and I waited anxiously for the results of the biopsy.

We were sitting on the couch in my family room, watching TV and trying to ignore that today was the day Dr. Kessler was supposed to call with the results of the biopsy. It was Friday in the late afternoon, which meant if she couldn't or didn't call today, it would be Monday before we heard. Or I'd get another Saturday call, maybe. The idea of spending a whole weekend with no information was devastating.

As usual, Cass was hanging out on Tom's lap. As it was summer, Tom was wearing shorts, and Cass was having trouble getting comfortable on his bare skin. She wanted to knead his legs, but he'd already dissuaded her from that idea once. I laughed because I was wearing sweatpants, which meant Cass would be more comfortable on my lap. She still wanted to sit with Tom. In many ways, she had become as much his cat as Brie was mine.

Sabrina was sitting on the side of me, nestled against my cloth-wrapped legs and as far away from Tom as she could get and still be next to me. This, too, was her usual perch. She'd warmed up to Tom enough that she hadn't hissed at him in several months. But she was still my cat, and she only tolerated Tom's presence in our lives. The fact that her sister, Cass, loved Tom seemed to have had no impact on Brie's opinion. At first Tom had been a little insulted. But after I explained that cats sometimes just had a single human they bonded with, Sabrina's predilection just became one of our inside jokes.

"I'm Brie. To do what I want. Any old time," Tom sang, to the tune of the Soup Dragons' *I'm Free*. Tom had dubbed it Brie's song because of her attitude toward him.

I laughed and smiled, and leaned into Tom's side a bit in affection.

Just then, my mobile phone rang, and both cats scattered. We'd had some concern about whether the signal would get through downstairs, which was partially below ground. We'd talked about not watching TV, but sitting upstairs instead. But I'd gotten calls before while we were downstairs, and I was trying to keep from being nervous by keeping to my usual routine. I was pretty sure the call would come through. And now it had.

The caller ID said "Dr. Kessler". I tensed as I answered.

"This is Tiffany." I always answered the phone that way, even when I know who's calling, except with my mother. With her, my answer is always, "Hello, Mom." Otherwise, she's insulted since she knows I know it's her. Apropos of nothing, I thought, as these random thoughts went through my head in the seconds it took to answer the phone.

"Hello, Tiffany. It's Dr. Kessler."

"Hello, Dr. Kessler. What's the word?" I had the phone on speaker, so Tom could hear what the doctor said. He had as much invested in the results as I did.

"I wish I had better news. The biopsy is concerning. It looks like the cyst is atypical cells. I recommend a lumpectomy to remove the cyst and allow a more precise biopsy. We'll know more after we get the tissue examined."

Tears started to stream down my face. "Thank you," I mumbled through my closed throat.

"Of course. I wish it was better news, Tiffany. The good news, though, is the cyst is very small. You may not even need reconstructive surgery. I recommend Dr. Peterson for the lumpectomy. We have a relationship with her practice, and she comes very highly recommended."

I nodded, but couldn't get words out.

Tom intervened, "This is Tom."

"Hi Tom," Dr. Kessler responded. "It's nice to meet you, though not under the circumstances."

"Tiffany is having some trouble talking. Is it okay if I ask some questions?"

"Sure."

"Can't you do the lumpectomy instead of another doctor? Tiffany trusts you."

I nodded at Tom's question. I did trust Dr. Kessler.

"I'm not a surgeon. Dr. Peterson is a skilled surgeon. She specializes in breast cancer. Tiffany will be in good hands."

I shrugged. It wasn't my first choice, but I understood.

"Thank you. Will Tiffany need to make an appointment with Dr. Peterson, or will your office do that?"

"I'll have my team contact Dr. Peterson's office. They should be able to get Tiffany in early in the week."

I nodded.

"Tiffany says that's okay. Thank you again."

"No problem. We'll be in touch, and I'll follow your progress the whole way, Tiffany. That's what a primary care physician does. Try not to worry too much this weekend. I know that will be hard. But try."

I nodded again, the tears still streaming down my face.

"We'll try," Tom replied. "Have a good weekend."

"My office will call on Monday, Tiffany."

"Thanks," I managed to croak out. "For everything."

"Of course."

Tom hung up the phone and put it back on the coffee table. He opened his arms again, and I dived into them, sobbing.

"I know this is scary," Tom said.

I nodded against his chest.

"Do you want me to come with you to see Dr. Peterson?"

I nodded again. "Yes, please," I choked out.

"Okay. Let me know when the appointment gets scheduled, and I'll make the arrangements with my work."'

"Thank you!"

The shock of the situation was starting to subside a bit, and my organizational self was starting to rise up.

"I need to call some people."

"Your parents. And Jack." Jack was my stepdad, Mom's husband after she and my father divorced in 1987. I liked Jack. He was good to my mom, even if did seem like they'd married awfully quickly after my parents' divorce had come through. They'd been married for 20 years now, though, so I guess it stuck.

"And Jane. And Peter, too, of course."

"Are you going to tell your brothers?"

"I'll send them an email. My mom would kill me if I just emailed her though."

He smiled. "Yes, she would."

I smiled in response.

"Are you okay?" Tom asked, very seriously.

I had stopped crying by now, but the tears were still very close to the surface. "I guess so. I'm trying really hard to take this one step at a time. The idea that I have cancer is terrifying, though."

"Yeah. I get that. I would feel the same way, I think."

"You would?"

"Yeah. It's a big word, isn't it? Cancer. Scary connotations. But this is small cyst. And a lumpectomy. We can research what that means."

"Thank goodness for Google," I said, with a laugh. Another of our inside jokes. We almost always ended up Googling something during our evening TV watching, either because something came up in what we were watching or because of our conversation. Smartphones and Google made it entirely too easy to get information these days, though one did have to check the source. I knew that would be particularly critical for me as I tried to figure out what was next.

"Tom," I said, "I wanted to talk to you about something else."

"Okay," he replied, his tone concerned.

"It's a good thing. At least I think it's a good thing."

"Okay..."

"I was thinking about you. About us. About moving in together."

"That's on hold now, I think."

"Yes, I think it probably is."

"You have enough to deal with, without the pressure of trying to sell your house."

"True. I'll have to put Sarah on the list of people I call this weekend. She should know. We'll have to rescind the offer on the new house, if we can."

In the midst of everything else this week had brought, there had been negotiations on the offer I had put in. The owners wanted more money; I had balked but coughed up a little more in exchange for some other improvements like fresh paint in a few of the rooms. We hadn't heard back on that counteroffer. Sarah had explained that, until both parties had agreed to the counter, we could withdraw it. It would be imperative to get her to get the owners' agent to understand that the circumstances had changed. I just hoped it would work.

"She'll understand."

"She will." I was trying to figure out how to get the conversation back on track, so I took a breath.

"But that wasn't what you wanted to say, was it?"

I did love this man!

But I knew I was going to push him in the next few minutes, because I wanted us to get married while Tom wasn't sure he ever wanted to get married. Live together, yes. For the rest of our lives. But the institution of marriage wasn't his thing, he had said more than once. Even though his sisters were both happily married. If anyone should be cynical about marriage, it should have been me. But it wasn't. I wasn't. I was the incurable romantic. And I'd found my man.

With the diagnosis facing me, I wanted the permanence of marriage. I wanted to hold on to Tom and never let go, and know that, if he decided to let go, it was going to be pretty hard for him to do so. Of course, I wanted him to want to get married, too. But I knew he wasn't a fan of the rite. I just hoped he was enough of my fan to say yes.

"Will you marry me?"

Tom's face betrayed his shock, though he didn't say anything. I didn't really expect him too, because he wasn't that guy. A loud resounding "Yes!" would have been great. But I knew my Tom.

"You really want to get married?"

"Yes, I really do. I know you're not a fan of marriage."

"I don't really see the point."

"It will make your being part of my journey with the doctors and cancer easier." I was appealing to Tom's practical side, which I shared.

"That's true. How soon were you thinking about getting married, though? You've got a lot on your plate already."

Valid point, I thought. "I don't want a big wedding."

"You don't?"

"No, I don't."

"But you love *Say Yes to the Dress*?"

I laughed. "I love the show, yes. But don't we usually end up talking about all the unnecessary drama that these brides have to deal with?"

Tom smiled. "True."

"I was thinking immediate family only."

"Even that is quite a few people."

I thought that comment meant Tom was onboard with the idea. My heart sang. "True," I said, mimicking one of Tom's favorite responses.

"What about a dress?"

"A wedding dress? Nah. Doesn't seem the thing to do at my age."

"But you really like some of the dresses on *Say Yes to the Dress*."

"I do. But I'd like to keep things more low key. Immediate family only. Justice of the peace. Find a hall somewhere; not a church. New outfit for me. New outfit for you. No fuss, no muss."

"Your mother is going to want more than that, you know."

"I know. But you know what? I'm 41, and I have cancer. I think I'll win."

Tom smiled, but didn't laugh. The C word was back in our brains.

"So, what do you say?"

"About what?"

"Will you marry me?"

Tom laughed. "I thought we'd already agreed about that."

"We had?"

"Sure. What have we been talking about for the past five minutes?"

I looked at Tom like he was crazy. I was talking about hypotheticals. I asked again, "Will you marry me?" My voice was pretty emphatic.

"Yes!" he shouted at me, knowing that was what I wanted and needed to hear.

I laughed. "Good!"

ᏳᏩᏳᏩᏳᏩᏳ

Not everything was in a good place, but with Tom's love, I knew I could cope. His caring nature and calm presence were the panacea for the irrationality of my cancer diagnosis. They were my foundation, my peace, my everything.

"If you want to build a ship, don't drum up people to collect wood and don't assign them tasks and work, but rather teach them to long for the endless immensity of the sea." -- Antoine de Saint-Exupery

TOM'S MOTHER (1996-2003)

Meghan told me the story of their mother, her fight with cancer, and her death. It was hard to listen to, but important for me to hear to understand Tom.

"Mom was originally diagnosed in 1996," she explained. "You have to remember that technology was very different then. And so was cancer treatment. In those days – well, I suppose it's still true to some extent – they almost killed you in order to kill the cancer."

"Yeah. I had a high school friend who had leukemia and died from the chemotherapy, not the leukemia."

"Exactly. Chemotherapy and radiation were much harder then. They can target the cancer now in ways they couldn't then. Detection has also gotten so much better."

"Like them knowing I had only a lump."

"Right. So they didn't need to take your whole breast. In Mom's day, they wouldn't even have thought of that. Breast cancer meant losing your breast. Sometimes both if they thought the risk was high."

"Scary."

"It was. We were old enough to know what was happening. Tom and I were in high school when Mom was first diagnosed. Lauren had just started college. She almost left to move back home, but Mom and Dad convinced her not to. We hoped for the best. And promised Lauren we would keep her informed. In those days, that meant a lot of phone calls."

"Right. Not much email and no texting."

"Right. Communication was harder. But Tom and I took that task on. It was easier for us to talk to Lauren anyway. And Dad had enough to do just taking care of Mom."

"Did he get any help?"

"Never. Wouldn't hear of it."

"That explains a lot about Tom."

"How so?"

"He anticipates my needs. He's always looking for ways to make my life better or easier. He must have learned that from your dad."

"Interesting. Yes, that makes sense. To him, love is taking care of the people you love."

"That much I've figured out."

She went on to tell me the whole history.

ᘓ ᘔᘓ ᘔᘓ ᘔ

"Mom got sick in 1996. Tom was 17, Lauren was 20, and I was 13. It was the summer before Tom's senior year of high school. Lauren was going into her sophomore year in college in California. I had just gotten to high school, so Tom and I were going to be in the same school again. That was good as we struggled with Mom's diagnosis and treatment for the next year.

"Mom had been run down for a while. She figured it was just a cold she couldn't shake, though she didn't really have a runny nose or a cough. Just the tiredness. You have to remember that, in 1990s, we knew a lot of about breast cancer, but not as much as we do now. Mom wasn't much on going to the doctor; neither is Dad for that matter. They tend to be stoic about getting sick, powering through, all that. So, because she just felt run down, Mom didn't go to the doctor for a while.

"Finally, when she just wasn't getting better, she went. The doctor asked a bunch of questions, and he was suspicious after Mom told him about this small lump in her armpit. She was also having some pain in her left breast, which she had attributed to normal hormonal changes. But since the pain had stayed throughout her monthly cycle, which was unusual, she mentioned it. The doctor put two and two together, and he ordered her to get a mammogram. Mom hadn't had one in a couple of years, apparently, though of course they were recommended, even in 1996, as part of women's health treatment. Like I said, Mom wasn't much into doctors.

"The mammogram showed a mass on her left breast that spread from the nipple to the lymph nodes under the arm. It was bad, but they thought with a mastectomy, radiation, and chemo, they'd be able to get all the cancer. She didn't have the option of a lumpectomy, like you did, since the cancer was pretty pervasive. I don't think lumpectomies were really a thing then, anyway. But I don't honestly remember. I just remember they suggested a mastectomy, along with chemotherapy and radiation.

"Mom was scared; we all were. But Dad was her bulwark. He was optimistic and really stepped up to take care of her through that first mastectomy. It wasn't until the second one that he fell apart. But I'll get to that.

"They took the whole breast and a fair amount of tissue under her arm, to get the lump there. When they did the biopsy of the tissue, it showed malignancy. They were pretty sure she was going to need chemo and radiation, but the malignancy confirmed it.

"Poor Mom, who was already feeling run down, did not deal with the chemo well at all. She got very sick and couldn't eat much because she was so nauseous. She wasn't a large woman to start with, but after months of chemo, she was a skeleton. She lost her hair from the radiation, too. She looked really bad. I remember that scared me the most. The way she looked so thin and frail. Mom was always athletic, so she was fit. Now, after the chemo and radiation, she had no muscle mass anymore. She could barely walk from being so weak. It was so scary!

"Tom and I spent most of our lunches together in the high school cafeteria, just to spend time together. We didn't talk about Mom's cancer very much. But I was comforted to have him there. We'd talk about all kinds of things at lunch. And he helped me acclimate to high school. Some of the other students thought it was weird that my older brother ate with me; he was a senior, after all. He should have been hanging out with the seniors. Or a girl. But Tom's priorities were never on being popular. He was more focused on being a good student, and he cares very much about family. To him, it made total sense for us to hang out together. Personally, I was fine with it. What was going on at home was kind of scary. I got strength from my time with my big brother.

"Aside from Mom's physical changes, she became a different person in psychological ways. Her fragility extended beyond her body to her emotions. She'd always been the center of the family. Dad, as you know, isn't the most emotional guy. But, boy, did he love our mom! She pushed his boundaries and made him do things he would never do now. They took trips together, adventures to other parts of the world and this country. When we were small, we stayed with our grandparents while Mom and Dad went off on these trips. When we got older, they took us along sometimes. You've heard some of this already. The infamous story of Tom getting lost, for example."

I nodded, but didn't say anything. I didn't want to interfere with Meghan's sharing.

"After Mom got sick, she never wanted to leave the house. She withdrew from everyone, including us kids. She and Dad still had a close bond. But she didn't take care of us anymore. Dad tried, but he wasn't really the type. So, Tom ended up being the one who helped me as I went through the typical teenage struggles. Lauren helped where she could, but she was in California at school at UCLA. She was distancing herself from us, even then. She loves us – don't get me wrong. But Lauren just doesn't have that strong sense of family – at least not with our family – that Tom and I do. She and Charlie seem to have the kind of bond that our parents had, which is great. And I've seen Lauren as a mother – she's a great mom. But when our mom got sick, well, I don't know whether Lauren couldn't handle it or whether she was trying to stay focused on school. But she didn't come home much, even for vacations. She spent her summer in Los Angeles, interning with a company there, rather than coming home to help with

Mom. I get it. Mostly. But at the time, it just meant that more of everything fell to Tom. Or at least everything to do with me and our growing up. Dad was wrapped up in taking care of Mom. Mom was incapable of taking care of anyone but herself for the better part of a year. So, Tom took up the slack. He made sure I got my homework done. He taught me how to make my lunches. He got money from Dad for clothes and other things that we needed, but Tom was the one who took me shopping when I needed stuff."

"That explains why you two are so close," I said, while Meghan took a breath.

"Tom became father and mother to me in that time. It's not like I was that young. I was a teenager, after all. But 13 is still young in a lot of ways. I had no idea about the world yet. I didn't know what I wanted to be when I grew up. I had to deal with puberty and boys, and all of that. Tom did his best. But being a teenager himself, it wasn't easy."

"I wouldn't think so."

"After about a year of surgery and treatment, Mom was 'cured', or so we thought. She had breast reconstruction. She started to get her strength back. I was looking forward to having my mom again.

"But it didn't happen. Whatever had made her withdraw didn't reverse itself. Dad came back, though. He took some of the parenting burden back from Tom. He recognized that he needed to, because it was time for Tom to go off to college that fall. I was going to miss Tom terribly. He'd been my best friend and my rock for the past year. But, even at 14, I knew it was important that Tom get the chance to be on his own, too. If Dad hadn't come back to being a dad, I don't think Tom would have gone away to college. He probably would have stayed local, gone to George Mason or something. But Dad did get his act together, mostly. And so that August, we went to Chicago with Tom to get him settled into the dorm before school started again for me. Dad, Tom, and me. Mom stayed home. She said she was still too weak. I'm not sure she was. I think she just didn't want to go anywhere. I think she was scared. I suppose that's not that surprising. But it was hard on Tom.

"I spent a lot of time with Dad my sophomore year of high school. I missed my lunches with my big brother. But I made friends in my grade, and I got through the year pretty well. Mom came to a few of my high school events. I sang in the choir, for example. Alto. She came to most of our concerts. I played soccer, too. But she didn't come to our matches. Sitting outside for several hours wasn't something she'd liked to do before the cancer. But after the cancer, she never let the sun touch her skin if she could help it. I guess she was paranoid about skin cancer? I'm not sure. Maybe someone had told her that she was more vulnerable after the chemo and radiation. I'm not sure. She never said.

"Dad came to everything he could. They were both still working; or rather, Mom went back to work once she was healthy again. I think work was good for both of them. It put some normalcy back in their lives. Anyway, Dad came to my high school events when he could, including soccer games. He cheered me on loudly. It was embarrassing, but sweet. I knew that, even at the time.

"Tom came home for every break from school. He spent time with me when he was home, making sure I was doing okay. He and Dad tried to do some things together. But they weren't really sports guys; you know that about them. They weren't the type – aren't now – to go to a bar either. Tom, of course, doesn't drink, and he hates crowds. Dad's not much better. Tom tried to get Dad interested in some of the TV shows he had found while he was at college. But Dad was never much of a TV person. They did find some books they both enjoyed, and they would talk about those. But they didn't spend a lot of time one on one.

"Lauren graduated from college, and she moved to Boulder to be with Charlie. As you know, that's where he was from, where his family still lived. They are inseparable, those two. Just like Mom and Dad. When Mom met Dad, they were working for the same company. She fell in love with him instantly, she always told me. 'He was so handsome, so strong. I needed that.' That's what she said. I'm not sure why she needed someone who was strong. But Dad's still handsome, don't you think?"

"I do. Tom, too, though not perhaps as classically as your dad."

"Tom got enough of Mom that he's not quite as handsome, as you say. Dad could have been a male model. Anyway, from the moment they met, Mom and Dad were, from all reports, a couple. Lauren and Charlie were the same. George and me, too. I guess that's one thing we all have in common."

"Except Tom."

"Except Tom. Tom had a few relationships. But he didn't have the 'big love'. Not till you."

"That's nice of you to say."

"It's true. He loves you in a way that's different from the others. I see it. So does Dad. We've talked about it."

"Really?"

"Oh yeah. Priya had Tom wrapped around her little finger. It wasn't a healthy relationship, as you know. We all tried to get him to walk away. But I think he thought Priya was his Mom – his chance for big love. Tom is also fiercely loyal."

"Yes, I've seen that."

"Anyway, Lauren and Charlie moved to Boulder. They found jobs and settled in. They came back here some, but they made their lives out there. His family has become her family."

"She loves you guys."

"She does. And the Davises come here for Christmas every other year. Lauren keeps in touch. But her life is in Colorado."

"Yeah. Okay. I see that."

"Anyway, Lauren graduated and moved to Boulder. Tom continued at the University of Chicago. I continued high school. Mom seemed okay. She went back to work. She and Dad didn't take any more trips, but she started to participate in a few more things outside our home. She wasn't back to herself, the person she'd been before cancer. But she was better.

"They say if you can pass five years cancer free, you can be considered cancer free. Well, Mom made it to that milestone. By then, in 2001, she was feeling well enough that she even went to see Tom graduate from the university. Lauren and Charlie made the trip from Colorado, too. We gathered as a family to see Tom get his bachelor's degree. He had been accepted to MIT's Sloan Program for graduate school. His plan, though, was to take a couple of years off. He wanted some real-world experience before going to grad school. He stayed in Chicago and got a job programming for a small company that was a subcontractor to SAIC. He loved it. MIT would wait, he said.

"In 2000, I graduated high school, and I went to college at George Mason. I didn't have a clue what I wanted to do!" She laughed. "So, I just applied to Mason. Fortunately, they accepted me. Otherwise, I'm not sure what I would have done after high school. I stayed at home. I just wasn't ready to grow up, I guess.

"It was early 2002 when Mom started to feel fatigued again. She had some pain in her right breast. The cancer was back. This time in her other breast. And this time, it had metastasized to her chest wall, as well as the lymph nodes under her arm. We all knew that meant it was really bad. We'd learned enough the first round to know this was Stage 3. Then they found cancer in her lungs. And that meant it was Stage 4.

"She didn't want to fight anymore. She just wanted to die. That was really hard to face. I get it now. But at the time, I wanted her to fight. I wanted her to be there – for my dad, for me, for all of us.

"But she was done. The doctor did convince her to at least get a mastectomy and some radiation, to give her a little more time with us. She had hated the chemo so much, though, that she refused to even consider it. That wasn't protocol. Protocol was chemo and then radiation. But Mom was stubborn. She said no. The surgery almost killed her. Her lungs were pretty compromised, so the anesthesia was tough. She did it for my dad. She did the radiation for him, too, she told me.

"Dad completely fell apart when Mom was diagnosed the second time. He knew he was going to lose his life partner. Remember, this was the woman he'd met and fallen in love with instantly. They lived for each other. Now, he was going to have to go on without her. I still don't think he's recovered."

"Has he ever dated since her death?"

"No. Some women have expressed interest. He's a handsome, nice guy. He's had opportunities to make connections again. He just doesn't want to. He's locked his heart in a box. He loves us, but that's different. He believes he's had his 'big love' and that you only get one."

"I wish he'd find happiness again," I said, though I wondered if I was overstepping my bounds.

"Me too. I worry about him. A lot. He lives in that house – our house – all by himself. There have to be a million memories in the family house. I've tried to get him to move. But he's as stubborn as the rest of us."

I laughed. "Yeah. Trying to get your brother to move was not easy. Even after he said he wanted us to live together. He dragged his feet on getting stuff done in the house that he needed to do, according to Sarah, to get the best price."

"We would have helped," Meghan insisted.

"I know. But you know Tom. He doesn't like to do that kind of thing. He'd rather pay someone else. I get it. But then he didn't make any plans for the longest time. I didn't want to be a nagging fiancée, so I didn't bother him about it."

"You should have."

"I think Tom needs to get to his own decisions in his own time."

"That's true. But he also needs to be pushed sometimes. Just like my dad."

"Okay. I'll keep that in mind." I smiled. Meghan's relationship with her brother was close, no question. But it also wasn't the same as our relationship.

"Anyway, Dad couldn't deal with Mom's cancer. He practically lived at the hospital when she was there. And he was there for her when she came home for hospice. But he wouldn't deal with the doctors or organize the hospice. All of that fell to me. And Tom."

"Tom moved back to Virginia at this point?"

"Right. He left Chicago and moved back home. He lived in his childhood room, just down the hall from me. It was like high school again. Including not having much parental support. I think Tom moved back more for me than for Mom."

"Interesting perspective."

"Mom was happy to have him there. But she and Dad, as they had often been, were an entity unto themselves. They were focused on each other.

"Anyway, Tom moved back here about four months after Mom had her surgery. Fortunately, the company he worked for in Chicago was okay with him being a remote worker. They had a one-person office in Virginia where he could go to get on the classified network, and of course, he worked a lot from home, too."

"As he has ever since, right?"

"Right. That feeds his inner introvert."

"Yeah. But as you said, he needs to be pushed sometimes. I think he gets more introverted if he doesn't try to be around other people. I know it happens for me. Other people get louder and more obnoxious when you don't spend time with them very often."

Meghan laughed. "Totally! We're all introverts. I'm the least introverted. But even I get tired of people sometimes."

"Funny for someone whose job is human resources." Meghan was the HR director for a small manufacturing company.

"Yeah. Isn't it? I care about other people. But they do drive me crazy."

I smiled. "Totally!"

We cracked ourselves up. It was cathartic to have a good laugh in the middle of what was a not-so-nice story. I was glad to hear all the details about Tom's family and his mom's battle with cancer. But it was a sad story.

After we settled back down, Meghan continued her narration. "Anyway, Tom moved back home, and he and I did everything for Mom. I mean, Dad was there. But he was her emotional support. Physically, we were the ones who got her to the bathroom, who tried to make her eat, who read to her when she didn't have the energy to do it for herself."

"And you were the one who dealt with all the insurance and hospice and all that, right?"

"Yeah. It's how I fell in HR, ironically. I learned that I was good at dealing with other people's messes." She smiled, but it was a little more ironic. "And insurance. And all that. Lots of HR is around messes and insurance, often at the same time."

I smiled. "I can believe that."

She sobered. "Mom died six months after she was diagnosed with cancer the second time. She had her surgery. She had four weeks of radiation. Then she went into hospice at the house where Dad still lives."

"That can't be healthy."

"Exactly the point I've made to him a bunch of times. He doesn't want to hear it. I do think he is able to focus more on the happy times. It's the house he and Mom bought after Tom was born. So there are lots of good memories there. Including, of course, bringing me home from the hospital."

"Ha! You never lived anywhere else?"

"Not till I moved out after Mom died. I spent 22 years in that house."

"You would miss it, too."

"Probably. But it's still the right thing for Dad to move."

"I'll add my voice to the mix on that, because I agree with you."

"Of course, getting that house ready for sale will be an even bigger job than Tom's house."

"You guys don't move much, do you?"

"Apparently not!"

"We moved a lot. My parents both moved a lot. I've lived in many different places."

"Very different than our family."

"Yeah. I need to remember that when Tom and I start house-hunting again."

"He's only ever bought the one house."

"Where I've bought three now."

"Right. When George and I bought, we ended up in Tom's neighborhood, Ridge Drive, which was nice. We'd have dinner with Tom once in a while, and sometimes we'd hang out at one house or the other to watch television or a movie with takeout."

"Funny. So, were you around during the Priya years?"

"Yes. George and I had a front seat for all the drama. At first, I was all for the relationship. Tom needed to be shaken out of his shell. But then it became toxic. But by then, Tom had become loyal to her. It took a long time for George and me, and Dad, to get him to see how bad she was for him."

"It's hard for people to see things when they are in the middle of them."

"Oh yeah. I see that all the time in my job. It's hard to listen to other people, too. Your heart says one thing, while your brain says another."

"Hard."

"Yup. And when you've just been through the trauma of losing your mom. And your dad locks himself away in his grief. We had a rough few years, all of us."

"Did you have to do all the funeral arrangements, too?"

"Oh yeah. Dad hardly spoke for months after Mom died. Tom helped, too. But yeah, I was the one who did all the arrangements – funeral, estate, cleaning out her stuff – all of it."

"I'm sorry. That can't have been easy on top of losing your mom. And your dad essentially."

Meghan shrugged. "It kept me busy. It was what it was."

"Where was Lauren in all of this? You've talked about you, Tom, and your Dad. Did she come home at all?"

"She called a lot. She participated as she could from halfway across the country. But, no, she didn't come back to Virginia like Tom did."

"Do you resent her for that?" The family dynamic was the same today. Lauren was just not actively involved in the McDonnells lives. It helped, of course, that Meghan, Tom, and the elder Tom all lived within 30 miles of each other. They saw each other in person about once a month. Lauren called or texted with their dad pretty frequently, I knew. But she didn't get involved in his life; she wasn't invested like Tom and Meghan were.

Meghan shrugged again. "Lauren is who she is. She's a good person. She just didn't want to deal with all of the drama. She had her own life. I get it. I got it. Though I guess I would have liked a little more support from my big sister. Tom is great and all. But he's still a guy. You know?"

"I get it. I have two brothers, remember? No other girls in my family. I would have liked to have a sister to talk to."

"Me too." And that comment told me everything about Meghan's relationship with Lauren. They were family. But they weren't close.

"Thank you for sharing all this with me. It can't have been easy."

Meghan smiled. "It's been a long time. I'm at peace with it now. But it is part of who I am, as it is for Tom."

"Which is why it was important for me to hear all about it."

"Yes. Tom was shaped by this experience, as much as I was. And by having to be a grown-up before he really was."

"I had to grow up, too, when my parents split up. But that was different. They are both still around. Still, both Tom and I experienced emotional trauma. I think it's one of the things that binds us."

"No doubt. And I love that you appreciate his way of showing love. Priya never could understand it. She wanted him to change for her, rather than accepting him for who he is."

"I think it helps that we met in our 40s."

"Probably. I know I'm a different person now than I used to be."

"Exactly. I was much more selfish in my 30s. I don't think Tom would have liked me much then."

"I can't believe you were ever that selfish."

"Oh, I was. Selfish and angry. I carried a lot of that from my childhood. I didn't really get past it until my late 20s and early 30s. When I finally learned to like myself."

"Well, I think you're fabulous," Meghan said with a straight face.

I laughed. "Thanks! I think you're fabulous, too."

"I can't wait till we are officially related."

"Oh, we are now, don't you think?" I replied.

"Yes, I do."

I got up from where I was sitting on the couch and came over to Meghan to give her a huge hug. It hadn't been an easy day for her, I knew. For all her bravado, and her strength, I knew that. Because it wouldn't have been for me. And in many ways, Meghan was the sister I'd never had and always wanted.

❧ ❧ ❧ ❧ ❧ ❧

We sat in silence for a little while after Meghan finished and I had sat back in my original position, each of us alone with our thoughts. I was sure Meghan was remembering those hard days, and I hoped that she wasn't sorry she'd revisited them with me. For my part, I filed the details of his mother's death away for future reference in my dealings with Tom. He was so strong in many ways. But his childhood, and particularly this period in his history, obviously shaped how he dealt with the world. According to Meghan, Tom had always been a conscientious person, concerned about others as much as himself. But having spent his high school and post-college years helping his little sister cope with growing up and dealing with their mother's death – well, it explained a lot about how he took care of me, like feeding the cats so I could sleep. And also helped me understand why it was so important to him to take care of me.

WEDDING PLANS (2018)

Sarah understood when I told her the house sales had to be put on hold for a while. Fortunately, she was able to talk to the new house's owners' agent, and equally fortunately, the new house's owners were understanding and didn't hold me to the offer. One hurdle had been removed.

Stopping the sale of my house was ridiculously easy. We hadn't had any offers yet, so we just took down the listing. And Sarah had the sign removed from the front yard and the hole patched. Unless you looked for it, you couldn't even tell the post had ever been there. We left my things in storage, though. We were being optimistic that this little cancer episode was going to be over soon.

We could have still rented or sold Tom's house. But then he would have had to move in with me, and we would have had to put his stuff in storage. He didn't really want to take on that extra expense, which I understood. He spent most nights at my place, though. Fortunately, I had all that extra room in my closets.

CR ᏇᏆᏯ ᏇᏆᏯ ᏇᏆ

My mother and I spoke at least once a week, sometimes more when there was something going on. So, I called her to tell her about the cyst. In typical Mom fashion, however, she'd turned the conversation to be all about her.

"Oh, Tiffany!" she'd wailed. "I don't know where the cancer might have come from. I've never had it, as you know. Nor my sisters. I wonder whether your father's genes contributed. His mother had cancer, you know."

"Mom," I had warned, "let's leave Dad out of this."

"Of course. You never want to blame him for anything."

I just rolled my eyes. Tom almost started to laugh. My mother was so predictable.

"What's next? Surgery?" she had asked, actually showing some concern for my health.

"Yes. A lumpectomy. I don't know when yet."

"Okay. Keep me posted. Love you."

"Love you, too." In Mom world, this phrase meant she was done with the conversation. I loved my mother, I really did. But she wasn't capable of expressing her emotions well. I figured she was going to go process my diagnosis, and I'd hear from her later, probably with some information from a not-so-trustworthy website about what I should have done to prevent breast cancer in the first place.

"Well, that went well," Tom had said, with just enough sarcasm. He hadn't been on the call, but had heard it all from his spot next to me. Mom's voice carried.

"About what I expected."

Tom nodded. He'd been around Mom often enough to understand her dynamics.

As expected, she'd sent me a long email with a long list of websites, some about preventing cancer by taking various drugs and supplements, and a few with information about cysts and lumpectomies that were actually useful. My mother wasn't a complete idiot. She just wasn't exactly the stereotypical, hug-you-till-it-hurts kind of mother.

A couple of days later, we called again with the good news of our engagement.

"Congratulations!" she said. "It's about time."

I let that one go. Mom was Mom.

"Thanks, Mom. We're very happy."

Tom nodded from his seat next to me.

"Love you," she replied.

So, I hung up, after saying I love you back, of course.

Once we'd told Mom about the wedding, she'd dived in with both feet into planning it, even though I had told her expressly that I only wanted a small wedding. She'd bought a hundred bride magazines. All right, maybe not a hundred, but a bunch. She started scanning and emailing me pictures of wedding dresses she liked, even though I told her I wasn't interested in a wedding dress.

"You'll change your mind as the date gets closer," she predicted.

"I'm 41, Mom. I'm past that stage in my life. And we are trying to keep things on the less expensive side."

"Jack and I will pay for the dress."

"Mom, I love you. But no means no."

"You'll see. When you start planning in earnest, you'll change your mind about a dress."

I let it go. My mother was who she was. I also suspected that diving into planning for a wedding that she had no business planning was easier than dealing with her daughter possibly having breast cancer.

Beyond the initial discussion, when Tom and I had called to share both pieces of news – one great and one not to so great – Mom never brought cancer up again. Instead, it was all wedding, all the time. I ignored her constant stream of advice. I wasn't ready to start planning anyway.

CR ℰꙨCR ℰꙨCR ℰꙨ

Tom and I did decide to buy a ring, though. Again, I wanted to go non-traditional and not get a diamond. I've never really liked diamonds. I would have loved a sapphire, but right now, they were more expensive than diamonds. So, I didn't think a sapphire was worth the expense, though I was willing to check into it more.

I had a habit of buying jewelry from artists at art shows. With Tom's encouragement, I reached out to a few of them and described my ideas for a different kind of engagement ring. One of those artists, Jean Metier, specialized in industrial style silver jewelry. She had an idea of a sculptural setting. She sent us a few sketches, and I loved all of them. My ring would be one of a kind and a work of art. I was thrilled. Tom, while not cheap by any standard, wasn't sorry that the price tag for the ring was also going to be considerably less than a traditional diamond ring would have been, even with a custom design. We were facing some fairly serious medical expenses. Our money was better spent on that.

Jean offered us prices for many stones, including sapphire. As expected, the price for a sapphire was considerably higher than any other stone, including diamond. Given the differences in costs and our upcoming medical expenses, I told Tom I was leaning toward amethyst, one of my other favorite stones.

"Will you be happy with an amethyst?" Tom asked.

"Yes!" I said.

But he could hear my hesitation.

"You really want the sapphire, don't you?"

"It's so expensive!"

"That's not what I asked you."

"I know. But I'm practical. The amethyst will be lovely in that setting. I'm so pleased Jean came up with it. I think we should go with that."

"Okay," Tom said.

Six weeks later, a package came special delivery. It was my ring. Tom had it delivered to his house, so he could bring it to me like a good fiancé, or so he said. But he had also included me on the shipping notifications, so I knew exactly when the ring arrived. He came to my house after work, shipping box in hand, and we opened it together. The ring was perfect!

Tom put the ring on my finger, mock-kneeling like the goofball he was. He didn't say the words. I'd already done that. But it was a lovely gesture, nonetheless.

Then, I looked at the ring, really looked at it. The stone was not the purple I had been expecting, but a clear, brilliant blue.

I looked at Tom with a question in my eyes.

"I called Jean back after you left. I changed the order. We can afford to indulge. After all, we're saving a ton on the wedding dress."

Tom knew my mother was still on me about getting a traditional wedding dress. Though I knew his reasoning was sophistry, I laughed. Tom laughed, too.

Then I cried at his kindness; I was a sentimentalist.

Tom got a little choked up, too.

"You're crying," I said, though he wasn't really. His eyes were just puffy with unshed tears.

"When you cry, I cry."

"Really? I don't think I've noticed that."

"When they are real tears."

"Don't spoil it," I warned.

"Sorry. Old cynicism dies hard."

"I know. I have my tender spots, too."

He smiled. "We'll work on them together."

"Deal!"

With the ring, the whole idea of marrying Tom became more real to me. I couldn't wait.

❧ ❧❧ ❧❧❧ ❧

Tom's family was more, well, McDonnell about the whole wedding thing. Meghan offered to help in any way I wanted. I appreciated her low-key approach after my mother's attempt to run the show. Lauren, being Lauren, was less committed. She said she'd be there with bells on and to let her know if she could help from 2,000 miles away.

Tom's father, thrilled for his son – and me too – offered to help pay for the festivities.

"Thanks, Dad. But we got this," Tom said.

"All right," the elder Tom replied. "But you need anything, you just let me know."

"We will," I added, for I was on the other line of Tom's old-fashioned landline.

After we hung up, I turned to Tom. Another idea had sparked in my brain. "We are sticking with a small wedding, right?"

"You sure you don't want a big wedding with all the pomp and circumstance? The kind your mother wants?"

"Tom, I love you, but you hate crowds."

"Yeah. So?"

"So, do you really want a couple hundred people at your wedding, a bunch of whom you haven't seen in years?"

"Not really. But I'm not the one who wants to get married."

I frowned. "You don't want to get married?" My voice betrayed my hurt.

"That's not what I meant. I want to marry you. I do."

"Really?"

"Really."

"Okay." Tears were on the edges of my eyes. Tom's reluctance to get married didn't have anything to do with me, I knew. He just didn't think it was important to be married. And that's honestly where the health scare did come in for me. I would much rather have Tom making those kinds of decisions for me than my mother. I had thought about having one of my brothers as my medical proxy. Phin would do it, I thought. Tom had been willing to do it as my significant other; we had talked about having each other listed on our advanced medical directives. But I knew being married would carry more weight. And besides I wanted Tom in my life for the rest of my life. By my side. As my husband.

"Tiffany, I'm sorry. I shouldn't have said that. It was reflex."

"I know. I'm okay. Really."

He cleared his throat. "So, small wedding?"

"Immediate family."

"Well, that's not very many people."

Which made me realize that Tom's family was smaller than mine. It consisted of exactly seven people: Tom Senior, Meghan, George, Lauren, Charlie, and their two kids, Sophie and Tyler. My family included not only my brothers, their spouses, and their kids, but also my mother, my stepfather, my stepsiblings, their children, and my father. The total was nearer to 20. I wasn't that close to my stepsiblings, so I immediately thought about excluding them to make the numbers more equal. But I knew my mother would be horribly insulted if I even suggested the idea. I could hear her in my head, 'Tiffany, Jack has been like a father to you. How could you!' I did love Jack. But Jack's kids and I had had little interaction over the years, as they lived in various parts of the country and only visited every once in a while. Still, I knew my mother would consider them "immediate family". Even if I hadn't talk to them in, literally, years.

"We could add your Young cousins to balance things out. They were as close as siblings to you, especially when your mom was still alive," I offered.

"Tiffany, that's a nice idea. But you already have your mother trying to take over the wedding planning. Do you really want Cathy involved too?"

We laughed. Cathy, the unforgettable cousin I'd met at Meghan and George's anniversary party, had adopted me as part of the family, saying "No one else in the McDonnell family ever shares anything!" Which was true, but also their choice. Most of what I shared involved my family, not Tom's. Still, Cathy had tagged me several times on social media, trying to find out more about what her Virginia cousins were up to. And then there was the infamous almost trip. It was all done in love, but it was a bit more than the privacy-loving McDonnells could deal with.

"Okay. You have a point."

"It's okay that your family is larger than mine."

"Not really. But let's put that aside for now. No church, right?"

"Right!"

Neither Tom nor I followed any religion. Our grandparents had been active members of different Protestant denominations. But our parents had not participated as adults. My siblings and I had been baptized when we were infants, but Tom's family hadn't even done that much. So, church as a location was out of the question.

"There are some lovely halls around DC, I'm sure. Historic properties. Jane and Peter got married in one."

"I know. I was there."

"Oh yeah. I forgot."

Tom and Peter had known each other since college, where Jane and I had only met five years ago when I started my current job. We'd become fast friends, though. And she'd told me all about her wedding, especially after Tom and I had started dating.

"I don't really want to get married in the city, though," Tom said.

"Really? Why not?"

"I'm not a fan of having to deal with the traffic."

"True. But for one afternoon?"

"I'm sure there are places in Virginia, right?"

"Lots of historic properties here, too. Okay. Virginia, it is. What about Maryland?"

I had spent part of my childhood in Maryland, so I wasn't opposed to crossing state lines. But Tom was a Virginian, born and raised. And I knew some Virginians would rather die than go to Maryland. Tom didn't seem to be one of them, as my mother and Jack lived in Rockville, and we visited them quite a bit. But getting married there was another story.

"What about the license? Can we get a Virginia license and get married in Maryland?"

"I have no idea, but that's a good question. I'm sure there's some reciprocity. I mean, once you're married, you're married in all 50 states. That was part of the problem with weddings like Phin and Joseph. The conservatives were all okay with it in places like Vermont and New Hampshire. But not in Utah or Wyoming."

"Tiffany, you're generalizing."

"I am. But you get the point. Legalizing same-sex marriages meant they had to be recognized in every state. So, if that's true for Phin, then surely it would be true for us."

"Of course. But we don't know what the paperwork might be."

"Valid point. I'll look into it. But Virginia locations are starting to look more promising."

"Probably better."

"So, we need someplace that seats about 30 people and is convenient to Fairfax."

"Sounds about right."

"And we need an officiant."

"Not a preacher."

"Of course not," I agreed. "I can figure that out, too."

"I can help, you know."

"Okay. Want to figure out the process for getting a marriage license?"

"Sure. Do we need to get blood tests?" The idea of more blood tests was not appealing. I had been stuck quite a few times in past weeks.

"I have no idea."

"I'll do that research."

"Great. I'll look into wedding locations and officiants. You're in charge of legal details."

"Got it."

CR ∞CR ∞CR ∞

It turns out you don't need a blood test to get married in Virginia. So, one less time I'd have to get stuck.

Which was good because the other news was not so much.

Because the ultrasound and second mammogram had shown the same result as the first mammogram, I was scheduled to meet with Dr. Peterson, the surgeon.

Tom, now my fiancé, came with me to the appointment. It was a magical word, fiancé. Not only did it mean he could be part of the discussions without issue, it also meant I felt a contentment that even the threat of cancer couldn't touch. Having Tom beside made everything better, including the idea of surgery.

I had assumed this appointment was just to talk through the particulars of the surgery and recovery. But not quite. They were going to do a physical exam, as well. When I thought about it, that made sense. Dr. Peterson hadn't been part of the original diagnosis, after all. But I'll admit I wasn't expecting it.

The nurse asked if I wanted Tom to be part of the physical exam. He, of course, would be part of the discussion that ensued about the logistics of the day of the surgery and my subsequent recovery. But I had the option of her doing the physical exam without him.

I thought about it. I didn't want Tom to feel uncomfortable. And I didn't want him to have the sense of my breast that I was developing – that it was somehow not me any longer. Although I hadn't been feeling very sexy lately, with all the worrying and stress of the cancer diagnosis, I didn't want Tom to be turned off in the future. On the other hand, I had invited him to participate fully in this scary thing that was happening.

"Tom," I said, "what do you think? Do you want to be part of the physical exam?"

"Whatever you want" was his unhelpful answer.

The nurse was waiting at the door, her face not showing the impatience I'm sure she was feeling.

"I think I'll leave you out of this part, if that's okay? Save a little of the mystery of the female breast."

Tom laughed as he nodded that he was okay with my decision. He and I had discussed before the male fascination with women's breasts and how we women sometimes didn't really understand it. We, of course, got pleasure from men touching our breasts. But Tom explained that men did too, much as they did from touching the rest of our bodies but somehow more.

So, I followed the nurse back to the exam room alone, where she took my vitals. Dr. Peterson arrived a few minutes later.

She checked the site of the cyst. She kneaded and poked at my right breast, just as Dr. Kessler had done, and the mammography technician, and the ultrasound technician. All of them had been women, which helped me feel a little less awkward. But it was still strange. It was almost as though my breast had become separate, no longer connected to the rest of me, as it was the subject of such intense scrutiny.

"No change in size or shape," Dr. Peterson explained, with a pleased look on her face.

"Thank goodness," I echoed.

"In fact, there has been little growth in the cyst since the original mammogram. So, if this is cancer, it isn't growing very quickly."

"I assume that's good news."

"Very."

I expected her to say more, but she just took off her exam gloves and said she would meet me and Tom in her office shortly. Then she left.

I put my bra and shirt back on, and then walked down the hall to Dr. Peterson's office. I startled a bit to see Tom already in the office, but it did make sense. I wondered if he'd been sitting in there during my exam, since it hadn't taken very long. He looked relaxed but interested. Perfect.

Dr. Peterson joined us in her office, sitting behind the desk and pulling out my chart. She explained she would perform a lumpectomy and remove the cyst. The cyst was small and near the top of the breast, so the surgery would be pretty straightforward. She would remove a little of the tissue around the cyst just to ensure we had clear margins. She reiterated for Tom's sake that the cyst had grown very little since it had originally been found.

Tom asked, "Does that mean it's not cancer?"

Dr. Peterson smiled a little. "We don't know yet. Once we have more tissue to test, we'll know more. But, yes, it's a good sign. At the worst, I would say you have Stage 1 cancer," she said, looking at me. "Do you know the stages of cancer?"

I nodded, having checked on all this in the past few weeks.

She continued, pulling over a pamphlet on cancer to show to me and Tom. "Stage 1, which is where I think you are, is where cancer is detected, but only in one area, in your case your right breast." She pointed to the next panel in the pamphlet. "Stage 2 and 3 mean the cancer has spread to nearby lymph nodes or tissue. We haven't seen any evidence of this in your case. Neither on the mammograms nor on the ultrasound."

I nodded again, only because I felt as though I should.

"Stage 4 is when the cancer has spread to another part of the body. It has metastasized. This, of course, would be the worse-case scenario, but we are not anywhere near there."

I thought of Tom and his mother's situation. Her Stage 4 cancer had spread from her breast to her lungs, Meghan had told me. I took Tom's hand and smiled at him. 'We're not there,' I thought. I hoped we never would be.

"Finally, we will test the cyst and the surrounding tissue. If the results are not benign, the next step would be an oncologist," Dr. Peterson concluded. "Though even if the results are benign, I would expect only some radiation therapy. That's the usual protocol."

"Not chemo?" Tom asked.

"The oncologist would make that determination. But I wouldn't think so. Radiation to kill whatever small, undetectable cancer cells might be left. Should the testing indicate that there was cancer at all. We still don't know for certain. We only know there is an invasive mass."

I didn't like the sound of that. 'Invasive mass.' I was liking my breast less and less.

"That's good about the chemo. That wiped my mom out."

"Oh, I didn't realize you had a family history with cancer," Dr. Peterson responded.

"My mother died of breast cancer in 2003," Tom explained.

"I'm sorry to hear that. Condolences on your loss."

"It was a long time ago," Tom said, his voice a little rough. I was reminded again that this was a subject about which he rarely spoke.

"What about recovery?" I asked, changing the subject back to the topic at hand.

"Time healing from surgery can range from a few days to a week or two. Every woman is a little different, but generally patients recover in a few days. We will give you post-op instructions, which will include how to clean the site, exercise instructions, and scheduling a post-op appointment."

"Only a few days' pain? I can deal with that," I said bravely.

Tom smiled. He knew I was reluctant to take pain meds, as was he. I liked that our philosophy about these things was similar. I wouldn't have to spend a lot of time or energy convincing the man in my life that I didn't want to take the pain medications any longer, that the pain was bearable, and I just don't like those kinds of drugs.

"Exercise instructions," Tom asked. "As in when she can start exercising again?"

"Well, yes. But also moving your arm on the same side as the incision to keep it from getting stiff. We will start you on those exercises the morning after surgery."

"Really? Interesting."

"Yes, and we recommend wearing a sports bra day and night for a few days, as well, for the support."

"At night? To sleep?" I asked.

"Yes. You'll find it more comfortable," Dr. Peterson argued.

"I haven't slept with a bra on since I was 12, and someone teased me about not knowing better," I explained.

Dr. Peterson smiled. I had a feeling I wasn't the only young woman who hadn't known that you generally took off a bra to sleep. "Keeping the breast stable during recovery will be helpful."

"Makes sense when I think about it," I admitted. "But how do you get the bra on in the first place? Sports bras are notoriously hard to get on and off. And they smush the breast when they go on."

"Do you have one that opens in the front or back, like a conventional bra?" Tom asked.

I didn't. But I thought I could get one.

"Yes," Dr. Peterson said, echoing Tom, "you should use a bra that has a back or front closure, but the support of a sports bra."

"Got it. I'll have to get one. Or two."

"Good," Dr. Peterson offered. "Any other questions?"

"I can't think of any. Tom?"

"Not at the moment," Tom responded.

"You are free to call with questions any time. I'll see you on the 24th."

"Thank you, Dr. Peterson. I appreciate your time today."

"Yes, thank you. It was good to hear Tiffany is likely to be fine," Tom echoed, his voice rough with emotion again.

"The prognosis is good," Dr. Peterson reiterated. "We'll know more after surgery."

ᏣᎵᏣᎵᏣᎵ

So, I prepared for surgery. I didn't like the idea. Not one bit. I wished we could go back to the time when I was normal. Boring, even. When Tom and I were just another couple planning to move in together.

I knew the prognosis was good. I knew there was little chance I would have more long-term consequences. But I was still scared. I bought several sports bras with back closures and scheduled a few days off from work. I mentally prepared, too. But in the deepest parts of my brain, fear sometimes took over.

Thank goodness for Tom. My rock. My solace. My warm arms to hold me when the fear came.

But there were times when even Tom wasn't enough. I wanted to be cancer-free, so I could live a long and fruitful life with my husband.

"You need to take risks. You never know the end results will be beautiful or strange. You need to be instantaneous, listening to every moment, without missing a scrap of the music" -- Brian Blade

TOM'S FEAR (TOM'S CHILDHOOD)

Part of the reason for a small wedding was Tom's fear of crowds. There are some who might scoff at that kind of fear. They treat their anxiety like they treat our being picky eaters – as just a personal preference. After all, we're just people, nothing to be frightened of.

But I had learned that Tom's anxiety about being in a crowd was not just part of his introversion. It was a very real fear, and therefore, we would not be having a large wedding under any circumstances. My mother be damned.

CR EOCR EOCR EO

The McDonnells traveled a fair amount when Tom and his sisters were youngsters. Mary and Tom Senior were adventurers, and they brought their children with them once the kids were old enough to participate. Tom and his sisters had been around the world, in one case literally as the family spent three weeks traveling from Virginia to Europe to Japan to California to Virginia again.

The adult Tom that I loved hated to travel. As a child, he hadn't had much choice about going on these trips. But as a picky eater, he found other countries' food problematic at best. And his introversion played a big role in his desire not to sight-see.

But it turned out, his deep-seated fear of crowds came from a particular incident when he was about 11.

The family was in Budapest, back when Hungary had just ended communist rule. The McDonnells had been staying in Vienna, Austria. The parents decided to take a day trip to see Hungary, now that the border was open again. Tom Senior had learned from their hotel's concierge that there was a festival taking place in Budapest, and he and Mary thought the children should experience it, being so close by. Tom mapped how to get to Budapest from Vienna, and the concierge provided advice on places to eat and sites to see before or after the festival.

Hungary was not a happy place. Inflation had been rampant, and the population had suffered. There were still Soviet troops in the capital, remnants of the previous regime.

Tom and Mary thought it would be educational for their family to experience the country, especially at this pivotal time.

What they hadn't counted on was the lack of English.

CR EOCR EOCR EO

The family of five crossed the border in their rental car. The parents showed everyone's passports as they left Austria and crossed into Hungary. One passport per person. All was well.

"We should let the children carry their own passports," Mary suggested. "They understand the importance of them, right, kids?"

The three children dutifully nodded, wanting to be trusted with this grownup responsibility.

"No, Mary. I think it would be dangerous. It would be terrible if one of the passports got misplaced."

"They are good children," Mary insisted.

"They are," Tom agreed. "But they are still children. Meghan's little pocketbook isn't even large enough for it, anyway."

Mary huffed, but stayed quiet.

The family drove through the city, taking in the dichotomy of architecture from the buildings that had survived the Soviet occupation to the more modern ones with their sharp edges and unforgiving facades.

"I'm hungry," Lauren whined.

"Me too!" young Tom chimed in.

"We'll stop in a bit. Do you want to experience authentic Hungarian cuisine?" Mary responded.

"Yes, please" Lauren said, as she was the most adventurous of the children.

"Sure," Meghan replied. She was too young to have much say anyway.

Tom knew he'd hate it, but he also knew his parents didn't really understand why. He didn't really either. He just knew he was unlikely to like the strange flavors. In Vienna, he'd been able to find food that was enough like the American foods he liked to get by. He had no such illusions about this strange place they were now. So, he remained quiet. There was no point in saying anything.

"I have a map from the concierge at the hotel with some suggestions," the elder Tom explained. "We have to find a place to park near the town center. It might take a while."

"That's okay, honey!" Mary said, enthusiastically. "We're taking it all in."

Meghan allowed as how she could barely see anything from the middle of the back seat. But she was seeing what she could see.

Tom feigned interest in his surroundings. He really didn't like this strange place where nothing was familiar.

Lauren, barely a teenager, echoed her mother's words, seeking approval. "It's wonderful!"

❧ ❧❧ ❧❧ ❧

The family parked the car not far from where Tom's map said the restaurant was situated. They had some challenges as most of the signs were not in the Latin alphabet they knew, but in Cyrillic, which they knew not at all, or Uralic with strange accents on the letters they thought they knew. The elder Tom spent a lot of time comparing the letters on his map and the signs in front of him before being confident they were in the correct location.

"It's this way," he said with more confidence than he felt.

"We'll follow you," Mary agreed.

The family headed west through the city center.

"Here's the restaurant the concierge suggested," Tom exclaimed with relief. He had been right.

"Dad, I need to use the restroom," young Tom announced.

"Fine," replied his distracted father as the hostess found them a table. "I'm sure it's toward the back."

Tom glanced at his family as they were headed to a table, to make note of where they would be. He wandered past the bar that was almost as tall as he was. He walked down a narrow hallway that did not smell at all inviting. His stomach started to heave, but he was able to get it under control. But his bladder was starting to be more urgent. And he couldn't figure out which door might lead to a toilet.

He opened a door and saw much more than he wanted to of a large woman peeing. He immediately shut the door and ran.

The woman came out of the bathroom, yelling in a language he didn't understand and trying to find the intruder.

Tom ran further into the bowels of the restaurant. He opened another door, desperately hoping it was the men's room. It wasn't. There was a wall of plates and silverware in front of him. A storage room, apparently. He closed the door behind him, hoping the angry woman didn't see where he'd gone.

Finally, the ruckus settled down. Not having found Tom, the woman had apparently settled down to her meal. Tom was mortified, of course. He hadn't intended to see what he saw. But why hadn't she locked the door, he wondered?

Carefully, he opened the door to the storage area. He didn't see anyone. So, he headed back to his family. Maybe his father would be able to ask which door was the men's room. Tom thought his bladder might burst, but he wasn't going to open any more doors!

He could just see his family when apparently the woman also saw him. She yelled and pointed.

Unthinking, Tom ran out the door of the restaurant and turned left. There were people everywhere. The festival was scheduled to start that afternoon, and the crowds were starting to gather. The organizers had put out barriers to demarcate where the festival was taking place. This made navigation for cars and people even more confusing.

Tom ran and ran, terrified of what might happen to him in this strange country. No one seemed to follow the decorum he was used to. He was bumped and jostled as he ran. Cars were honking, trying to get through the streets now blocked by barriers and people walking. Hordes were speaking languages Tom had never heard before in his life. It was frightening.

He made so many turns, he was now well and truly lost. He couldn't read any of the signs, even if he did remember where they had left the rental car. He had no idea how to find his family, even if he could figure out which direction was which. He had lost track of all the turns he'd taken. He recognized nothing.

He sat down on a bench in a small park, shaking with fear. What could he do now? Where should he go? Should he stay still and hope his family found him? Were the police chasing him now? Maybe he should keep moving?

'Dad always said, if we got lost, we should just stay where we are,' he remembered. 'So, I will stay here. And they will find me.'

It didn't seem like the park was a very important one, though there was a large statue of a man on horseback that loomed over it. Tom was sitting on one of four benches that circled the statue. The park reminded Tom of the ones he had seen in Washington, DC, when his family had visited memorials and museums there. That little bit of home made Tom feel just a little less like he was in an alien world. He clung to that familiarity as he fought to catch his breath and stop his feelings of sheer panic.

But Tom still needed a toilet. The idea of peeing on the street – which they'd seen others do in their travels – was both embarrassing and terrifying. He wasn't sure he could hold it much longer.

To his right, we saw a sign that looked like a male stick figure near a small building at the other end of the park. Men were coming and going from the entrance. 'Maybe?' he thought. Daringly, he crossed to the building, which was indeed a toilet. It stank horribly. But Tom hardly cared. He was just relieved.

He returned to his bench and his vigil. Surely, someone would find him soon?

People passed by, some of them staring at the child on the bench who obviously did not belong there. Tom was suddenly very aware of the differences in his clothes from the people around him. An older woman – not the one from the restaurant, thank goodness – tried to talk to Tom. Though her tone was gentle, he didn't understand anything she said. He replied in English. But she just shook her head that she didn't understand him either. Eventually, the language gap being too much, the woman moved on.

Tom saw some kids his own age, perhaps on their way to the festival? He watched them walk by and decided to try to talk to them. He waved, but they didn't see. The young men just laughed amongst themselves and kept walking.

As the noise picked up from a few blocks away, Tom's watch told him it had now been about an hour since he had sat on the bench. He longed to do something, to try to retrace his steps, to keep moving. But his father's words echoed in his head. 'If you get lost, stay where you are. We will find you.'

Tom despaired of this being true. But he didn't know what his alternatives were. He had no money. No identification of any kind.

A soldier walked by, his rifle slung over his shoulder. Tom froze, willing himself to be invisible. The soldier moved on.

Another half hour passed.

"Tom!" he heard his father yell. Tom didn't think he'd ever heard anything better. He cried in his relief.

"Dad!" Tom said, running to his father's arms, uncaring whether his father saw him cry.

"Tom! Oh, I'm so happy to see you!" the elder Tom said, tears streaming down his face.

"Am I in trouble?" Tom cried, scared of the answer but needing to know.

"No. We explained everything. The woman is very nice. She understood, through the restaurant owner's translation, that it was an honest mistake. It's all okay."

"Okay," Tom said, in a small voice. He was still horribly embarrassed, but so relieved.

"Let's go home," Dad offered, cheerily.

"Home?" Tom sniffed.

"Well, the hotel in Vienna."

"All right."

Tom held his father's hand tightly as they walked back to the restaurant, where his mother and sisters were waiting. They had to go past the festival, where there was loud music, off-key singing, and so many people. It was all chaos. Tom hated the whole thing. Every fear he had was now projected on the crowd, and he could hardly walk past, even with his father there.

"Oh, Tom!" his mother cried when she saw him. She opened her arms wide, and Tom let her hold him as tightly as she wanted. He needed her too.

The family got back in the car and crossed back to Austria without further incident.

"Dad?" Tom said, once they were back in what he saw as civilization.

"Yes, Tom?" the elder Tom asked.

"I'm starving."

The family laughed at this statement, because of course he was, having missed lunch.

"Can you wait another hour till we get back to Vienna?" Mom inquired. "We can get gelato!"

Tom thought about it. "I can wait. But I'd really like a hamburger first."

His parents and sisters laughed at him. But that was okay. He was safe again. They could laugh if they wanted to.

⚬ ⚬⚬⚬ ⚬⚬⚬ ⚬⚬

Back in Vienna, the McDonnells found a hamburger for the young adventurer. Tom felt much better with some food in his stomach, though he still had a touch of nausea. He didn't tell his parents that part, though. His family was chatting happily, teasing Tom about the incident. That was the McDonnell way. They tended to make light of trauma as a way to minimize it.

"Ready for some gelato?" Mary asked, once Tom had finished his cheeseburger.

Tom just nodded, though in truth he wasn't sure he wanted any. He just wanted the day to end and to wake up tomorrow back in Virginia. Knowing that wasn't going to happen, he figured maybe some gelato – though he wished it would be good, old-fashioned American ice cream – would be better than nothing.

The family walked to Stadtpark from their hotel. They had seen many gelato vendors plying their trade throughout the park.

In the late afternoon sunshine, the park was full of people. Tom watched everyone, but there were too many people to keep track of them all. There were families, somewhat like theirs and yet not quite the same, walking through the area, enjoying the scenery and the views of the Weintal Kanal from the various bridges that crossed it.

Tom tried to stay close to his father, though the elder Tom didn't seem to notice. Tom Sr. seemed more caught up in the romance of the location and kept stealing kisses from his bride as they walked. Mary would titter, but complied with Tom's requests for affection. Meghan and Lauren just rolled their eyes, used to their parents' behavior. Normally Tom would have joined his sisters in this reaction. But right now, he wasn't really in the mood.

"Tom," his mother said, pointing to a stall not far away, "how about that one?"

Tom shrugged. He didn't want to be here. He just wanted to go back to the hotel. He'd never been much for crowds, but now he was anxious at every sound. A woman screamed with laughter, as her partner pretended to pick her up and toss her into the water. Tom was horrified. Had people always been this mean to each other?

Lauren got a chocolate gelato, her favorite. Meghan opted for mocha. Tom stuck with his favorite, vanilla. Mary and the elder Tom shared a pistachio.

"Let's sit down to eat," Tom's father suggested, gesturing with his spoon toward a cluster of benches along the Kanal.

The children took one bench, while Tom and Mary cuddled and ate on another. Tom's sisters were commenting on the passersby, their clothes and their shoes. Some of their comments were not all that polite.

"Excuse me?" said a huge man with his outraged wife, glaring at the two girls. His English was heavily accented, but understandable, nonetheless.

Lauren blushed, while Meghan cowered. Tom shrank, though he hadn't been participating in his sisters' observations.

"Is something wrong?" the elder Tom said from the neighboring bench.

"Are these your children?" the strange man shouted. "You should teach them manners!"

Tom rose from the bench to stand in front of his children. Behind his father's body, young Tom again wished he was invisible.

"I'm sure they didn't mean anything. Just children being children," Mary said, joining her husband and trying to diffuse the tense situation.

"My children would never behave in such a way" came the indignant response from the huge man's wife. Her English also showed she was not American, but clearly both people spoke the language.

"Apologize for whatever you said," Tom ordered his children.

"I'm sorry," Lauren immediately responded.

"Sorry," Meghan complied.

Young Tom stayed silent. He hadn't said anything.

"Tom!" the elder Tom barked.

"But I didn't say anything!" Tom wailed.

"You don't even know what your children did," the foreign man said. "You Americans have no manners."

Mary huffed, while Tom – being a diplomat – remained calm in the face of the couple's anger.

"The girls know better. We apologize if you were insulted. Now, can we please put this incident behind us and have a nice rest of the evening?

The huge man nodded and led his wife away.

As soon as they were gone, Meghan stuck her tongue out at them.

Mary laughed. The elder Tom chided his youngest, "That's not nice, Meghan. Did you learn nothing from what just happened?"

Meghan just shrugged.

Tom Jr. stood up. "Can we please just go home now?" He meant to their Virginia home, but the hotel would be better than nothing.

"Yes, honey," Mary responded.

The two girls got up, and the five McDonnells headed back to their hotel. Tom took his book and sat in the corner of their suite for the rest of the evening. He wanted nothing to do with anyone.

 CR ꙮCR ꙮCR ꙮ

I wasn't much of a traveler either, fortunately. For many of the same reasons as Tom – strange food and places. Added to these elements was Tom's anxiety about crowds. Not to mention Tom's clearance meant there were places in the world it would be better if we didn't visit. Thus, our wedding would be limited in size. If we did take a honeymoon, I knew it would be a domestic location.

SURGERY (2018)

The day of surgery arrived more quickly than I could have imagined. Per instructions from Dr. Peterson, I had taken a leave of absence from work.

"You may feel fine in a week. You may not. Every body behaves differently. It's best not to have high expectations and be pleasantly surprised."

I told my boss a little about what was going on, but not all the details. He wasn't comfortable with personal stuff like that. And he only needed to know that I was having surgery and was expected to be out three weeks. HR had to be involved, because I was taking a formal leave of absence, with all the accompanying paperwork to get disability pay. I probably could have afforded to take off three weeks of work without disability. But not to pay the hospital and doctor bills on top of that. Even with insurance, this experience wasn't going to be cheap. We weren't really focused on that – we were focused on getting to a positive outcome – but the reality loomed. I was too practical not to consider it.

Outside of HR, of all my colleagues, I'd told only Jane what was really going on. And I had sworn Jane to secrecy about my diagnosis, not always her strong suit.

"It's no one's business, and I don't want anyone to know unless I have to go through more procedures, okay?" I had emphasized.

"Got it. Really. I understand."

"Thanks! I know you have my back."

I prepped my team on all my accounts and any activities that needed doing in the next few weeks. My staff were good at their jobs, and they would be fine for a few weeks without me. They knew I was having surgery, but not for what.

I wasn't sure what I was going to do with myself for three weeks though. I hadn't taken off that much time sequentially since I started working 20 years ago. Under the disability agreement, I wasn't allowed to even check my work email. The firm was very strict about that. It was a rule for disability, apparently. I would try to be good.

Jane said she would let me know via my personal email if anything went completely haywire. And my second-in-command, Jim, promised to send me an update every week, even though he wasn't supposed to. We had long since exchanged personal emails, if only for trips and other times when getting to work email was tough. Between Jim and Jane, I was sure I would be kept informed.

But I wouldn't be able to solve any problems directly, only offer advice. I wouldn't be able to talk to customers or even most of the staff. I would be cut off. The idea was alarming.

So, to keep myself from going completely insane, I bought several books to read. I loved books. Unlike Tom, I still read physical books. I enjoyed the act of turning a page. It felt like I had accomplished something at the end of every chapter. But I knew myself. I could read a book in a day if I put my mind to it and it was a good book. I didn't think even my love of books would sustain me for three weeks.

I also had a wedding to plan, such as it was. Tom and I were still adamant about keeping things simple, though. We had enough other things going on, what with surgeries and buying and selling houses. If we had gotten married a decade earlier, even, I might have been more inclined to give into my mother's constant machinations and have a bigger wedding. But the idea of wedding dress shopping and spending literally thousands of dollars for a wedding Tom wasn't sure he even wanted and when all I wanted was for Tom to be my husband? It just didn't make sense.

I knew we wouldn't be able to get away with eloping, though we talked about it. My mother would never forget and would be unlikely to let the subject drop, even if asked repeatedly. I thought Meghan might object as well, as close as she was to her brother.

But small was still the plan. And as such, wedding planning was not going to take every hour of three weeks. I was reasonably sure I could arrange most of it in a day, once I found a place to get married. And even that was so not important. As far as I was concerned, we could get married on the courthouse steps. Yeah. Wedding plans were not going to work as a distraction.

Tom had surprised me with a new iPad.

"I put all the streaming services on it," he said. "So, you can watch pretty much anything you'd like – TV, movies, podcasts, whatever."

I kissed Tom to thank him for his kindness.

He was always doing this – thinking of things he thought I needed – like reading glasses when I started struggling reading small print – or just fun things he'd thought I'd enjoy, like a new iPad!

For the few weeks after surgery, Tom would come over after he finished work and spend the evenings with me, as he usually did. He'd even stay the night if I asked him to. He'd also offered to work from my house, too. But he was limited in what he could do in an unclassified environment. And it would make me feel guilty if he couldn't work. I had my books. I had some movies to watch. Hopefully it would be enough.

So, I was worried I was going to be bored out of my mind, which I mentioned to Meghan and George, one evening when the four of us were having dinner, which we did about once a month.

"I can come over a couple of times," Meghan offered. She was my favorite sister-in-law-to-be. Lauren was nice, but Meghan was nice and also fun. Lauren was more formal; Meghan was anything but, which made her easier to be around. Especially when I knew I wasn't going to be feeling well.

Lauren also had the disadvantage of being halfway across the country. We hadn't gotten to know each other all that well, as a result. We mostly kept in touch via social media and the occasional text or email. So though I enjoyed her company, and I thought Charlie was a nice guy, I didn't have much of a relationship with them. Meghan and George lived about ten miles away, and we had spent quite a bit of time with them in the years Tom and I had been dating. Their proximity also made Meghan's coming by relatively easy.

"It's the days that I'm worried about," I confessed. "Evenings, Tom and I will still watch TV with the cats. But I tend to go through books quickly. And I can only watch so many soaps." I sighed. Tom shrugged. He didn't think I was going to be as bored as I thought I was.

"I'll bring over some movies. We'll make popcorn and veg. I have Tuesdays and Fridays off. We can figure out what works best after you have the surgery."

I had forgotten Meghan only worked half the week. She had found a great company to work for, after a couple of real duds. But they were small, and they only needed her part time. Fortunately, since George was a partner in a medium-sized law firm, money wasn't an issue and Meghan could afford not to work full time. "That would be phenomenal. Especially the second week."

"Yeah. The first week, you'll probably sleep a lot. Or be in pain and not want company."

"I really am not sure. That's what they tell me, though."

"I remember Mom would spend a couple of days recuperating after surgery. She wasn't as strong as you are, certainly not for the last one. But just going under knocks you on your butt a bit."

"I'm sorry. I wasn't being sensitive to your history with your mom. If you don't want to hang out with me, that's perfectly okay."

"I volunteered, remember," Meghan assured me. "Besides, I do know what you'll be going through. And I can help if you have questions." Meghan had been her mother's final caregiver. Tom, their father, had been there. But he struggled with his wife's pain, much like Tom had trouble with mine or anyone else's. It had fallen to Meghan, as the local sister, to deal with the messier side of their mother's illness and death.

I smiled, if not fully. "Thank you. It can't be easy. The memories."

"It's not. But you're not my mother. You're Tom's fiancée. And my friend."

I smiled more fully. "Thank you. You're my friend, too."

CR ℰƆCR ℰƆCR ℰƆ

So, I had my plan. Tom would drive me to the hospital for the surgery and stay until I was in recovery. Mom wanted to come to, but I convinced her not to. Tom was a calmer presence.

I was having outpatient surgery, so after a few hours in recovery, the plan was for Tom to take me home. Tom was worried about adverse reactions to the anesthesia. I did have a history of nausea from being under general anesthesia, which Tom had reminded me about when we were talking to Dr. Peterson about the surgery.

"Remember how sick you got after your shoulder?" he said, as Dr. Peterson was reviewing our hospital instructions with us.

I had had my right shoulder scoped a few years ago to remove the tissue that was keeping it from moving freely. It was called adhesive capsulitis. Though I remembered that description, I had conveniently forgotten that I had thrown up in front of Tom for the first time when they brought him back when I was in recovery. That had been mortifying! But then again, if we were going to be together for the rest of our lives, he was going to have to get used to my bodily functions. And I was going to have to get used to him being used to them. As someone who had spent the majority of my adulthood living alone, the idea was daunting.

"I had forgotten."

Dr. Peterson made a note during our pre-op surgery consult. "We'll give you some anti-nausea meds. I've made a note for the anesthesiologist. He'll talk to you about that once we're at the hospital. It might not completely eliminate the nausea, but it should help."

"Thanks, Dr. Peterson. And thank you, Tom, for remembering." He was good at that.

"You'll be sore for a while. I've prescribed some pain medications, which you should absolutely take if you have any pain. Preventing pain from developing is important, so take the medication at the first sign."

"I'm not good at that."

"She's really not. Doesn't like to take even aspirin."

Dr. Peterson had frowned at me. "This is important, Tiffany. You really are going to be uncomfortable, and you really don't need to feel pain. Take the drugs. I promise you won't get addicted."

I had smiled wanly. Addiction ran in my family. I used to say the only two things we inherited from my dad's side were addiction and depression. One, naturally, fed the other. It was part of why I was very leery of pain medications. Dr. Peterson had that right. What I had learned, though, from my shoulder surgery is that I also have a very high threshold for physical pain; I had only ended up taking one day's worth of meds. It wasn't that I avoided the meds and was in pain. I just didn't experience pain. Whether I was just lucky or had a high threshold, who knew?

I still couldn't quite believe it was possible I had cancer. We wouldn't know for certain until the pathology report came back, a couple of weeks after the procedure.

The reality was I did have cancer in the sense that I had cells in me that were growing where they weren't supposed to and in a way that wasn't healthy. That, by definition, was cancer. How invasive the cells were and whether they were benign or malignant was still to be determined.

Also still to be determined, whether the cancer had spread elsewhere. It didn't appear to have. It appeared the cancer was only in my right breast. But they would take some of the lymph nodes, called sentinel nodes, from next to the lump to test. The goal was what they called "clean margins", that the tissue around the lump would be cancer-free.

I was also worried that the surgery would leave me, well, uneven. They were taking some of my breast tissue, after all. Dr. Peterson assured me that I wouldn't be able to tell. But I wasn't convinced. And part of me was worried that Tom would see me as damaged, even though he was so not the kind of guy to even think that way. Still, it was natural to worry, I thought. So, I let myself worry, and I let myself off the hook for worrying.

ଓ ଛାଓ ଛାଓ ଛା

And so it was the day of surgery, faster than anyone wanted it to come.

We arrived promptly at the surgical center at the ungodly hour of 6 am. Surgeons, apparently, like to get their surgeries done early in the morning. Tom was, of course, wide awake. I was too but mostly because my adrenaline was high. I was not a morning person.

The surgical center wasn't far from my house, which was good because Tom had to drive me, and he hates to drive. I had actually driven by the building several times over the years, but had no idea what was in it. It was an innocuous two-story brick building, not that much different than many other buildings around it. There was a small sign that mentioned "medical offices". But no indication of the surgeries that went on inside.

I found that both comforting and annoying. A place that was going to change my life should be more grand, I thought. And yet, the fact that it was so ordinary, that surgeries were performed there every day, day in and day out, made my surgery seem more mundane. And that was somehow comforting.

I tried to explain this line of reasoning to Tom as we sat in the waiting room for them to call me back. He just shrugged, and I let it drop. I knew he was nervous, and while I had a tendency to babble when I was nervous, I had learned Tom preferred quiet. And in this moment, I was more inclined toward silence.

Finally, they took me back, and we started to get the show on the road, as it were. I had on comfortable clothes, what Tom and I called our 'indoor clothes' despite the fact that I was outdoors. Everything had elastic to make getting in and out easy. I knew I would eventually be put into a hospital gown. But for now, the nurse had explained, I could stay in my own clothes.

The nurses confirmed I hadn't had anything to eat since midnight. I was not even remotely hungry. Too many other distractions, which was good.

Dr. Peterson came by the pre-op room to let me know she was here.

"As we discussed, you'll be meeting Dr. Jones, the anesthesiologist, shortly. He's very good. I've already told him about your problem with nausea from the general. He's got a plan for that."

"Thank you, Dr. Peterson."

"I'll send the lab results to Dr. Kessler as soon as I get them. My office will schedule a follow-up in two weeks, and we'll go over the results then. In the meantime, try to relax."

Easy for her to say!

She left, and a nurse came in to do more of the prep. He had me change into a hospital gown and then attached me to a monitor to measure my heart rate and blood pressure. He had taken the same readings when I first arrived, but this time he did not disconnect me. I guessed I was going to stay hooked up now until after surgery. Interestingly, that made me anxious enough that both readings went up slightly. The nurse just raised his eyes at that, but didn't say anything. Again, I suspected that was a normal reaction.

"Your pulse is lower now than mine is normally," Tom complained. "Even facing surgery."

I shrugged. My pulse had always been slow, but years of martial arts had slowed it down even more. It hovered around 50 normally, though currently it was around 60. I concentrated to see whether I could bring it down. It didn't work. I let it go. I was sure my pulse would return to normal after the anxiety of today was over.

"Your BP is low," one of the many nurses said. "Is that normal?"

"Yes," I replied.

"Okay. I'll tell Dr. Jones."

I looked confused.

"The anesthesiologist," Tom clarified.

'Oh yeah.' Aloud, I replied, "Got it. Why?"

"When people go under general anesthesia, they can have their blood pressure drop. It can be a bad thing. So, we measure now what is normal for each patient. And Dr. J will try to keep you in that range."

"Okay. Thank you for the information."

"It's my job." He left.

Tom and I then waited for what seemed like a very long time. The clock on the wall was an old analog one that literally ticked off the minutes. It was kind of annoying.

Finally, Dr. Jones came by. He was a very handsome man, I thought. Nearly as handsome as Phin's Joseph. Married, I noted as well. It reminded me that I didn't have my engagement ring on – no jewelry was allowed for the surgery. I missed it.

"I understand you have some problems with anesthesia," he said.

I nodded. "My fiancé reminded me that I vomited after my last surgery. I thought it was from the Percocet. But it could have been the anesthesia."

"Reactions to anesthesia are pretty common. We'll fix you up, I promise." Dr. Jones smiled. He really was ridiculously handsome. I kept my face as neutral as I could.

"Okay. Sounds good."

"You have low blood pressure too. You're a challenge." He smiled again to let me know he was kidding.

I laughed. Tom chucked. "Sorry to be difficult."

"Keeps me on my toes. And makes me earn my pay. Seriously, though, you'll be fine. You got this!"

He gave me a high-five, which was not normal doctor behavior as I had experienced it. But it did help relieve some of my stress, so I appreciated the gesture. Then he left, and Tom and I were left to wait again.

"I'm as straight as they come, but that guy was really handsome. Don't you think?"

"I didn't notice," I said with a straight face, before laughing out loud. "I wasn't going to say anything. I didn't want to make you jealous."

"Can't be jealous of that. Can't compete with that."

"He's married though."

"You noticed that? Should I be worried?" Tom said, teasing me.

"I'm not even close to his league," I replied, being sassy back.

Tom got serious. "Yes, you are. Tiffany, you are beautiful!"

I was shocked. Tom had never said that before. And here I was with no makeup, in a hospital gown, and it was very early in the morning. "Really?"

"Really! You know that."

"Not really. I mean, I think I'm reasonably okay. Sometimes even pretty. But beautiful? I don't aspire to such heights." I was serious, even if my tone was joking.

"Tiffany, you are one of the most beautiful women I've ever known. No, don't blush. It's true."

"I can't help blushing. And thank you. It's very nice of you to say."

"I'm not good with compliments."

"No, but I know how you feel most of the time anyway. And you show your love in actions, not words."

"That is definitely true."

I had read an article a few years earlier about love styles. It opened my eyes to the realization that, even if Tom didn't say the words all the time, he showed he loved me by taking care of me, by feeding my cats on the weekend mornings so I didn't have to get up, by taking out my garbage, and in a million other ways. I took care of him too, don't get me wrong. But I also instigated the words more often. Tom always responded in the affirmative, that he loved me too. But he was more comfortable showing his feelings than expressing them.

After a seeming eternity, they came to start my anesthesia. Tom had to leave me then, and I was sad to see him go. I tried to hold onto his quiet strength.

I don't remember being wheeled into the operating room. I certainly don't remember the surgery. The next thing I remembered was waking up in the recovery room. And there was Tom again, sitting with his ebook, waiting patiently for me to wake up.

"Hey there!" he said, when he noticed my eyes were open.

"Hi?"

The nurse heard us talking. "Hello again," he said to me. I remembered him as one of the ones who had taken care of me earlier. "The surgery went well. Dr. Jones said you reacted to the anesthesia just fine. Dr. Peterson will be by in a little bit to check in on you."

"Thank you."

The nurse left.

"Dr. Peterson came to see me after you were done," Tom told me. "She said she thinks they got good margins."

I smiled. Good margins were what this was all about.

"As we discussed the other day, she said the lab report wouldn't be back for a couple of weeks."

"I hate waiting."

"How do you feel?"

"Okay. Groggy."

"I'm sure that's normal."

"Yeah."

"Any nausea?"

"Not yet. But as I recall, it didn't hit last time until I was more with it."

"I was hoping you didn't remember that."

"Not remember throwing up spectacularly in front of a guy who was barely my boyfriend? I'm afraid it's emblazoned in my mind."

Tom smiled, as I had intended. "It was quite spectacular."

I smiled wanly. "Gee. Thanks."

Tom shrugged. "I still like you."

"No, you don't," I replied.

Tom looked concerned. "Yes, I do!"

"No, you don't. You love me!" I teased.

Tom laughed. "Yes, I do. But I also like you."

"Well, I guess that's a good thing."

"Definitely."

About ten minutes later, I threw up. Fortunately, there was a basin by the bed, and Tom, hearing me heave, got it under my mouth in time. That was, perhaps, more embarrassing than throwing up in the first place. I tried to take the basin from Tom, but he batted my hands away. The nurse, having heard me throw up, came in with a fresh basin and took the dirty one away.

"I'll see if we can get you some anti-nausea meds," he said, as he left use once again in the curtained enclosure.

"I guess there's nothing we can do about my nausea, huh?" I said to Tom, as he stood with the basin ready to help once again if I needed it. There was a chair for Tom to sit in, but he preferred to stand. I had learned that about him too.

"If Dr. Good-Looking couldn't fix it, I guess not."

I laughed at Tom, before throwing up again.

Dr. Peterson came in. "Still nauseous?"

"A little," I said.

"Well, we can give you something to hopefully help with that. I don't want you to pull your stitches."

"That would be great."

"Tom has your other prescriptions for pain medications. I made him promise to get them filled."

I shrugged, and Tom grinned. "I will get them filled today, after I drop her off and makes sure she's comfortable."

"Thank you, Tom. Try to get her to take them."

"I can't promise that," Tom replied.

They were both teasing me. "I promise I will take the meds if I start to feel pain."

"That's all I ask." Dr. Peterson pulled up a rolling stool and sat down next to my bed. "I told Tom the margins were clean. I didn't see any evidence of cancer in the lymph nodes, but we took some of the ones around the lump just in case. My office will call when we have the results to share. Rest. Call if you have any questions or something comes up. Dr. Kessler will be in touch soon, too. I spoke to her after the surgery, so she's up to speed on everything."

"Thank you again, Dr. Peterson. I appreciate it."

"Talk to you in a couple of weeks. Rest!"

"Got it."

And she stood up, rolled the stool away, and left. The nurse came in with some other anti-nausea medications. They got me up and walking, too, which helped. About an hour after surgery, I was discharged, and Tom took me home.

ርጽ ዎጽ ዎጽ ዎ

My recovery plan worked pretty well. Tom took care of me in the evenings. The first week, as everyone except me had expected, I wasn't good for much. I slept a lot, though finding a comfortable position wasn't easy, and I felt very funny wearing a bra to sleep. I read a bit, watched a little TV, used my new iPad, and called a few friends who were home during the day because they worked in retail or restaurants. That was all I had any energy for. By evening, I was usually dozing. Tom would come by after work, but we just lolled in front of the TV. Xan and Phin called, and I tried to talk to them. But I just couldn't muster much energy. Tom filled them in on the details and promised he'd let them know when I was up to company.

The second week, Meghan came over on Tuesday, and we watched a movie. She had brought three with the intention of it being a marathon kind of day. But after the first one, I just didn't have the energy for two more. So, she and I talked a bit instead.

"Tom tells me you're not planning on much in the way of a wedding."

"Low key. That's what I promised him. No church, of course."

"Of course."

"Justice of the peace or some other non-religious type. Not sure of where yet. And then as few people as we can manage."

"What about a reception?"

"I guess we have to?"

"Usually. Maybe you can find a place to do both?"

"Yeah. That was my thinking too. I'm not sure location means a lot to me, and I know Tom doesn't care."

"No," Meghan said with a laugh. "Will you invite the Young cousins?"

I was connected to all of them on social media now. And of course had met most of them at Meghan's anniversary party. "I was thinking about that. Immediate family only would be my preference." I'd already decided not include my stepsiblings either.

"Yeah. Not many of us. Dad. Lauren and Charlie, and their girls. Me and George."

"Right. Mom, Jack, Dad, my brothers and their spouses, and my two nieces and one nephew."

"The Youngs won't be happy not to be invited."

"I know. But if I invite your cousins, then I have to think about mine. Unlike your dad, my parents are both from large families, and I have a zillion cousins."

"And you're trying to keep things small."

"We are not spring chickens anymore. And Tom is the introvert's introvert."

She laughed. "That's true."

"If I could get away with it, I'd just have it be us. No one else."

"Why not do it that way then?"

"My mom would kill me. And your dad would be sad, too, I think."

"Probably. We never thought Tom would get married, to be honest."

It was my turn to laugh. "I'm sure my family feels the same way about me. Even Phineas got married before me, and he never thought he'd ever get married!"

Meghan smiled. She knew I loved my gay brother very much and that I was thrilled that Joseph and Phin had been legally allowed to wed finally in 2015. "So, small wedding. Immediately family only? Low key reception."

"That's my plan. No fancy wedding dress. No tuxes. Just Tom and me before the officiant with a handful of family in attendance."

"No bridesmaids or groomsmen?"

"I don't think so. Everyone who would be there would be in our bridal party!"

"Good point." She laughed.

"I did a little internet sleuthing the other day when that was about all I could handle, energy-wise. There's a cool old farmhouse not far from here that does weddings. As long as we don't do it in June or July, they seemed to have openings. They even have a barn for a reception. Only seats about 20, but that should be plenty for us."

She thought for a second, doing the math as I had. "True."

"Lots of kids, so no alcohol for them, or Tom."

She laughed. "Right. But you'll need plenty for the rest of us."

I laughed. "I guess so. At least for my mother and Jack."

"Let me know if you need any help."

"I will. Thanks."

"What are sisters-to-be for!" she said, with a laugh.

"Never had one, but I guess that's right."

We laughed.

CR SOCR SOCR SO

So, there I was. In recovery and, if the margins were really good and the biopsy benign, things in my life could start moving forward again. Until we knew, though, all my carefully laid plans were for naught. There were so many variables – houses to sell, wedding plans to make, cancer to beat – before I would feel settled and secure.

Except Tom. Tom was the one thing I was sure of. He was my rock. My lodestone. My center.

"The drums tell me everything. Everything else registers a millisecond later."
-- Adam Clayton

GRADUATE SCHOOL (2001-2004)

I'd graduated from college with the intent of becoming a college professor. To do that, I knew I'd need to get a PhD. I applied to both MA graduate programs and PhD graduate programs.

But first, I thought it would be good to get some "real life" work experience. I had worked summers while I was in college. Mom had insisted that all of us work in the summers, rather than being bums. Also, it had given me money to pay for the extras at college. My father, having done well for himself professionally, had paid my tuition and room and board at Boston University. But, if I wanted something more than just the bare minimum, I had had to pay for it myself. I had appreciated my father paying for school enough that I wasn't going to complain about having to work and earn the extra money. Fair was fair after all.

So, I found my first real job out of undergraduate school working as a receptionist for a firm that raised money for nonprofits. The company wasn't a nonprofit, which was good in terms of my salary. But I liked that we were helping the nonprofits. It seemed like a good balance of doing good and getting paid for it.

But I hated being a receptionist. At heart, I'm an introvert, though I can play extrovert as needed. In truth, I'm on the cusp of the two. But when it comes down to it, being "on" wears me out. And being a receptionist, where I was required to be "on" all day, was exhausting. I would come home every day, and I would just lie on the living room floor. My roommates were concerned, because they liked me and they worried it was too much.

It was, but I had plans. The company was growing, which is always a good thing. They were hiring two new company representatives, managers who worked with specific nonprofits on their messaging in their fundraising materials, etc. I knew those two new managers were going to need an assistant. And I was positioning myself for that job.

Luckily enough, I got it. No more coming home to collapse on the floor. It was still hard work, but I wasn't afraid of hard work. And I was learning from the managers both how to manage relationships with clients and how to improve their communications to be more appealing. The fundraising materials also had to reflect the nonprofits' overall messaging, the way they presented themselves to the public. Their brand.

I became fascinated by brand management and strategy. Most companies had several routes by which they communicated with the public, and nonprofits were no different. It was critical that the tone, style, and wording be similar across all platforms, as I learned they were called. Here was a way to use my love of words and my eye for details in a way that could also pay well. Suddenly, my career plans changed.

So rather than going to graduate school for a PhD and becoming a college professor, I decided to get my MBA and learn even more about how businesses work.

I took my GMATs so I could get into the kinds of programs I thought I'd want. Several of the MBA programs I looked at didn't require taking the standardized test. But all of the good ones, the ones whose names I knew, did. Because I was still naïve and a little arrogant, I applied to these top-level schools.

Now, I had been a good student in high school and college. I had graduated with a decent grade point average at both levels. But I was not at the top of my class. Top ten percent, probably. Maybe. At least in high school. College, well, there had been good grades and okay grades. My GPA equated to a B+, which I thought was pretty good.

The rejection letters started to come in, and I was crushed. So much for my naivety.

Thinking better of things, I applied to some other programs at less prestigious but still good schools. I did want my MBA to count for something, after all. And even the less-well known schools' programs were pretty darned expensive. If I was going to go into debt to get my MBA, I wanted it to be worth every penny.

I ended up at Boston University again. For three reasons. One, as an alumna, I was pretty sure I would be accepted, and I was. Two, they had an MBA program I could take in the evenings and weekends. That meant, I could still work and be in school. I would still end up in debt, but not quite as in debt as I had been contemplating. Third, I didn't have to move.

I started the program in Fall 2002 with plans to graduate in Spring 2004. For two years, I would do little besides work and study. But I could do it. I was sure I could.

CR ℰ)CR ℰ)CR ℰ)

I met Patrick on my summer break between the two years of my MBA program. As I was able to have a life again for a few months, my friends and I were catching up. Fortunately, they had been pretty understanding of my lack of time from September to May. It was now June, and I was planning to take advantage of it.

Patrick played bass in a band. There's just something about musicians that I was drawn to. Perhaps it was their artistic flair. After all, I considered myself something of an artist too – with words and music. I had sung all my life, mostly just for myself, but also in high school and college choir. Music had always been part of my life, sometimes a refuge when things weren't going all that well. I paid attention to music, too. I had taken musical theory in high school. I knew most of the rock and pop artists, and I appreciated a well-crafted song. In other words, I was a sucker for guys like Patrick.

So, my friends and I were at this club, watching the band play. One of my friends thought the lead singer was just her type. She started making plans to meet him somehow. It wasn't that big a club, and they weren't that big a band. It was possible.

The lead singer was cute enough, I suppose, but then that's part of their job. Most lead singers have a touch of the egotist. They almost have to, to be able to do their job, don't they? They are the "voice" of the band, and the one who draws in the fans. This one was stereotypical of the type with blond hair, blue eyes, and a serious swagger as he strutted around the stage. Susan was smitten.

I tend to like the quieter guys. Less showy. Maybe it's just my own insecurities, but I don't like the guys who need to be front and center. I prefer the ones who are supportive. So, while Susan was plotting how to get the attention of the lead singer, I was focused on the bassist. He was still a handsome guy, though perhaps not as classically handsome as the lead singer. He had longish black hair, which I liked, and light-colored eyes, though I couldn't tell if they were blue or green. I noted he didn't have a ring on the telltale finger. I took that as a good sign.

Susan and I stayed after the show ended, trying to figure out how to get backstage to meet the guys in the band. We were milling around, not really clear in our approach, when the band came out from backstage. They were laughing amongst themselves. When they saw us, they immediately went into "stage" mode, no longer the laughing casual guys we'd just seen, but now focused on the fans – i.e., the two women standing there.

One of the guys didn't stick around. I assumed he had other plans, or was married already, or some such. He wasn't the bassist, so I was fine with that.

Susan made a beeline for the lead singer. He smiled at her – she was an attractive female – and they started to talk. He started to lead her backstage, where they'd just come from. But she said no and looked at me.

Susan and I had a deal. Neither of us would leave the other unless we got a good vibe from the guys. The last thing we needed was the guys to be jerks, or worse. We weren't that smitten.

Fortunately, the guy seemed not to be that much of a jerk, though I got the impression he didn't mind having an adoring fan, but wasn't all that interested beyond what he could get from her. I tried to tell Susan my impression of the guy wasn't positive. But she was still enthralled.

I was trying to be much cooler with my interest. The two remaining guys – the bassist and the drummer – were sizing me up. I was dressed for an evening at a club, so I had on more makeup than I normally would wear, and my clothing was definitely the sexiest clothes I owned. I thought I looked good, without looking too slutty. I wasn't really interested in the drummer, though. He seemed like a nice enough guy in the few minutes we'd been talking. But I'd gotten the bassist into my head, and he was the one I wanted to get to know better.

The drummer got the message, and with a laugh and a wave, he headed backstage, leaving Susan and I with our respective conquests. Sort of.

We sat at tables, near each other, but not close enough to hear the actual conversation taking place.

"Hi! I'm Tiffany," I said as we sat down.

"Patrick. Nice to meet you, Tiffany. That's a nice name."

I'd heard this line before. All too often. I was disappointed he hadn't come up with better.

"Thanks. I've learned to embrace it."

"Embrace it meaning what? You don't think it's a nice name?"

"It's a name that gets attention, and that's not always what I'm after."

"It isn't?"

I blushed. It was obvious he meant himself, or attention from him. "I don't use my name as a calling card, no."

Oh dear. This conversation was not going the way I had intended. I was supposed to be all fun and cute. Not serious and whiny.

"Sorry. I think we got off on a bad foot. Shall we try again? I'm Patrick." And he held out his hand.

It was such a genuine thing to say and do. I was pleased. Here, it seemed, was a real human.

I shook his hand. "My name is Tiffany. It's nice to meet you." And I smiled a genuine smile. Not a flirtatious smile, though it was probably that too.

"You too. What brings you to Good Habits tonight?"

"I'm escaping," I teased.

"Oh? Husband? Bad boyfriend?" He looked pointedly at my unadorned left hand.

Laughing, I explained, "No, I've been in school. Just ended for the year in May. And working full time. So, I haven't had much chance for fun."

"Wow. I can imagine you haven't. Full time school and work?"

"Yes. It's grueling, but worth it. I hope."

"What are you studying, if I might ask?"

Politeness. I liked this guy. "I'm getting my MBA."

"Smart and beautiful."

Okay, that was another line. "I do okay," I said, hoping for something other than another line. I was hoping to be more than just a groupie. If this guy could be sincere, that was.

"Sorry, I slipped into band mode again."

"Is that what it's called?" I said with a laugh.

"Well, that's what I call it."

"Girls often waiting for you after a show?"

"Often enough, to be honest."

"What do you do with them?"

"Depends. Usually just talk and flirt. Occasionally more, but not very often. I'm not the 'love 'em and leave 'em' type."

"Kind of sounds like you might be," I replied honestly.

"Well, I am a guy," he responded with a smile. "If things are offered, well, sometimes a guy just needs to be a guy."

"Really? That seems pretty shallow."

"Definitely. But as long as she knows that's all it is, too, isn't that okay?"

I hadn't really thought of it that way. "I suppose."

"I'm careful. I don't just fool around indiscriminately. Not like Tim." He pointed to his friend, the lead singer, who now had his arm around Susan. She was laughing at something he said. I wondered if I should warn her about what Patrick was saying about Tim.

"That's my friend he's with."

"Does your friend want a little something or a relationship? Because Tim is definitely not the relationship type, if you get my meaning."

"Oh, I do. And honestly, I'm not sure. Susan likes guys. She's not loose, as they say. But she isn't tight either." I laughed at my witticism, and so did Patrick.

"What about you? You looking for a little something or more?"

"I'm probably on the tight side of things," I replied honestly.

"That's what I thought. You don't seem like the 'love 'em and leave 'em' type either."

"Not really."

He laughed. "At least you're honest!"

"New concept?"

"Whoa. I'm not THAT bad."

"I was teasing. You seem more genuine than I sensed at the beginning."

"Like I said, band mode."

"Putting on a show for the fans?"

"Exactly."

"So, who's the real Patrick?"

"He's a guy who plays bass in a band, and works selling cars to make a living."

"Not easy to make a living as a musician, huh?"

"Not at all. But I love it. We have this regular gig on Friday nights, here. It pays okay, but not enough to live on."

"Do you want more? To be a musician full time?"

"Sometimes. Sometimes not. It's a hard life. Tim and I have known each other since we were kids. We write our own stuff, and we appreciate that Good Habits lets us play about fifty percent original material. Lots of clubs only want you to play covers."

"Because that's what people know."

"Yeah. And if you're good, you can draw in a crowd, and that's what they want. But since we're regulars, we get a better deal."

"Good Habits seems like they let more original stuff than not."

"They do. Luke, he's the owner, he's a good guy. He is a musician himself, so he gets it."

I noticed Tim was starting to eye the backstage again. I wanted to check in with Susan, though I didn't want to ruin things with Patrick. They were going pretty well, I thought. "I have to check in with my friend. We promised to take care of each other. You understand."

"I do. Go see what she's into."

I approached the table and got the evil eye from Tim. He definitely didn't appreciate my interruption.

"Susan, are you ready to go?"

She laughed. "This is Tim. Tim, this is my friend, Tiffany."

"Hey, Tiffany," Tim said, his eyes telling me to go away.

"Nice to meet you, Tim. So, what do you want to do, Susan? Stay or go?"

Susan looked at Tim, who smiled his best smile at her. "Stay," she replied.

"You sure?"

"Yes. I'll call a cab later."

"Be careful," I said.

"I will. I'm a big girl, you know."

"I know. But be careful anyway, okay?"

Susan laughed. Tim smiled at me, happy with Susan's choice. She was right. She was a big girl. And I had a feeling she knew what she was getting herself into. Her call.

"Okay," Susan responded.

I walked back to where Patrick was now standing beside the table. "What's the answer?" he asked.

"She's going to stay. I don't think she thinks Tim is very sincere, but that's okay with her," I said, continuing my streak of honesty with Patrick.

"Good. As long as she's aware."

"How about you? Band mode or human mode?"

"I quite like human mode. You?"

"I prefer it."

"Patrick Jameson," he said, holding out his hand again. "From Southie."

"Tiffany Johnson. From Brookline by way of Virginia."

"I didn't think I heard any accent," Patrick Jameson said, with his definitely Southie accent.

"Just WASP."

He laughed, a full bellied laugh. It made his blue eyes sparkle.

"What are you doing tomorrow night?" Patrick asked.

"I don't know. What am I doing?" I flirted back.

"Dinner?"

"Love to. Where and when?"

"Here?"

I laughed. "Good Habits is okay, but how about someplace else? I mean, don't you get the food here once a week anyway?"

"Yeah, but I got a buddy playing tomorrow. Solo gig. I told him I'd be here for support."

"Not to play?"

"No, just be in the audience. A friendly face. Luke will let me sit upfront. The advantage of being a regular."

"That actually sounds like a lot of fun. I love music."

"Then you'll love Matthew. He's the genuine deal. He's really trying to make it in the musician's world, where I dabble my toe in."

"Seems like you do a little more than dabble."

"Like I said, I go back and forth. For right now, I'm happy with the balance. I get to play, which I love. And I get to eat and have a roof over my head, which I also love. And I don't have to travel all the time."

"Yeah. That could get old."

"You have no idea."

"Tell me about it. Tomorrow."

"Show's at 7. Dinner beforehand, when we can talk."

"No talking when the performers are on stage," I mimicked the announcement that had been made before the show started and that was posted on all the tables.

"Luke's rules. But I like them."

"Me, too. I hate when people are talking, and you can't hear the music."

"It's nice to have the attention of the audience. It's why we play."

"I get it. Really."

He nodded. "So, dinner at 6? I'll put your name on the list, so you can get in any time."

"That's a nice perk."

"One of the few. See you at 6."

"See you then."

I looked over to see that Susan and Tim were kissing. And it looked like he was about to reach down her shirt, something I really didn't want to see.

"Will he hurt her?" I asked Patrick.

"Not physically. He's a good guy, really. He just is, well, a little indiscriminate."

"Okay. She's a big girl."

"He's maniacal about protection."

"Good to know."

The loving noises the two were making were getting excessive. It was time for me to leave.

"I'll see you tomorrow, Patrick Jameson."

"See you tomorrow, Tiffany Johnson."

I walked out, still worried about Susan's heart being broken. But recognizing that she was an adult. And I hoped reasonably smart about men.

CR &)CR &)CR &)

Patrick and I saw each other the next night. And the next weekend. And the weekend after that. The weekend after that, I invited him to my apartment. He, too, was maniacal about protection, which I appreciated. I wasn't on birth control, so condoms were it. For both pregnancy protection and sexual disease protection.

I spent most Fridays that summer at Good Habits, watching the guys play. Dog Park was their name. It wasn't the greatest name, though I thought the band was really quite good. I'm pretty snobby about music, and Tim could really sing.

He'd broken Susan's heart, though. She had been foolish enough to think that he wanted more than just a one-night stand. He said he'd been clear with her, and for all I know, he had been. That's not the way she remembered it, though. I tried not to hold Tim's lothario nature against Patrick. They might be best friends, but Patrick had shown himself to be a genuine guy.

We'd been dating for a couple of months now, and the summer was winding down. That meant I was going to lose my free time. I hadn't dated at all last year, and I wasn't sure dating, working, and school was even possible. But, for Patrick, I was willing to try. School starting up again did mean I was going to miss Good Habits, though. I only had so much time in my life. Patrick and I planned to see each other Saturdays during the day, as he had gigs a lot on Saturday nights, and maybe Sundays, depending on whether he had to work and how much schoolwork I had. We planned to talk often, too. It wasn't ideal, but it was the best we could come up with.

෬ ෨෬ ෨෬ ෨

By November, I sensed Patrick was losing interest. He did, after all, have access to a bevy of beauties weekly, and my time was very limited. I was pretty sure he'd been faithful to this point. But the time apart was taking its toll on our fledgling relationship.

November proved fateful for another reason. The protection we'd been using failed. I was pregnant.

I panicked when I started to realize it might be true. I didn't have time for a baby. Patrick and I were not in a place where we wanted to have a child. We'd only been dating four months, for crying out loud. This was bad. Very bad. I mean, I loved the man, at least I thought I did. But this was bad. Very bad.

I bought a pregnancy test at the drug store. I peed on the stick, as instructed, and got a plus sign. The pamphlet talked about the plus sign like it was a good thing, which I supposed might be the case for a lot of women who took these home pregnancy tests. Just not me.

I also started to experience morning sickness. All the time, not just in the morning. Thank goodness for the Internet, which told me to eat salted crackers to combat the nausea. I managed to get through work and school, though sometimes it was a close call and sometimes I ran to the bathroom and threw up anyway.

No one knew. I didn't tell anyone. No one in my family. None of my roommates. Not until I told Patrick, I told myself.

In the meantime, I was researching clinics. Massachusetts was a liberal state, thank goodness. I had options.

I showed up at Good Habits on a Friday night. Patrick saw me sitting there when he was playing, as by now, Luke knew me, and I was at one of the reserved tables near the stage. His look was questioning, but glad to see me. Good.

The set ended, and the band headed backstage. I was allowed back there, too, but I didn't want to interrupt their night. I was planning to wait until after the show to give Patrick the bad news. He needed to be told. And I needed to get on with it.

Second set over, the band came out for their usual two encores. The audience was appreciative tonight, more hooting and hollering than usual. I was pleased for Patrick.

After the show ended, I did go backstage. I didn't want to have this conversation in public.

I found Patrick in the green room, with the rest of the guys.

"Didn't expect to see you tonight," he said, as he gave me a quick kiss hello.

"A surprise!" I said, with some enthusiasm to mask my nerves. I waved at the other guys, who I had gotten to know in the past few months. They were really okay guys, even Tim.

"Can we go somewhere? Talk?" I said to Patrick.

"Sure. There's a little space over here. We can be private there."

He took my hand and led me to a room I'd never noticed before. He closed the door behind me and gave me a more enthusiastic kiss. And started to reach up my shirt for more.

"We're not in band mode," I said coldly.

"Sorry. I'm still on my show high. It takes a while to get out of it."

"I know. Not my first time, you know."

"I know you know. Geez. What's going on? You seem really angry."

I took a deep breath. The tears were brimming in my eyes. This was the hardest thing I'd ever done. Well, that and coping with being pregnant while working full time and going to school full time. "I have bad news. Maybe we should sit down."

There wasn't really much in the way of chairs in this room. It seemed to be a storage closet as there were shelves with plates and other things on them. We sat down on the floor. I tried not to think too hard about how dirty the floor probably was. That was beside the point at the moment.

"What's going on?" Patrick asked. "Why are you really here? I don't think it's just you're taking the night off from school."

"Not at all." The tears started again.

"Tiffany," Patrick said, taking me in his arms, "what is going on?"

I blurted out my news. "I'm pregnant. You're the father, in case you were wondering."

"Pregnant? But we've been careful."

"Yeah. Careful, but not quite good enough apparently."

"What are you going to do?"

'What are YOU going to do?' I heard the words echo in my head.

I stood up, tears drying up as anger set in. "I was hoping for some sympathy. And support. But I guess that's too much to ask." I reached for the door handle.

"Wait! You took me by surprise, is all. What do you need? Do you need money?"

I winced. "Will you go with me?" I asked quietly. I was scared, and I wanted him to comfort me.

"I don't know, Tiffany. That's not really a guy thing, is it?"

"It's your kid too, you know." The question of whether I would get an abortion hadn't even come up. Patrick seemed to take it as a given that I would. It was the smart thing to do, of course. But part of me had hoped Patrick would be a little more interested in supporting me through this.

"Geez. Don't say that."

"Well, it is. You made it just as much as I did." I was furious.

"Stop yelling. Do you want everyone to hear? To know?"

I said through clenched teeth, "No, I don't. But don't you care enough about me to help me through this."

"So, you do need money?"

"No, I don't. I have money and very good health insurance. Goodbye, Patrick."

And I dramatically opened the door and walked out.

I half expected Patrick to come after me. And I half knew he would not.

I did expect him to call the next day, though.

He didn't.

He didn't call the day after that either.

I made an appointment on Monday for the following Friday, which I took off from work. That way, I'd have the weekend to recover. I assumed I'd need a few days, based on what I'd read. But I could study and be in pain. And then it would be over.

I really wanted to call Xan or Phin to be here with me. But I was too ashamed. I was so stupid! How could I have been so stupid!

One thing was certain. I was getting birth control as soon as I could.

CR ℘ CR ℘ CR ℘

I never heard from Patrick again. I picked up the phone a bunch of times to call him, but I never went through with it. What was there to say?

I recovered physically quite well. None of my roommates knew more than I had a bad stomachache, and I was going to be in bed for a few days.

Emotionally, the worst of the pain was over Patrick and his reaction. And lack of support. I never regretted my decision to abort. It was really the only choice to make, and I was grateful the choice was mine.

But I never told anyone other than Patrick.

CR ℘ CR ℘ CR ℘

I finished my MBA program. I graduated at the top of my class. Somehow because I was paying for it, school was more important this time. Also, I just loved what I was learning. I didn't care all that much about operations management; running factories didn't have much appeal. But I loved strategic management. And brand management. And change management. I loved it all. I had found my world. I had moved on from my original dream of teaching college. I was going to be in marketing and communications.

I moved back to Virginia as soon as I graduated. This, too, was part of moving on. Phin and Xan were right. Virginia was home.

THE COURSE OF TRUE LOVE... (2019)

As she promised, Dr. Peterson followed up with Dr. Kessler, who followed up with me once they had the biopsy results.

Neither doctor would tell me the outcome over the phone. I had to come in for an appointment. I took that as a bad sign.

"If the news was good, wouldn't Dr. Kessler just tell me?"

"I don't know," Tom admitted. "Maybe there's a protocol they have to follow to tell patients in person – either way. Don't panic until you know."

"I guess so. Can I panic just a little?"

Tom laughed, as I had intended. "I guess a little is okay."

"Will you take the cats if I die?"

"Tiffany…"

"Okay, I'm joking. Well, mostly. I know you would take Cass. But would you take Brie, too. They're sisters, you know."

"Cheese Omelet would be safe. She and Little Mama would come live with me. Though Sabrina wouldn't be happy, probably. She's come to tolerate me. But love me? Maybe not."

"Thank you. That's a load off my mind. And Brie would come around. I think. Especially if you feed her more often."

Tom fed the girls most weekend mornings as he left to go do his thing in the morning before I got up. Often, he worked. Sometimes, he got in a quick workout. He and Meghan also went to have breakfast with their father about once a month. It was a McDonnell thing, so George – who also liked to sleep in on weekends – and I weren't invited. The three of them would meet early at a diner near the elder Tom's house. I didn't mind these excursions. I figure it was good for the family to bond. I wondered sometimes if Lauren felt excluded. But there wasn't much of a way to include her from Colorado. Tom did say they'd often call her when they got back to their father's place, just so everyone could talk together for a bit.

"Food is definitely the way to the cats' hearts," Tom teased.

"And my fiancé's heart, too."

"Okay. You got me there. Does that mean I'm just another cat to you?"

"Not at all. You take care of me as much as I take care of you. Especially right now."

"Well, these are extenuating circumstances."

"Yeah. Well, there may be more."

"Don't think that way!"

Tom was more of an optimist than I was. "I'm trying!"

"I'm confident in Dr. Peterson's work. And Dr. Dreamboat."

I laughed. "He just kept me under."

"His mere presence made you better," Tom teased.

"Didn't hurt," I responded.

෬ ෨෬ ෨෬ ෨

My appointment with Dr. Kessler was scheduled for three weeks after surgery, on my last day of disability leave. We were now in a new year, though Tom and I had barely noticed to be honest. Our New Year's Eve had been spent on my couch, watching television and petting the cats, much like virtually every other evening of the year.

My sutures were healing well, and I generally felt fine. I was, however, very nervous about what this appointment was going to reveal.

Christmas had been rough. We'd done our family events separately again this year, even though we were engaged. We hadn't wanted to take on the extra challenge of figuring out which family's Christmas to go to, and therefore which family was going to be peeved.

The reality is that the McDonnells probably would have been fine if Tom had come to the Johnson-Kelly family Christmas celebration at my mother's house with Jack, Xan, Phin, and everyone's broods. But Tom would have been sad to miss the day with his family, which included Lauren, Charlie, and their kids, who had flown in from Colorado. Tom had already given me so much of his time, and his family had been so understanding, I didn't want to deprive them of this time together.

In addition, when the whole Johnson-Kelly clan got together – with Mom, Jack, my brothers, their spouses, and their kids – it was a lot. Tom had experienced it several times already. But that many people constituted a crowd for him, even if they were all family. He was much happier in the quietness of the McDonnell family celebration.

Now, we were facing the day we had dreaded during the holiday season. The day we would find out whether I needed more medical intervention. Whether I still had cancer. I was terrified.

Tom had taken the day off to come with me. The appointment was in the morning. Depending on the news, I might need his support in the afternoon.

I was mentally prepared for the worst. I consoled myself that, even if I did have cancer, it was likely to be in the very early stages. Which meant I had a really good chance of beating it. I wasn't looking forward to chemotherapy and radiation. But if that's what I had to do, then that's what I would do. I wasn't going to play games with my health.

Dr. Kessler's office was about 30 minutes from my townhouse. I drove, mostly because I could now. Also because Tom didn't like to drive. And my car was more comfortable, anyway.

As we were driving, I said to Tom, "I wonder if I'll ever see Dr. Peterson again."

"Yeah. Kind of interesting how that works with surgery. The surgeon does their thing, and that's pretty much all you see of them."

"That's not how it works on *Grey's Anatomy*."

Tom chuckled. "I wouldn't know."

"You've watched it with me a couple of times. Haven't you?"

"If I have, I blocked it from my memory."

"Oh fine," I responded with mock indignation as he intended. "The main characters are all surgeons. But they take care of their patients from admittance to discharge."

"Maybe hospitals are different?"

"In my limited experience, in the hospital, you mostly only see nurses and orderlies. Even the regular doctors only stop by once or twice a day, at most."

"Guess that wouldn't make for very good television."

"Not for a show about surgeons!"

We arrived at Dr. Kessler's office 10 minutes early. You could count on Tom and me to be early to just about anything. We couldn't seem to help it. We were both like that. Always early.

We sat in the waiting room, waiting to be called. Tom read a news magazine, while I played games on my phone and responded to social media.

So far, I had been silent on social media about my diagnosis and subsequent surgery. My immediate family knew, and Tom's immediate family knew. And a select group of friends like Jane and Peter. But I did not want our extended families involved. Not at this point. I would just get a lot of unsolicited advice, most of it bad. I had a few friends who had had breast cancer, and if I did have it, I would probably reach out to them – not in public – to learn from their experiences. But I wasn't up to broadcasting the news. Social media had its benefits, but it also had its drawbacks.

We had "announced" our engagement on social media, after we had told all the important people face to face or over the phone. Or rather, I had changed my status, followed by Tom changing his. Immediately, Cathy had offered to help with planning, as I knew she would. I had a few other friends who offered, too, of course. And some of my cousins had said, passive-aggressively, they looked forward to getting Save the Date notifications. But most people had just congratulated us. The whole experience made me realize that, while I loved many of the people with whom I was connected on social media, I tended to share my life in less-intense chunks online. Posts about the cats. Frustrations with clients, with no names of course. That kind of thing. Nothing that was so deeply personal. Until the engagement. And that had been enough.

I thought about all this as I sat in the doctors' waiting room, browsing through social media. I could have "checked in" at the doctors. I often did that in places where I was eating and even at the cats' vet and other places like that. But checking in at the doctors would invite commentary and questions about why I was there. And so I didn't. I tended toward the dramatic, which Tom liked to tease me about. And it would have been nice to get the "hang in there" kind of posts and affirmations from friends and family. But there was also the very real chance that comments would go awry. And I was in much too vulnerable an emotional state to deal with that!

Finally, Dr. Kessler's nurse called me back. As this part was just to check my weight and other vitals, I suggested Tom just wait some more. Once I was called into the office for the consult, I would ask the nurse to get Tom. Both the nurse and Tom agreed with this plan.

My pulse and blood pressure were back to their normal lows. Even with the anxiety of waiting to hear about the cancer, I was still in the bottom of what is considered safe for both vital statistics. The nurse, who knew this was my history, just chuckled as she noted the information down. "Wish I had your genes," she said under her breath.

"It's nice, but I do have to watch it a bit. If they get too low, that could be dangerous too."

"Yes, sorry to have said that aloud."

"Don't worry about it. Lots of people remark on their being so low. Back when I was doing martial arts regularly, I actually had to stop giving blood because my pulse was so low, I didn't make their threshold of 50 bpm." Today's pulse was about 55.

"Yes, you will need to keep an eye on that. As you say, it's possible for these things to get too low."

"My father has a pacemaker," I offered. "It's a genetic thing."

The nurse just smiled. "I'll call you to Dr. Kessler's office in a moment. She's just finishing up with another patient."

"Thank you."

I sat in the exam room for another five minutes. My anxiety was getting higher the longer I was alone with my thoughts. I kept telling myself I would be fine in the end. But I was still nervous.

Finally, the nurse came, with Tom, to take us back to Dr. Kessler's office.

We sat down across the desk from Dr. Kessler. She opened the file with the results. I tried not to rush her as she read the information again. I was sure she knew the overall answer – cancer or no – but perhaps was wanting to make sure she remembered the details.

"How are you feeling, today, Tiffany?" she asked, looking up from the file. "Any residual pain?"

"No. I'm pain free. And am able to move around just fine. I haven't tried any strenuous activities yet, as Dr. Peterson said not to until after we met with you three weeks post-op. But day to day, I feel fine."

"Wonderful!"

"And what is the biopsy result?" I asked, not being able to wait any longer.

"Good news! You had a cystic lump. If I had to classify it, I'd say Stage 0. But really it was precancerous."

"No cancer?" Tom asked.

I had tears in my eyes.

"No cancer. The margins were clean. The lymph nodes showed no signs of cancer," Dr. Kessler continued, checking the file again.

"No cancer?" I echoed Tom and Dr. Kessler. I couldn't quite believe it.

"As a precaution, though, Dr. Peterson and I recommend a short course of radiation. Eight weeks, at least three times a week. I will refer you to an oncologist who will confirm that recommendation."

My heart dropped a bit. "But if it's not cancer…"

"There were some precancerous cells. We'd just like to make sure they don't develop."

"Oh. Okay."

"The technical term is ductal carcinoma in situ or DCIS. This means atypical cells were found in the milk ducts of the breast, but have not spread to anywhere else in the breast."

"That sounds good."

"Yes, but DCIS can mean the cells could spread to other tissue and develop into breast cancer. A short course of radiation should keep that from happening.

"Should?" Tom asked.

"There are no guarantees. But with this type of atypical cells and some radiation, I believe you could consider yourself cancer-free. We will want you to continue to have annual mammograms. And we will pay attention carefully to any other abnormalities, of course. But all in all, you would be considered cancer-free."

"Really? Cancer-free?" That was a possibility I hadn't even considered.

"Yes."

"How does the radiation work?" I asked.

"I'm giving you a referral to Dr. Okino. She's an oncologist and better qualified to give you all the details. Her office is in this building. I've worked with her a few times before. She's very good and very thorough. We will want to get you started as soon as possible. So, I would ask that you go make an appointment today. She's expecting you."

CR ∞CR ∞CR ∞

Still in something of a daze, Tom and I left Dr. Kessler's office and headed straight to Dr. Okino's office one floor down. The scheduler made an appointment for three days from today. I told Tom I thought I could handle it by myself.

"If you're sure," he said, as we walked to the car.

"I'm sure. It's just a consultation. Then I'll know about the radiation treatments and what I might need from you for support."

"Okay. If you're sure."

"I'm sure. But I love you for offering to come."

"Of course! I love you, too."

We were quiet for a while as I drove us back to Tom's townhouse. He would go back to work this afternoon, since the news had been good. There wasn't much of the day left, but there were a few hours. And he wanted to take advantage of them.

As I pulled into the parking area in front of his townhouse, I shouted, "I'm cancer-free!"

Tom laughed. "Yes, you are!"

"Sorry. I was so focused on the radiation and the appointment with Dr. Okino I almost lost sight of the most important thing!"

"You are cancer-free!" Tom shouted at me.

I kissed him vigorously. "I'm cancer-free!"

"You need to call your mom. And dad. And Xan and Phin."

"I do. I'll do that when I get home. I'll call Meghan, too. If you don't mind."

"Of course I don't mind. She may be my sister, but she's your friend."

I smiled broadly. "She is!" I was giddy with relief. "I'm cancer-free!" I shouted again.

Tom chuckled. "You're a nut!"

"That too. See you later."

"I'll come by around dinner. Warn Cheese Omelet."

"Ha! She knows that by now."

"You should warn her anyway."

"I will."

Tom went up the outside stairs to his door. He turned to blow a kiss at me before opening the door. I blew a kiss back, and then pulled out and drove the two miles to my house, with a huge grin on my face.

Once inside, I called Meghan. I wanted to call her first because I knew she would be the most on my side, well except Xan and Phin. Mom would be supportive, but also more emotional. Meghan would just plain be happy for me. And I needed that to bolster me for the other calls.

"Hey, Meghan!" I said, when she picked up her cell.

"Hey, Tiffany! What happened at the doctors?"

I guessed Tom must have told her today was the day. I hadn't, but the two siblings were very close, and I wouldn't have it any other way.

I took a deep breath. "I'm cancer-free!" I shouted into the phone.

"Really?" came Meghan's response. "That's fabulous!"

"I'm very happy. I do have to have some radiation, though, which sucks."

"That does sound like no fun. But cancer-free is awesome. What happened?"

"Just atypical cells. Nothing had spread outside of the breast or even very much with the breast, as I understand it. The radiation is more precautionary than anything. To kill the atypical cells."

"That makes sense. So, no cancer?"

"That's what the doctor said. She said I could consider myself cancer-free. I can't seem to stop saying it!"

"Well, you should! It's great news."

"Thank you. It is."

"Anything you need for the radiation?"

"I don't think so. My appointment to talk with the oncologist is Friday. I'll know more then."

"Okay. Let me know. I'll help however you want."

"I know you will. Thanks, Meghan. I'm going to go now. I have a bunch of other phone calls to make."

"Of course. Congratulations again! That's great news."

"Thank you! I'm cancer-free!"

Meghan laughed as we hung up.

Next, I called my brothers. First up was Alexander.

"Hey Xan!" I said cheerily.

"What's up, Tiffany? Long time, no talk."

It was true it had been a while since my brother and I had talked. We tended to text more often, in between life happening. But mostly I knew he was teasing me.

"Good news! Just got back from the docs. Turns out the cyst was just that, a cystic lump. No cancer, though perhaps precancerous."

"That's amazing. I'm so happy for you!"

"Thanks. I'm pretty happy too. Looks like I'll have to have some radiation just to be sure to kill the bad cells, though the surgery went really well too."

"Then why the radiation?" Xan was concerned.

"Just precaution. I'll know more on Friday when I meet with the oncologist. But Dr. Kessler said I'm in good shape. In fact, she said I could consider myself cancer-free."

"Well, that's awesome! Glad to hear it! Woo-hoo!"

I blushed. "Thanks, Xan. Gotta go. Gotta call Phin and Mom and Dad and give them the good news."

"I'm very happy for you, little sis."

"Thanks again. Me, too. Love you. Love to the wife and kids. Bye."

"Love you. Love to Tom. Bye."

One brother down, I called the other one.

"Hey, Phineas!"

"Hello, Tiffany! How's my sister today?"

"I'm great! I'm cancer-free!"

"What?"

"The doctor said the surgery went really well, and the lump was just a cystic lump, possibly precancerous, but not cancer."

"That's fantastic!"

"I know. So, I'll have some radiation to be sure to kill any atypical cells. But overall, I'm considered cancer-free!"

"Wonderful!"

"Gotta run. More calls to make. Love you. Love to Joseph and Eliza. Bye."

"Love you. Talk to you soon."

I was getting tired, and I felt like I was repeating myself. But I had to call Dad and Mom, and Jack, though I rarely talked to Jack on the phone.

"Dad?" I inquired when he picked up.

"Tiffany? How are you?"

"I'm good, Dad. Really good. The doctor said I'm going to be just fine."

"They got the cancer, then?"

"Turns out it wasn't cancer yet. Precancerous if anything."

"That's great, honey!"

"Yeah. I think so, too."

"You feeling okay after the surgery?"

"I'm pretty good. A little twinge every now and then. But generally, almost back to normal. I go back to work next week."

"Well, that will be good for you. You like to work."

"That I do. Got that from my dad."

He chuckled. "Yeah, well, probably. Though your mom is no slouch in the working department either."

"True. Speaking of whom, she's my next call."

"Tell her hello from me. And that handsome fiancé of yours."

"Will do. Thanks, Dad. Love you."

"Love you, too, baby girl." My father wasn't one for terms of endearment, but I could hear the tears in his voice. He hung up before I could get mushy on him.

I dialed Mom's number. I knew this would be the most taxing of the calls, which is why I did it last.

"Tiffany?" she asked, knowing who it was from the caller ID.

"Hi, Mom."

"Everything okay? You're not at work?"

"Still on disability leave. I go back next week."

"Oh, that's good then. You'll be happier once you're back to your routine."

"Probably. Say, Mom," I said, taking a deep breath.

"What's wrong?" she pounced.

"Nothing's wrong."

"Did something go wrong with Tom? Please tell me you haven't done something to drive that sweet man away."

"Mom, it's nothing like that. It's good news," I replied, shaking my head at my mother's passive-aggressive behavior. I'd learned to ignore it over the years, though it was still annoying. I just refused to give in to her fearmongering. "We went to the doctor this morning."

"Oh, no! Is it cancer? I'm so sorry, honey. What can I do?"

"No, Mom. It's not cancer."

"What do you mean? Why did you have surgery then? They don't just cut people open for no good reason."

"Mom, I had a lump. They did a biopsy, though, and found out it's not cancer."

"Well, what was it then?"

"Just some atypical cells."

"Well, that doesn't sound good."

"Better than cancer." I couldn't help myself. This was supposed to be a happy conversation.

"Yes, of course. I didn't mean anything."

"Anyway, I just wanted to let you know." I decided I was not going to tell her about the radiation. She would just make too much of it. I'd have to tell my brothers not to mention it either in front of her. I'd text them both as soon as I got off the call.

"I'm glad to hear. I don't get to hear all the details of your life much anymore."

I just shook my head and was glad she couldn't see my face. "Gotta run, Mom. It's been a long day."

"Are you sure you're okay? You don't normally get this tired."

"I'm fine, Mom. It's just been an emotional day. I have to go. Love you."

"Love you, too. Keep me posted."

"Sure will." Though I thought I just might not.

I texted Xan and Phin to let them know not to tell Mom about the radiation treatments.

"She doesn't seem to believe me," I wrote.

"She's just worried about you," Phin responded. He always gave Mom more credit than I did. Came from being the youngest, I suppose.

"I won't tell," Xan replied. "Let us know if you need anything."

"Thanks, guys! Appreciate the support!"

ରେ ၄ଠରେ ၄ଠରେ ၄ଠ

Dr. Okino was a small woman of Asian descent and quite beautiful. She wore her black hair long, but had it up in a bun, for work I presumed. Underneath her white doctor's coat, she was dressed in a magenta shirt that was a wonderful shade against her skin, with black pants and shoes. She smiled at me as she came into the exam room, and I liked her immediately.

"I have ordered radiation three times a week for six weeks. That should kill any remaining atypical cells," she explained to me.

"Will I lose my hair?"

"You shouldn't. It's a fair low dose of radiation. You might see a few more strands come out in the shower. But I wouldn't expect to see anything that noticeable. In fact, if you do get that kind of reaction, I would want to know immediately."

"Okay. Good to know. Any other side effects?"

"You might be a little more tired than normal."

"I've been tired since the surgery."

"Yes. That, too, is normal. This will just be a little more of the same level of fatigue."

"Okay."

"I scheduled your radiation for late afternoon, so you could work the day and then get the treatment. Will that work for you?"

I appreciated her consideration of my working schedule.

"That should work. I haven't worked in three weeks, so I appreciate being able to get back to it."

"A little advice. Ease back into work slowly. You will probably be more tired than you realize."

I nodded. "I believe you. Just going to see Dr. Kessler the other day was more exhausting than I expected."

"Yes. It's normal. Don't push yourself too hard. Take the time to heal. Your body has been through a lot. The radiation will add to that. But in the end, you will recover."

"Dr. Kessler said I could consider myself cancer-free."

"Medically, that is true. If anything, I would characterize your cyst as Stage 0. But even that is probably too much. Precancerous is a better word. Nothing to worry about for now, after the radiation. But we will want you to get annual mammograms, to check."

"I planned to. I have for years."

"Yes, I saw that in your file. That's good. That's why this was caught so early."

"Thank goodness."

"Exactly. Breast cancer is one of the most survivable cancers in large part because women have mammograms."

"You don't have to sell me on them, Dr. Okino. I'm a walking billboard!"

She smiled. "Good."

We were silent for a moment. I wasn't sure if the appointment was over.

"Please make an appointment for two months from now for a final follow-up. Assuming the radiation goes well, that should be it."

"Thank you, Dr. Okino. I'll do that right now."

"Good."

I stood up. "Thanks again." I shook her hand. And went to the front desk to make my appointment.

The first week of radiation went well. I didn't notice any appreciable hair loss. I was tired, but I attributed that to going back to work as much as anything.

I was amazed at how exhausted I was at the end of every day. Was work really this hard all the time, and I just didn't realize it?

My clients were pleased to have me back. All reported that my staff had taken fine care of them. But they knew me better, and they were glad I was back to take the reins again. I suspected that the truth was they would have adjusted just fine if I had been out longer. But I was also grateful that they missed me. Job security and all that.

My boss checked in with me on my first day back, as a good boss does. And he was that. "Everything okay?" he asked. He didn't know why I had been out. HR told me he didn't need to know. But Rob and I had a more congenial relationship than that. So, not to offend HR, I hadn't told him the details then. But now I did.

"I had a small lump in my right breast, Rob. I had it removed, and I'm fine now."

"Oh my. I had no idea, Tiffany. Cynthia had a lumpectomy about five years ago." Cynthia was Rob's wife.

"I didn't know. She's okay now?"

"Yes, she's fine. She had some chemo and radiation. But they got the lump early."

"Same here. Though technically I didn't have cancer. Just some atypical cells. I will have to have some radiation, though, for the next few weeks."

"Take whatever time you need. Your clients will be fine."

I smiled. "They were happy to hear I'm back," I teased.

"Of course they were. You have a great rapport with them. It's why they love you."

I blushed, though I knew it was true. "Thanks. Anyway, I'll be fine in another month or so."

"Good to hear. I hated not knowing what was going on, but I knew it wasn't my place to know. I'm glad you were comfortable enough to tell me, though."

"I'm glad too. It's nice to have a good boss."

It was his turn to blush, though I only knew because I knew him so well. For the most part, Tom was very good at hiding his emotions. Much better than I was.

My computer pinged. It was Jane IM'ing me.

"Well, I'll let you get back to work. Nice to have you back, Tiffany. Let me know if you need any help."

"Thanks, Rob. I will."

And he left my office.

I pinged Jane back. "Rob was here."

"Oops. I just wanted to say hello again. Nice to have you back."

"Thanks."

Jane, of course, knew all the details of what had happened. In fact, she and Peter had been by for dinner while I was on disability, though the office didn't know that. Or at least HR didn't. No offense to my lovely sister-in-law-to-be Meghan, but our HR was borderline nosy. I told them as little as possible. Jane had given me a full report on what was going on in the office. Since fortunately nothing untoward was happening, I was able to just listen and ignore it all while I was recovering. The beauty of hiring good people.

The second week of radiation was not as good. I was so tired. And it was making me cranky. I soldiered through the days, but I was very happy when Friday came.

Tom tried to help. He brought me things I liked to eat from the store. And he was very supportive when I said I needed time to recover. Time alone.

Week three was worse. I could hardly work, I was so tired. I started working from home on the days I didn't have radiation treatments, so I could spend the day in sweatpants and a t-shirt. My skin was very sensitive normally. But the radiation made it even more so. I could hardly stand to wear clothes. Aloe vera helped. The radiation was like having a sunburn, which fortunately or unfortunately, I was quite familiar with.

By the fourth week, I was starting to feel really sorry for myself. I just wanted this whole thing to be over with. I was sick and tired of being sick and tired.

"How do people with chronic illnesses stand this?" I whined to Tom.

He was being very patient, but he was kind of tired of me being whiny. "I suppose they just do. I mean, what choice do they have?"

"They could be miserable all the time."

"They could. I'm sure some are. I'm sure some drive their loved ones crazy." He smiled, to try to make it a joke, though we both knew it wasn't entirely a joke.

I couldn't help myself. I was miserable. My skin was flaking and itchy. And irritated all the time. I had to go to the office sometimes, and wearing 'real' clothes was very hard to do. I kept a large bottle of hand cream in my desk, which I applied liberally whenever I could. It helped. But I was much happier when I was at home in my 'indoor' clothes.

"I'm sorry I'm a pain. I know I am. I'm just so tired. And my skin is driving me crazy!"

"I know. I would hate that too. I wish I could help."

"I know you do."

"Little Mama wishes she could help too," Tom teased, as Cass sat on his lap contentedly purring.

"Ha! She and Brie don't help. They still want to snuggle. They don't understand I can't right now."

"They don't like change. You taught me that."

"Yeah. And they had me all to themselves for three weeks."

"They got spoiled."

"I suppose they did. Well, for now, they've been locked out of my bedroom."

"Poor kittens!" Tom declared.

I frowned. He didn't seem to understand the depth of the problem. "I need to try to sleep!"

"I know. I was teasing."

"Sorry."

"Maybe I should go."

"Maybe you should."

"Okay. I'll see you tomorrow."

I didn't want Tom to go home angry. But I wasn't in the mood to mollify him either.

Week five, I was about to jump out of my skin. Tom and I were still communicating, but not well. I was so miserable, I was miserable to be around.

I had talked to Rob and my team, and I explained I had to work from home. My clients didn't even know where I was working from, I told them. And it was much easier to manage the side effects from the comfort of my house. Fortunately, the office was understanding. More understanding than my fiancé, who was close to losing his patience with me.

That sixth week, I got through only because I knew it was the end. I kept telling myself, 'Only one more week!'

But my relationship with Tom was one of the things on which I depended. He was my rock, my strength. And now I didn't feel his love and acceptance.

I fell into a depression. I still worked, but that was as much as I could do in a day. I spent more and more of my evenings alone, having begged off Tom's visits. It was a downward spiral. The more I pushed Tom away, the more I needed him. But I couldn't reach out. I didn't have the energy. All I could do was cry, which I knew Tom wouldn't understand. So, I kept him at bay.

Little Mama meowed at me in the evenings, missing her favorite lap. Even Cheese Omelet seemed to feel Tom's absence.

My mother called often, but I was terse with her. I didn't want her advice. I tolerated her calls only because she was my mother.

Tom left me alone. He texted me, and I returned his texts in short bursts of energy. But I couldn't make myself do more than that. And even that was more than I could do some days.

A week after I finished the radiation, my skin started to return to normal. I was peeling a lot, as after a bad sunburn, and it itched. But the aloe vera and other moisturizing helped. I started to wear other than "indoor" clothes.

The middle of the next week, I finally felt like I could tolerate getting dressed enough to go to work. My staff was glad to see me, though they also didn't ask too many questions. Which was good because I was still barely functioning. Rob asked if he could help. But I declined. He was a kind man, but I didn't want him any further into my personal life than he already was.

Tom texted me when he thought I would be home, asking if I felt up to a visit.

"Not tonight," I replied.

"Soon?"

"I don't know."

"You feeling better?"

"My skin is recovering," was my non-answer. The truth was my emotions were still in a bad place.

"I wanted to tell you something."

'This is it,' I thought. 'Tom is going to break up with me.' I clutched my phone waiting for his next text and dreading it at the same time.

The next text didn't come. I guess he was waiting for me to respond to his last text. But I couldn't. All I could do was stare at the phone.

Finally, a new text appeared. It was not the breakup I dreaded, but it was also not good news.

"Your mom called me."

"WHAT?" I typed. How dare she!

"She's worried about you. I am too."

I didn't know how to respond to that. To be honest, I was worried about me too. I was in a funk I couldn't seem to get out of. I was cancer-free. I was finished with the horrible radiation. I should have been dancing on air. Instead, I was barely eating and sleeping more than I usually did.

"Tiffany?" Tom wrote when I didn't write back.

I couldn't bring myself to say anything more. I just sank further into the morass that was my heart. I curled up with the cats in my bed and cried until I couldn't cry any longer. I lay there torturing myself going over everything I'd ever done wrong in my relationship with Tom. I was still convinced he didn't love me anymore. Why would he? I was damaged. I was no fun. I was no longer worthy of being loved.

Suddenly, I realized I was really thirsty. I figured I was dehydrated from crying. So I went downstairs to get myself one of my sports drinks with electrolytes to replenish myself.

I heard the front door unlock. I panicked. Someone was breaking into my house! On top of everything else! I went for the butcher knife in the knife block on my kitchen counter. Not being much of a cook, I wasn't even sure why I had such a lethal weapon. I think my mother had given me the knife set one year when she decided I needed a fully functioning kitchen even though I didn't cook. I wasn't sure I'd ever used this knife, though others from the set had proved useful for cheese and such.

My phone was upstairs, I realized. I had a landline, still, thank goodness. But the kitchen phone would make me too vulnerable. And I couldn't get to the stairs to get to any of the other phones in the house.

My heart was racing. How did this person get in the front door!?

"Tiffany?" a voice called.

It was Tom.

"What are you doing here?" I asked.

"That's a really big knife," came the reply.

"I thought you were an intruder. I almost stabbed you!"

With that, I collapsed to the ground.

Tom came over quickly to where I was on the kitchen floor. He carefully took the knife from me and put it on the island. Then he pulled me into his arms.

'Oh, how I missed those arms!' I thought. The old 3 Doors Down song, *Your Arms Feel Like Home*, came into my head. Tom's arms were my home.

I cried for a while. Tom got me the drink, and I drank the whole bottle in one long pull. He got me another one from the fridge.

"What are you doing here?" I asked, once I was settled again. The profound sadness was still there, though a little more remote than it had been a half hour earlier.

"I was worried about you."

I didn't respond. I just kept looking at him.

"I know you needed some space to deal with the radiation. I didn't want to bother you. I know you couldn't stand to be touched. So, I left you alone. But these past few days, really the past week, you just haven't been yourself. Your mom noticed it too. That's why she called me. She thought you might become depressed. Did you?"

"I don't know. I don't know if that's what you call this. I just couldn't deal with anything else."

"Or anyone else?"

"I guess. I thought you didn't want to be here."

"Tiffany…"

I just started to weep again. "I'm sorry. I know how you hate crying."

"Tiffany, I love you!"

I cried harder.

"I love you. I love you. I love you," Tom repeated.

"How could you? I'm horrible. I'm so mean to you."

"No, you are not!"

"I am. I'm always telling you what to do."

"Well, sometimes I need you to tell me what to do," Tom teased.

"I cry all the time. You hate crying."

"I've gotten over that."

"You have?"

"You don't weaponize your tears. You cry when you are genuinely in pain. I know that now."

"You do?"

"I do. Now, what else do you do to me that's so awful."

"I'm forcing you to marry me. You don't want to get married!"

"Tiffany, do you really believe that?"

"Isn't it true?"

"Do you think I would marry you if I didn't want to? If I didn't love you?"

I thought about it for a minute. In the cold rationality of my kitchen, I believed him. I just wasn't sure I could hold to that belief. "Why do you love me?" I asked because I really needed to hear his answer.

Tom smiled. "Because you are the strongest woman I know. Because you laugh at my lame jokes. Because you care so much about everything. Because you love me. Because you let me be me."

I smiled, though the tears were right there too. "You really love me? You're not here to break up with me?"

"I love you. I'm going to marry you. As soon as you're ready."

"Really?"

"Really. I love you, you silly woman."

And Tom kissed me. Through the tears that were streaming down my face again. And he held me on the floor for a while longer.

Finally, I said, "This floor isn't really comfortable."

Tom laughed. "You just noticed?"

I smiled. "Will you stay with me even though it's a school night?"

"You couldn't talk me out of it."

I leaned into Tom's strong body as we made our way upstairs. He tucked me into bed. Then he went to the bathroom and used the toothbrush he'd left here. Then, he came to bed. He had to displace the cats, who complained bitterly for a minute before jumping back on the bed and settling in their usual spots. Tom reached over and pulled me into his arms. I resisted for a minute, feeling the tears starting again.

"No, you don't," he said sternly. "You need me."

And I realized that I did. And I started to believe that maybe he still loved me. At least a little.

❦ ❦ ❦ ❦ ❦

I didn't recover from my depression for another month. Tom was with me every step of the way. I think he realized how close he'd come to losing me to it.

The recovery process made us stronger. We found the joy of being together again, the joy that had been pushed aside by the worry of cancer. We learned to talk again, about things other than my health. We found peace in each other's arms. We built a new foundation that was stronger than the original one.

And I knew in the depths of my being that Tom was mine and I was his. And I found my strength.

"But I don't think any arranger should ever write a drum part for a drummer because if a drummer can't create his own interpretation of the chart and he plays everything that's written, he becomes mechanical; he has no freedom." -- Buddy Rich

...Never Did Run Smooth (2003-2004, 2005-2006, 2005-2015)

Love isn't easy. Under the best of circumstances, it can be tricky to navigate through to a happy place. When the circumstances are less than ideal, love is tested.

CR ℰℂℝ ℰℂℝ ℰℂ

Peter and Tom had been roommates in college, two young, attractive men making their way in the Chicago area. Both had been studying computer sciences, though Peter, like Jane, had gravitated toward the creative side. Where Tom programmed algorithms and looked for patterns in words and language, Peter made patterns and images, for Peter designed computer games. Where Tom was dark with light blue eyes, Peter was a blond with deep caramel-colored eyes. Both grew beards every winter to protect against the harsh climate. They had grown up together and become best friends.

Peter had found a way to combine his art and love of all things technical in high school. He had loved to draw since he was a child, creating comic books, now called graphic novels, with his invented superhero. In 1998, when Silicon Graphics released Maya, and subsequently won Academy Awards for graphics in film, Peter found his calling. Once he learned how to use these sophisticated programs, of course.

The beauty of the relationship between Tom and Peter was that Tom grounded Peter's creativity by asking reality-based questions, while Peter pushed Tom to dream bigger. Listening to the two of them was a master class in friendship.

Peter had moved to Boston after college. He had met Jane in Cambridge, where she was a free-wheeling artist working in a local theater doing set design. Peter's job was to create lifelike graphics for computer games, and he got inspiration from going to see plays and musicals. There was no lack of such inspiration in Cambridge, with students associated with Harvard and MIT putting on productions as well as independent theater, not to mention numerous venues in nearby Boston. Being impressed with the set of one of the more avant garde productions, Peter went backstage to find the artist. And that's when he met Jane.

Jane looked every inch the artist. She had wild, dark, curly hair, that hung to her waist when it wasn't tied up to make painting easier. Her blue eyes sparkled with challenge. She moved with exuberance, with grace, like a dancer, which she was along with a painter and poet.

She had finished college with a degree in the creative arts from Emerson College, across the river from where she now lived in Cambridge. She worked for whichever theater needed her and had at least some money to pay for her art. Sometimes, she worked for free, too, if the art director tugged at her creative juices or the show was irresistible. She didn't have much, but she didn't need much. She had her art; it was all she ever wanted.

For them, it was love at first sight. Or at least it was attraction at first sight. They went for coffee at midnight, which fortunately was not hard to find. They talked for the next several hours, jazzed not by the coffee but by meeting someone whose thoughts mirrored their own. From that day, they were inseparable.

They moved in together three months later. Tom was happy for his friend, though if he hadn't been distracted by his mother's illness, he might have warned Peter against committing so quickly. But Peter was as impulsive as Tom was cautious. And Jane was, if anything, more so. If friends and family had said they were crazy, Jane would have taken that as a sign that she was doing it right. Nothing conventional for Jane. She wanted to live her life without rules.

In that way, Peter was a mainstay for Jane. He was creative, but responsible. He never told her to get a full-time job; he was fine with her working in the theater and making a little money here and there. But she watched Peter getting paid substantially for his creative skills. And she wanted in.

Where Peter excelled in animation, Jane's strengths were in two-dimensional design. With a gift for conveying ideas through images.

They lived and loved in Cambridge, with their artistic lives, keeping their toes in the theater world with an occasional set design. His current work project was based on a new movie franchise based on a series of wildly successful books. He wasn't allowed to talk about it, even to Jane. She understood that, though, because she was working on a marketing campaign that was super-secret as well. Both of them were thriving in their careers, able to mesh art and commerce.

Life for Jane and Peter seemed ideal. For three years.

Then, came the unimaginable loss.

They were thrilled when Jane became pregnant, even as they wondered how they would blend their artistic world with the practicality of a child.

And then Jane miscarried. There was blood and pain and incredible sadness.

Peter wanted to talk to his best friend. But Tom was dealing with enough already. Peter didn't want to burden his friend with more troubles. So, he didn't share the grief he was feeling.

Jane's whole world was Peter. She had friends, of course. But no one she trusted with this deepest of secrets.

She and Peter found some solace in their art. And each other. Their projects had both been well accepted. Peter was going to get to work on the series' next iterations and offshoots. Jane got a promotion to lead designer.

Six months later, they got good news. Jane was again pregnant. Surely, this time it would be different. They counted the days. Jane took extreme caution with her health.

But the gods were not kind. They miscarried again.

This time, Jane ended up in the hospital when the bleeding wouldn't stop. Peter worried he might lose her. He couldn't imagine his life without this woman. He would do anything to save her.

The doctors were able to stop the bleeding, but at the expense of Jane's fertility.

Afterward, Jane didn't want to talk about it. She refused to discuss anything but art with Peter. She made him bring her sketchpads, and she created drawing after drawing of the children they would never have. It broke Peter's heart.

Finally, not knowing where else to turn, Peter called Tom.

"Tom," Peter started.

"Peter! I'm so happy to hear your voice. It seems like it's been a while."

"Tom…" Peter started again. He really didn't know what to say. The tears were rolling down his cheeks.

Though Tom couldn't see them, he sensed Peter's pain. Tom knew all too well the signs of sorrow. "Is Jane okay?" Tom asked.

"No. Oh, Tom!" Peter wailed.

"What do you need?" Tom asked. "I can be there tomorrow."

"No, thank you. You have your own problems."

"I do. But you're my best friend. If you need me, I'm there. Can you tell me what's going on?"

"Jane is shutting me out."

"Why? What? That doesn't sound like Jane," Tom sputtered. Jane was the most open person Tom knew, so open she sometimes drove Tom a little mad.

"I haven't told you what's been happening here. I didn't want to add to your burden."

"Peter, what happened?" Tom asked quietly.

"We lost a baby. Twice."

"Oh, Peter! Oh, man. I'm so sorry. When did this happen? Twice?"

"Yeah. The first one about seven months ago, and the second one two days ago."

"Oh, man. Oh, man. What can I do? Are you okay? How's Jane?"

"The second one was bad. Worse than the first miscarriage. Jane had to have surgery to stop the bleeding. And they had to take out her uterus. She's not going to be able to have any more kids."

Tom was shocked. This was beyond his depth, but Peter was his closest friend. He struggled to find the words. "I'm sorry, buddy. And that's what's causing her to run away?"

"Yeah." Peter's voice was so sad.

"That must be hard. I wish you had called, but I understand why you didn't."

"You have a lot going on," Peter responded.

"It's only a matter of time now," Tom replied.

"I'm sorry, friend. I wish I could help."

"Right there with you, Peter. But I feel like I should be able to help you. Should I talk to Jane? I mean, I'm more your friend than hers. But we are friends."

"I don't know. Maybe I shouldn't have said anything."

"No, of course you should have told me. There's nothing to be ashamed of!"

"Jane won't talk about it."

"I can imagine it would be hard. If I was a woman, I'm sure I'd have more insights. Can I tell Meghan? She might be able to help."

"That's a good idea. Maybe Meghan can tell me what to say. What to do. I just want Jane back. I want her to be herself again. I want to tell her I love her. I want her to know that I love her no matter what."

"Have you told her that?" Tom asked.

"Well, she knows."

"I'm sure she does. But it wouldn't hurt to say the words aloud."

"I suppose so. Will you tell me what Meghan says?"

"I'll talk to her right now."

"Thanks, buddy."

"Peter?"

"Yeah?"

"I love you."

"Love you, too. Sorry about your mom."

"Thanks. Sorry about the babies."

"Thanks."

When Tom told Meghan what was going on, she agreed that Peter being more open about his feelings with Jane was a good strategy. "And let her draw all she wants, I think. Let her process her pain in whatever way makes sense to her. Has Tom talked to the hospital staff? I'm sure there are support groups."

"I'm sure there are. But Jane doesn't seem like the support group type," Tom replied.

"Maybe not. But you never know. I think this is like any grief. It's different for each person. I mean, look at Dad. Would you have predicted his reaction to Mom's dying?"

"Yes and no. Mom is his life. But I get what you're saying."

So, Tom called Peter and told him Meghan's advice, to share his feelings, to let Jane experience hers in her own time and her own way, and to see if talking to others would be helpful. Peter was grateful for the counsel. He said Jane hadn't responded directly to his explanation of what he was feeling, but that she seemed better for hearing it. Tom told Peter explicitly to call with regular updates.

"Just because I have my own crap going on, doesn't mean I don't want to be involved in yours."

"Oh yeah?" Peter teased.

"You know what I mean."

"I do. Thanks."

Jane allowed as how it couldn't hurt to go to the support group sessions while she was recovering. There, they met other couples who had recently learned they wouldn't be able to have children. The reasons were varied and many.

Finally, Jane was healthy enough to be discharged. She still refused to talk about children outside therapy, but Peter was just pleased that the nonstop drawing had subsided. He thought that was a positive sign. He continued sharing his feelings, and he found it was therapeutic for him. He'd been so focused on Jane and Jane's pain that he hadn't really processed his own. Telling Jane what he was feeling, and talking to the others in group, gave him a safe place to talk. He started to heal.

"Let's move," Jane said about a week after they got settled back into the apartment.

"Move?" Peter was confused. "To another apartment?"

"No, another city."

"Where?"

"I don't know. Anywhere that's not here."

Peter worried that Jane was trying to run away again. She didn't run away from him anymore. And she seemed to be happier, though she still had her bad times. But moving?

"If it would make you happy," Peter said, not knowing what else to say.

"I think it would be good. For both of us. We've done all we can do here."

'Have we?' Peter wondered. Aloud, he said, "I guess I could talk to my job. They have offices all over the country."

"Exactly. And I can do my job from anywhere."

"I just want to be sure we are moving toward something, not away from the past," Peter offered.

"Does it have to be one or the other?" Jane asked. "I'm sad. I think it's going to be a while before I'm happy, though I can see the end of it coming. But we are not the same people who moved into this apartment. Not anymore."

"I suppose we aren't. We've changed and been changed."

"Right. So, let's take our new selves and build a new life. Somewhere else."

In some ways, that sounded like his old Jane, Peter thought.

Peter's phone rang. It was Tom. Peter had a feeling he knew why his friend was calling. "Hi, Tom," he said.

"Hi, Peter. I just wanted to let you know Mom is finally at peace."

"I'm sorry for your loss, but happy she's out of pain."

"Me, too. How's things in Cambridge?"

"We're thinking about leaving Cambridge, actually."

"Oh yeah. Where to?" Tom asked.

"Maybe DC?"

"I'd love to have you here," Tom said.

Peter looked at Jane for confirmation. She was smiling. She nodded. DC sounded like a great plan. They, at least, would have Tom there. And Meghan, who they had met several times through the years. It was the best plan they had.

"Count on it. When's the funeral?" Peter asked.

"No funeral. Mom didn't want one."

"Memorial service?"

"No. Nothing. She just wanted us to remember her in our own ways."

"Okay. How's your dad?"

"Not good. But we'll get through this. Together."

"I'll be in touch as we make plans to get there. But in the meantime, I love you, Tom."

"Thanks, Peter. Love you, too. And Jane."

Peter's job had been fine with his move. It really didn't matter much where he lived, as far as they were concerned.

Jane quit her job, knowing she would find another when they got settled in DC. With Peter's income, she didn't need to rush to find a job, so she was able to be picky. She found this great job in a marketing firm, where she got to use her skills to help companies find just the right messaging.

She also found a therapist. Not because she felt broken, but because she needed to continue her recovery. To learn to accept her new reality.

Six months after they moved, Peter asked Jane to marry him. He hadn't wanted to do it while they were recovering from their pain. He didn't want Jane to think of marriage as a consolation prize. But he loved Jane, and he wanted to be sure she knew that. Every day of their lives.

Jane accepted Peter's ring. She loved him, too. But she had one more thing she needed to be sure about.

"Peter?" she said after he asked her to marry him and before she accepted.

"Yes, love," Peter responded.

"I think I don't want to have children. Not just because we can't have our own. But because I don't think I can be a mom without thinking about the ones we lost. Are you okay with that?"

"Of course!"

"Peter, think for a minute. Don't just tell me you're okay without thinking."

Peter looked at Jane, looked deep into her eyes, which were brimming with unshed tears. "Jane," he said, "you are my life. My love. My everything. I want you. Kids or no kids."

"So, you would like to have kids?" Jane asked. Her therapist had told her this was something they had to discuss. They had to be in sync on this, or it would eat away at their relationship.

Peter took Jane's hands in his. "I had never really thought about having kids or being a father. Then you were pregnant, and I was happy with the idea of kids. Because they would be with you. And then we lost them. And I almost lost you. And I realized that I could live without children. But I couldn't live without you."

Silent tears were streaming down Jane's face. She nodded.

"You're okay with no kids then?" she asked quietly.

"I'm okay with no kids. All I need is you," Tom responded equally quietly.

"Then let's get married!" Jane cried out. She threw her arms around Peter and gave him a big kiss. She was learning to be the woman she had been, with big emotions and a strong sense of self.

"Yes, let's!"

Peter and Jane had had a small wedding at the Women's National Club. In keeping with Jane's sense of the avant garde, she hadn't worn a traditional gown, but a fabulous light blue dress that made her eyes pop. Tom had worn a suit, rather than a tux. Tom had been there, of course, as Peter's best man. But he hadn't been an attendant, hadn't stood next to Peter as Peter said his vows. Instead, it had been just Jane and Peter in front of the justice of the peace.

And, so, they were married. Happily and creatively.

CR ℰℛCR ℰℛCR ℰℛ

It would tough to find a couple more different than Meghan and George. She's boisterous. He's quiet. She's quick-tempered and sarcastic. He's calm and laughing most of the time.

From outside their relationship, people often wondered how it works. But I can tell you, as the "new kid on the block", theirs is one of the strongest relationships I've ever seen. They move through life in sync, like yin and yang, or black and white, each the other half of a whole.

They met when they worked companies in the same building. George was just finishing law school and was interning at the law firm where he hoped to get an offer once he passed the bar. Meghan worked for a brokerage firm on the same floor. They usually arrived at work at the same time and rode the elevator up to their respective offices. After a few weeks of seeing each other often, Meghan introduced herself, well, because, that's Meghan.

"Hi! Seen you around. I'm Meghan," she started, putting out her hand.

He looked at the hand in front on his body and then up to the face with a big smile. "George. Yeah, we seem to be on the same schedule." He looked down again.

But that wasn't enough to discourage Meghan. George was a reasonably good-looking guy about her age, with dark hair and dark eyes and what looked like a very nice body under his suit. She knew he worked at the law firm, so she assumed he was a lawyer, though he was on the younger side for that. Maybe he was super-smart? She wasn't sure. "I work at the brokerage," she went on. "You're at the law firm. I applied there, but they didn't need anyone for HR at the time. Fortunately, the brokerage firm did."

George didn't respond. That didn't discourage Meghan. She could keep up a conversation all by herself if need be.

"Do you like being a lawyer?"

"Not a lawyer yet? Still in law school," George replied in short sentences. This woman seemed nice enough, but he wasn't really looking for a friendship or whatever she might be looking for. He still had a lot of work to do. Relationships weren't on his list right now. She was pretty, he had to admit, with dark reddish hair and blue eyes. He was pretty sure that wasn't her natural hair color, though, as he was pretty sure that shade of red wasn't found in nature. He thought it was interesting that someone in human resources would be a little alternative. It rarely happened with lawyers. Most of them wore lawyer-y clothing and had lawyer-y haircuts.

"Oh, that's cool. I know it takes a lot of energy to do that. Good luck!"

And she left him in peace for the next five floors of elevator ride.

He was intrigued.

As the elevator approach the tenth floor, their floor, he said, "It was nice talking to you."

Her smile could have powered the whole building, he thought.

"Nice to meet you, too, George. See you again tomorrow morning."

And that was the beginning.

From that day onward, George found himself milling around the elevator lobby, looking at whatever decorations were there and ostensibly looking at the list of other offices in the same building, until he saw Meghan coming down the street. Then, he would quickly trot to the elevators and push the up button. He knew from experience, it took a few minutes before there would be a ding that the elevator had arrived. Most mornings, he timed it just about perfectly for Meghan to dash into the car just before the door closed. He thought he was playing it cool. He didn't show he was waiting for her. And yet he was.

But Meghan knew. She saw him scurry to the elevator plaza from where he was oh-so-casually looking out the windows. She had changed her walk to the building to be sure to walk past those particular windows. She never acknowledged that he was there before her.

If there were others in the elevator, Meghan and George nodded to each other good morning, without conversation. If it was just the two of them, they would exchange pleasantries. He would ask her about her evening or weekend if it was a Monday. She would ask about school. In this way, they learned that each other was not attached. No dates were mentioned. No live-ins. No spouses.

This went on for a few weeks. Meghan was fine to let George play this game. She was just thrilled he wanted to. And she had sensed, because she was a people person, that he was shy. This was his way of courting her, without actually asking her out.

Then a week went by without George. Meghan was trying to figure out how she could stop in the law firm and inquire about him to the receptionist. She missed him.

But she only knew his first name. And didn't want to seem stupid as there might very well be more than one George at the firm. If the receptionist asked for a last name, what was she going to say? 'I don't know. I only know he's in law school'? Meghan didn't want to be embarrassed. So, she just hoped that George would show up again. Soon.

Another week passed; still no George. Meghan stopped walking her changed path and went back to the way she had entered the building before she met George. She was sad at the idea that he was gone for good. But she was resigning herself to the idea.

After three weeks, she moved on mentally. Maybe George's internship was up. It was almost summer, and assuming his law school operated on the same semesters as most universities and colleges, he ought to be finishing up. That made sense. The internship ended when he graduated. Now, he was probably studying madly for the bar exam. She wished she knew George's name so she could send him a pizza and wish him well. But alas.

One Monday morning, Meghan dashed into the elevator just as the doors were closing. The event made her smile in memory of her "relationship" with George. She was standing at the front of the elevator, which was more crowded than usual. Monday morning, she supposed.

As the elevator moved up the floors, it emptied out, one or two people at a time. Her offices on the tenth floor were two from the top, so most of the time, there weren't many people who worked on the eleventh and twelfth floors.

"Hello," Meghan heard someone say from the back of the car.

She knew that voice. "George!" she yelled before she could stop herself. Fortunately, they were the only two left in the elevator at that point. She blushed.

"Hey there, Meghan. Nice to see you." George blushed too.

And because Meghan is, well, Meghan, she said, "Where have you been? Graduating?"

George smiled. "Yes. And studying. Took the bar last week."

"And?"

"And I don't know. Won't know for several weeks."

"Oh, that sounds like torture."

"It is, of a sort."

"Well, here's our floor," Meghan said, because she wasn't sure what else to say, which was unusual for her.

George smiled at her. He held the door, as he usually did, while she stepped out. He turned right, and she turned left.

"Meghan!" he yelled. And started to head back toward the elevator. She walked back toward him as well.

"Yes?" Her heart was pounding.

"Would you like to have dinner?"

"I'd love to. When?"

"Tonight?"

"It's a school night."

"Yes, of course. Never mind," George said, as he turned to walk away.

"George, I was just teasing. Tonight would be fine. Shall we meet at the elevator and find a place from there? There are lots in the neighborhood, of course."

"That sounds wonderful," George said, with relief. "Say, 6 o'clock?"

"Could we make it 5:30? I get off work at 5." It was 8 am now.

"Sure."

"Unless you have to work later?" Meghan backpedaled.

"No, 5:30 is fine. See you then!" George said with a wave, as he headed back to the law firm's suite.

"George?" Meghan shouted.

"Yes?"

"What's your last name?" Meghan asked, with a laugh.

"Smith. You?"

"McDonnell."

"Well, that's a little more interesting than Smith," George observed, with a smile.

"A little, but not very."

They both entered their respective offices.

Meghan ducked into the floor's ladies room at 5 pm that evening and redid her makeup. She fluffed her hair and considered putting it up so it would be a little more conservative. George was a lawyer. Maybe he liked women who looked more traditional. Meghan was not that woman. And she liked this guy. Or so she thought.

'No,' she told herself, 'he likes you for who you are, or he doesn't. You shouldn't pretend to be anyone other than yourself.'

Of course, Meghan had told herself that before. But she wasn't entirely convinced it was really a good strategy as she didn't have much luck with dating. A few guys in college. But nothing much recently. Her elevator flirtation with George had been the highlight of her life for the past few years.

She paced in the bathroom for a bit, willing herself not to put too much pressure on a first date. And to waste some more time. She didn't want to be waiting for George by the elevator. She thought she should play it cool, as she had all those mornings getting to the door just in time.

'Screw it!' she thought, and she left the bathroom and headed to the elevator, determined to really be who she was. If George couldn't handle it, well, that was too bad for George. She was worth it.

She was taken aback to find George already at the elevator, waiting for her. "I couldn't wait any longer," he admitted. "I hoped you might be a little early."

It was 5:15. They were both early. "I get off at 5, so I was just primping."

"You look great," George said. "I love your hair." He blushed at his honesty.

Meghan blushed, too. Her hair was her place to play. She loved the vibrant red. It was her signature. And indicative of her personality. It was a good sign that George liked it.

"Not very lawyer-y," she admitted.

"Best part."

The elevator dinged. They rode down together.

"Where to?" Meghan asked. "There's the Mexican place in the next block. I think the sushi place is closed for the evening. Pizza, of course."

"How about the nice Italian place a few blocks east? A little nicer than tacos or pizza."

"Sounds good."

They started to walk down the street, side by side. Then Meghan, being Meghan, took George's arm as they walked over a grate in the sidewalk and her heel started to get stuck.

"All good?" he asked, once they were past the grate.

"Fine," Meghan responded.

"Good," George said. He put his hand over hers. "Very good."

And that was their "meet cute". Over the course of a month or so.

George passed the bar exam and became one of the youngest lawyers in the firm on the tenth floor. Meghan continued to work down the hall.

They met for coffee every morning at the lobby cafeteria. George confessed about his watching for her in the mornings.

"I know," Meghan told him. "I walked that way so you would see me."

"You did?!" George exclaimed.

"I did."

"I thought I was being so cool."

"I thought you were adorable." Meghan was comfortable telling George this now. They'd been dating for a few months.

Six months later, they decided to get married. Everyone, including Tom, thought it was too fast.

"What's the rush?" Tom asked his sister when she told him the good news.

"I love him."

"Yeah. So. He's not going anywhere."

"Do you know that? For certain, sure?"

Tom shook his head. "No, I don't. But he's a good guy, George. He's honest. He's not going to leave you. At least I don't think so."

"I don't either. But I love him. And I'm not losing anyone else that I love if I can help it," Meghan insisted.

"He's not dying," Tom reminded Meghan.

"No, he's not. And I'm not. And I don't care. I love him. He loves me. We're getting married. You can be happy about it, or not."

"Oh, Meghan! I'm thrilled for you. Really."

"Really? Doesn't seem like it." Meghan pouted.

"I am. Really!" Tom shouted.

Meghan smiled. "That's better. Geez. I thought Lauren was going to be the tough sell."

"Sorry about that. I just want the best for you."

"And that's George," Meghan said firmly.

"Yes, dear."

It took months to plan the wedding, however. And by the time the actual day arrived, whatever fears Tom had had about George and Meghan getting married so quickly had evaporated. Their love was inspiring, if sometimes a little too much. But then again, that was Meghan.

And so a year to the day after their first date, Meghan McDonnell married George Smith on a beautiful Saturday afternoon, surrounded by hundreds of friends and family. When they said "I do", the crowd roared. Even Tom. They knew Meghan would love it, though I suspected George wasn't opposed to the show of enthusiasm.

CR ℰℭR ℰℭR ℰ

Phineas had known he was gay since he was quite young. Xan and I figured it out early, too. It wasn't that Phin was effeminate. It was just that he liked boys. When most young boys have their first girlfriend, at age six or seven, Phin didn't. Maybe he wanted to have a boyfriend or maybe he did and just called him friend. Whichever. The reality was Phineas never showed any interest in dating girls. Ever. Not even to pretend.

I think our parents assumed Phin was just a "late bloomer" or some other nonsense. When we were in high school, Mom and Jack tried to set Phin up a couple of times, inviting him to things where there were young ladies to meet. The same thing happened to me with guys, and I didn't mind so much. Mom had terrible taste, but Jack was better. Xan always had a girlfriend, so he wasn't subjected to these fixups.

Needless to say, Phin never followed through on any of these relationships. He loved his family, but he wasn't going to pretend to be anyone other than himself for them.

Junior high school and high school were hard for Phineas. Xan and I tried to protect him, as best we could, but he didn't even want that.

"I am who I am," he said.

He came out to Dad his senior year. He had asked Alexander and I to be there. So, even though the subject was awkward – who wants to discuss sex with a parent? – we went to support Phineas.

Dad took the news surprisingly well for a guy who didn't seem all that evolved on such topics. He asked Phin if he'd ever been in love, to which Phin carefully responded no. Dad said he hoped for Phineas that the time would come when Phin would find love. Real love. I thought that was pretty amazing of Dad to say. Phin cried. I even saw Xan choke up a bit.

Next, Phin told Mom and Jack. He again asked us to be his support system. Xan and I readily agreed, knowing that we would always have each other's backs. Always. We loved our parents, but we weren't oblivious to their flaws. We knew we needed to be the support for each other that Mom and Dad, and even Jack, could never be.

Jack just laughed at the announcement. "I've known for a long time," he said.

"You have?" Mom asked. "Why didn't you ever say anything?"

"You Johnsons have to say things in your own time, in your own way. For example, Tiffany here hates my kids. She'd never be so rude as to say so to my face. But I know they were mean to her, and she's not found it in her heart to forgive them."

I started to deny Jack's words, but stopped. He was right. And since Phin was living his truth this day, I supposed I should too. "I'll get there eventually," I equivocated.

"Maybe. Someday," Jack replied.

"Phin, are you sure?" Mom said, plaintively.

Jack just laughed.

"I'm sure," Phineas said calmly and carefully.

"You're only 18. Maybe you just haven't met the right girl," she tried.

"No, Mom. I am who I am. I always have been."

Mom frowned, but didn't say anything more. Which was amazing all by itself. I rarely got away with so little "advice".

Xan drove us back to his apartment, so we could regroup without our parents. He had just gotten his first place. Phin and I were so proud of him. And jealous too. Jenn was there, of course. She had understood that talking to our parents was a Johnson-only thing. But otherwise, she was pretty much with Xan at all times. We had resented her at first, for horning in on our sibling bond. But then she just became one of us. And I got a sister for the first time. It was fabulous.

As I had, Phineas went away to college. We kept in touch, grateful that communication in 1998 was easier than it had ever been. With cellular phones, the siblings could talk often, though we did have to watch our minutes. Cell phones were convenient, but not cheap. Dad paid for Phin's, while Mom paid for mine. Xan was on his own now, as he was in so many things.

Phineas graduated with honors with a degree in finance. He moved to New York, determined to make his way on Wall Street. He worked at a trading company, tracking stocks for the brokers. He studied for his brokerage license. When he got it, Xan and I drove to NYC from our respective homes to help celebrate. Jennifer came with Alexander, of course. They were a matched set.

Phin tried to love New York. He tried to embrace the cutthroat world of Wall Street. But that's just not who Phin was.

"I'm leaving New York," he told us when we came to help him celebrate.

"Where will you go?" I asked.

"Home" was his response. That meant Virginia.

"It won't be the same," Alexander argued.

"I know. I'm counting on that! Besides, you're there, and Jennifer. And I have a feeling Tiffany will be back after graduate school."

I wasn't sure yet. I loved to write, and I loved to be creative. But my MBA had shown me that I loved business, too. I was hopeful I'd find my way, whether there or in Boston.

"Maybe. I'm not sure, to be honest."

"I just know NYC isn't the place for me," Phin argued.

"I agree, little brother," Xan said. "I just wanted to be sure you knew what you were getting into."

"I know I won't make the same money. But that's okay. It was never about the money for me. I think I might try working for the federal government."

"Really?" I asked.

"Yeah. For the SEC or somewhere else to help make fiscal policy. I like that."

"Hard work," I said.

"Yes. But much more of an impact that making a millionaire into a billionaire."

"I can appreciate that."

"I think it sounds wonderful," Jenn weighed in. "You'll be doing important work, and that's admirable."

"If I can get the job," Phin said.

"Is it hard? To get that kind of job, I mean," Xan asked.

"My boss knows someone. I have an interview in a week. We will see."

"An interview is a good first step."

"Yeah. I've already packed, and there are a hundred people waiting for my apartment already. That shouldn't be a problem."

"We have a couch you can sleep on for a week or two," Jennifer offered. I knew she was our kind of people.

"Thanks. I may take you up on that. I have some friends still in the area, but it's good to have a backup plan."

"Always."

One of our other childhood carryovers. Mom and Dad didn't always see eye to eye in child rearing, and sometimes we would think we were going to stay with Dad for the weekend, until Mom said no. Or Jack came to pick us up after we'd only been at Dad's place an hour or two. We learned to be resilient. We learned to take care of each other. And we learned to have a backup plan. When you grow up in chaos, you have to have a plan.

So, Phin moved back to Virginia. He got that job at the SEC. He stayed with friends for a couple of weeks until he could find a more permanent arrangement. He and a few of his friends, all of them gay men, moved into a townhouse together. One of the friends' parents had bought the place as an investment, so the rent was a little cheaper than typical. But not much, and the parents expected the guys to keep the place in good shape.

"Ironically, they are convinced because we are all gay, we will be neater," Phineas explained to me when he called to give me his new address and a landline phone number.

"Have they seen your room?" I teased. Phin might be gay, but he was a slob.

"Never!"

"Oh dear."

We laughed. "We will keep the place neat, though. Ryan is a neat freak, stereotypical gay man. We promised him we'd help with keeping the house clean."

"Good for you."

"What are your plans?" Phin asked.

I graduated soon. I thought about staying in Boston. But I knew I wouldn't. Too much of my heart was in Virginia now. "I guess I'll be next to move back," I admitted.

"Woo-hoo!" Phineas responded.

"I need a job."

"Yeah. I'll take a look at *The Post*."

"Thanks. I've been applying to jobs in Maryland, Virginia, and DC. Even to the feds. No luck so far."

"We will figure it out," Phin offered.

I laughed. "What's my backup plan."

"We have an attic," Phin teased.

As it turned out, I lived there for a few weeks.

Phin and his roommates were sweethearts. I had met most of them before, but I didn't know them well. I was just glad Phineas had found his tribe. People with whom he could truly be "who he was". Things were getting better in society writ large for homosexuals. But it was still not an easy path. And I wanted only the best for my baby brother.

Joseph arrived in our lives through one of these roommates. Ramon was his name. He was from Honduras. He had fled when he figured out he liked men. It wasn't safe to stay in his country.

Ramon had a thick accent, but spoke beautiful English. He worked as a nurse because his medical degree wasn't accepted in the U.S. He was working on that. But in the meantime, he helped people by being a nurse.

Joseph Rodriguez was from Argentina. His accent was lighter than that of Ramon, but it was still there. He and his family had emigrated when Joseph was in high school. He'd gone to college in the United States, and had become a citizen once he finished medical school. Ramon told all this before we even met the man. Ramon had a crush on Joseph, who was a doctor. Ramon had been talking to Joseph about how to get his degree transferred. Joseph had told Ramon he needed to take his boards to become licensed in Virginia. Ramon wasn't sure he wanted to study all that again. "Maybe being a nurse isn't so bad."

"Didn't you have to pass a bunch of licensing exams to be a nurse?" I asked, as I was pretty sure he did.

"Yeah. But I was younger then."

"Ramon, that was two years ago!" Phineas argued.

"Right. I was younger."

Anyway, Ramon was infatuated with this Argentinian doctor he'd met at the hospital. "We should have a party," he suggested.

"I'm not sure Ryan's parents would be happy about that," the third roommate, Dave, argued. "We are supposed to be nice to the house."

Ryan wasn't there, but I was pretty sure he'd agree.

"Just a small party. 20 people at most," Ramon said.

"Ramon, that means you could only invite two or three people," Phin pointed out. Ramon knew everyone. He was so much the opposite of Phin and me.

Ramon frowned. "Only two or three?"

Dave nodded. "If we each invite two or three people, that's 20 already."

Ramon frowned. "Well, okay. For Joseph."

The plan was to have the party in two weeks. Xan and Jenn were my guests. Phineas invited a couple of work friends. Dave, who was a programmer, also invited some work friends. Ryan, who had had to be talked into the party at all, had invited some friends from college who lived in the area. His guest list included the only other females besides Jennifer and me. Ramon kept changing his mind about his two other guests. We had had to remind him often that he could only invite two more people besides Joseph. Ramon insisted he was onboard with the plan. But we heard more than two names being bandied about. I had a bad feeling.

It was Saturday night, the night of the party. This was to be a quiet, elegant affair. We had cleaned the house from top to bottom. We had wine and appetizers for our guests. We had borrowed chairs from Xan and Mom, so we had enough places for 20 people to sit, spread between the living room, dining room, and downstairs rec room.

Xan and Jenn arrived early, of course. It's a Johnson trait. They helped with the last-minute touches. Phin was surprisingly nervous.

"Introvert?" I asked in our shorthand for our shared aversion to being with lots of people.

"It's more than that. I feel like something is going to happen."

"Well, we are all afraid Ramon has invited the world."

"No, this is something else."

Phineas was not the type to have feelings or see omens. I wasn't sure what to make of his comment.

Ramon came downstairs dressed in a beautiful shirt and very tight pants. He actually looked quite beautiful. It wasn't my style. But I appreciated that his butt looked really good in those pants, an important thing in gay man world. Or so was the stereotype.

The doorbell rang, startling us all. Phin being closest to the door, opened it.

On the other side of the door was perhaps the most beautiful man I've ever seen. I knew in an instant, this must be Joseph. It helped explain Ramon's obsession. This man was gorgeous! For once, I was glad I wasn't in the running.

Phineas politely but coldly invited Joseph in. I looked at Xan, who shrugged. This was not normal behavior for Phin.

Fortunately, more people arrived just then. Ramon led Joseph to the kitchen for a drink, chattering all the way. I had to laugh at his attempts to woo his quarry. Phin was still at the door, letting people in when I noticed Joseph was barely paying any attention to Ramon. He was looking back at Phineas. Interesting.

As expected, Ramon had invited many more than his two or three guests. But fortunately, he'd kept the list to seven. So, the house seemed reasonably safe. Also fortunately, they had all brought food and wine. Otherwise, we might have been in danger of running out.

The evening went well, for the most part. One of the people Ramon had invited was a young lady who was also a nurse. She decided that Xan was going to be her next conquest. Despite his complete lack of interest and Jennifer's presence. This young lady made a point of cornering Alexander in the kitchen when he went to refresh his and Jenn's drinks. I could hear him raise his voice, something he very rarely did. I was the one who was more likely to lose my temper. But when faced with someone who refused to take no for an answer, Xan had no choice.

"Leave me alone!" he yelled.

The noise in the living and dining room silenced.

Apparently, the young lady either got the message or was mortified, possibly both. She ran out the door without even remembering to take her coat.

Ramon said, "I'll bring her coat to work. It's fine."

Xan was so upset, he made his apologies to Phin and the others, and he and Jennifer went home.

I was standing by Phineas after the drama subsided and conversation started up again. Joseph walked up. He had eyes for no one but Phin. I took my cue to leave, but Phineas grabbed my hand. So I stayed. We had each other's backs. If Phin needed me, I wasn't going anywhere. Joseph looked at me inquiringly, but I didn't move.

"I'm sorry Marian caused such a fuss," Joseph said, just starting a conversation.

"She seems a little high strung," Phineas observed.

"She is young," Joseph offered. "And it was a long day."

"You worked today?" I interjected. I was standing there, after all, even if Joseph was barely acknowledging my presence.

He looked at me, and I was mesmerized for a moment by the depth of his brown eyes. He conveyed wisdom somehow. It was fascinating. "We had a 12-hour shift that ended at 6," he explained. "Like many in the ER, it was not an easy one."

"Oh, I didn't realize you worked in the ER," Phin blurted out.

Joseph nodded. "Yes. Ramon works on the post-surgery ward. But we have met often in the cafeteria. He is a nice man, though I'm afraid his interest in me is more than platonic."

I laughed. "You noticed that, huh?"

He turned those eyes on me again. "I did. And while I share his appreciation for our sex, I do not find him of interest."

"He's going to be very sad to hear that," Phin said, with the first hint of laughter I'd heard from him since we started talking to Joseph.

"He has been told this before. I will tell him again, though I'm not sure he will hear me any better this time than he has before."

"He can be stubborn," Phin replied.

This was my charming brother. His death grip on my hand also let go. I sensed it was my turn to leave.

"It was nice to talk to you, Joseph. Another time you'll have to tell me all about working in the ER."

"I'm afraid it's not like in TV."

I laughed. "I'm sure it's not. But I'm also sure it's fascinating."

"It has its moments." Joseph smiled at me. I felt my knees buckle a little under the weight of all that beauty. I silently wished Phineas good luck resisting that man. And then I decided I was on Joseph's side. As long as he was good to my brother, why shouldn't Phin have the best-looking guy in the room?

I kept tabs on Phin and Joseph as the night progressed. They talked to other people, but it was rarely very long before they would gravitate back together. I knew Joseph was interested in Phineas, of course. But I saw Phin softening toward Joseph.

At the end of the night, Joseph was one of the last to leave. He'd crushed Ramon's hopes once again, as Ramon had told me as he poured himself another glass of Pinot noir.

"I think he quite likes your brother," Ramon said. His words were a little slurred. I was glad the party was winding down.

"I agree. Are you okay with that?" I didn't want there to be any animosity between the roommates.

"If I can't have him, at least Phin can. My god. Isn't he beautiful?"

There was no question about whom Ramon was speaking. "Yes, he is. Quite the most beautiful man I've ever seen."

"The sad part is he's just as beautiful on the inside as out."

"Sad part?"

"Yes. I mean, if he were ugly in the inside, it would be so much easier to resist him, don't you think?"

I laughed. "Yes, of course."

"But he's not. He's a wonderful doctor. So patient with all the craziness in the ER. I've come down to watch him sometimes. He didn't know it, of course."

I had a feeling Joseph knew every time Ramon just happened by. "Of course."

"The patients love him. The nurses love him. Even the administration loves him."

That was good to know. My brother was in good hands, it appeared.

"Ah. He's leaving. I should say good night," Ramon said, as he headed to the door.

I watched the drama as Ramon tried to give Joseph a quick kiss. Joseph turned his head so that kiss landed on his cheek, rather than his mouth as Ramon had intended. Ramon turned with a laugh, and caught my eye from where I was standing in the kitchen. He winked at me and shrugged.

We both noted that Joseph was lingering over saying goodbye to Phineas. Ramon looked at me with regret but a smile at Phin's good luck. Then, he went upstairs.

I started to turn back into the kitchen when I saw Phin kiss Joseph. I had actually never seen my brother kiss a man before. For that matter, I had never seen two men kissing. It wasn't anything shocking, and I was thrilled for Phin.

Joseph became a fixture in the house after that. I moved out a few weeks later, but Ramon kept me posted on the situation. Phin did, too, but Ramon's perspective was more fun.

I knew it wasn't easy dating, given Joseph's schedule. Fortunately, Phin worked more normal hours, with only the occasional late night. Still, they figured it out. Just as Jennifer had become the sister I never had, Joseph became another brother. Sort of.

Phineas couldn't quite believe his dumb luck.

"My first real relationship, and it's him?" he'd said to me more than once.

"You deserve the best, Phin," I replied.

"He is that. Oh, Tiffany. How did I get so lucky?"

I just smiled. Phineas was funny in love.

Still, all was not perfect.

"We want to get married and have a family, too," Phineas complained to me months later. Jenn and Xan had just announced their engagement. "Why can't we do those things? We're just who we are. We love each other. We just want to be a family. Like everyone else."

"I know. Someday, maybe. You could have a commitment ceremony." In 2005, that was the best we could do. Marriage wasn't legal for gay couples. Adoption was possible, but very hard. Joseph and Phin applied often. And they had finally been successful in the wake of Hurricane Sandy. There had been so many children left without parents, that the agencies were willing to let Phineas and Joseph adopt. And little Eliza came into our lives. Those two men loved that little girl so much. Xan and Jenn had their kids, too, so she had cousins. And doting grandparents. They even took her to Argentina when she was a year old to meet her Argentinian side of the family. Phin and Joseph felt like a family, no different than Xan and Jennifer. It sucked that they couldn't be married.

Then, in 2015, a miracle. The Supreme Court ruled that gay marriage couldn't be banned, effectively making it legal. In all 50 states.

You never saw two people plan a wedding faster. And a big wedding, too. Joseph's Latino background came out. He wanted a big, big wedding. The wedding to end all weddings. The wedding he didn't think he'd ever have.

Phineas was not so sure. It was a lot. His introversion came out. He told Joseph to make things smaller. It was one of the few times I'd ever seen them fight. Phin just couldn't cope with all that fanfare, the spectacle where he'd be front and center. He just couldn't.

Joseph, loving my brother, took his feelings into account. He scaled back the festivities, much to the chagrin of my mother, who had been with Joseph whole hog on making things as big and as extravagant as possible. She'd missed out on that with Xan's wedding to Jennifer, as Jenn had planned it with her own mother and let our mother help only because she knew she had to. Somehow, she had managed to keep Mom under control. I still don't know how.

I knew I was in trouble, if I ever decided to get married. Tom and I been dating for a while. But we weren't at that point. Not yet. Still, Tom was my date for the Phin and Joseph wedding of the year.

It was wonderful, I have to say. Tasteful, and yet over the top. I wasn't sure how Joseph managed that. But then again, as Ramon had pointed out all those years ago, the man was pretty much perfect.

But then again, so was Phin.

Eliza was a proud maid of honor. Peyton and Samantha also participated in the wedding. A few of Joseph's nieces and nephews rounded out the wedding party. It was adorable.

I thought Phineas' face might split in two from smiling so much.

"Happy?" I asked him as we danced.

"Delirious!"

"That's wonderful. I'm happy for you."

"Your turn next?"

"We will see."

"Tom is good people."

"That he is."

The seed was planted.

FINDING A GOOD FIT, PART TWO (2019)

When I finally felt well enough to deal with strangers coming to see my house, I called Sarah again.

"We're ready now."

"You healthy?" she asked. She wasn't quite a friend. But she was a caring person, and I knew her question came from that place, not from any nosiness.

"All better. The doctor said they got it all, and the radiation made sure of that."

"Radiation sucks."

I remembered then that Sarah had had her own bout of breast cancer. "Yes, it does."

"Energy draining."

"Very much so. But it's been a month since my last treatment, and I feel very much more myself."

"Ready to put the house on the market, then?"

"Yes. And to start looking for new ones too."

"Great! What about Tom's house?"

"Tom will give you a call about his house."

"So, he is interested in selling?"

"His decision. I gave him your number, though, at his request. So, my guess is yes. But it's completely up to him."

"That's great! When do you want to start looking?"

"This weekend too soon?"

"Not at all. I'll do some research and send you some listings to review."

"We have some we already scoped out, too. I'll forward them along."

"Okay. Sounds good. What time on Saturday?"

"Open houses or other arrangements?"

"Do the listings you are interested have open houses?"

"Most of them do, I think."

"Okay. So, we can go out Saturday and look. And then Sunday, I'll do an open house at your place. 1-4 pm okay?"

"Perfect. I'll go to Tom's for the open house."

"Or you can go to other open houses, anything we don't see on Saturday."

"We'll think about it. We might just need to relax and recharge, though."

"Whatever you think is best."

"Thanks. Talk to you soon."

CR ℰꙞCR ℰꙞCR ℰꙞ

Sarah and I exchanged a bunch of texts and emails over the next few days. We made a list of five houses to see on Saturday, most of which were in the same relative location. Three in Reston and two in Herndon.

The house we'd wanted in 2018 wasn't for sale any longer, of course. It had long since been bought and presumably the current owners didn't want to sell after only a few months of owning it.

So, we were starting fresh. Same parameters, though. Three bedrooms. Three bathrooms. Two spaces for a television. Easy access to main roads, but not on one. Two-car garage.

Sarah met us at my townhouse. She arranged for the For Sale sign to be put in place this week, too, along with the placard about the Open House tomorrow. If nothing else, coming home to see the notification of sale in my front yard and signs pointing to my house from the main roads made the decision to sell very real.

She gave me a hug when she saw me and whispered, "I'm so happy you're healthy."

I nodded past the lump in my throat. The reminder of what I'd been through and the relief of it not being any worse than it was, was still very raw. "Thanks," I whispered back, though Tom could hear me as he walked past us to the car.

"We're all very happy with where we are."

Then, Sarah noticed the ring on my left hand. As she grabbed it and asked me the question with her eyes, I realized I hadn't mentioned the change in our status. "Yes, we are getting married!" I crowed.

Tom laughed. "She's very excitable," he teased.

"Congratulations!" Sarah shouted. "You didn't tell me that part."

"Well, I think I kind of forgot. The house thing and the health thing were enough."

"I suppose. But, wow."

"I know. A couple of 40-year-olds getting married," I teased Sarah, as well as Tom.

"I'm very happy for you," Sarah said, as the two of us moved to get into her car for our day of house-hunting.

"Thanks. We're getting married in a couple of months," I explained.

"What about the house then?"

"Oh, and moving, too."

"You're crazy," Sarah argued, as she buckled up and put her car in reverse.

"You have no idea," Tom replied.

"I'm just trying to get everything in place," I countered.

"Do you have to get married so soon, though? Just moving is going to be a lot of work."

"Well, no one is pregnant, if that's what you mean."

Sarah gasped. "I didn't mean that!"

"I know," I said with a laugh. This was part of what Tom had brought to my life. Teasing was a natural reflex now, and it felt good. "Tom, as you heard, thinks I'm crazy to try to do so much." I glanced over my shoulder at Tom where he was sitting in the back seat of the car, while I was in the passenger seat. Back seat was Tom's preferred position, and my sitting up front made Sarah feel less like a chauffeur.

"You just got healthy, so yes, I think we don't need to get married quite so soon."

"I just don't want you to run away."

Tom laughed. "You're stuck with me now."

I could see Sarah's smile, though I wasn't sure if Tom could since he was sitting behind her. She'd known me a long time, and she could tell I was happy. And that made her smile.

"That I am," I replied, a broad smile on my face too.

"And to answer your question, Sarah, no we don't have to get married. I'm just so happy that Tom wants to get married that I want to get it done!"

Tom laughed, as I had intended him to. "Stop giving away family secrets."

I stuck my tongue out at him, like a 6-year-old.

"Seriously, though," Sarah intervened, "you know how this house-hunting thing goes. It's very stressful, and you have no way of knowing when you'll find the perfect house, your offer will be accepted, and you'll be able to move. Planning a wedding around that seems crazy to me."

"Amen" came from the back seat. I knew Tom was mostly teasing me because I kept insisting we could do all these things virtually simultaneously. But Sarah, of course, did not know that.

"We're doing immediate family only, and a justice of the peace. I've already reached out to the ones on the Fairfax County website. A couple have already replied. We still need a location, though. That's only big item that needs planning."

"So, no big church wedding? Photographer? Flowers?" Sarah asked.

"No. We are not church people. I'm not sure we need much in the way of photographs. We don't much like pictures of ourselves."

"Amen" came from the back seat.

I chuckled. "As for flowers, I may just go to a craft store and get some silk ones. We're not having any attendants, so that eliminates the need for bridesmaid dresses. And no tuxes."

"Amen" came from the back seat.

"Just a nice suit or something for Tom, and a nice dress or something for me. I mean, we're in our forties. Do people at our age do the big wedding thing?"

"Some do. Doesn't sound like that's important to you," Sarah added.

"The important part is being married. The actual wedding is almost immaterial." This was essentially the same thing I'd said to Tom when I'd asked him to marry me.

I was pleased to see Tom nod. He was finally onboard with the whole idea of marriage. He'd realized during my treatments that, not only did he love me a lot, he wanted to be involved in the decision-making regarding my health. The best way to make sure that happened was to be married. Our lives would be intricately intertwined from now on.

By now, we had arrived at our first destination in Reston. As we'd seen many times before, this house was mid-century modern. Interestingly, it was also set catty-corner on an intersection, which was one of the things I'd loved about the house we had had to give up.

"Not too many trees," Tom commented as we got out of the car. There were quite a few large trees around the house, but set away from it. The skylights we could see would get good light. A nice sign.

"Yes, and I like the wide driveway. And the street is quiet," I echoed one of Tom's requests.

"I thought you'd like it, that's why I put it first on the list," Sarah explained.

We opened the door with Sarah's magic realtor code. I was immediately stuck by the layout. It was a split-level house, which I liked very much. The stairs were hardwood, and we took the flight up to the main floor with the kitchen, dining room, and living room.

I looked at Tom to see his reaction, to see if he was getting as excited as I was. He was smiling as he looked around the space.

"I like that it's open," he said.

The living and dining rooms formed a "great" room on the left side of the house, giving it a very open feel. There was a large bay window off the living room, with a small nook and built-in seating. 'Perfect,' I thought, 'for curling up with a good book.'

The kitchen, which was just at the top of the stairs in the middle of the house, had been updated from when the house had originally been built in the '60s. The appliances were all full-sized stainless steel, which was one of the things we'd not seen in other Reston houses from the same era. We didn't cook much, but I did want the kitchen to be fully functional. The kitchen had a large window above the stove, which looked out over the forest that was behind the house. As Tom had noted, there were lots of trees, but none that close to the house. At this time of the year, the leaves were bright green, but I could imagine the beauty that would come in the fall. "Nice view," I said. Tom nodded.

The other half of the floor included a large family room on the front side of the house, almost as large as the great room, and a small room facing the forest that could be an office or another bedroom.

"We could put the TV in here," I said, "and leave the living room for, well, living."

Tom smiled. "I have my TV in my living room, and I can still live in it," he teased.

"You know I like the TV to not be in the living room," I pouted.

Tom gave me a quick kiss, as I had intended. This, too, was part of our normal interactions, part of our teasing.

"I do, and you know I don't mind it. I was just giving you a hard time."

I stuck my tongue out at him again, while I took his hand to lead him to the next floor.

We went up the flight of hardwood stairs to the bedrooms. The master bedroom was the width of the house, with a beautiful en-suite bathroom. I was falling in love with this house. There was also a balcony the length of the back of the house from the back of the master bedroom to the adjacent guest room. I wasn't sure I would ever be able to take advantage of it, given my fear of heights, but I loved the floor-to-ceiling sliding glass doors that let in great light.

"Does the balcony let you get into the guest room?" Tom wondered. He wandered out on it and, sure enough, was able to come inside into the guest room next door.

"That's a little weird," I said. "I'm not sure I'd want our guests to be able to come into our bedroom!"

"That's why there are locks on the doors," Tom teased.

"I know. But it's still a little weird."

"You could put a small barrier between the two halves, if you wanted," Sarah offered.

I nodded. That might work.

We went to see the guest room Tom had walked through, but hadn't really seen.

"Nice size," I said. "You could fit my queen bed in here."

"That would be nice for couples who might visit," Sarah agreed.

"I'm still not sure who will visit us," Tom argued. "Everyone we know lives here."

"Well, not your sister," I pointed out.

"Yes, but they would probably stay in a hotel, with the kids."

"What about when the kids are grown and out of the house?"

"True. They are in high school now."

"Phin and Joseph could use it, too," I commented. They didn't live that far away in Annapolis. But it was just far enough that they did sometimes stay overnight when a family function ran late. "Eliza could use the other guest room, I think."

Which prompted us to go to the other room. It was essentially the same size as the one we had just left. "We could put two twin beds in this one, so we could have Xan and Catherine and their kids visit, too." I said.

"Tiffany, your brother lives in Bethesda. He doesn't need to stay with us," Tom insisted.

"Well, probably not. But you just never know."

Tom just smiled at me indulgently. Sarah knew better than to say anything.

We glanced at the hallway bathroom between the two bedrooms and the master bedroom. It wasn't large, but it did have a full shower/tub. Serviceable for guests, I thought. And I liked that the bathrooms, master and guest, were adjacent. So, you wouldn't hear a flush in the middle of the night from the bed in the master. I just hoped the walls between were reasonably soundproof. From a layout and plumbing perspective, having the two bathrooms in this configuration made all the sense in the world.

Next, we went down two flights to the downstairs. Here was another great room, obviously intended to be another family room downstairs. It was essentially under the same rooms above, but with a slightly wider space because it included part of the kitchen, as well. But what really made the house interesting was that, under the other side of the house was yet another bedroom and then there was lots of storage. The unfinished part of the downstairs housed the furnace and water heater. But beyond those two appliances was a very large, very open, storage room. That was one of the things my current townhouse lacked – storage. I tried not to be a packrat. My minimalist father had rubbed off on me in that way. But just the idea of all that space for storage – it made my heart go pitter-pat.

"Tiffany loves this, don't you?" Tom said, as we walked through the unfinished space.

"I do!"

"It's a very nice feature of the house," Sarah agreed. "Most houses either have a finished basement or an unfinished basement. This house has both!"

I nodded. "It's a huge house," I said.

"4,000 square feet," Sarah reported.

"Wow!" Tom said. "That's huge."

"And in our budget?"

"Yes. Also, they just redid the roof and the air conditioner."

"Oh, that just adds to the value," I agreed. "Fewer things that need updating, even in this older house."

"Exactly. The kitchen is newer, too, as you noted."

"Right. Definitely not original to the house, based on the others we've seen" Tom said.

Sarah looked at the listing paperwork. "It says it was remodeled in 2016, so everything is still pretty new."

"Why are they even moving?" I asked. "It seems like they put an awful lot of money into the house in the past few years."

"I don't know. Maybe one of them got a new job in a different town. People move all the time after renovations."

"I guess." I was skeptical. I thought the job situation might be a logical answer. All I knew was Tom and I could potentially be reaping the benefits of the owners' displacement.

"Well, I love it," I stated. "Love everything about it."

"Even the balcony," Tom asked.

"Even the balcony."

"Well, we have four more on our list to see today," Sarah pointed out.

"I know. I'm just saying I think this is the one. Tom? What do you think?"

"It's a very nice house. It checks everything on our list, right?"

"Garage?" I asked. We hadn't seen that yet.

"Oh, yes, we should check that out," Sarah agreed.

We found the door to the garage off the finished side of the downstairs.

"This means carrying your groceries up a flight," Sarah pointed out.

"I do that now," I added. "I've gotten used to it."

"My car parks outside," Tom said. "And it's a flight of stairs outside to my front door. I'm just going to be spoiled by being able to park out of the rain!"

Sarah laughed. "Yes, you will get very used to having a garage."

"I know I have," I agreed.

"You're going to make me soft," Tom teased.

"I'm going to try," I countered.

The garage itself was unremarkable, just the space for two cars. There were no built-in shelves or anything. But I was fine with that. There was a lot of storage just inside.

We went to see the other houses that Sarah and I had agreed to, but I'll admit my heart wasn't really in it. I suppose if I had seen another house that I liked better, I would have been more enthusiastic. But I didn't.

Tom appeared to be less excited about the other houses too. We toured them, remarked on their good and bad features. But we spent less time at all the other houses than we had spent at that first one.

At the end of the touring, Sarah drove us back to my house.

"Well," she said, "I think the first house won the day. You?"

"I think we'd agree."

"I think we'd like to make an offer," Tom said. "If Tiffany agrees."

"I do!"

"Great. Let's go inside and fill it out. Then I can fax it from my office."

"You fax it from here," Tom offered. "We have an app for that."

Tom and I laughed. Another of our favorite expressions.

Sarah looked confused.

I explained. "I have a fax application on my laptop."

"But the files will be electronic on mine."

"You email them to me and then they will be on my laptop."

"Okay. But then will the fax look like it came from you?" she asked.

"Possibly. Is that a problem?" I inquired.

"I don't think so. Let me think about it while we do the paperwork."

"Okay," Tom said. "I could probably change the parameters of the program, too."

"It's what he does," I explained to Sarah.

"Good to know."

As we filled out the paperwork, I realized that Tom and I were truly buying this house together, even though technically it was my money being used. True to our plans and previous agreements, we decided together what our down payment would be. We already knew what our interest rate would be, because we had been prequalified for over a year. I did check that it still held, and it did.

Most importantly, we had decided which house we wanted to buy – together. And we were doing the "fun" task of making the offer – together.

ᘓ ᘏᘓ ᘏᘓ ᘏ

It then became ever more critical to sell my house. We'd put in a contingent offer, contingent on my house being sold. Sarah was again nervous about whether the owners would accept that. We could only try.

True to our plans, Sarah held an open house at my townhouse the day after we put in the offer. I went to Tom's house, since I wasn't allowed to be home. It was anxious time, especially since we were now working against a deadline. Assuming our offer on the Reston house was accepted – we hadn't heard yea or nay yet.

I had brought books and my laptop to Tom's house. I figured they, along with my phone, would be enough to keep me busy. They were, but I was still very aware of the slowness of time. The open house was from 1-4 pm, and by 3:30 I was very ready to go home.

It's not that I didn't like being with Tom. I loved being with Tom. But I wasn't very comfortable at Tom's place. For one thing, it was a little musty, though he had started to get it cleaned professionally again, which was helping. For another, his couches were really old and didn't have much support left in them. As he spent 90% of his time at one of the three computer desks that inhabited the dining room instead of a dining room table, he perhaps didn't care. But in the almost three hours I sat on the couch, I squirmed quite a bit trying to find the most comfortable position. But mostly, I was just anxious to know whether the open house was going well. It would be amazing to get an offer after the first open house, so I was trying not to count on it.

I went home around 4:30, to give Sarah a chance to shoo all the people out before I showed up. The house looked the same, which I'll admit I was also a little worried about. I mean, Tom and I had been very respectful in the open houses we had gone to, but I wasn't sure if people always were.

Sarah was still there, which I also found interesting. She was packing up the marketing slicks that she had put out on the kitchen island.

"I'll leave a couple of these here, just in case anyone stops by."

"Aren't people supposed to call you for an appointment?"

"They are. That's what the sign says. But you never know."

"Okay. Does that mean I have to keep the house clean all the time?"

I'm not a messy person, but keeping the house completely tidy all the time might be exhausting.

"I would think that someone who just drops by would be tolerant of a little mess. But generally, neat is always better!"

Ugh. I wasn't sure I was up for more pressure. But I was the one trying to sell, so I guessed I was just going to have to cope.

"I guess there weren't any potential offers?" I asked, trying not to sound too hopeful.

Sarah smiled. "Not yet. A couple of people seemed interested. We'll see if any offers come in this evening. I will keep you posted."

"Thanks!"

Sarah left, and I settled in for an evening alone. Tom and I had decided, after the day together, that our introverted selves would appreciate some alone time.

I fixed myself a little dinner, and the girls and I settled in to watch some of the television shows Tom didn't enjoy.

Tom texted an hour or so later. "No offers?"

"No. Sarah said there was some interest, but nothing firm."

"Bummer."

"Guess you'll have me as a house guest again next weekend."

"I'll suffer through somehow."

Which reminded me that I needed to find out from Sarah if she planned on an open house every weekend. I sent her a quick email, to which she promptly replied, "Let's see how it goes."

Unfortunately, no offers came in the next few days. So, the following weekend, Sarah planned another open house. Liz would be the one to lead this one, however, as Sarah had some kind of family event or something.

In the meantime, we were in negotiations on the Reston house. The sellers had countered with an ask for a little more money. We had countered with not quite as much money and a request for some other considerations, namely getting the chimney cleaned. The house had an old-fashioned wood-burning fireplace. Tom and I weren't sure we would use it, but it was a nice amenity to have. Sarah had mentioned, however, that it looked like it hadn't been cleaned or used in a while. Which could have meant there were critters in the chimney. We didn't want to find out the first time we used the fireplace.

The sellers agreed to the chimney cleaning, but countered for just a little more money. We were considering our options while waiting to see what this weekend's open house might bring.

Unfortunately, the second open house didn't yield any offers either. I was somewhat disheartened by that, but Liz assured me that, even with the hot housing market we were experiencing, it could take several weeks to get an offer.

We countered again to the Reston house sellers and hoped that would be the end of that. We agreed to their modified asking price. If they accepted, we would be on our way to purchase. Assuming we could sell my house!

On Tuesday, I was sitting downstairs watching TV with the cats. Tom had a bit of a stomach thing, so he wasn't there. And the doorbell rang about 7 pm.

Now, my doorbell almost never rang. I about jumped out of my skin. I debated about whether to answer it. But then I remembered Sarah's advice about drop-bys. And I decided I could at least go see who it was.

Fortunately, I had a peep hole. Outside, I saw a youngish man. He didn't appear to be selling anything, though I was mentally prepared to be rude if it turned out he was. I opened the door.

"May I help you?"

"I'm very interested in living in this neighborhood," he said excitedly. "And I saw your sign." He pointed to the For Sale sign. "Can I come in and see the house?"

Sarah had told me to tell anyone who stopped by to make an appointment, but that it was up to me if I wanted to offer them a tour too. "You should really call my agent," I responded.

"Okay. I just really want to see the house. Okay?"

I assessed that this guy was harmless, and I said, "Sure. What's your name?"

"Kai," he said. "Kai Yu."

"Okay, Kai. A quick tour. And then you should call my agent."

"Got it. Thanks!"

I sent a quick text to Tom and to Sarah.

Tom's response, "Do you need me to come over?"

"I think I'm okay. I'll let you know if I get a bad vibe."

"Okay!"

Sarah's response, "Is his name Kai or something?"

"Yes!"

"He called me a few minutes ago. I told him I would make an appointment, but he said he was going to knock on your door anyway. Sorry."

"It's okay. Nice try, though. :)"

"Tell him to call me."

"I did, and I will."

"Okay."

Kai was standing in the dining room waiting for me. I gave him points for not just wandering on his own.

"I was just talking to my agent. She said you called her?"

"Yes. She said to wait. But I really want to get a house in this neighborhood."

"It is a nice neighborhood," I said, though I wasn't sure what the big draw was. It was nice enough, but nothing all that special. Just a townhouse community. It was near several major roads, for easy access to everywhere. That was part of what I liked about it. But there were several other neighborhoods not far away with the same access.

I showed Kai around, upstairs to the bedrooms – I was glad I had made my bed! – and then downstairs to the family room and garage.

"It's perfect!" Kai crowed. "It's my dream house. Really. I'm very excited. How much?"

As we were now in the kitchen, I handed him one of the flyers Sarah and Liz had left behind. "This has the information. I'm glad you like the house."

"It's great. I'll be putting in an offer today. Don't sell to anyone else, okay?"

"I don't have any other offers right now," I confessed, though I realized I probably shouldn't have said that. I could have pretended and been more hardcore about negotiating. But that wasn't my style.

"Good, good," Kai said. "Thank you again for letting me see the house. I'm going to go call my agent right now!" He ran out the door and drove off.

I texted Tom. "His name was Kai. He's interested in the house!"

"Great! Is he still there?"

"No, he left. I saw him drive off."

"Okay. Be careful."

"I will."

To Sarah, I texted, "He said he's going to put in an offer. He wants to be in this neighborhood."

"I'll let you know if something comes in."

"Okay!"

A couple of hours later, my cell rang. It was Sarah.

"Well, they did put in an offer. Full asking price."

"Wow. That's amazing."

I texted Tom the news while still talking to Sarah.

"His agent said he loved the house, and he really wants it."

"Should we counter?"

"Do you want to risk him bolting? If you counter, he can withdraw his offer."

"No, I guess not. Asking price is what we wanted anyway."

Tom confirmed his agreement via text.

"Exactly. It's a fair price."

"Right. I'm okay with it. Let's not counter."

And so, we ended up selling my house to a guy who just "stopped by".

CR ℰℭℛ ℰℭℛ ℰℭ

The contingency was met. We planned to close on the new house a week after Kai bought mine. Both of those events were scheduled for a month from when we accepted Kai's offer.

CR ℰℭℛ ℰℭℛ ℰℭ

That just left the decision of what to do with Tom's house. And packing and moving. And finishing the wedding planning, not to mention getting married.

The beauty of staging my house meant that about a third of my possessions had already been packed and were in storage. I started packing up the rest of my townhouse. Tom helped, especially because he wasn't sure I was fully recovered from surgery, though I had clearance from Dr. Kessler. Tom was like that, though. Long before I had been diagnosed, he was more cautious about my health than he was his own. The past few months had only exacerbated his anxiety about my well-being.

One evening, as we were packing up the downstairs books, Tom asked, "What do you think we should do with my townhouse? Sell or keep and rent out?"

We'd had this conversation several times already. In my heart of hearts, I wanted to sell. But it was Tom's house, and I wasn't going to tell him what to do with it. He'd lived there for a very long time, and I suspected he was going to have some challenges adjusting to our new house and location. So, I struggled with how to respond. I replied with a non-answer. "I think it's your house, your call."

Tom just looked at me.

I responded to his look. "It's really not my decision. Some people have a terrible experience. But other people, Xan and Jenn for example, have had great success with keeping a previous house for the cash flow."

We had talked to my brother and his wife about their experiences, so Tom knew this already.

"But who knows? For you, it could be a great thing. So, I really think it's up to you if you want to keep the house or not."

"I would get a manager to deal with the renting out and advertising. But you know this neighborhood" – Tom and I thought of our adjoining communities as essentially the same neighborhood – "is very transient. The house wouldn't be empty much."

"That's true. And it would be a good source of income."

"On the other hand, we'd still be responsible for everything that might go wrong with the house."

I nodded.

"And we'd have to get quite a bit done to rent it out."

I didn't respond to that. Tom knew how I felt about the current condition of his house.

"On the other hand, if I sell, I'd have to get even more things done to fix it up."

"I guess that depends on how much you want to sell it for."

"Meaning?"

"Meaning you could sell as-is. You might not get as much, but Sarah would be able to advise you on that. If you want to use her."

"Sure. Might as well keep things in the family, as it were."

I nodded again.

"Maybe the first step is to have Sarah walk the property and tell me what she thinks she could get," Tom answered himself.

"Makes sense to me. That way, you'll know at least that half of the equation."

"Third."

"What?"

"That third of the equation. Second third is what would be needed to rent it out. And the third is whether the cost-benefit analysis of renting is worth it."

"Okay. You're making my head hurt!"

Tom laughed. "Sorry. Lots to think about."

"Definitely."

We finished packing up all the books except the handful I thought I might want to have in the next month.

A couple of days later, Tom texted, "Talked to Sarah. She's going to come by this evening. So, I may not be by."

"Okay!"

Around 8 pm, I got another text, "Sarah told me what she thinks. Too much to text. Will talk to you tomorrow. Going to bed now."

I laughed and replied, "Sleep tight!"

The next evening, Tom came over at dinnertime, and he filled me in. "She gave me a list of what she thinks needs to be fixed."

"She does that. Remember she did that with me. You don't have to do it all, though, you know."

"It was actually less than I would have done."

"Really? Like what?"

"She didn't think I should take down the mirrors you love."

I hated the mirrors in his dining room. "Really?"

"Really. She said they make the space look bigger."

"Well, that's true. But they are pretty dated."

"Just telling you what she said."

"I know. I'm just surprised. What else?"

"Well, I would have upgraded the hot water heater. She said I didn't need to do that either."

"Interesting. Why?"

"She said long as it works, I wasn't obligated."

"Fascinating. I guess that's good, then."

"Yeah. So, I think I'm going to sell."

"Really?"

"I think it makes the most sense. Then we don't have to worry about anything going wrong with the house. Or bad tenants."

I nodded. "Your call."

"I know you said that. And I also know you're just as happy I decided to sell."

I shrugged. "You know me too well."

Tom laughed.

It took another month for Tom to get the repairs done. This time, he didn't drag his heels. I guess he was in "get-it-done" mode. Several of the rooms needed fresh paint and a few needed wallpaper removed before painting could be done. All in all, the house looked much nicer when the changes were finished.

Sarah was the listing agent, of course. With Liz. Before the first open house, however, Sarah got a call. There was someone really interested. Like Kai with my development, the person had been waiting for a house in Tom's community. Tom had the advantage of his house being across from the neighborhood pool. He had the disadvantage, from my perspective, of not having a garage. I guess the pool access was more important to the prospective buyer.

Tom came to stay at my house on Saturday while Liz showed his house to the buyer. An offer came in later that night. It was a little lower than asking, though.

"What do you think I should do?" Tom asked me. "Counter?"

"It's $2,000 below asking?"

"Yes. Not that much on the scale of things. I wonder why they didn't ask for more?"

"Some people just always want a discount," I offered.

"Could be. But what do you think?"

I looked at Tom.

"I know. It's my house, my decision. But we're in this together now, right? Isn't that what marriage is all about?"

I grimaced, as I was supposed to. "Nice. Throw my desire for security in my face."

Tom laughed. "Figured it was worth a try!"

I laughed, too.

"Seriously, what do you think?" Tom asked again.

"If it were me…"

Tom nodded.

"…I'd take it. A couple thousand? Not a big deal, right? You'll make enough to cover your outstanding mortgage."

"And then some!" Tom said, enthusiastically.

"Then why quibble?"

"It's not like I really need the money. You're going to be taking care of me, right?"

"Right! You can be a gentleman of leisure."

"Looking forward to it."

Tom picked up his phone and called Sarah. "We'll take the offer," he told her.

"Sure you don't want to counter?"

"We don't need the money."

"Your neighbors might not appreciate the less-than-asking price."

"Comps," Tom said.

I nodded, not having thought about that.

"Right," Sarah argued.

"Okay. Ask for asking."

"I'll fax you the paperwork tonight."

"Thanks!"

Fortunately, the buyer accepted our counteroffer.

And so Tom's house was sold. With a closing a week after mine on my townhouse.

CR ℰℐCR ℰℐCR ℰℐ

We were very lucky. The two major house dominos that needed to line up and fall in order – the sale of my townhouse and the purchase of our new single-family house – had done just that. Tom's house selling was just the icing on the cake. Now, to packing!

"You know the drum was the first instrument besides the human voice." --
Billy Higgins

Finding a Good Fit, Part One (2015-2016)

People often wonder how to find the perfect person, your forever love. I'm not sure how to find the perfect someone. Goodness knows, I've dated some people who were just wrong for me. But the one thing I found really interesting was how I knew I found the man who was perfect for me.

The answer was: it was easy.

It being "the relationship".

Not that we haven't had our fights and disagreements. But being with Tom was easy in the sense of not having to prove myself, like I did with Richard who always wanted the ideal woman. Or not having to worry that some other woman would catch his eye, like with Patrick. Or from Tom's perspective, not feeling like I had to change the core of who I was to match the other person's vision of what I should be.

⚜ ⚜ ⚜ ⚜ ⚜

One of the first things that drew me to Tom was his kindness. Not just to me, but to everyone. It showed in everything he did, and it was obvious that it wasn't for my benefit or to impress me. It was just him.

I saw it from the start, when he left that large tip on a check for almost no money after our first date. A tip equivalent to what it would have been if we'd eaten dinner, and then another party had been sat and left a tip, and another.

Once we really knew each other, I mentioned to Tom that I was impressed by this kindness to our server.

He was genuinely shocked that I would comment on it. "It was only fair," he argued. "We'd taken the table for the whole night!"

"I know. And having been a server in my lifetime, and having had friends who were servers and bartenders, I knew what that meant. But I was impressed that you did, too. You've never been a server. You started working for your customer as soon as you graduated!"

"True. But I'm not stupid either. Honestly, it was just the right thing to do."

"I agree. But not everyone sees it that way. You'd be amazed."

"No, I probably wouldn't be. I've seen others be unkind. But it's not right."

"I know." And I kissed Tom for his kindness and his caring, and his perplexity that others could be cruel.

Tom's kindness showed up in a million little ways. He fed the cats for me on the weekends to save me from having to get up quite as early. He took out my garbage on "garbage night". He bought me roses for Valentine's Day even when I told him all I wanted was a card. He bought me reading glasses when my eyes started to be fuzzy first thing in the morning. He remembered when I was going to have a big meeting with a customer and would text me "good luck" beforehand. He sympathized with the craziness that is dealing with my mother, though he never said a bad word about her.

He might not know my favorite color or comment on my new dress. But I found that wasn't as important.

CR ЄƆCR ЄƆCR ЄƆ

Another thing that made our relationship easy was our shared dislike of most food. To call us "picky eaters" is both an understatement and insulting.

In my 30s, I stopped apologizing for my food choices. And I stopped accepting the kind, but annoying "just try it; you'll like it" gibes. I liked the food I liked. I didn't like the food I didn't like. And that was okay. It was part of who I was. I was fine with my choices.

But it did usually mean some accommodation by a guy I was dating, and I sometimes worried that would be a problem. I certainly could never date someone who loved to cook or thought going out for the latest food craze was the perfect date night. When I was doing online dating, I shied away from anyone who talked about food a lot, knowing that their interest in all things food would likely make us incompatible.

But most people have preferences in other areas, and those are accepted. It's part of what makes us who we are. It's just that, when it comes to food, people seem to have a bias against others who don't eat the same foods they do. Maybe it's a leftover from when we were children, but just saying you don't want to eat something isn't acceptable.

When I was dating Chris, who had Celiac disease - an acceptable reason to not eat certain foods – he told me even he got comments. Even after knowing it was a health concern for him, people still tried to get him to eat food he knew he should not. He and I were largely compatible when it came to eating because of his restricted diet. We didn't date long for reasons other than food choices.

So, I really appreciated that Tom's eating habits were, if anything, more constrained than mine. And he appreciated that I didn't try to change his habits. Or try to make him eat foods I liked that he didn't.

CR SOCR SOCR SO

Another area of compatibility was music. Not that we had the same taste in music. We didn't, though there was a great deal of overlap.

It was more that Tom appreciated that I loved music because he also loved music.

Growing up, music was a big part of my life. I sang in my high school and college choirs. I went to lots of concerts, for large and small acts. I sang and played acoustic guitar with a local youth group, mostly around campfires and such. And I owned hundreds of albums and knew the lyrics to every song. Most of the time, I could also tell you who wrote the song and who played on it. I was very into music.

Tom is tone deaf, or so he says. He's not or he wouldn't appreciate music. But he says he can't sing, though he whistles on key. I've never heard him try to sing, so I couldn't say. But he appreciates music, and he has an amazing memory for songs, including jingles and television theme songs.

I always thought that I'd end up marrying a musician or at least someone who played an instrument or sang, like I did. I dated musicians, Patrick being one of them. But I also knew being a professional musician is a very tough thing and not many who try that profession achieve any kind of stability. So, that's why I thought I'd end up with someone for whom music was more of a hobby.

That's not the case for Tom. He loves music and has hundreds of albums, just like I do. But he doesn't play, and he doesn't sing. And I realized that's okay.

One of the interesting things I found in dating musicians or even musician hobbyists was a competitiveness in myself. I consider myself a pretty good singer, but I'm not professional grade. I'd love to be, but I'm realistic enough to know that my voice is more choir grade. Maybe it's just because most of the singing I've done for any kind of audience has been geared toward trying to blend my voice, rather than being a soloist. When I would sing along with some of my favorite female singers, I found myself almost imitating their style, rather than developing my own. And I have a good range, but not an outstanding one. I sing on key, and I used to be able to read music pretty easily. That's what I mean by choir grade – good enough to blend in, but not really unique or special in tone or quality.

But I had a fantasy about singing in public, about being that person called on at the last minute to fill in for someone who fell ill or whatever, and just nailing the performance.

Except I have terrible stage fright. I choke up when asked to sing by myself. I have no problem singing in a group or a choir. But solo? Can't do it. So, the fantasy remains a fantasy, and will never be reality.

This doesn't stop me, however, from being jealous of other people's abilities and presence. When I was dating Patrick, part of me wanted him to call me up from the audience to harmonize on a song. He knew I sang. We'd sung together a few times. But Tim was the lead singer, and Patrick sang harmonies with him. If Tim hadn't been able to perform, for whatever reason, I wouldn't have been a good substitute. But it didn't stop me from the desire to be asked.

Maybe it's just that I wanted to be seen as good enough? Patrick said he loved my voice. But he was the professional musician, and I was a student and worker bee. And part of me was jealous of that.

In college, I dated a guy, Vic, who played a bunch of instruments and sang. But his thing was classical music. He thought rock and pop was drivel. Or most of it, at least. So, in his case, even though we had a love of music in common, the fact that he didn't think the kind of music I loved was worthy was a huge problem. He'd listen to it when we were in my room. Sort of tolerate it. But, given the choice, he'd prefer his classical music. So, in the case of this relationship, I not only felt inferior for not playing multiple instruments, but my singing skills weren't appreciated because he didn't appreciate the music being sung. He appreciated my choir singing. But not anything I did "solo" in my room when he was around.

Sad to say, Tom's lack of musical skills probably made it easier for me to appreciate his total love of music without being jealous.

CR ꜱꝋCR ꜱꝋCR ꜱꝋ

I told Meghan more than once that Tom is an introvert's introvert. When we were house-hunting, one of the critical components of our new house was a space for each of us to just be. Not that we don't love each other. But introverts need their time, even from the ones they love. When I told Sarah that, in front of Tom, Tom laughed heartily.

"I don't think it's that bad, is it?"

"You don't think we need to each have some space for ourselves," I asked.

"Well, I didn't say that," Tom replied.

"I think we'll be happier. Neither of us has lived with anyone else in a very long time, too. I think having separate space might be important for that reason, too."

Sarah just took it all in.

In the end, our perfect house included an office for Tom in the downstairs bedroom – I vetoed not having a dining room – and one for me, for the days when I got to work from home. My office doubled as a guest room with a futon sofa, though the number of times we expected to have guests was minimal.

The other accommodation we looked for in our new house was two spaces to be able to watch television. Dating, Tom and I had spent many nights watching TV together. We'd found we had a lot of the same tastes in shows, and we explored our love of documentaries and nature-based shows together. But Tom loved horror movies and shows about people behaving badly; I couldn't watch those. I loved nighttime dramas and procedural shows that drove Tom nuts for how quickly they solved mysteries. He didn't call me out for liking those shows; he just didn't want to watch them, much as I didn't want to watch the comedies where everyone is making fun of everyone else. I found it fascinating that Tom, who was one of the kindest people I knew, would enjoy watching people being less than kind. But he said it made him feel good in comparison.

For this reason, I thought we should have two television rooms. Again, the house we'd bought was perfect for this. There was a family room on the middle floor, on the opposite side of the kitchen from living room / dining room great room, and another downstairs, with the door to the garage. We both had televisions from our respective households, so we planned to set up Tom's downstairs and mine upstairs. Perfect.

CR ꙮCR ꙮCR ꙮ

Finally, Tom and I both agreed early on that, while neither of us was a gym rat, that was okay. We were both average, not fat but not slim. We didn't go to the beach, so there was no feeling inadequate in comparison with the bikini bods or washboard abs. We lived like normal people – trying to be sure not to eat too much junk, but not being obsessed by every bite going into our mouths.

Tom didn't really like to exercise, though he did occasionally. Mostly, he walked a lot and always took the stairs when he was out. And drank almost exclusively water. And he had never had any alcohol, so he didn't have any of the side effects from that. His fitness came from these things.

I exercised, but I wasn't fixated on it. I ran a little, but not far and not fast. That was okay. I wasn't interested in training for marathons. I did yoga several days a week, which I did more to keep myself moving and somewhat limber, rather than for weight control or trying to have the perfect beach body.

With other men, I had been very aware of my hotness compared to their hotness. In some cases, I felt like I won that competition. Vic, the guy from college, was one of those. He was super smart and, as I said, played lots of instruments and sang. But he wasn't a beauty. He wasn't ugly, but his nose was too big for his face and he wore thick glasses that didn't do much to help his appeal. He didn't care; he was more interested in intellect. So, in that case, I felt I was the more attractive of the two of us. But as looks were not the basis of our relationship, who cared?

In other cases, I failed miserably at being the better-looking one. Richard was an example of that. Richard was a beautiful man, and he knew it, reveled in it, used it to his advantage in every aspect of his life. He had shoulder-length curly brown hair that most women swooned over. He had a gorgeous face to go with the lovely hair. He also was a fitness instructor, so his body was not only perfect, it was his job. When I was with him, I felt like the other women in the room envied me, and I'll be honest, I enjoyed that. But I also knew he was sizing them up for conquest. And I never felt as though I was quite good enough to keep him from straying. And I was right.

But Tom and I were attractive to each other, and that's really all that counted.

⚘ ❧⚘ ❧⚘ ❧

Some people enjoy conflict, but Tom wasn't one of those people. There had been times when I enjoyed the drama of a good fight. It took Tom to teach me how to disagree and not fight.

I grew up with emotional parents. My mother and father were both yellers who didn't do a good job of listening to each other. It's why they ended up divorced. But that was the environment Xan, Phin, and I were raised in, and honestly, we didn't know any different until we were teenagers.

Alexander is naturally more laidback than Phineas and me. He was our rock in the days of fighting. Phin and I looked to our big brother to help us make sense of the chaos. Once our parents divorced, and we shuttled back and forth between houses, Xan was old enough by then to speak for all of us when there were things that made us uncomfortable or we just needed a little more from one parent or the other. The fact that Xan doesn't get easily annoyed was key to our adjustment.

I spent a good portion of my 30s unhappy. I wasn't depressed, at least not in any sense I've ever read about. But I was alone a lot, and I was convinced I was unlovable. I mean, my family loved me, but they were supposed to. Men, in many cases, ran away. I took it personally.

My unhappiness manifested as anger a fair amount. I had a short fuse, and though I didn't like it, I didn't seem to be able to control it. I started getting more exercise, because I read somewhere that would help. Maybe it was the exercise, maybe it was the exhaustion that followed the exercise, or maybe I was just growing up, but I ended my 30s nicer than when I started them.

I have told Tom a time or two that he wouldn't have liked me then. It's hard for him to understand, I think, though he's seen some touches of the way I was.

But I learned after our first fight that Tom would rather walk away than yell. He took his emotional pain from his mom's passing and his relationship with Priya, and decided he didn't have to deal with anger and manipulation. In the years I've known Tom, I think I've only heard him raise his voice twice. And only when he was very, very angry.

I didn't know how to deal with that at first. I was used to people who yelled at each other and, though neither party would really feel satisfied, someone had to be the winner.

Tom didn't think that way. To him, there were no winners in fighting. We could argue, sure. Have a serious discussion about a delicate topic. But yelling accomplished nothing in Tom's mind.

So, I learned – as the kids say – to use my words. Instead of huffing and puffing, and trying to blow the house down, I approached Tom with the problem, and we discussed it. Most of the time, calmly.

This also meant I had to really examine my feelings. What was I really upset about? Was it something Tom had done or something that had happened between us? Was it something that was just the way Tom did things – letting Tom be Tom – or was it something I needed him to change? Or was the anger or annoyance or whatever residual from a stressful day? Was my mom getting on my nerves again? Or had something happened that had nothing to do with Tom? If I really thought about what was going on before I got mad, I often found that I wasn't really mad. I was annoyed or upset. But I could work through those.

On those occasions when there really was an issue that needed to be addressed, I brought it to Tom's attention in a quiet moment, not in the heat of anger. I reasoned my side of the discussion, and I really listened when Tom told me his side. Because, like all humans, we did have places where we disagreed. We just talked things through, instead of yelling to defend our position.

I liked this new Tiffany, as I'm sure did the other people around me. It wasn't that I was less opinionated. I just knew better how to approach disagreements.

And I thank Tom for that.

CR Ƨ)CR Ƨ)CR Ƨ)

But most of all, the thing that I loved about Tom was laughter. And silliness.

Tom's family is made up of punsters. If there's a pun to be made, they will make it.

They also love to tease each other mercilessly. Stories from childhood, like Tom's getting lost in Budapest, are not hidden away, never to be discussed. Rather, they are made part of the family lore and the whole incident becomes a source of amusement. Even though Tom's dislike of crowds stems from that day of getting lost, and even though he still hates traveling in part because of it, that doesn't mean the story isn't told. Often.

This is not how things worked in my family. Perhaps it's because of Mom's tendency to be passive-aggressive, but stories the McDonnells would make into funny tales in the Johnson family just don't get raised again. If I were a McDonnell, for example, I think I'd get called Tiff fairly regularly. I would perhaps have come to tolerate the name again in that case. I just don't know.

But the punning and the teasing are part of an overall drive for silliness, for not taking life all that seriously. Particularly between Tom and Meghan. There is no animus in their relationship.

With Tom, I remembered how to laugh at myself. And with him. We developed our own inside jokes, like calling the cats Cheese Omelet and Little Mama. We joked about how all nature documentaries ultimately seem to include penguins, even ones set in about Africa (there are penguins in the southern part of Africa). Tom teases me about my love for drama in television. I tease him about the zombie apocalypse.

CR Ƨ)CR Ƨ)CR Ƨ)

So, finally, at the ripe old age of 42, I liked myself, and I loved Tom.

FINAL WEDDING PLANNING (2019)

With the houses on their way to being sold and bought, the last thing to do to settle into our new life was get married.

Unfortunately, nothing was as simple as we wanted it to be.

$$\text{CR } \text{EO}\text{CR } \text{EO}\text{CR } \text{EO}$$

"You're not inviting David and Anne?" my mother wailed on the phone, as I talked to her about our immediate-family only wedding plans. "Jack will be heartbroken."

My stepfather might well be upset with me, but he also knew the realities of the situation, which was that my stepsiblings and I didn't really get along. My wedding day was supposed to be a joyous occasion. I honestly didn't want them there.

"We are limiting the guest list, and they aren't on it," I said firmly, hoping to end the topic.

"Why are you so set on having a small wedding? I'd be happy to help with planning. Now that you're healthy again, you should celebrate it! Have a big party. Invite all your friends. Get lots of gifts."

"Mother, we don't need gifts. Tom and I both have fully stocked households. The last thing we need is more plates!"

"There's no such thing. You need fancy dishes for entertaining. Those are expensive. I got mine from marrying your father. We had everyone buy a setting. It worked out beautifully."

'Except for the whole divorce thing,' I thought but didn't say. All these years later, and Mom still didn't like to be reminded of that time in her life. "We don't do much entertaining. What we do is usually just small groups of friends. So, not much need for fancy dishes."

"But you love to entertain!"

"Mom, I love you, but sometimes I feel like I'm talking to a stranger. I do not love to entertain."

"Sure you do. You've had many open houses and parties at your home."

"I've had a few, and I always get super stressed about them."

"It's Tom, isn't it? He's the one who really doesn't like parties."

I sighed. "No, Mom, he doesn't. But I'm also an introvert."

She had her mind made up now. She ran with it. "Is Tom the reason you aren't having a big wedding? He is, isn't he? His shyness."

I took another big breath. It was true that Tom was part of the reason for a small wedding. He wouldn't have enjoyed having 300 people staring at him for a few hours. To be honest, I wouldn't either, though I would cope better than Tom would.

But the more I had started planning a smaller wedding, the more I had come to love the idea. For one thing, it was a whole lot cheaper. For another, it meant we didn't have to fight over who did and didn't get invited. With the exception of my mother, who would have been a thousand times worse if I had opened the guest list up. Most importantly, though, we were going to be able to get married without the whole Save the Date drama. We were picking a date about six months from now, when we hoped our respective families would be available. Lauren was the only one who had to travel, so her schedule was in some ways the driver. We'd checked in on dates with a select few of the family and were now trying to find a venue that was available for those same dates. Once we had those two in line, we would be set. None of this waiting for a couple of years for me. I loved Tom. Tom loved me. I wanted that formalized. The rest was just hooey.

"Mom, at 41, don't you think a big wedding would be ridiculous?"

"I did it." Her voice was flat.

Oh yeah. I forgot about that. She and Jack had had a fairly large affair. Oops.

"And it's your first wedding. All the more reason to have a big one. Celebrate!"

"Celebrate that I'm finally getting married? Is that what you mean, Mom?"

"Of course not. Well, maybe a little. I didn't think it would ever happen."

I didn't either, but that didn't let her off the hook.

"Mom, I'm done with this conversation. It's my wedding. Mine and Tom's. We are having only immediate family, and that does not include Anne and David. You're invited. But I'm not going to have this conversation again."

"Very well, Tiffany. You don't have to be rude about it."

I sighed, but to myself. "Thank you, Mother."

☙ ❧☙ ❧☙ ❧

I decided we would do formal invitations. I talked to a local stationery shop who said they could get them done in around two weeks.

We didn't need very many printed, which was why the timeline was shorter. Tom's father; my mother and stepfather Jack; my father; Meghan and George; Lauren, Charlie, Sophie, and Tyler; Phin, Joseph, and Eliza; Alexander, Jennifer, Peyton, and Samantha. A total of 17 people, plus Tom and myself.

I asked Tom which color scheme he preferred and font choices, but his eyes just glazed over. "You're the creative one," he argued. So, I made the choices and made sure Tom didn't object.

"I think the language should be simple. Only the date, time, location, and that kind of thing. None of the 'my parents and your parents have the honor of requesting your presence…' nonsense. I mean, we are our own people, right?"

"Absolutely. That seems very antiquated."

"Yeah. Left over from when fathers gave the bride away."

"You're not going to have your father walk you down the aisle?"

"Oh, goodness! I hadn't really thought about that. Maybe both my parents?"

"And Jack?"

"Well, all three would be a bit much, don't you think?"

Tom laughed. "Yes, I agree. But your mom won't."

"Yet another source of contention. Maybe I'll just walk myself."

"That works for me. I'll only have eyes for you anyway."

I chuckled. "Nice of you to say."

"It has the advantage of being true, though also totally sentimental."

"I like sentimental sometimes," I confessed.

"I know. That's why you got a sapphire for your ring."

I looked down at the beautiful ring on my left hand and knew Tom was right. Practically, I advocated for the amethyst. But deep down, I was really glad I got the sapphire. I kissed Tom to let him know I appreciated his decision, impractical as it was.

"Well, I'll figure out the whole walking me down the aisle thing later."

"Okay!"

"Now, how about vows?"

"Nothing religious."

"Agreed. And no promising to obey."

"Ha!"

I smiled. "The rest is okay, I think. I honestly haven't looked at the words."

Tom pulled the traditional vows up on his phone. Thank goodness for search engines.

We read them together and agreed the rest was fine. Love and cherish. Honor and keep. Sickness and health – well, we'd already done that. Death do you part. All that was okay.

"Photographer?"

"Meh," I responded. "We could just have family members take pictures."

"On their phones?"

"Sure. We've seen some really good ones from Phin and George. We will pose for a few, of course. But mostly I want to experience the wedding, not stand around for hours taking the perfect picture."

"Will you regret that when we're old?"

I thought about it. Tom was right to make me think beyond my gut reaction. I hated pictures of myself, as did Tom. But this was an important event. And I did like to have some photos of those kinds of things. The question was did they need to be professionally taken? I didn't think so. "I think we can do it ourselves. We will also have the advantage of seeing them in the moment, so we can decide if they are okay or not."

"Good point! How about flowers?"

"I was serious when I said I'd get them from the craft store. I see no point in paying a lot for flowers that will be used for an hour."

"Okay!"

"But I probably do need to make sure I get the right colors."

"Yes, that's really important," Tom said very seriously, teasing me for my color obsession.

"We want things to look good in the pictures!" I teased back.

"Speaking of which, I guess I need to get a new suit?"

"That would be nice. I have an idea for a skirt and top for me."

"What color suit?"

"Oh, charcoal gray, I think. Do you have one of those?"

"Nope. Brown and blue are all I have."

"Then a charcoal gray, with a small pinstripe, maybe?"

"You'll come with me?"

"If you want me to."

"I think it will be better if you do. You know more about these things than I do. What about shirt color and tie?"

"Tie? Do you want to wear a tie?"

"Not really. But it's a wedding. Shouldn't I wear a tie?"

"Only if you want to. I'm not planning to be that fancy. I'll show you what I'm planning to get."

I pulled up the website of one of my favorite stores. There was a beautiful magenta skirt with multiple godets. It was flowy and floor length, two of my favorite things. The website had paired it with a light gray shirt, which I thought looked very nice. That's why a charcoal gray suit would work out great. And gray and pink was one of my favorite color combinations. This would be the strong versions of those colors. But I thought it would work.

"Very nice."

"And practical in a good way. I will be able to wear both to work afterwards."

"I won't wear my suit to work," Tom teased. Tom's company was business casual, much as mine was.

"You don't ever wear a suit when you meet with your customer?"

"Oh, I do sometimes. When it's not just our customer. He wouldn't care and, most of the time, he's just in a polo. But when there are other government types in the room or if we are presenting our findings to an audience, then yes."

"Great!"

"So, that's flowers, clothes, photographer, invitations. What else?"

"Still need to find out dates from the old farmhouse venue, Huntingdon Manor."

"And match those to the family dates we've been debating."

"Right. So then we can finalize the invitations."

"Cake?"

"Oh, reception! Good point!"

"We need food!"

"Our kind of food. I'll ask the farmhouse people what caterers they recommend. Again, with a small number of people, it should be easier. And cheaper."

"Cake!" Tom shouted again.

I laughed. "Yes, I will find out about cake too. I don't know that we need a multi-tiered extravaganza though, do we?"

"I wouldn't think so. Chocolate cake."

"Yum!"

"Yum!"

CR ℰↄCR ℰↄCR ℰↄ

"Tom," I said as we were watching television one night a few days later, "could you do me a favor?"

"Sure! What do you need?"

"Now that we have the date and location picked, could you get the invitations finalized? I haven't had a chance to get to the stationers. I'm afraid if we wait too much longer, they won't be able to get them printed in time."

"Sure. I'll go this week."

"Tomorrow?"

Tom looked at me. "All right. Tomorrow."

"Thanks!"

"What else can I help with?"

"Want to call the officiant and confirm she's available that day. She said so in our first call, but now that we booked the Huntingdon venue, we need to lock her in."

"Okay!"

"I'll send you her contact information." I picked up my phone, and I sent the latest email exchange to Tom. He'd been included in the previous email exchange, but this way it would be at the top of his inbox.

"Invitation. Officiant. Got it."

"Great!"

The next evening, I reported that I had talked to the caterer, who agreed to a simple menu of heavy hors d'oeuvres and chocolate cake. The cost wasn't outrageous. Things were coming along.

"I got the invitations done," Tom explained. "They will be ready in a week. We should be able to get them in the mail in the next week after that. Though pretty much everyone already knows the possible dates."

I frowned. "Officiant?"

"Didn't get a chance to do that today. It was crazy at work."

I thought about saying he could just have sent an email, five seconds. But I reminded myself that Tom did things in Tom's way, and that was okay. A day or two shouldn't be a problem. And if the officiant couldn't do that date, I had backups.

"All right. If Regina isn't available, there are others on the list."

"We liked her best, though. Right?"

"Right. But just in case."

"I should have time tomorrow. I just could only do one thing today, and you said the invitations were the priority."

"They absolutely were. Thanks!"

I realized I hadn't thanked Tom for that.

"Oh, I talked to Meghan, well, texted with her. She has a friend who is a photographer. She said he could take the pictures for a nominal fee."

"Instead of the family?"

"I'm worried the family's photos won't be good enough. Professionals know about lighting and posing. We have a better shot with getting a decent picture if we have someone who knows what they are doing."

"I hadn't thought about it that way. You have a point. Could we do photos before the wedding? Just us? Or do we want pictures of the reception too?"

"Oh, reception photos can totally be the family taking them. I was just thinking of the formal bride and groom portraits. Sean can do those. Before?"

"That sounds great! Thanks for thinking of that."

"I have my moments," Tom teased.

"You do at that."

I realized that I was getting better at this shared responsibility thing. Jane's advice to think about it like I do my job really helped. That, and trusting Tom. Or deciding that doing things a different way than mine was okay. All these things combined into a more relaxed Tiffany. That was good!

CR ᔕꊌCR ᔕꊌCR ᔕꊌ

"I'm in trouble," Tom Senior said to Tom without preamble. Tom Junior was on his smartphone, but the elder Tom talked loudly enough that I could hear.

We were at Tom's house, watching television on his uncomfortable couches. I frowned at the elder Tom's words, so the younger Tom put the phone slightly away from his ear, and I tilted my head to listen. "What's up, Dad?" Tom asked.

"The Young cousins are in the know," Tom's dad said.

"Uh-oh. What happened?"

"He doesn't call often, but he does every once in a while. Your uncle, John. He checks in on me. The last time we talked, he asked about you and Tiffany, wanting to make sure things were going well. I had just gotten the invitation, so I didn't think about it, but told Uncle John that you had chosen a date. Wasn't that exciting? That kind of thing. I forgot the Youngs weren't invited."

"What did Uncle John say?" Tom asked.

I was frowning. I knew the Youngs wouldn't be happy, but we also were hoping that they wouldn't know about the actual wedding date until after it had happened.

"He was congratulatory and all that. He loves you, you know. But I'm afraid he'll tell Cathy and Martha."

"I'm sure he will. It's okay, Dad. We'll deal with the fallout. Thanks for the warning."

"Sorry for spilling the beans, Son. I was just so tickled to finally see the invitation. I'm so happy for you, and Tiffany of course. I'm so happy you found someone to love like I loved your mother." There were tears in Tom's voice. Mary had been gone for over a decade, and he still missed her every day.

My Tom cleared his throat. He missed his mother, too. "Thanks, Dad. I'm very happy."

"Well, gotta run. Talk to you soon." Tom's father signed off.

Tom turned to me. "You prepared for the onslaught?"

"No, but I will be. Good thing your father warned us. I'm not so worried about Martha. She doesn't pick at things the way Cathy does."

"Yup. I'll call or email them. They are, after all, my cousins. You shouldn't have to deal with this."

"I'm sure they will find me on social media to complain."

"Probably."

"What's the expression? I've girded my loins."

"Really? That's the expression you pick?"

"First one that came to mind. What's yours?"

"Knowledge is power."

"Good one!"

"We'll deal with Cathy. We're not changing our plans," Tom insisted.

"We can't really. We have booked the room and the caterer. We could add more food to the menu, I suppose. But the ceremony room is only big enough for 20."

"Good to know. I can use that as leverage."

"Will Cathy really care? Won't she just say we can relocate?"

"Maybe. But we don't want to."

"Agreed! It's such a lovely spot, that old farmhouse. And I'm not much of a country girl, as you know."

"Yes, I know. You're an indoor cat."

I smiled. I really was. "But I just love the way they've restored Huntingdon Manor. It's charming without being overly done."

"And I like that you can use the barn for the reception, with the intimate feel of the ceremony room."

"I won't tell Cathy about the larger hall. She would pounce on that."

"Oh dear, yes. Don't mention that."

"She might look the location up, though."

"Did your dad tell Uncle John the location? I thought he just said date."

"Oh, that's true. Then we can claim anything we want about the location, right?"

"Well, no need to lie exactly. Just tell Cathy, and Martha if you're going to email them, that the location is small, intimate as we wanted, and only seats 20."

"Good. Sounds like a plan."

Despite our preparations, the Young cousins were relentless in their grievances. Cathy started it, in response to Tom's email, but Martha – surprisingly – was just as bad.

"Another email, this one from Martha," Tom said, when his phone binged as we were talking and eating.

"What's the complaint this time?"

"They'd invited us to their weddings."

"Did you go?"

"We did. Meghan and I did, at least. Dad didn't go to any of them. He's talked to Uncle John, but I don't think he's seen the Youngs since Mom died. Too hard on him, he says."

"That's too bad. He could use some more friends."

"I don't think he sees it that way. And of course, you now know the Youngs can be a bit overwhelming."

"Yes, and you McDonnells are a quieter people."

"Yes, we are." Tom smiled.

"So, Martha is arguing that since you were invited to their weddings at least a couple of decades ago, we owe them an invitation to our wedding?"

"That's the gist of it, yes."

"Well, I wasn't around then. So, I wasn't invited. Were they big affairs?"

"Martha's was huge. There must have been upwards of 200 people there. Her husband came from a large family. They were very boisterous. Meghan and I spent a lot of time outside at the reception, trying to keep our equilibrium."

"Oh my. I have no interest in that kind of a wedding."

"Completely agree with you. There were people there neither of them knew. Friends of their parents. That's just crazy."

"I think that was more of a thing in that day and age. Or maybe it's just more of a thing when you get married in your 20s."

"Could be. Cathy's wedding was smaller, but still over 100. I knew a lot of the people there from our annual visits to their hometown. Since she and Mitch both teach in town, there were lots of younger folks there – presumably their students or ones who had graduated. It was pretty fun, actually, if still overwhelming at times."

"Did you have a date?"

"I took Priya."

"Oh my. That would have been interesting. Cathy and Priya? Deadly."

"You have no idea," Tom said, running his hands through his hair. "Cathy assumed a lot, of course. And she expected that I was going to marry Priya. She was very mad at me when she found out I had 'let Priya go'."

"She didn't know about all the manipulation?"

"Not really. I mean, we're friendly, but I don't tell her much about my life."

"You don't tell anyone much about your life."

Tom laughed. "True. Anyway, I didn't want to badmouth Priya to Cathy. For all I know, they are still in touch. So, I just told Cathy it didn't work out."

"Are Cathy and Priya still connected on social media?"

"I don't know. I don't really do social media."

"Yes, I know." I checked it out on my phone. Sure enough, Priya was still connected to Cathy on more than one platform. "Well, they are still connected." I showed the results to Tom.

"Dang!"

"Yes. But not material to this conversation." I took a breath. Cathy's connection to Priya was problematic, but not my business. "Just tell Martha that we're having a small wedding. And that's that. That's what I had to do with my mom."

"How's that working out for you?" Tom teased.

I frowned. Mom still brought it up periodically. I'd learned to just change the subject.

"Martha and Cathy should be better than this. It's not like they are your sisters!"

"I agree. But they aren't being good. So, I will just respond to this email. And then not respond to any others. Agreed?"

"Agreed."

Cathy replied to Tom's email. She just said they were sad that they didn't count enough in Tom's life to have been included. True to his plans, Tom didn't respond. Guilt was never a good way to get to Tom, anyway. Priya had been the master at that, and he'd built a thick skin from her manipulations.

Then Martha wrote again. Followed by Cathy again. Tom was infuriated. "What do they think they are going to gain by bugging me?"

"I have no idea. It's certainly not ingratiating them to us, huh?"

"No! I'm not sure I want to have anything more to do with them after this."

"Well, let's not go that far," I said, trying to calm the waters. Tom was as angry as I'd ever seen him.

"I've had enough!" he shouted when his phone binged again.

"Tom," I said quietly. "I have an idea of how to make all of this go away."

"You do? How?"

"Let's cancel the whole wedding thing."

"You don't want to get married anymore?"

"I don't want to deal with this wedding thing!" I was upset, too. My mother had been on my case again. I tried to ignore her, but she was my mother. It was hard.

"I think I'm missing something," Tom said, calming down.

"Let's get married. But just the two of us. Regina said she'd marry us at her house. Quick, easy, no fuss."

"But your mother would blow a gasket."

"I don't care!" I was frustrated. "We are grown adults. We don't need anyone's permission to do anything!"

"I'm right there with you. Meghan might be hurt, though. And Dad."

"Not if we explain it to them. They will understand, I think."

"Probably. But your mom won't. She will harangue you to the ends of the earth."

"We won't tell them until afterward," I said.

"That might be even worse," Tom offered.

"Okay. You're probably right about that. But, honestly, all this fuss is driving me crazy!"

"I agree. And I like the idea of just us. Would we lose money with the farmhouse and caterer?"

"Huntingdon Manor? A little. I had to put some down to reserve the room, and there's a cancellation clause. I'll have to look at it. We could keep the caterer, though, and just have a party on the original date in our new home. A housewarming. We could expand the number of servings pretty easily. What do you think?"

"I like it. Not the party idea. You know how I feel about parties."

"I do. But this would be lower key than the wedding would be. We'd keep the guest list small, still. But we could invite the Youngs – they probably wouldn't come – and get them off our backs that way. I might even invite David and Anne, my stepsiblings."

"It has possibilities. Let's think about it some more."

So, we did. And we decided to change the plans.

Tom talked to Meghan first. She understood completely, which I thought she would. Lauren was fine, too, especially since they hadn't bought plane tickets yet. Tom's father was just as happy not to have to be in the midst of the event. I had a feeling he wouldn't come to our housewarming, but we would see.

I talked to my brothers, who also got it. Mom didn't, of course. She cried and yelled at me. She complained about how she never got to participate in my life anymore. I told her it was what it was. She could come to the housewarming or not. Her call. She whined a bit more, but let it go. My father didn't really care either way. He was just happy for me, happy that I had found the right guy. He said he looked forward to seeing our new home when we were ready.

Huntingdon Manor had a 60-day cancellation policy. As long as you canceled before 60 days out, you got your money back. Getting our deposit back covered the cost of changing the catering. The caterers were happy to have the extra business and didn't much care about the change of location.

"Will we still have cake?" Tom asked.

"Of course!"

"Yum!"

Tom and I called Regina together. She was pleased that we wanted to use her house. And she was available any of several weekends in the next month. Would any of them work?

They would.

Ironically, but appropriately, we would end up getting married after closing on our new house, after closing on our two townhouses, and just after we moved.

It would be a whirlwind. But so worth it!

In some ways, this was better than the original immediate-family plan. The wedding would be just another thing. Not a big deal. Which was just how we wanted it.

The important thing was not the getting married; the important thing was to BE married.

CR ℰℭ ℰℭ ℰℭ ℰ

"Music shouldn't be just a tune; it should be a touch." -- Amit Kalantri

WHAT'S IN A NAME? (TIFFANY'S CHILDHOOD)

My parents divorced when I was 10, Xan was 12, and Phin was seven. Us three kids were both scared and relieved. Scared because we didn't really want our world disrupted nor were we sure how we were going to split our time between our parents. But relieved because the house had been nothing but anger for a long time.

My dad was an ambitious guy. He worked long hours and usually brought home work as well. He consulted on the side, too, spending time with his additional clients on the weekends and sometimes in the evening. The only sacrosanct family time was dinner. I think that was Mom's insistence. Dad was always home for dinner, which she always prepared. It was typical of couples who had gotten married young and of their midwestern heritage. Though they both lived through the '60s, and all the cultural changes that had happened in that decade, when they married in the early '70s, theirs was still a pretty traditional relationship.

When Phineas went to preschool, however, Mom decided to go to graduate school. She'd gotten her undergraduate degree in education, typical for a woman who might or might not end up working outside the home at some point. I give her credit, though, for getting her degree. She'd met my father her freshman year of college, and they'd gotten married between her sophomore and junior years. She could have easily just succumbed to the housewife mentality and gone on to have a bunch of kids and raise them, probably with little help from my father.

Once Mom started school again, though, she began to evolve. It was 1983, and the societal changes from the turbulent decades that preceded the '80s were starting to sink in as more normal than revolutionary. Mom's version of becoming a modern woman was to enroll in a part-time master's degree program and start working part-time, as well.

I remember very distinctly the first time my mother wasn't home for dinner. She'd told Dad at least twice in my hearing that she was going to a university function that evening. It included a dinner. Dad had no interest in going. Mom thought it was important for her to go. The conversations hadn't gone well. Xan, Phin, and I had listened without really trying, to the fights, even though they happened in our parents' bedroom. It wasn't that big a house. We tried to ignore what was going on. We turned up the volume on the TV we were watching in our family room. But when the language got particularly vile, all we could do was look at each other and wonder when our parents started being so mean to each other.

Not that they hadn't fought before. Dad had more than his share of a temper. And I was sure that the amount of pressure he put on himself to succeed – and to work so hard – didn't help the situation. When he came home from work, he would put his briefcase down in the front hall and hang up his coat. Just those two gestures were usually enough to give us kids a sense of how his day had gone. And whether to be extra quiet at dinner so as not to trigger him.

Mom, though, didn't seem to care about Dad's moods. She had her ideas of what the right way to do things was, and she expected Dad to be her husband and our father the minute he walked in the door. She didn't needle him; not much. But she didn't seem to give him space either. Even if they didn't always yell at each other, theirs was not a caring relationship. More of a tussle for control.

I was pretty sure there hadn't been any resolution to the question of Mom's going to the reception without Dad. Or rather, I was pretty sure Dad assumed that his insisting she not go would be the end of it. I was equally sure that Mom's newfound sense of self meant she was going whether Dad liked it or not.

Dad came home that night, and the briefcase landed with a thud and the coat hanger clanged against the metal bar. We knew what that meant. Dad was in a foul mood. And he didn't even know Mom wasn't here yet.

Mom wasn't completely irresponsible. She'd arranged for Mrs. Leibowitz, the woman who babysat us after school while she and Dad were at school and work respectively, to stay until Dad got home. Mrs. Leibowitz, however, was not a cook and didn't consider putting dinner together part of her babysitting duties. She'd read to us and helped Phin with his homework. But she hadn't made dinner.

I was starving. But my stomach was also in knots waiting for Dad's temper to flare.

"Catherine?" he shouted.

Obviously, he either hadn't remembered that today was the day Mom was going to be late or he had expected her to be home at the usual time per his instructions. Either way, it wasn't going to be good when he realized what had happened.

Phin, Xan, and I were sitting quietly in the family room with Mrs. Leibowitz, which was upstairs from the front door. The television was still on, but we'd stopped paying much attention when we'd heard Dad come in.

Mrs. Leibowitz heaved her way out of her chair. She was not a small woman; I didn't think she missed many meals. She also didn't believe in yelling. She'd told us many times, "Go into the room where the person you want to talk to is sitting. Do not shout across the house to get someone's attention."

She lumbered to the top of the stairs, looking down into the foyer of the house, where Dad was standing having deposited his briefcase on the floor and his coat in the closet. She had just started to make her way down the stairs when Dad noticed her.

"Mrs. Leibowitz," he said, "what are you doing here? Where's Catherine?"

"Mrs. Johnson is at a school function. She asked me to look after the children a little longer than usual until you got home. I'll just be going now." She continued down the stairs at her normal pace, which was not quick.

The three of us kids stood at the very edge of the staircase, where we could hear but not be seen. Xan and I had shared a look of concern. Phin was just about to say hello to Dad, when we shushed him. We weren't ready to bear the brunt of Dad's temper.

By now, Mrs. Leibowitz had made it to the landing, though she was out of breath. She went to the hall closet to get her coat, preparing to leave.

"Where are the children?" Dad asked, his voice constrained with anger.

"They are upstairs watching a bit of television," Mrs. Leibowitz responded, seemingly oblivious to the danger. Xan and I exchanged worried looks again. Ignoring Dad's temper usually only made it worse.

We were so focused on the tension, we had left Phineas to his own devices.

"Hi Daddy!" Phin greeted as he made his way down the stairs. "I'm hungry. When is dinner?"

Alexander and I immediately ran down the stairs to where six-year-old Phin was making Dad's foul mood worse. I stepped in front of my younger brother and put him out of arm's reach of our father, while I too stepped just a little bit further away. Xan did the same.

Dad looked at us, as we strived to have neutral looks on our faces. Phineas was peeking out from behind me. He seemed not to realize the situation. Perhaps he didn't at that. He was, after all, only six.

"Xan, please take your sister and brother to the kitchen. I will meet you there in a moment," Dad ordered.

The three of us skedaddled to the kitchen, but kept the door opened just a crack. Dad sounded almost calm, but we knew it might be an act for Mrs. Leibowitz.

"Thank you for staying with the children," Dad said, as he helped Mrs. Leibowitz into her coat.

"Glad I was able to arrange my schedule to help out. Mrs. Johnson asked me over a week ago, so I was able to arrange for Mr. Leibowitz to pick up something from the diner next to where he works. He'll be waiting for me to have our dinner. So, if you don't mind, I'll just be going." As usual, Mrs. Leibowitz told more than was necessary.

"Thank you again," Dad said politely. I listened hard to see if I could hear anger. I just wasn't sure.

The front door closed, and Alexander and I took Phin to the kitchen table, though generally we used the dining room for dinner. The other two meals – breakfast and lunch if it was a weekend – were served at the kitchen table. But Dad had told us to go to the kitchen, so that's where we were. We sat down quickly, pretending we had been there all along, not listening on tenterhooks to the conversation in the front hall.

Dad pushed the swinging door to the kitchen. It thwacked against the wall. Clearly, Dad's temper had not dissipated. He had just managed to suppress it in front of Mrs. Leibowitz. We sat frozen in place, not saying a word to him or to each other.

"Where is your mother?" he asked Xan, his voice raw with emotion.

"School," Alexander stammered. At nine, he was trying to be the man of the house when Dad wasn't home and protect me and Phin. "There was a reception."

"Yes, I remember," Dad gritted out.

"I'm hungry!" Phin shouted.

"Shush!" I said before I could stop myself.

Dad's face turned bright red. He crossed the room to the table. He'd never struck us, but it sure looked like he wanted to. He stood over me, as I quaked in fear.

Alexander stood up. "I don't know how to make dinner, but I could make a sandwich," he volunteered.

"No, I'll make dinner!" Dad shouted. He stomped to the refrigerator and opened it so hard the door flew back and hit the cabinets behind it with a bang. There, on the top shelf, was a casserole with a note on it. "For dinner. Heat for 20 minutes at 350" in our mother's handwriting.

Dad took the dish and put it on the counter with a thud. He turned on the oven with a hard twist of the knob. He clanged the oven door open; I was afraid it might fall off. He put in the casserole and started the timer.

"I'm going upstairs for a minute," he said. "Alexander, you're in charge till I get back."

"Yes, Father," Xan replied.

The three of us stayed at the kitchen table, listening to the timer ticking away the minutes. Dad came back into the kitchen after 15 minutes had passed. He was dressed in casual clothes, having taken off his suit as he usually did before dinner.

"Tiffany, set the table," he barked.

I jumped up, resenting that as the girl, setting the table was my job. My mother would have made Xan help too. But my father was more old-fashioned. I grabbed the silverware from the drawer and put it on the table. I gathered the plates and put them around the table, with the silverware on either side, as I had been taught.

"Where are the placemats?" Dad asked.

"Mom keeps them above the fridge," I responded. "I can't reach them there."

He looked at me, trying to decide if I was being a smart-aleck, or just factual. Honestly, it was a little of both.

He reached up and handed me the placemats. I silently put one under each place setting. Then I got out glasses and the milk from the refrigerator. Dad went into the dining room and came back with a scotch. He took a sip as he inspected my work. He nodded at me.

The timer dinged, making all of us jump.

"Sit down, Tiffany."

I sat as Dad went to get the casserole out of the oven. He put it on the kitchen counter without a trivet. Xan and I looked at each other, knowing what Mom would say but being fearful to say it.

"Dad?" I started.

"What is it?"

"Will the dish burn the counter?"

"Damnit!" Dad yelled. He popped up from his seat and grabbed the dish. He was in such a hurry that he forgot to put on the potholders. He immediately dropped the still-hot pan, and it sloshed all over the counter, which also had a mark from the heat.

"Damnit!" he shouted again. Dad tried to salvage what he could, scooping it back into the pan. He put a trivet under the dish, too.

Alexander cringed in his seat. I sat as impassively as I could. Phineas had his eyes peeled on the ruins of dinner, wondering if he was going to get dinner after all.

"Plates!" Dad shouted.

We immediately handed him all four plates.

He served us each a helping of the beefy mess that had been the casserole. We ate in silence.

The front door opened as we were just about finished. Mom was home.

Phin jumped down from the table and ran into the front hall to greet our mother. Dad started to stop him, but decided not to. Xan and I just stayed where we were. The look on our father's face said another mutiny would not be tolerated.

Mom walked into the kitchen, holding Phin, a happy look on her face. She didn't bang the door. She was talking quietly to her youngest.

"Did you eat the dinner I left for you?" she asked.

Then she looked up to see the chaos on the counter and the look on her husband's face.

"I told you I was going to be late," she insisted. "And I left you dinner. All you had to do was reheat it." She crossed the room, putting down Phin as she went, to see what was left of dinner spread on the counter.

"And I told you not to go to that stupid reception. Your job is to be here, to make dinner for your family," Dad replied. His temper, which had been only simmering as we ate, was about to blow again, I could tell. I really wanted Mom to let it go, but I knew she would not.

"I did make dinner," Mom rejoined.

While this was technically true, it wasn't even remotely what our father meant. Mom knew that. Maybe she did needle him more than I realized.

"You left dinner. You did not make dinner," Dad argued, his voice rising.

"Don't lose your temper with me, Christopher Johnson. I told you I wasn't going to be home for dinner tonight. It was not a 'stupid reception'. My review committee was there, and it was important for me to be there too. I was able to impress the chair with my knowledge of my thesis subject."

"What do I care about your thesis subject?" Dad yelled.

"Well, considering what we are paying for me to get my master's degree, I would think you would care quite a bit," Mom responded.

"You should be home with the children!"

Mom laughed. "Do you hear yourself, Chris? We aren't living in the '50s. My career is as important as yours."

"You are my wife!"

"Not for much longer!" Mom's temper had finally gone.

Xan and I cringed. Mom had never said that before. Even Phin could tell something had changed.

"What does that mean? You're my wife, Catherine!"

"The day I graduate is the day I leave you!"

"Don't be ridiculous!"

"I'm not being ridiculous. You don't care about me! You don't love me, or you would want me to thrive!"

"Of course I love you!" Dad screamed. It didn't sound much like love to me.

"Now who's being ridiculous. You don't love me anymore, Christopher. And I'm not sure I love you either." Mom's tone was not angry; it was resigned.

Dad's red complexion suddenly turned white. "Catherine…"

Mom didn't respond. She just cleaned up the mess on the counter.

CR EOCR EOCR EO

That was the first time I heard my parents talk about divorce. It wouldn't be the last.

True to her word, our mother filed for divorce within weeks of getting her master's degree in 1987. She'd gotten a full-time job, too, and I guess that emboldened her to break things off with her husband.

She bundled us kids and our things into the family station wagon, and we'd driven across town to a much smaller apartment. Phin and Xan shared a room, which neither of them liked but both tolerated. I think we all knew money was a concern, and we did what we could to help out, even if it meant just being quiet.

To Dad's credit, he didn't fight Mom on the divorce. Or for custody of their children. The divorce went through with a minimal amount of court time, though it still took well over a year to be finalized.

Dad picked us up every other weekend for a visit. He had moved, as well, as there was no real need for him to keep our house. His new two-bedroom townhouse didn't have nearly enough space for all of us, though. Phin slept in Dad's bed with him, Xan was on the sofa bed in the living room, and I got the guest room. Again, though, we didn't complain. At least not to our parents.

A year after the divorce, Mom introduced us to Jack Kelly. He had been a student at the same university, we learned. Though I wondered when their relationship had actually started, I didn't ask about that either.

"Jack, this is my oldest, Alexander. Alexander, this is Jack," she started.

Xan shook Jack's hand, standing as tall as he could. The look in his eyes said, 'Don't mess with my mother.' Jack just smiled.

"This little guy is Phineas," Mom continued.

Phin was eight, but he didn't think of himself as little. He grimaced at Mom's description. "Not so little," he said under his breath.

"Of course not," Mom said with a laugh. "My big boy."

Phin was not really mollified.

"And this is my Tiffany," Mom finished her introductions with me.

Jack laughed. "Such grownup names!"

Mom chuckled. "Chris' idea. He hated being Chris Johnson. He wanted the children to have what he called 'substantial' names."

"Well, they are that. Phineas, Alexander, and Tiffany."

"We call them Phin, Xan, and Tiff," Mom explained.

"Tiff? As in a fight? Yes, I can see that in her eyes," Jack said. He'd now alienated all of us, as Xan fiercely defended his siblings.

I'd never thought about my nickname that way. To me, it was just "Tiff" a shorter version of my name, just like Phin. But from that day forward, I associated my nickname with fighting. I'd had enough of fighting, and so I came to hate my nickname.

ભ ૹભ ૹભ ૹ

Jack and Mom married about a year later, in 1989. Xan was asked to be one of Jack's groomsmen, and I was one of Mom's bridesmaids. Phin bristled at being left out, though Mom did invite him to be an usher.

It was a large wedding, though both Mom and Jack had been married before. They wanted to celebrate their new life in style. Mom got another wedding gown, and Jack wore a tuxedo. There were about 150 guests invited, including people from the university because Jack worked there.

Jack's first marriage had included two children, Anne and David, who were also in the wedding. Such simple names, I thought. They seemed nice enough, but we really hadn't had much interaction in the months since Jack and our mother had become an item. They lived in Connecticut with their mother and only visited every once in a while. The wedding was the first time we'd really spent any real time with them. We'd all been seated at the same table for the reception.

"Hey Tiff!" David teased, "think you'll ever fill out that dress?"

Xan laughed, which I resented. He was my brother; he was supposed to defend me. But David was a year older, a full-fledged teenager at 16 to Xan's barely a teenager at 14. Xan was trying to be cool in front of our new stepbrother.

"She doesn't like that name," Phin offered helpfully.

I cringed. I knew what that would mean.

"She doesn't like 'Tiff'? Oh, isn't that too bad. Tiff! Tiff! Tiff!"

He started chanting my nickname. The other teenage boys at the reception, including Xan, joined in. I blushed to the roots of my hair. I wanted to run from the room, but was trying to be above it all instead.

"Tiff! Tiff! Tiff!" They were now circling the table and chanting. It was humiliating.

Mom looked over from her place at the head table and grimaced. She knew she was the only one who could still get away with calling me by that nickname, and then only infrequently. She shrugged at me, as if to say, I'm sorry.

Phin stood up and blocked the boys as they started another circle. "She doesn't like that name!" he shouted with all of his nine years showing. He was tall for his age, but he was no match for four teenage boys.

"Sit down, Phin," I pleaded. I didn't want to call attention to this situation. It was awful enough.

"Can I help you?" the server asked carefully, coming over to the table and noting the four boys clustered around my younger brother, behind where I was sitting.

I silently blessed him for being an adult, though he was not as old as our parents. Maybe 20?

"It's nothing," Xan said sheepishly. He knew he had behaved badly.

David looked belligerent, but didn't say anything. He just sat down.

The other two boys dispersed to wherever they had come from.

"Thank you," I whispered, not sure if the server even heard me.

He winked at me as he walked away.

"Tiff! Tiff!" David whispered.

But Xan didn't join in this time. And so the humiliation receded.

I never forgot, though. And although I came to enjoy Anne's visits, I steered clear of David.

To his credit, though, he never called me "Tiff" again.

෩ ෪෩ ෪෩ ෪

"That's funny about your childhood nickname driving you crazy. Do you suppose that's what nicknames are all about?" Tom asked.

"I think some people like their nicknames. Phin still uses his, for example, as does Xan. I just hate Tiff. It reminds me of all the fights we heard when we were kids. I think my mom uses it on purpose for that reason. It's her little dig at me and the way we argue all the time."

"Makes sense, I guess. I've never been particularly fond of Tom-Tom either."

"It doesn't seem to fit you very well," I agreed.

"Why do you say that?"

"Well, maybe it's because I've only known you as an adult. But Tom-Tom is very childish, and you don't seem like the kind of person who was ever very childish."

Tom laughed. "No, I'm afraid I was always a pretty serious kid."

"So, perhaps your nickname – like mine – was something of a subtle dig. A reminder that you needed to be more childlike?"

"I never really thought about it that way."

"So, I won't use Tom-Tom if you don't use Tiff," I teased.

"Deal!"

Tom was quiet for a few minutes. I'm afraid I was reliving my childhood anger, but also experiencing gratitude that I wasn't that angry person any longer. She had been just a miserable person.

Tom smiled at me, in that cat-like way he had which meant he had an idea or joke to make.

"What?" I asked, using a mock-angry voice. Now it really was a mock-angry voice. A decade or two ago, it wouldn't have been.

"I have a terrible idea."

"I figured."

"You did?"

"You get this look on your face when you have a terrible idea or joke."

"I do."

"You do."

"You know me too well."

"I'm getting there."

Tom laughed. "Goes for both of us, huh? Well, we'll have a lifetime to figure each other out."

"Sounds good to me. What's your terrible idea?"

"Oh yeah. So, your name is Tiffany, right?"

"Right..." I wasn't sure Tom was going with this.

"And I was Tom-Tom."

"Right..."

"You know what those words have in common?"

"They're names? Or nicknames? I have no idea where you're going with this."

"Think, Tiffany." Tom had the look on his face again. Whatever it was, he was very pleased with himself for coming up with it.

"I have no idea."

"You're the one who had a thing for musicians."

I laughed. I did have that tendency in my younger years. So, I tried to think about our names from a musical perspective. It didn't help. "I'm not getting it."

"Forget about them being our names. What else is a tom-tom?"

"Indian drum?"

"Right."

"And..."

"Think about Tiffany. What kind of drum could that be?"

"Timpani!" I crowed.

"Right!"

"Oh, that's terrible."

"I know. We're the drum set!"

We laughed quite a while at that idea.

"It works, though," Tom argued. "Because we are a set. We aren't the same. We have different ways of thinking. We have different points of view. Different styles. Different noises?"

"And yet, when you put us together, you get beautiful music?"

Tom laughed. "Okay, so maybe the metaphor falls down a little bit there. But I still think it works."

"I agree."

And from then on, between the two of us, we called ourselves 'the Drum Set'.

HAPPILY EVER AFTER (2019)

So, in the end, we sold two houses, bought a new one, and got married in the same month, well, same four-week period.

It was a lot. Even with all my planning, and Tom's help.

♋ ♋ ♋ ♋ ♋ ♋

After all we'd been through and all the family fuss, we ended up with a super small wedding. Just the two of us and a justice of the peace.

Regina Thompson, our officiant, had explained when we met with her to discuss her marrying us that she lived in a beautiful house on a lake in Reston, and she often married people with the lake as a backdrop. After we punted on our immediate-family wedding at Huntingdon Manor, we planned a "just us" wedding on her backyard deck.

Back when I had first contacted her, Regina had requested us to tell her about ourselves so she could personalize the ceremony. I sent her an email with a little of our history. She asked a few more probing questions in the exchange.

Tom had been included on all these emails. He rarely interjected, though I made him respond to the questions that were directed at him. It was important for him to be included. For him and for me. No longer would I make any major decisions about our lives without his input. Even when he wasn't so sure he wanted to be involved.

Once Tom and I made the decision to pare the wedding down to just the two of us, I sent an email to Regina to make sure her offer to use her house still stood.

"Of course!" she replied enthusiastically. "When were you thinking, so I can tell my wonderful husband to make himself scarce?"

"We were hoping to move up the timeline," I replied. "If you're amenable, the sooner the better."

"Oh! I love the spontaneity and that you two can't wait to be married. It melts my romantic heart."

I hadn't told Regina about my health scare. She didn't need to know everything about our lives!

"Let me check with my husband. I think we could probably accommodate a date in the next few weeks. We aren't going anywhere, and the pond is brimming with frogs and turtles."

Regina lived on Turtle Pond, so that just made us laugh.

A day later, we got another email from Regina.

"Hubby says any weekend of the next three is fine with him. I'm open to them all. Check the weather, and let me know!"

We chuckled at Regina's use of the word "hubby". I had started teasing Tom that he was going to be my "hubby". He'd started calling me "wifey". It was somehow perfect that Regina used the same word. It solidified our faith in our choice of officiant.

We checked the weather for the next few weekends. There were no major storms due, but one just never knew with early summer. We had the three closings, too. First, mine with Kai to sell my current townhouse. Then, ours to buy our new house. And finally, Tom's to sell his house. We also had the movers scheduled. Kai had been very accommodating and would wait to move in until I could move out a week later, so we could move my furniture into the new place. There was a lot going on.

But we wanted to be married. And as we'd said from the beginning, the actual wedding was not the point. Being married was. So, somehow it was even more perfect to do it in the midst of all the other craziness. It reinforced the emphasis on the rest of our lives, rather than just this one day.

We picked the Saturday after we bought our new house. Closing was on Thursday, so all the paperwork could be filed on Friday. The movers were coming to move me from my old house to our new house on Sunday. Tom's house wouldn't be moved until after his closing. But that was okay. He'd practically been living with me anyway. We'd moved enough of his belongings into my townhouse that when the house was moved, Tom could live in the new house comfortably.

Therefore, by getting married on Saturday, we would move into our new house as husband and wife. It was perfect.

CR ℰↄCR ℰↄCR ℰↄ

"Does that make sense?" I emailed Regina with our thinking, including Tom as always.

"It's wonderful! I'll tell Hubby. One more request," she replied. "I'd like an email, 25 words or less, about why you love the other person. Send it to just me, without letting the other person see. Please send it no later than the Wednesday before the wedding."

"Okay," I replied for the both of us. Tom was sitting across the room from me and nodded in agreement at my response.

I tried very hard in the next week not to ask Tom whether he'd sent his email to Regina. Me, being me, I sent mine the next day, a week in advance of the deadline. Which is what I told Tom.

"I'll do it tomorrow," he promised.

When tomorrow came and went, and he didn't say whether he'd sent the email, I was quiet. He would or he wouldn't. If he didn't, it was up to Regina to follow up with him. She had his email after all. I was going to let it go.

I couldn't help but wonder, and worry more than once. But I didn't say anything. I trusted Tom.

The happy day came. Tom's dad called us around 9 am knowing the ceremony was scheduled for 10:30 at Regina's house. We would leave about 10 to drive over.

"Ready?" he asked Tom.

"Yes, sir."

"How about Tiffany?"

Tom had the phone on speaker. "I'm ready, too, Tom."

"Good. Can't wait for you two to make it official. Wish we could be there, but we understand why we're not."

I looked at Tom to make sure this was true. He nodded and mouthed, "They really do."

I nodded in response.

"We'll talk to you later today, okay?" Tom replied.

"Have fun! Talk to you when your husband and wife." Chuckling, Tom Senior hung up the phone.

Immediately after we hung up, my phone rang. It was my mom, or so caller ID said. I worried she would try to argue my choice with me again. It had been a trying few weeks since we changed our plans.

"Tiffany?"

"Yes, Mom."

"You got a good man there. Don't forget that."

I blushed, as the phone was again on speaker, but Mom didn't know that. "I'll remember. You're right about that."

"Thank you, Catherine," Tom replied, letting Mom know he was on the line.

"Oh, hi Tom. Didn't realize I was on speaker." She cleared her throat.

"It's okay, Mom. Tom knows us by now," I teased to relieve her embarrassment.

"Yes, he does. You are good for each other. I knew that all along."

I rolled my eyes at Tom. "Yes, Mom. I love you, but we have to go now."

"Love you both," she said, and then hung up.

We piled into my car and drove over to Regina's via GPS. We'd given ourselves some extra time, knowing we were going to be nervous and in case we got lost. Because of course we would.

As a result, we were early. So, we sat in the car for a minute, each of us alone with our thoughts, Tom in his new suit, me in my new skirt and blouse. We looked very nice, I thought. I glanced at my engagement ring again, loving Tom for having bought the sapphire. We had two bands for us to exchange at today's ceremony. Jean had made them to match my engagement ring.

Finally, after about five minutes, Tom said, "Ready?"

"Yes, I am!" I said enthusiastically.

He kissed me quickly, careful not to smudge my lipstick. We got out of the car and walked to Regina's house. It was indeed a lovely spot. She hadn't exaggerated about that. We could see Turtle Pond behind the house, though not the deck.

We sat in her living room for a minute, waiting for her to arrive. "Hubby" – whatever his name was – had answered the door. "Regina will be right with you," he said, leading us into their living room and to a sectional couch where we sat in expectation. He left us without another word.

Then, Regina strolled in. She was an elegant woman in her late 60s, with coifed white hair. She was wearing a simple black dress, which made her look like a wedding officiant without looking like a minister, and a beautiful multicolored scarf in bright hues that was very summery. Her smile was infectious and helped dispel some of my nerves.

"We have to do a little paperwork," she explained as she sat down on the couch opposite the couch on which Tom and I were sitting nervously. "It's been my experience that after the ceremony, the couple generally doesn't want to stay here any longer. You want to get on with your married lives."

We smiled. I was sure she was right.

"I've been doing this a long time," she explained. "You two are the 514th couple I've married."

"That many!?" Tom exclaimed.

"Yes, dear. I've been a wedding officiant for Fairfax County for 25 years. I keep a log." She showed us where she had listed our names.

"Now, this isn't a legal wedding certificate," she said, as she pulled out what looked like an official marriage certificate to me, "but it's my gift to you."

She carefully calligraphed our names, asking us before each word to be sure she was spelling it correctly.

"We'll just set this here to dry during the ceremony," she explained. "Shall we?"

We followed her down a set of outdoor stairs from her living room to the lower deck. The day was a perfect summer day, with the sun shining down and glistening on the water. It was an idyllic setting.

"This is lovely," I said.

"We like it. My husband and I moved here when Reston was new. Even got to meet Mr. Simon back in those days. He was particular about who moved into his creation."

"Did he have to approve the sale?" Tom asked.

"No. But he still liked to meet the residents. I think we passed. We raised our family here. And I've married many people on this deck."

"It was nice of you to offer. It simplified our plans."

"When it's just me and the couple I'm marrying, I've found this location works well. It doesn't work if there is a large wedding party, of course. The deck isn't that big."

We laughed, which again relieved some of the tension.

"Shall we begin?" she asked.

"Sure," I managed to choke out, tears starting to well in my eyes. I was very happy.

Tom just nodded. Tears were in his eyes too.

Regina stood with her back to the pond, and with Tom and me on either side of her, facing each other. She put our hands in each other's and opened her book to start the ceremony. It felt every bit like a wedding.

"Tiffany, repeat after me."

And then Tom and I repeated the traditional vows – without mention of God or obeying – we had discussed earlier with Regina.

Vows exchanged and new rings placed on our respective fingers, Regina paused for a second. I was curious, because as far as I knew, the wedding rites were completed.

"I asked you each to send me a few words about each other, why you loved the other person. I do this with most of my couples. It often tells me a lot."

We nodded, tears threatening again.

"In your case, the emails told me how perfect you were for each other. Are you sure you didn't let the other person see what you sent?"

"No, ma'am," I replied. "I didn't clue Tom in on what I was going to write."

"You know I was late," Tom admitted.

I laughed.

"But, no, Tiffany doesn't know what I wrote. Why?"

"Because you both said the same thing in your last sentence," she explained. She unfolded a piece of paper. "Tom, you wrote that you appreciated Tiffany's willingness to let you be who you are."

"I do!" Tom crowed.

"Tiffany, you said you loved that Tom was clever with words and loves your cats."

"Yes, very much," I said more quietly than Tom. Tears were streaming down my face.

"Can you guess what you both said next?"

We nodded.

Regina continued. "'We are the Drum Set. Two parts of a whole.' That's what Tiffany wrote. Tom wrote, 'She's the timpani to my tom-tom. Together, we are the Drum Set.'"

And she smiled at us. "Be happy. Love each other well. I think you're on the right track."

We kissed each other spontaneously, tears spilling on our cheeks.

"Drums all have their own particulars - each drum has a place where they sound the best - where they ring out and resonate the best..." -- Chad Smith

DENOUEMENT (2029)

Ten years on, and we're as happy as we were that day. Not that it's all been sunshine and roses. But more often than not, we've been happy. And that's really all you can ask for.

I'm also pleased to say that I continue to be cancer free. I've never had a recurrence of breast cancer or any other kind of cancer. Tom, too, though he didn't have the same scare I did.

It's funny how things work out sometimes, though. I wouldn't wish a cancer scare on anyone. And yet, in my case, it brought me to my greatest happiness.

I'm sure Tom and I would have been happy living together. We might never have gotten married and done just fine. But I'm thrilled to the core of my heart to be his wife.

There's nothing quite like the inevitability of life to make you rethink things. I've heard the same is true about having children, that you just don't prioritize things the same way after having a kid. But Tom and I didn't have children, so I can't speak to that.

What I can speak to, however, is that our experience with my breast cancer irrevocably changed both of us. Fairly early in our relationship, I'd realized that I was going to have to be the one to bring up difficult topics, as it was Tom's tendency to avoid them. Presumably his fear of being left contributed to that behavior, along with a natural introversion and reticence. But Tom has learned that, to share his life truly, he has to be more open, to not be afraid to talk about the things that bother him, to trust that I'm not going anywhere. I'm pleased to report that – most of the time – he gets it.

For my part, having faced my mortality made me appreciate what I already had even more than I already did. I knew I was living a great life before the diagnosis. I had finally found love; not the fairytale kind of love I'd thought I wanted, but a deep, honest kind of love. I was who I was, and Tom was who he was, and we loved each other because of and in spite of our flaws and strengths. The fact that I loved my job, was financially stable, and continued to be healthy was like dark chocolate icing on top of the gooey chocolate cake. Just like we'd had at our housewarming / wedding reception all those years ago.

The Drum Set keeps on beating.

CPSIA information can be obtained
at www.ICGtesting.com
Printed in the USA
BVHW031036230220
573073BV00001B/82